image comics presents

THE WALKING DEAD™

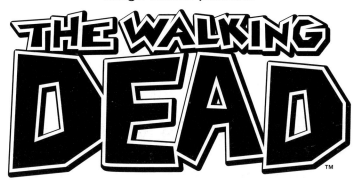

ROBERT KIRKMAN
CREATOR, WRITER

CHARLIE ADLARD
PENCILER, INKER

CLIFF RATHBURN
GRAY TONES

RUS WOOTON
LETTERER

CHARLIE ADLARD
&
CLIFF RATHBURN
COVER

SINA GRACE
EDITOR

SKYBOUND

For SKYBOUND ENTERTAINMENT

Robert Kirkman - CEO
J.J. Didde - President
Sean Mackiewicz - Editorial Director
Shawn Kirkham - Director of Business Development
Helen Leigh - Office Manager
Robert Pouder - Inventory Control
Feldman Public Relations LA - Public Relations

For international rights inquiries,
please contact: foreign@skybound.com
WWW.SKYBOUND.COM

image

IMAGE COMICS, INC.
Robert Kirkman - chief operating officer
Erik Larsen - chief financial officer
Todd McFarlane - president
Marc Silvestri - chief executive officer
Jim Valentino - vice-president

Eric Stephenson - publisher
Todd Martinez - sales & licensing coordinator
Jennifer de Guzman - pr & marketing director
Branwyn Bigglestone - accounts manager
Emily Miller - administrative assistant
Jamie Parreno - marketing assistant
Sarah deLaine - events coordinator
Kevin Yuen - digital rights coordinator
Jonathan Chan - production manager
Drew Gill - art director
Monica Garcia - production artist
Vincent Kukua - production artist
Jana Cook - production artist
www.imagecomics.com

PRINTED IN THE USA

ISBN: 978-1-60706-615-6

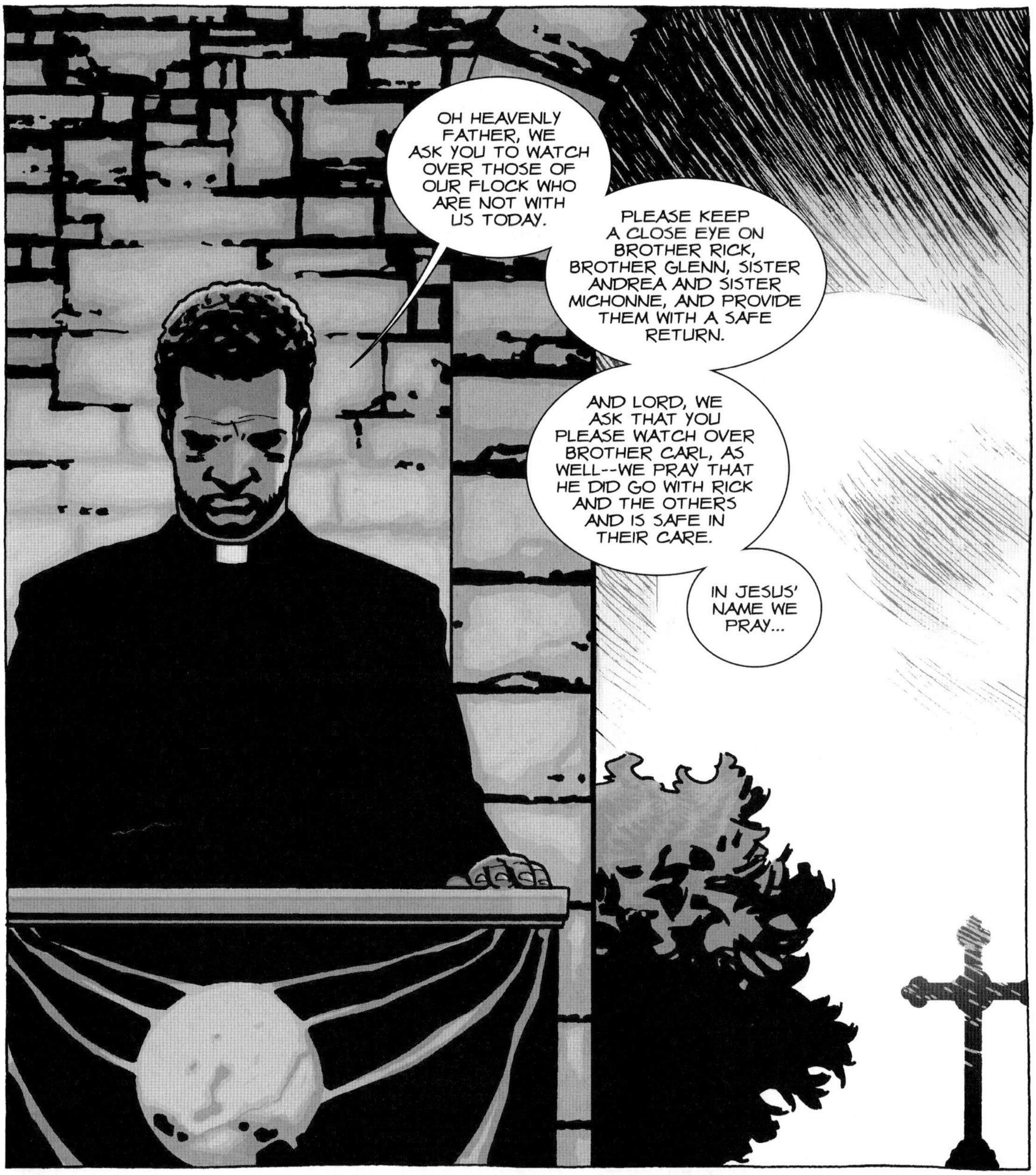
OH HEAVENLY FATHER, WE ASK YOU TO WATCH OVER THOSE OF OUR FLOCK WHO ARE NOT WITH US TODAY.
PLEASE KEEP A CLOSE EYE ON BROTHER RICK, BROTHER GLENN, SISTER ANDREA AND SISTER MICHONNE, AND PROVIDE THEM WITH A SAFE RETURN.
AND LORD, WE ASK THAT YOU PLEASE WATCH OVER BROTHER CARL, AS WELL--WE PRAY THAT HE DID GO WITH RICK AND THE OTHERS AND IS SAFE IN THEIR CARE.
IN JESUS' NAME WE PRAY...

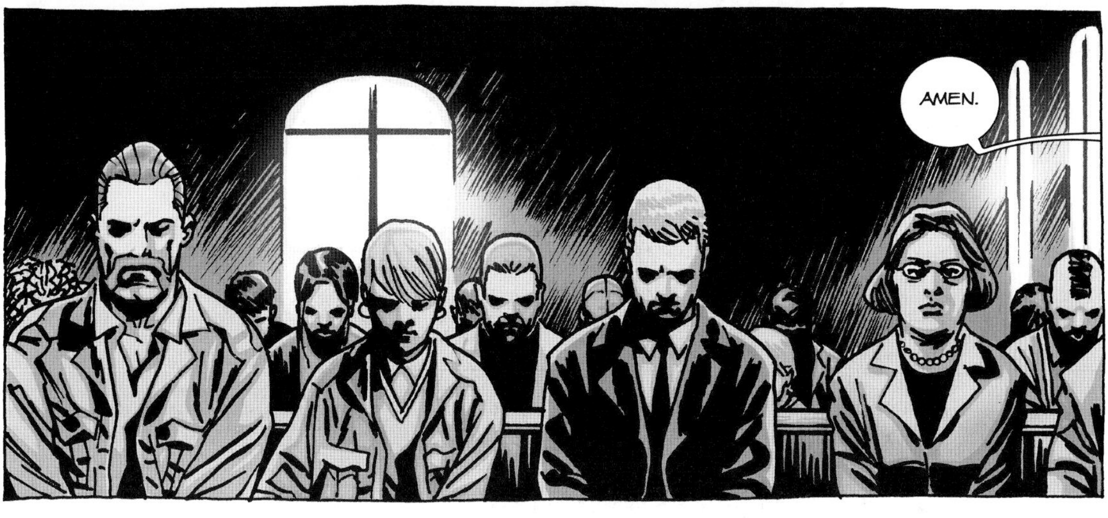
AMEN.

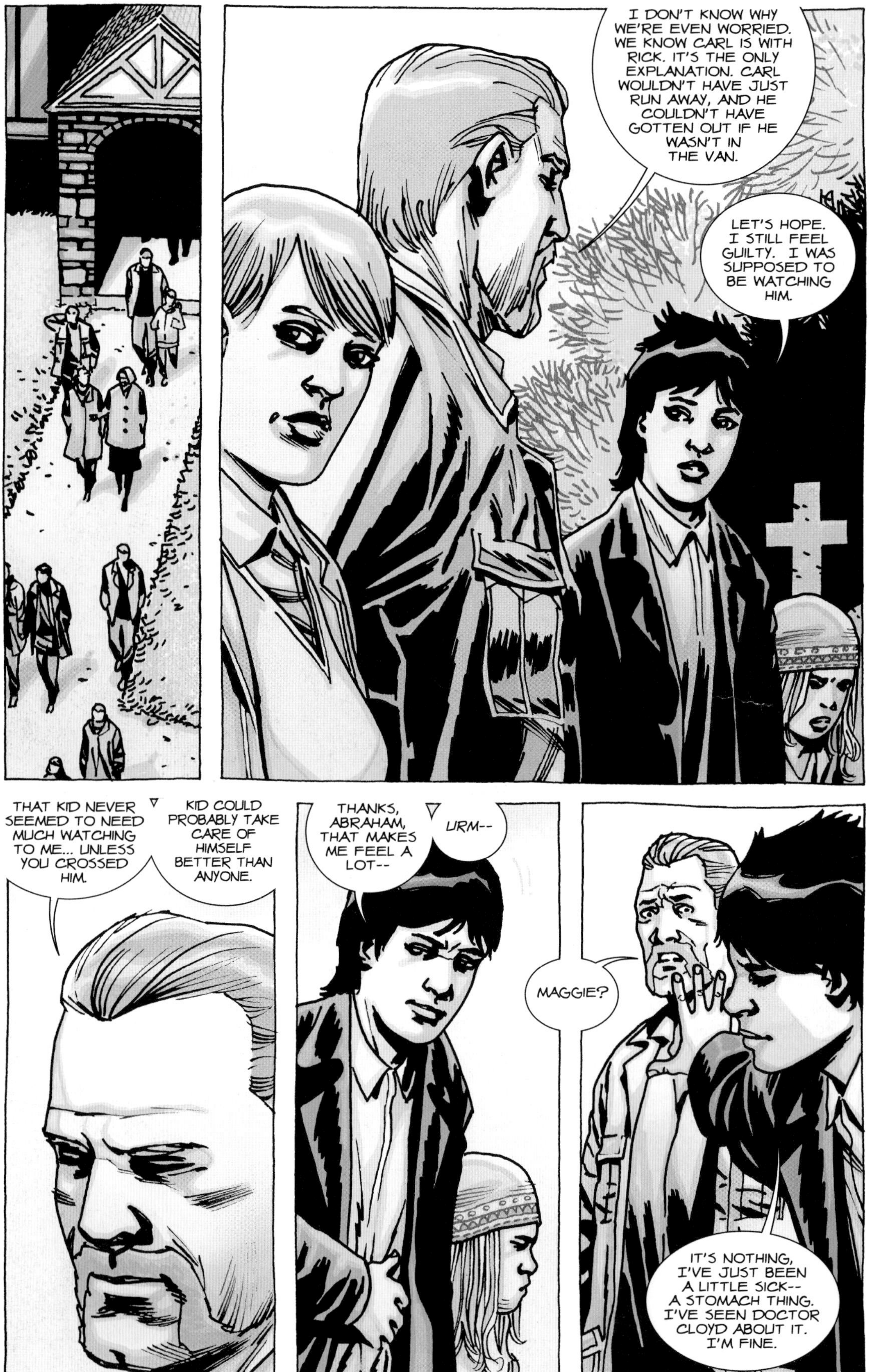
I DON'T KNOW WHY WE'RE EVEN WORRIED. WE KNOW CARL IS WITH RICK. IT'S THE ONLY EXPLANATION. CARL WOULDN'T HAVE JUST RUN AWAY, AND HE COULDN'T HAVE GOTTEN OUT IF HE WASN'T IN THE VAN.
LET'S HOPE. I STILL FEEL GUILTY. I WAS SUPPOSED TO BE WATCHING HIM.
THAT KID NEVER SEEMED TO NEED MUCH WATCHING TO ME... UNLESS YOU CROSSED HIM.
KID COULD PROBABLY TAKE CARE OF HIMSELF BETTER THAN ANYONE.
THANKS, ABRAHAM, THAT MAKES ME FEEL A LOT--
URM--
MAGGIE?
IT'S NOTHING, I'VE JUST BEEN A LITTLE SICK-- A STOMACH THING. I'VE SEEN DOCTOR CLOYD ABOUT IT. I'M FINE.

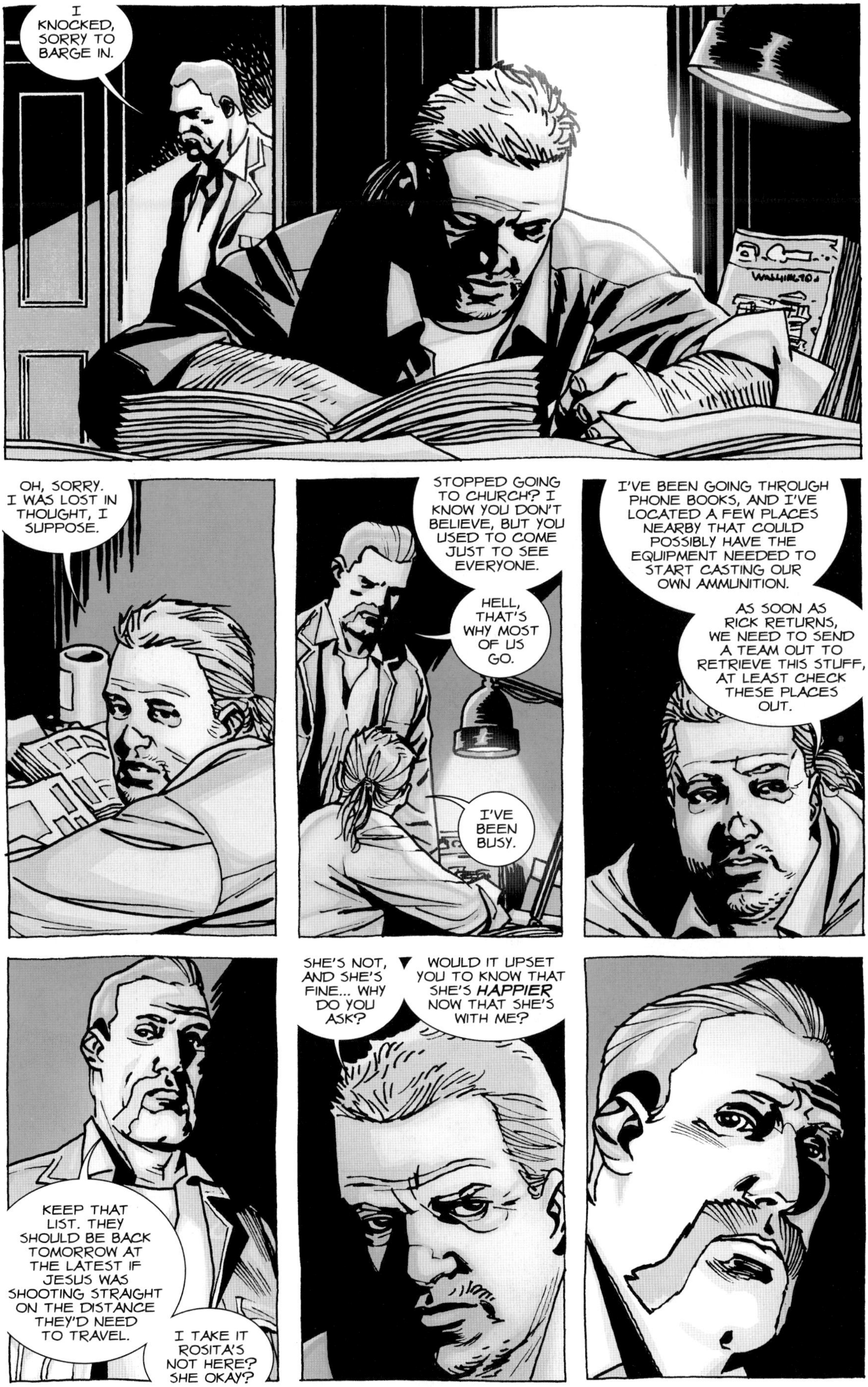
I KNOCKED, SORRY TO BARGE IN.
OH, SORRY. I WAS LOST IN THOUGHT, I SUPPOSE.
STOPPED GOING TO CHURCH? I KNOW YOU DON'T BELIEVE, BUT YOU USED TO COME JUST TO SEE EVERYONE.
HELL, THAT'S WHY MOST OF US GO.
I'VE BEEN BUSY.
I'VE BEEN GOING THROUGH PHONE BOOKS, AND I'VE LOCATED A FEW PLACES NEARBY THAT COULD POSSIBLY HAVE THE EQUIPMENT NEEDED TO START CASTING OUR OWN AMMUNITION.
AS SOON AS RICK RETURNS, WE NEED TO SEND A TEAM OUT TO RETRIEVE THIS STUFF, AT LEAST CHECK THESE PLACES OUT.
KEEP THAT LIST. THEY SHOULD BE BACK TOMORROW AT THE LATEST IF JESUS WAS SHOOTING STRAIGHT ON THE DISTANCE THEY'D NEED TO TRAVEL.
I TAKE IT ROSITA'S NOT HERE? SHE OKAY?
SHE'S NOT, AND SHE'S FINE... WHY DO YOU ASK?
WOULD IT UPSET YOU TO KNOW THAT SHE'S HAPPIER NOW THAT SHE'S WITH ME?

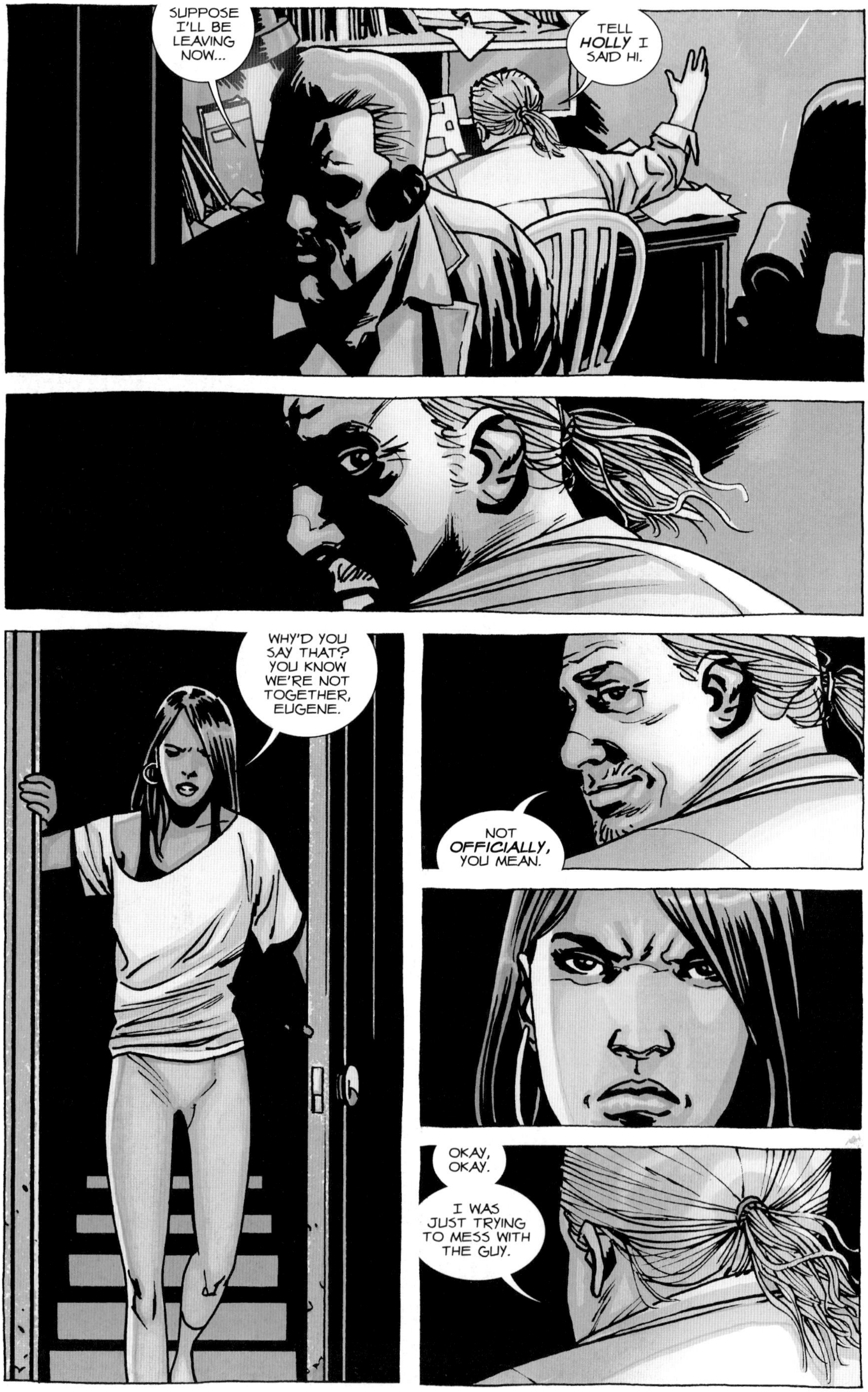
SUPPOSE I'LL BE LEAVING NOW...
TELL *HOLLY* I SAID HI.
WHY'D YOU SAY THAT? YOU KNOW WE'RE NOT TOGETHER, EUGENE.
NOT *OFFICIALLY,* YOU MEAN.
OKAY, OKAY.
I WAS JUST TRYING TO MESS WITH THE GUY.

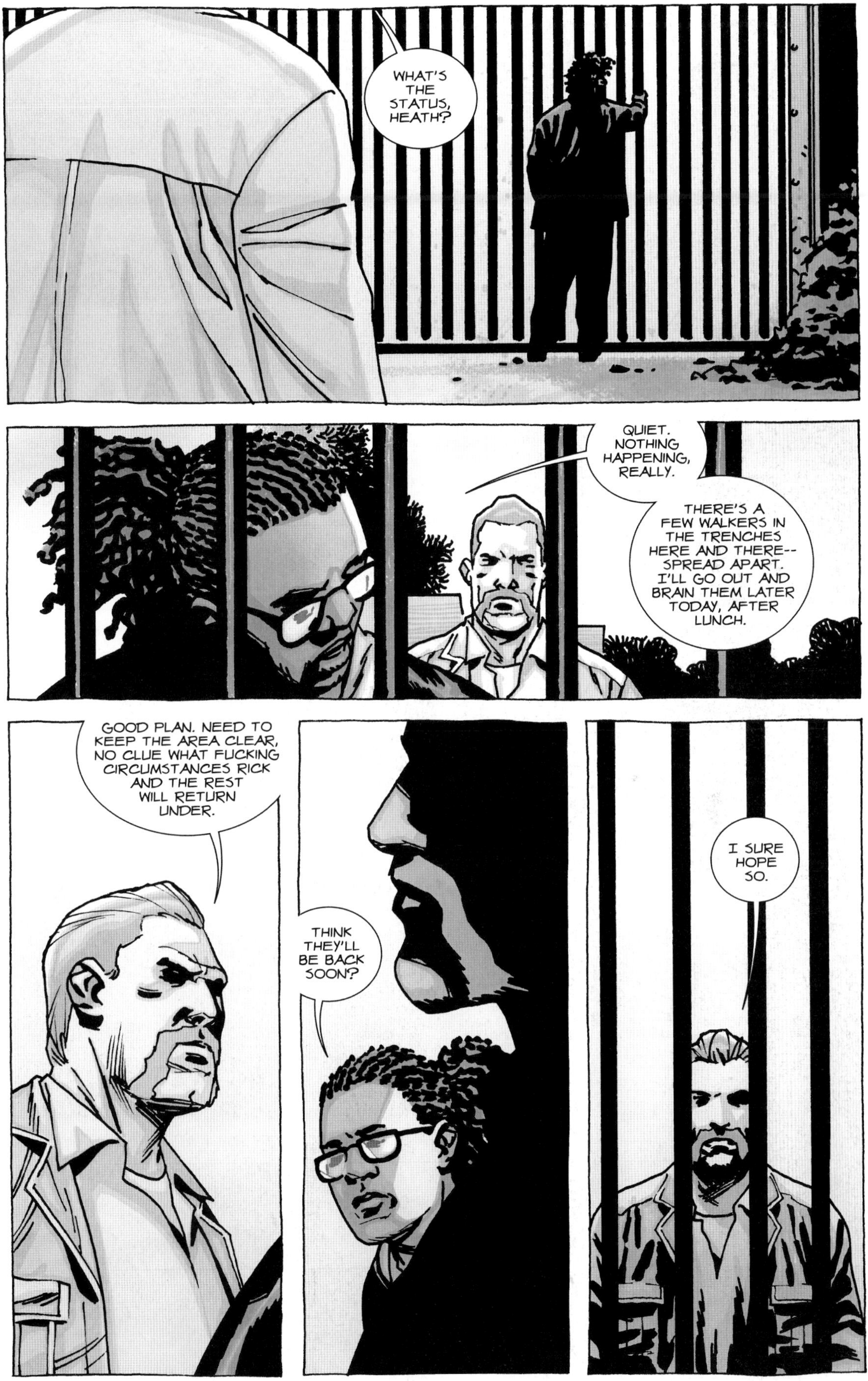
WHAT'S THE STATUS, HEATH?
QUIET. NOTHING HAPPENING, REALLY.
THERE'S A FEW WALKERS IN THE TRENCHES HERE AND THERE-- SPREAD APART. I'LL GO OUT AND BRAIN THEM LATER TODAY, AFTER LUNCH.
GOOD PLAN. NEED TO KEEP THE AREA CLEAR, NO CLUE WHAT FUCKING CIRCUMSTANCES RICK AND THE REST WILL RETURN UNDER.
THINK THEY'LL BE BACK SOON?
I SURE HOPE SO.

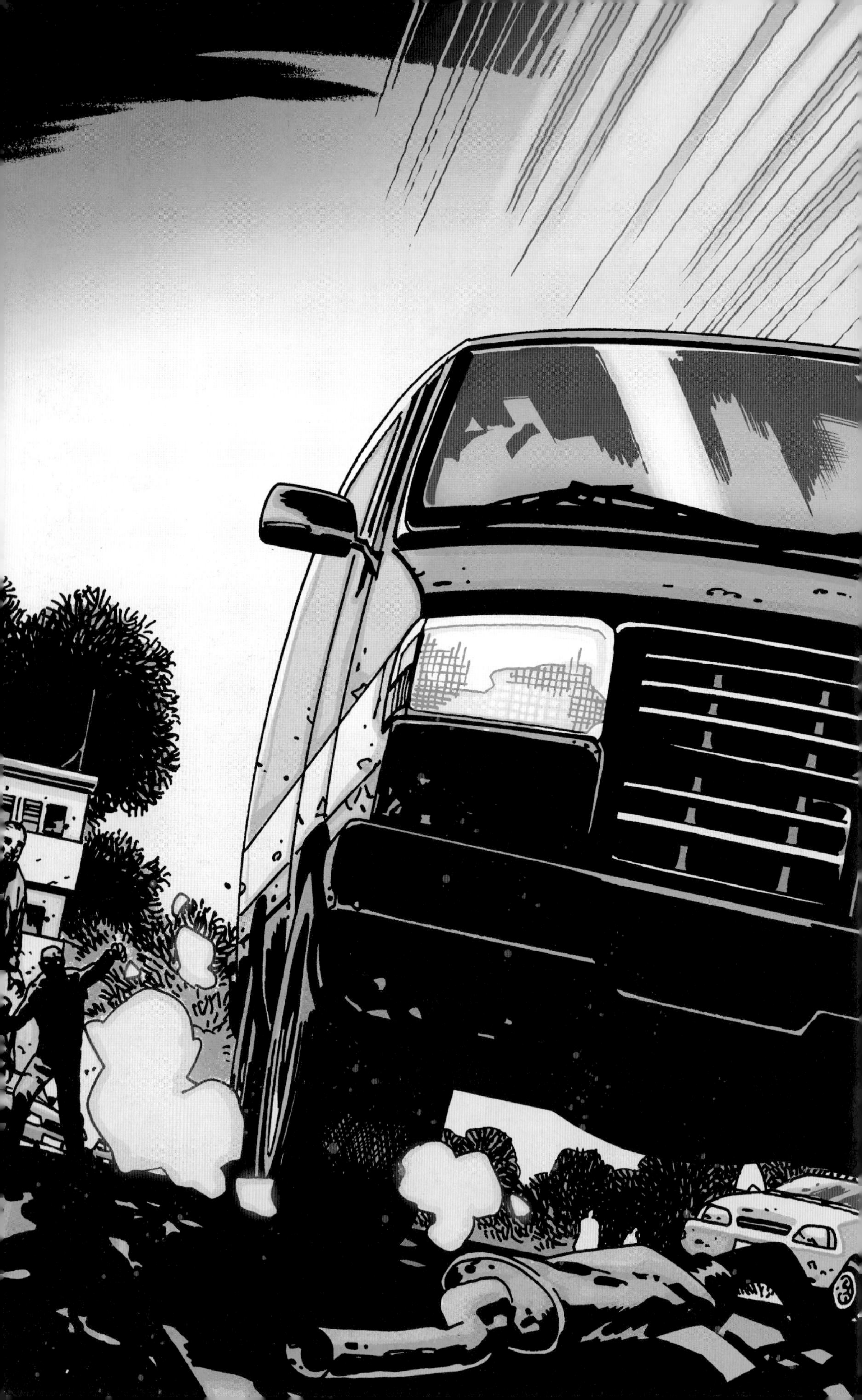

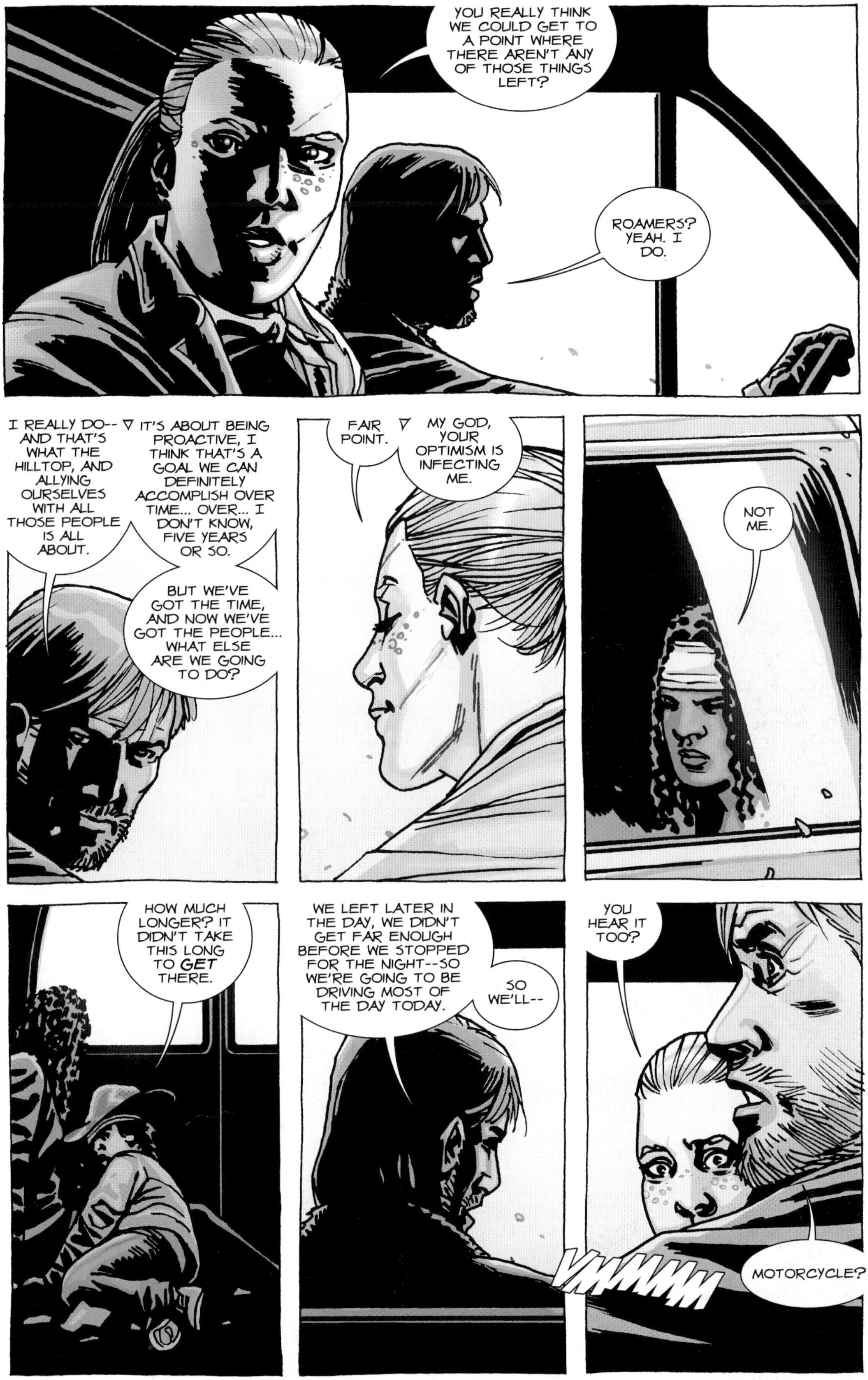
YOU REALLY THINK WE COULD GET TO A POINT WHERE THERE AREN'T ANY OF THOSE THINGS LEFT?
ROAMERS? YEAH. I DO.
I REALLY DO-- AND THAT'S WHAT THE HILLTOP, AND ALLYING OURSELVES WITH ALL THOSE PEOPLE IS ALL ABOUT.
IT'S ABOUT BEING PROACTIVE, I THINK THAT'S A GOAL WE CAN DEFINITELY ACCOMPLISH OVER TIME... OVER... I DON'T KNOW, FIVE YEARS OR SO.
BUT WE'VE GOT THE TIME, AND NOW WE'VE GOT THE PEOPLE... WHAT ELSE ARE WE GOING TO DO?
FAIR POINT.
MY GOD, YOUR OPTIMISM IS INFECTING ME.
NOT ME.
HOW MUCH LONGER? IT DIDN'T TAKE THIS LONG TO GET THERE.
WE LEFT LATER IN THE DAY, WE DIDN'T GET FAR ENOUGH BEFORE WE STOPPED FOR THE NIGHT--SO WE'RE GOING TO BE DRIVING MOST OF THE DAY TODAY.
SO WE'LL--
YOU HEAR IT TOO?
VMMMMM
MOTORCYCLE?

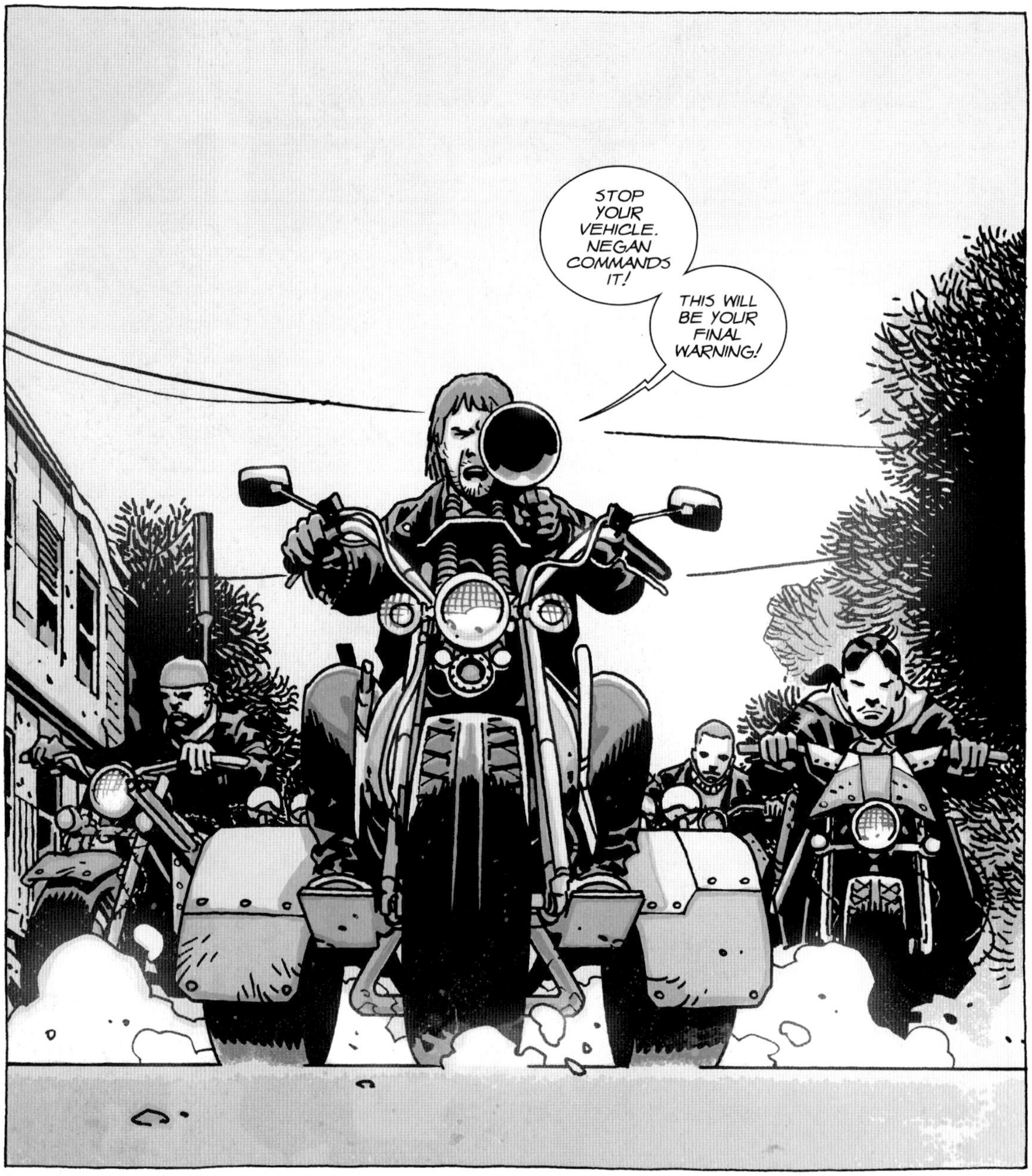
STOP YOUR VEHICLE. NEGAN COMMANDS IT!
THIS WILL BE YOUR FINAL WARNING!

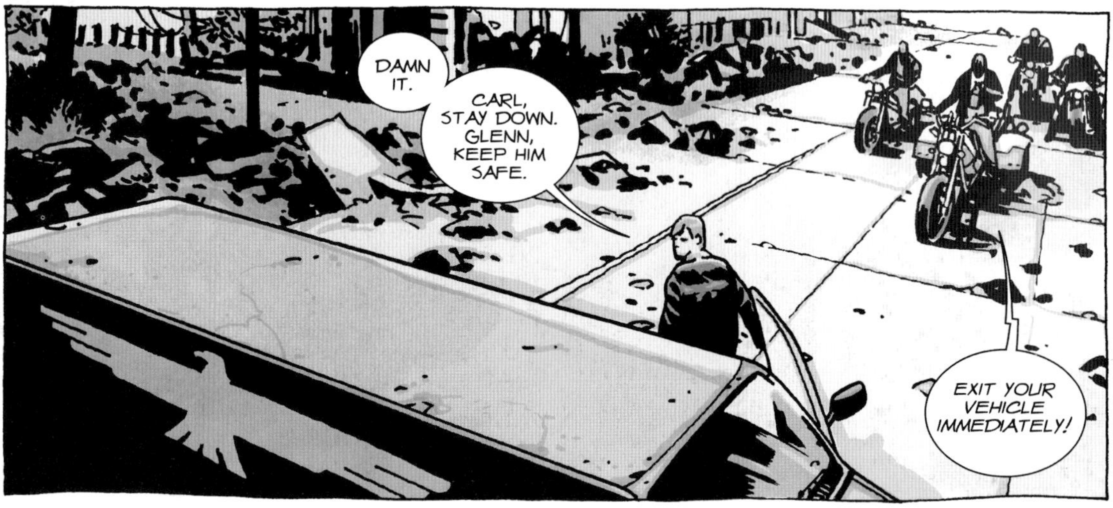
DAMN IT.
CARL, STAY DOWN. GLENN, KEEP HIM SAFE.
EXIT YOUR VEHICLE IMMEDIATELY!

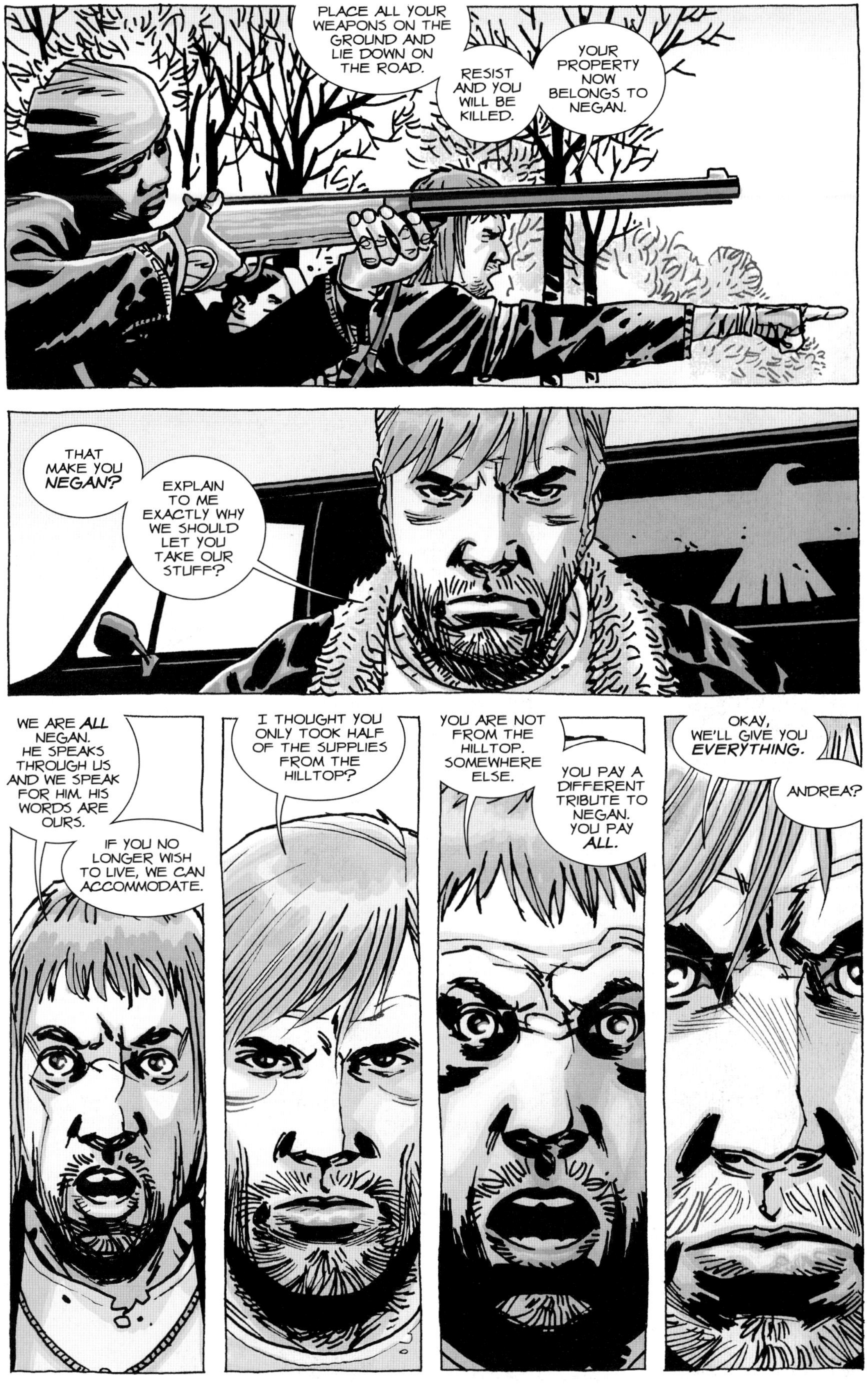
PLACE ALL YOUR WEAPONS ON THE GROUND AND LIE DOWN ON THE ROAD.
RESIST AND YOU WILL BE KILLED.
YOUR PROPERTY NOW BELONGS TO NEGAN.
THAT MAKE YOU *NEGAN?*
EXPLAIN TO ME EXACTLY WHY WE SHOULD LET YOU TAKE OUR STUFF?
WE ARE *ALL* NEGAN. HE SPEAKS THROUGH US AND WE SPEAK FOR HIM. HIS WORDS ARE OURS.
IF YOU NO LONGER WISH TO LIVE, WE CAN ACCOMMODATE.
I THOUGHT YOU ONLY TOOK HALF OF THE SUPPLIES FROM THE HILLTOP?
YOU ARE NOT FROM THE HILLTOP. SOMEWHERE ELSE.
YOU PAY A DIFFERENT TRIBUTE TO NEGAN. YOU PAY *ALL.*
OKAY, WE'LL GIVE YOU *EVERYTHING.*
ANDREA?

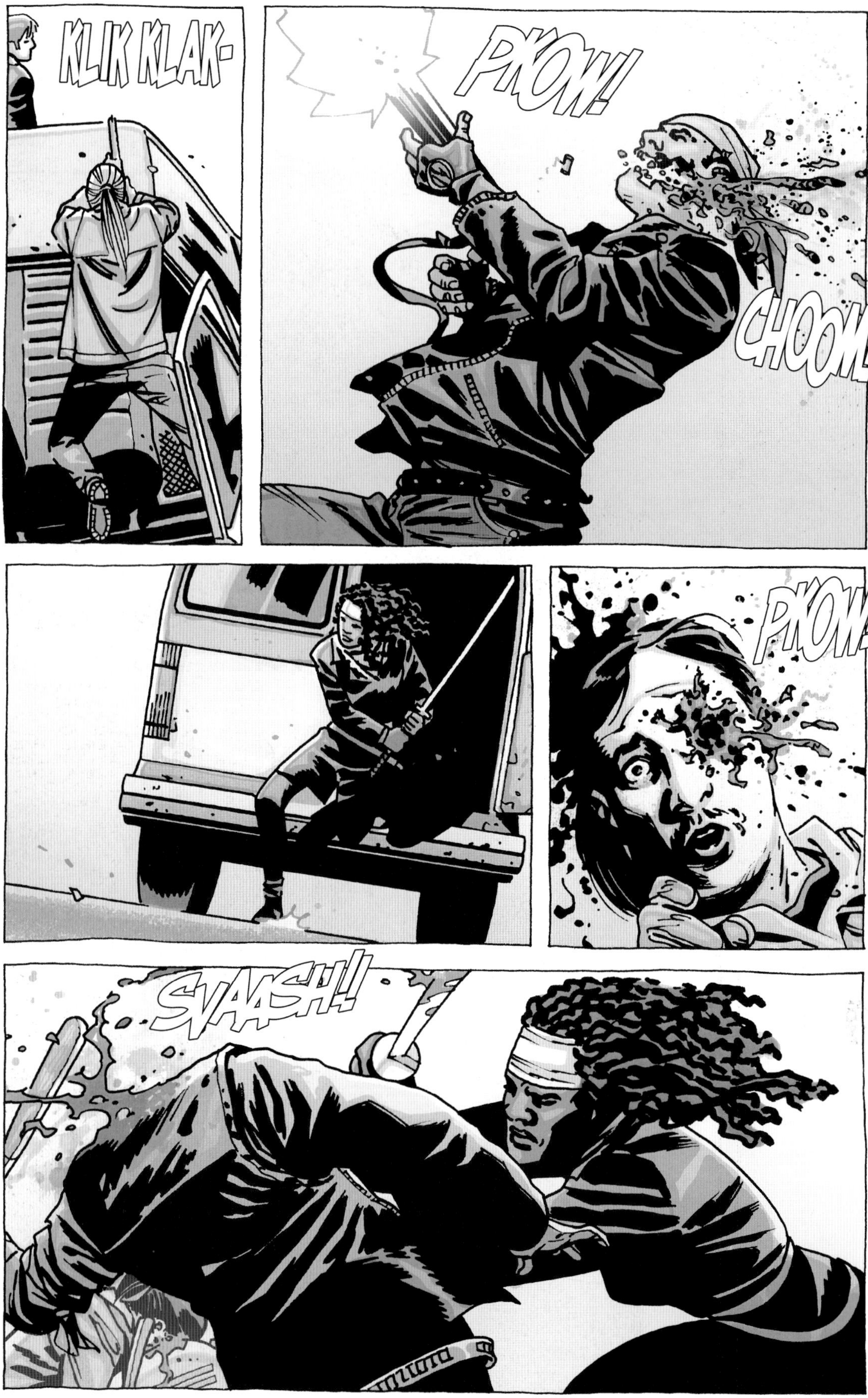
KLIK KLAK-
PKOW!
CHOOM!
PKOW!
SVAASH!!

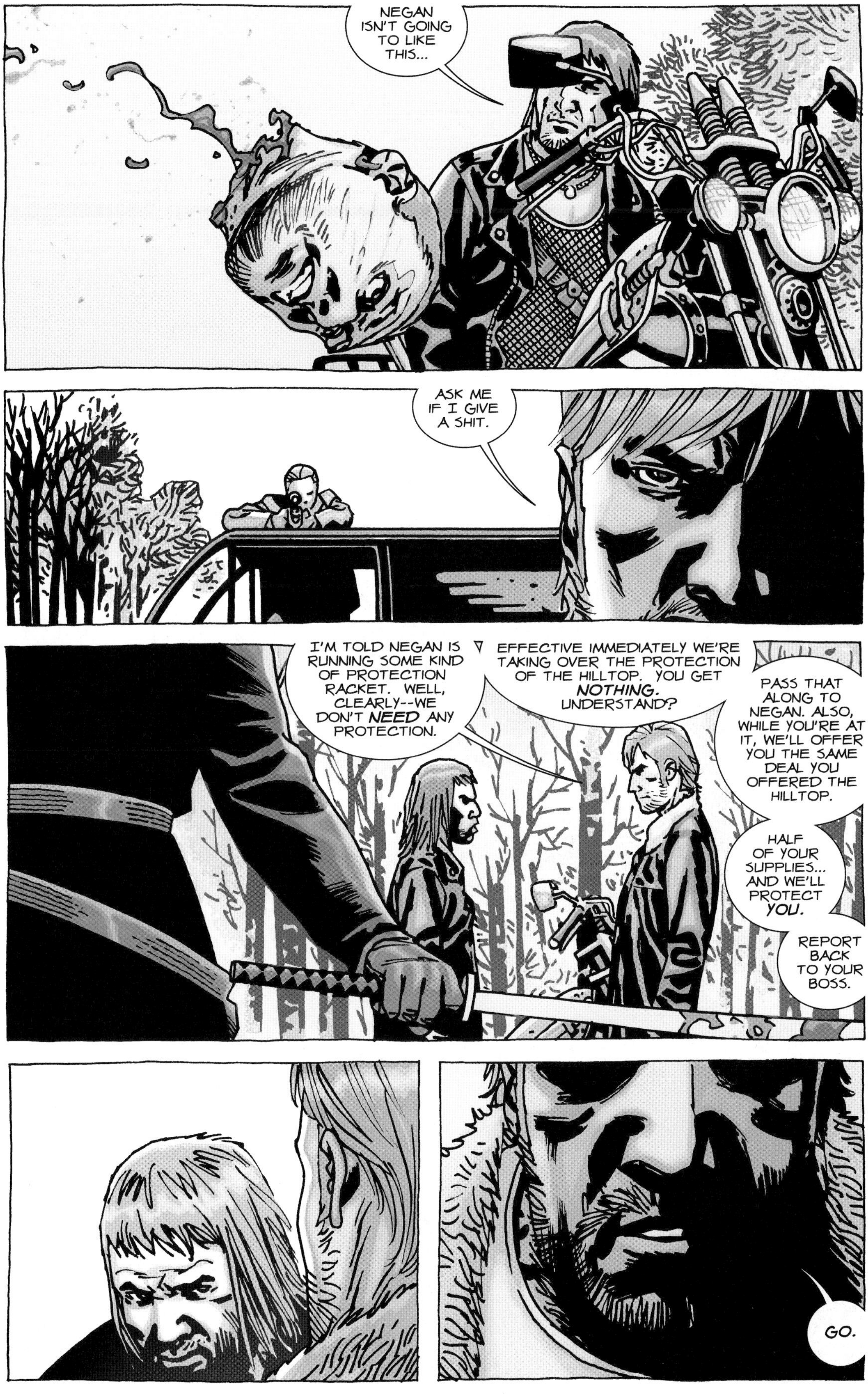
NEGAN ISN'T GOING TO LIKE THIS...
ASK ME IF I GIVE A SHIT.
I'M TOLD NEGAN IS RUNNING SOME KIND OF PROTECTION RACKET. WELL, CLEARLY--WE DON'T NEED ANY PROTECTION.
EFFECTIVE IMMEDIATELY WE'RE TAKING OVER THE PROTECTION OF THE HILLTOP. YOU GET NOTHING. UNDERSTAND?
PASS THAT ALONG TO NEGAN. ALSO, WHILE YOU'RE AT IT, WE'LL OFFER YOU THE SAME DEAL YOU OFFERED THE HILLTOP.
HALF OF YOUR SUPPLIES... AND WE'LL PROTECT YOU.
REPORT BACK TO YOUR BOSS.
GO.

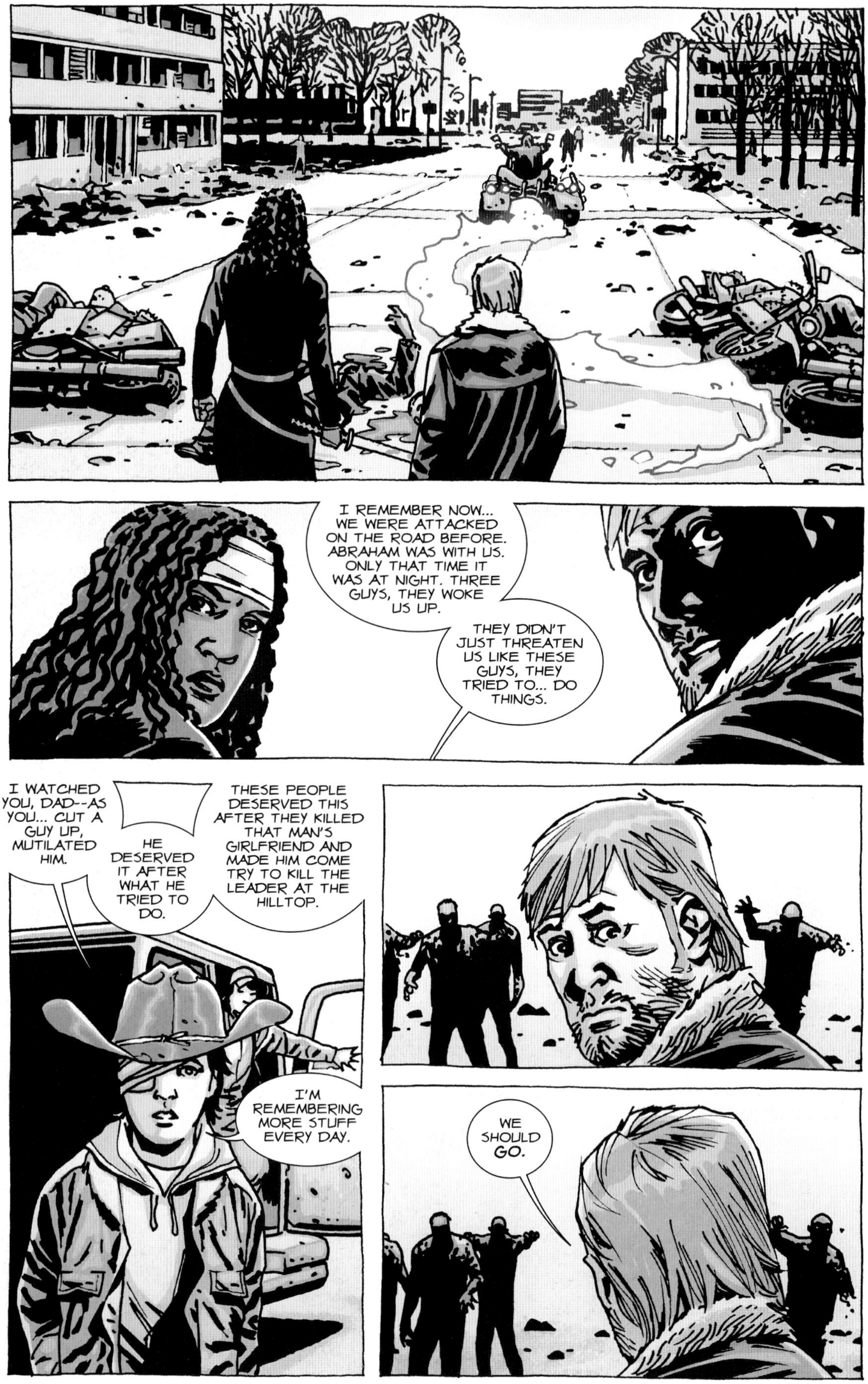
I REMEMBER NOW... WE WERE ATTACKED ON THE ROAD BEFORE. ABRAHAM WAS WITH US. ONLY THAT TIME IT WAS AT NIGHT. THREE GUYS, THEY WOKE US UP.
THEY DIDN'T JUST THREATEN US LIKE THESE GUYS, THEY TRIED TO... DO THINGS.
I WATCHED YOU, DAD--AS YOU... CUT A GUY UP, MUTILATED HIM.
HE DESERVED IT AFTER WHAT HE TRIED TO DO.
THESE PEOPLE DESERVED THIS AFTER THEY KILLED THAT MAN'S GIRLFRIEND AND MADE HIM COME TRY TO KILL THE LEADER AT THE HILLTOP.
I'M REMEMBERING MORE STUFF EVERY DAY.
WE SHOULD GO.

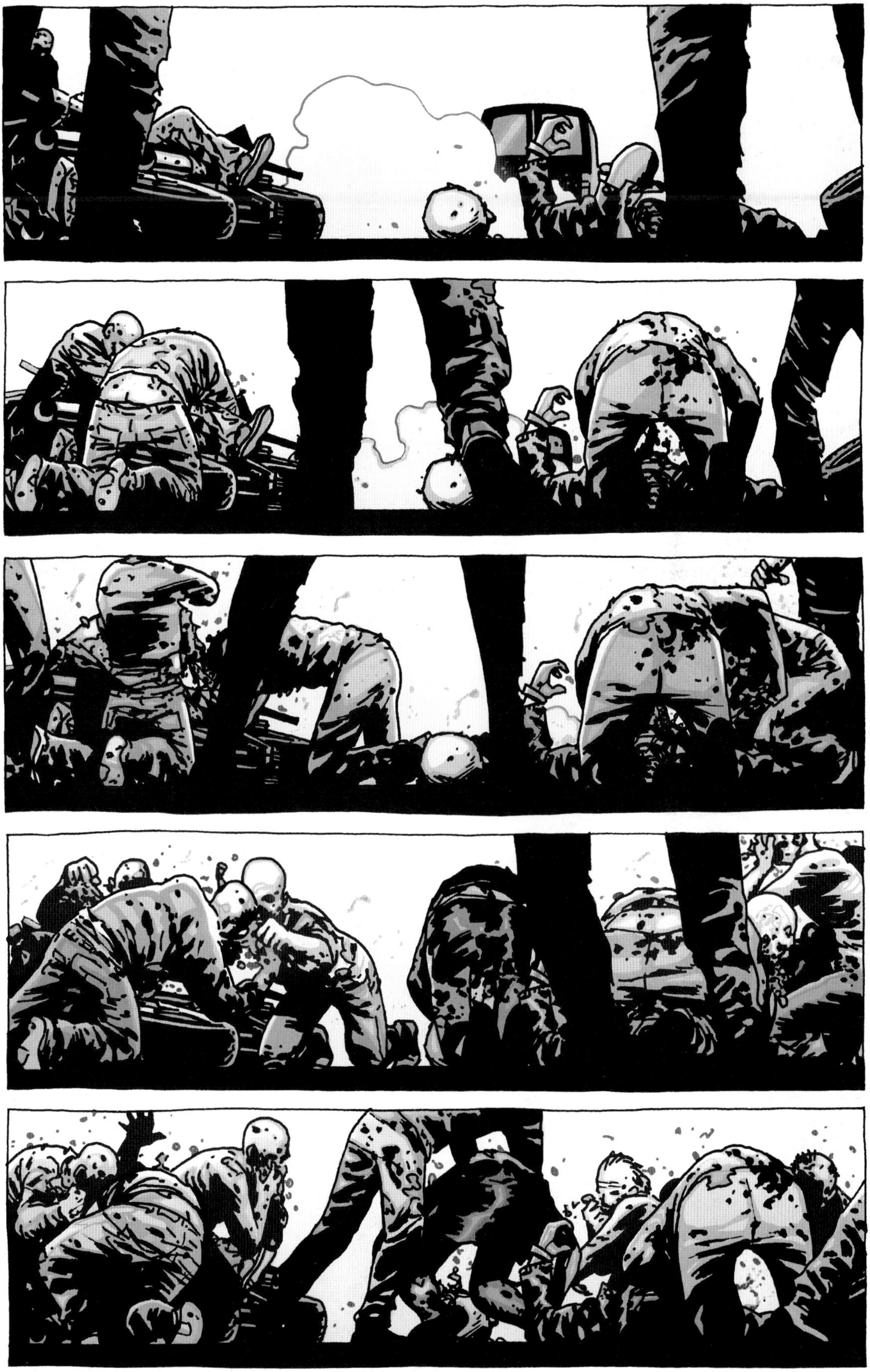

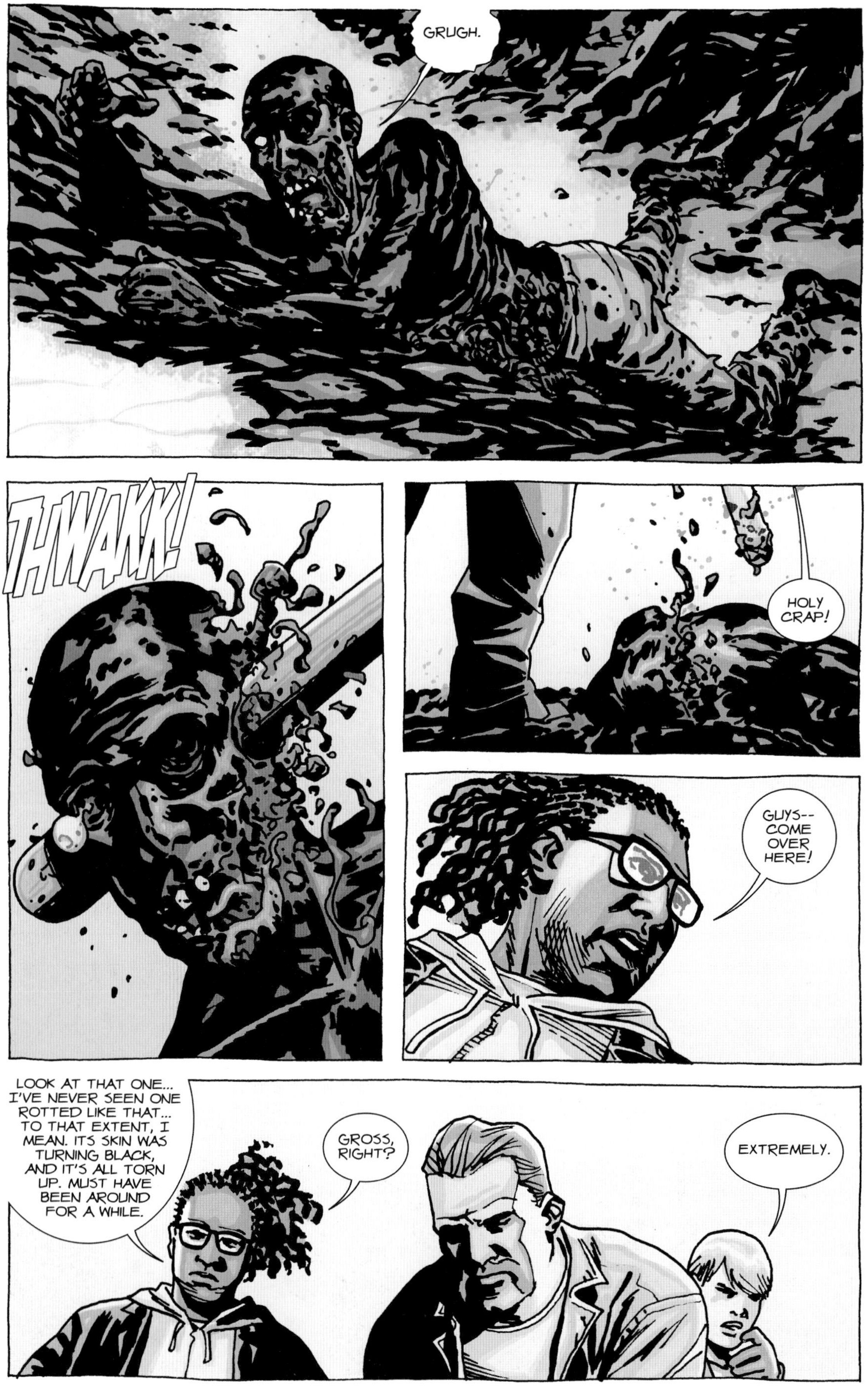
GRUGH.
THWAKK!
HOLY CRAP!
GUYS-- COME OVER HERE!
LOOK AT THAT ONE... I'VE NEVER SEEN ONE ROTTED LIKE THAT... TO THAT EXTENT, I MEAN. ITS SKIN WAS TURNING BLACK, AND IT'S ALL TORN UP. MUST HAVE BEEN AROUND FOR A WHILE.
GROSS, RIGHT?
EXTREMELY.

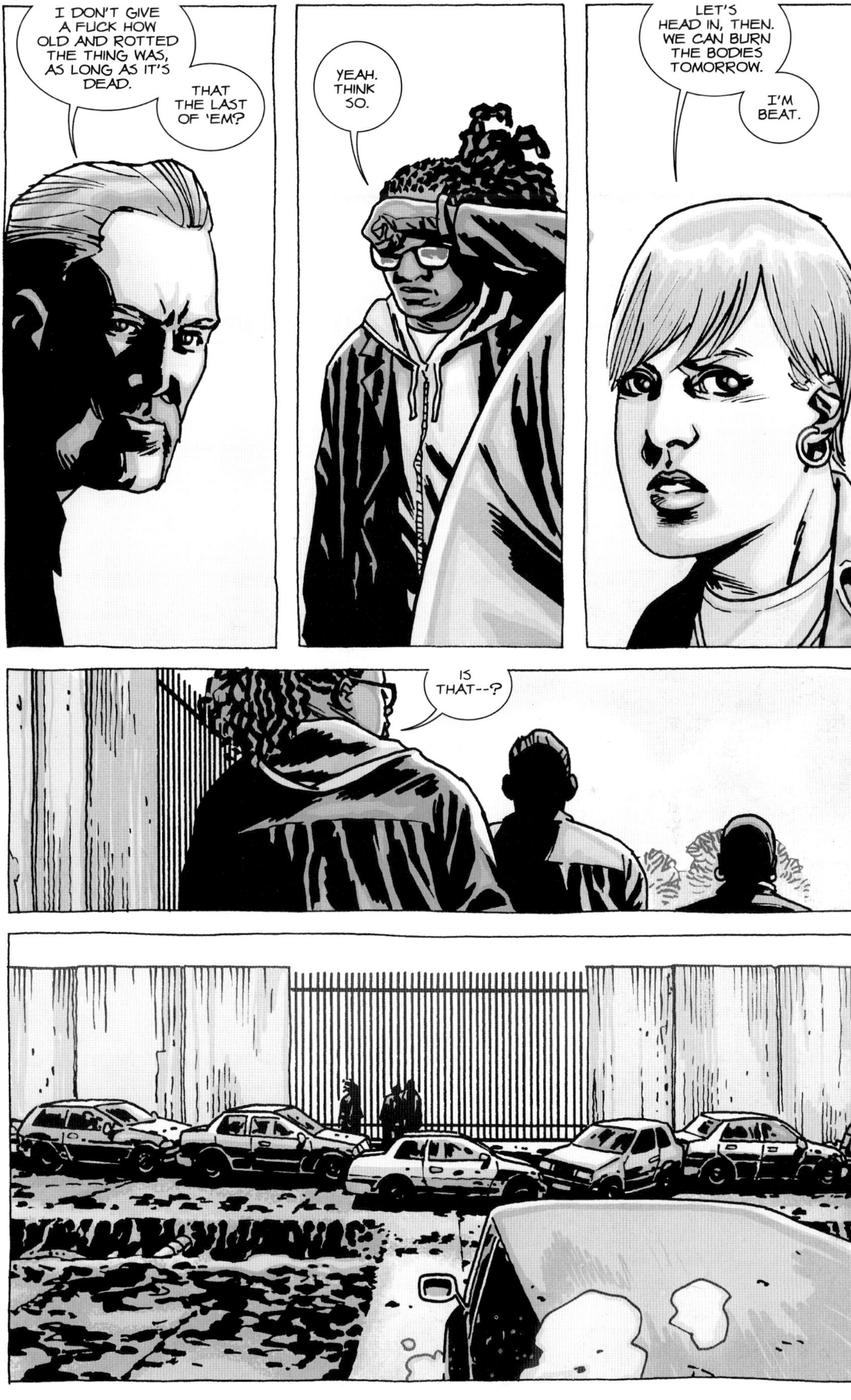
I DON'T GIVE A FUCK HOW OLD AND ROTTED THE THING WAS, AS LONG AS IT'S DEAD.
THAT THE LAST OF 'EM?
YEAH. THINK SO.
LET'S HEAD IN, THEN. WE CAN BURN THE BODIES TOMORROW.
I'M BEAT.
IS THAT--?

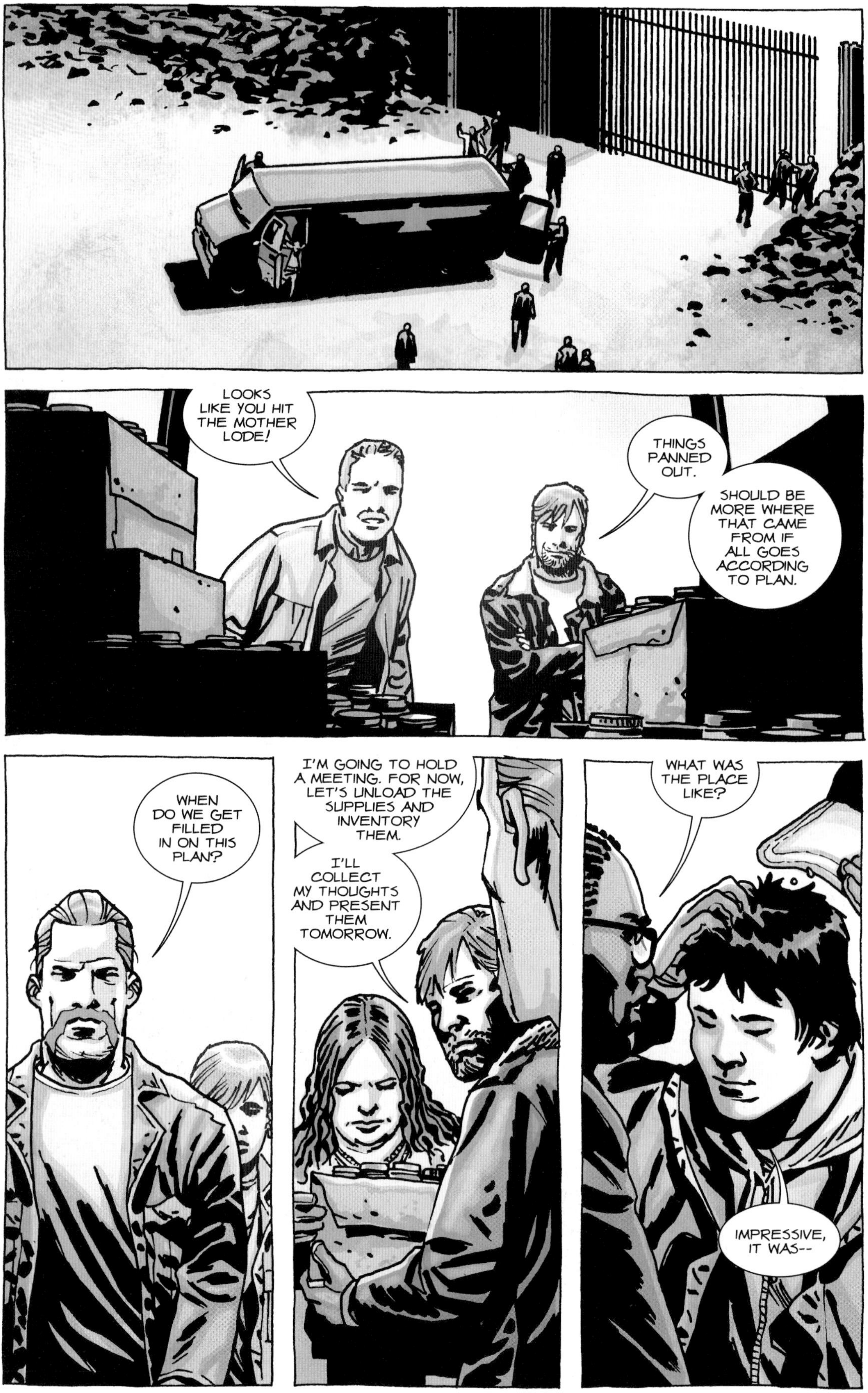
LOOKS LIKE YOU HIT THE MOTHER LODE!
THINGS PANNED OUT.
SHOULD BE MORE WHERE THAT CAME FROM IF ALL GOES ACCORDING TO PLAN.
WHEN DO WE GET FILLED IN ON THIS PLAN?
I'M GOING TO HOLD A MEETING. FOR NOW, LET'S UNLOAD THE SUPPLIES AND INVENTORY THEM.
I'LL COLLECT MY THOUGHTS AND PRESENT THEM TOMORROW.
WHAT WAS THE PLACE LIKE?
IMPRESSIVE, IT WAS--

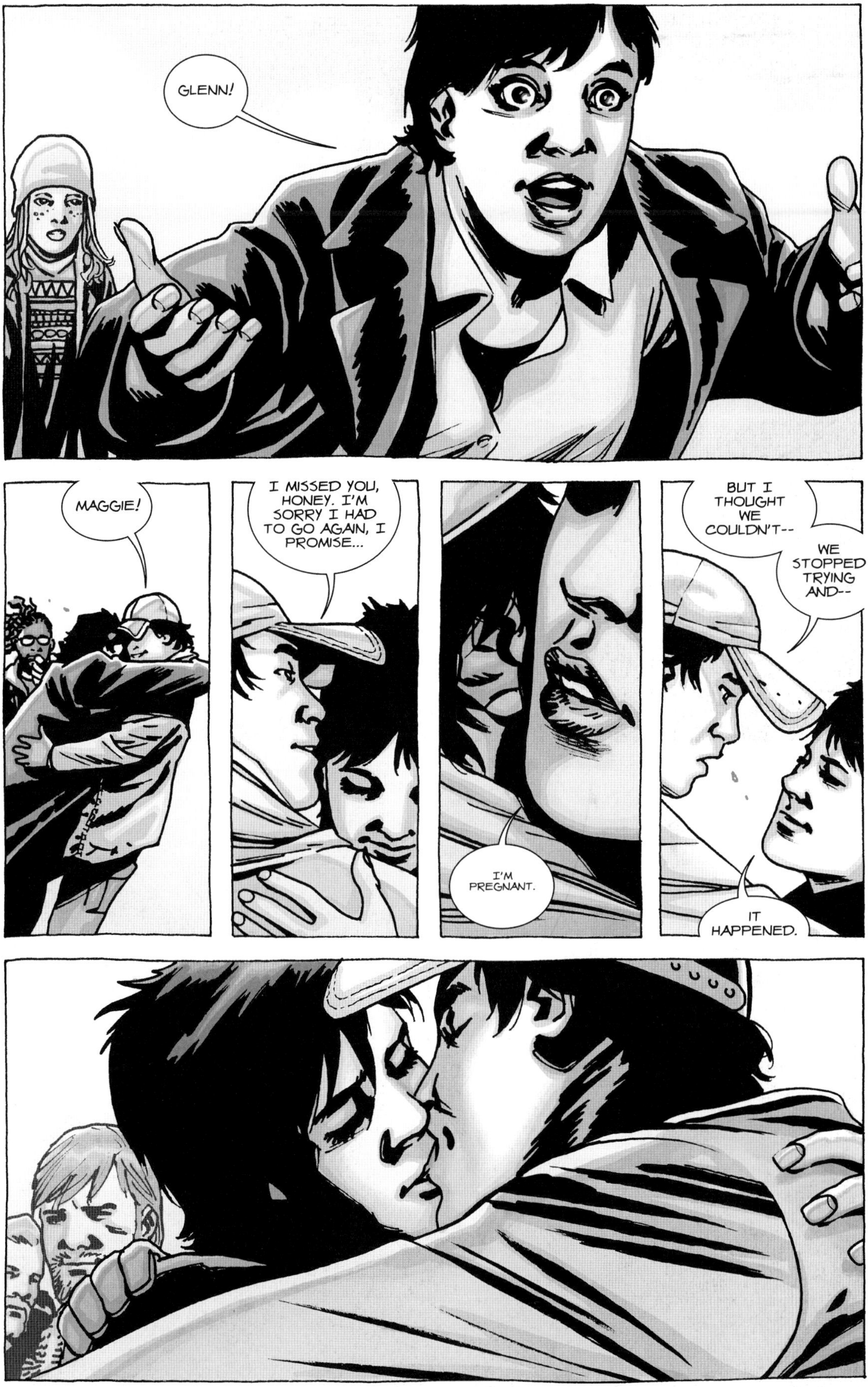
GLENN!
MAGGIE!
I MISSED YOU, HONEY. I'M SORRY I HAD TO GO AGAIN, I PROMISE...
I'M PREGNANT.
BUT I THOUGHT WE COULDN'T--
WE STOPPED TRYING AND--
IT HAPPENED.

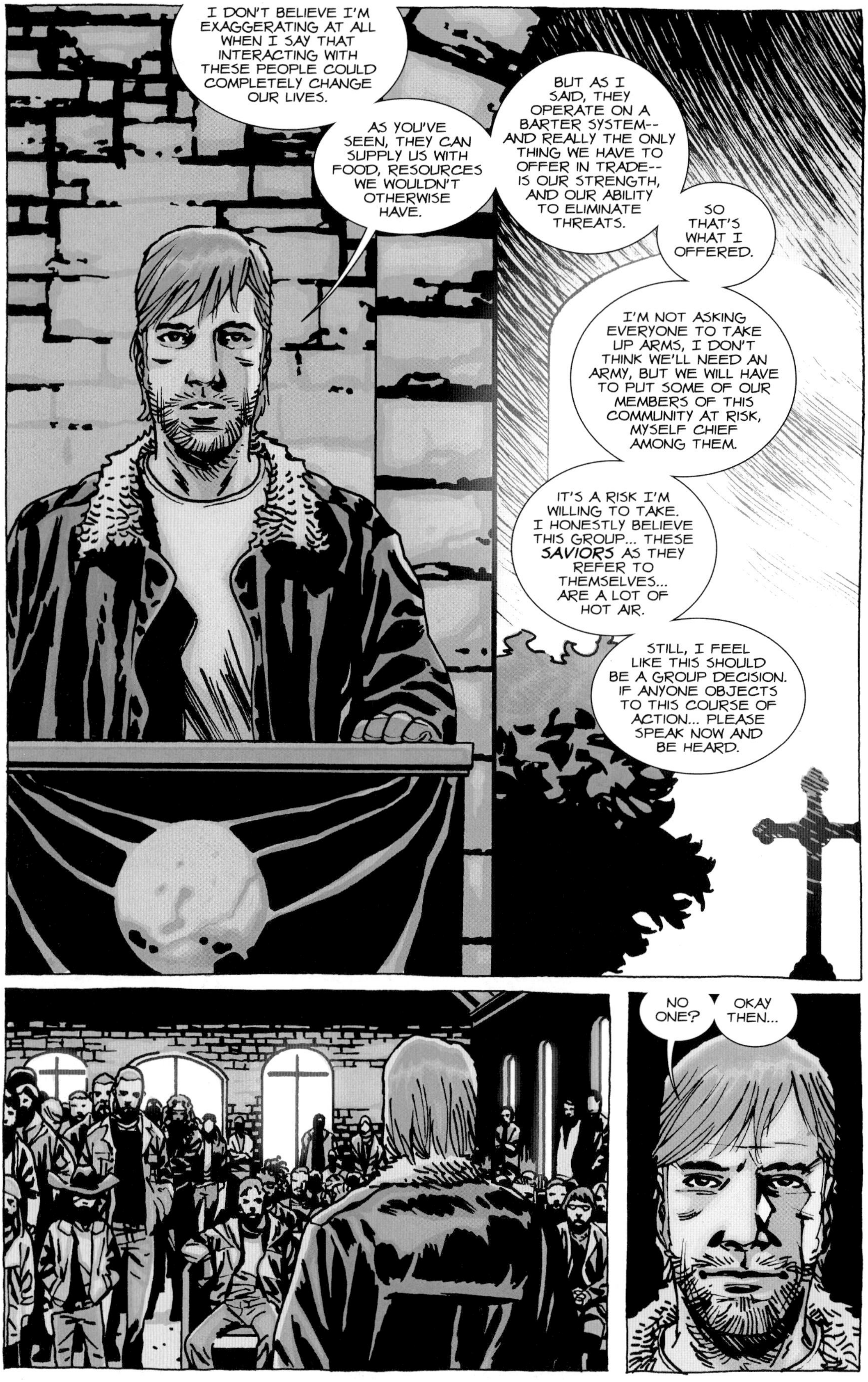
I DON'T BELIEVE I'M EXAGGERATING AT ALL WHEN I SAY THAT INTERACTING WITH THESE PEOPLE COULD COMPLETELY CHANGE OUR LIVES.
AS YOU'VE SEEN, THEY CAN SUPPLY US WITH FOOD, RESOURCES WE WOULDN'T OTHERWISE HAVE.
BUT AS I SAID, THEY OPERATE ON A BARTER SYSTEM-- AND REALLY THE ONLY THING WE HAVE TO OFFER IN TRADE-- IS OUR STRENGTH, AND OUR ABILITY TO ELIMINATE THREATS.
SO THAT'S WHAT I OFFERED.
I'M NOT ASKING EVERYONE TO TAKE UP ARMS, I DON'T THINK WE'LL NEED AN ARMY, BUT WE WILL HAVE TO PUT SOME OF OUR MEMBERS OF THIS COMMUNITY AT RISK, MYSELF CHIEF AMONG THEM.
IT'S A RISK I'M WILLING TO TAKE. I HONESTLY BELIEVE THIS GROUP... THESE *SAVIORS* AS THEY REFER TO THEMSELVES... ARE A LOT OF HOT AIR.
STILL, I FEEL LIKE THIS SHOULD BE A GROUP DECISION. IF ANYONE OBJECTS TO THIS COURSE OF ACTION... PLEASE SPEAK NOW AND BE HEARD.
NO ONE?
OKAY THEN...

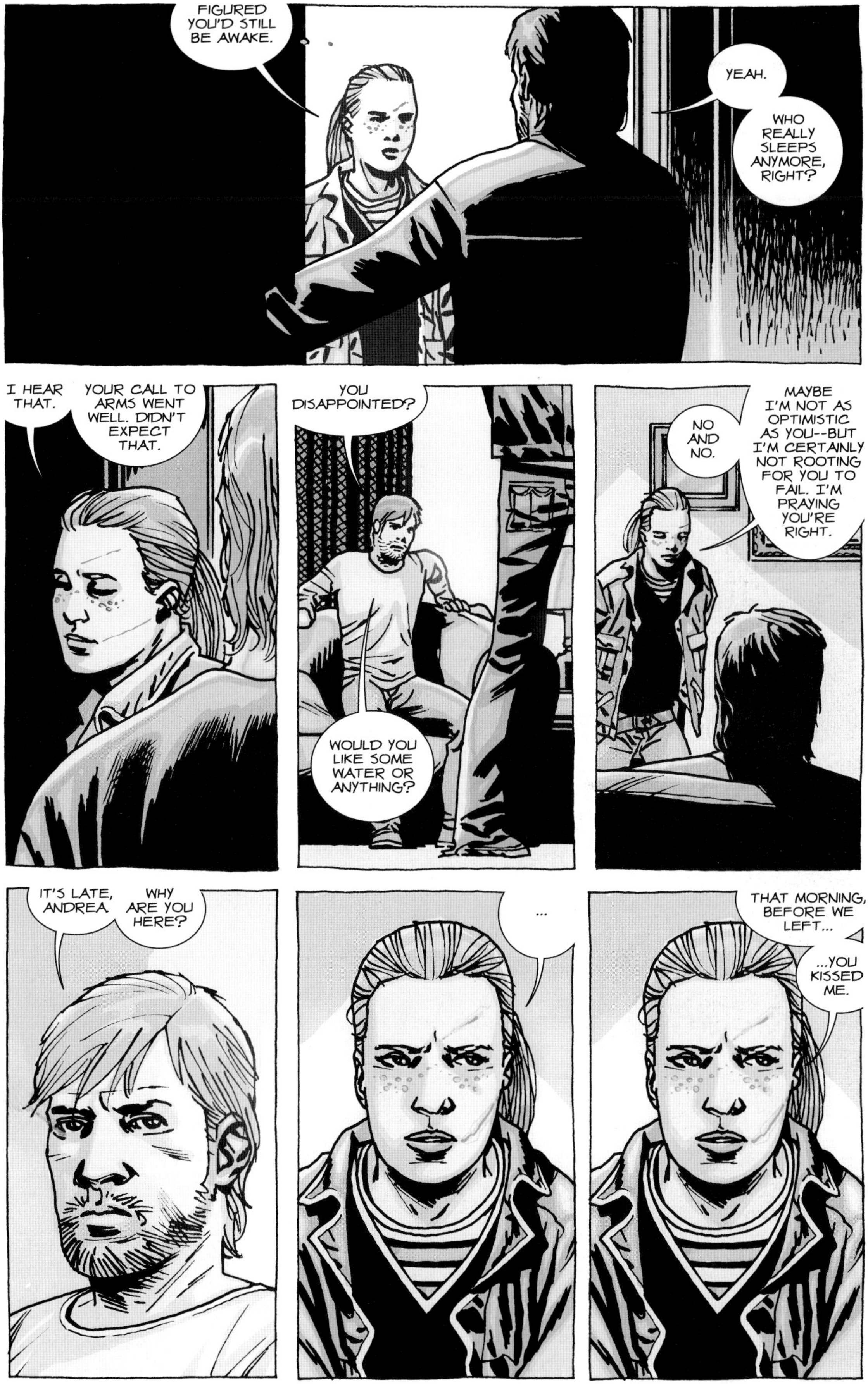
FIGURED YOU'D STILL BE AWAKE.
YEAH.
WHO REALLY SLEEPS ANYMORE, RIGHT?
I HEAR THAT.
YOUR CALL TO ARMS WENT WELL. DIDN'T EXPECT THAT.
YOU DISAPPOINTED?
WOULD YOU LIKE SOME WATER OR ANYTHING?
NO AND NO.
MAYBE I'M NOT AS OPTIMISTIC AS YOU--BUT I'M CERTAINLY NOT ROOTING FOR YOU TO FAIL. I'M PRAYING YOU'RE RIGHT.
IT'S LATE, ANDREA.
WHY ARE YOU HERE?
...
THAT MORNING, BEFORE WE LEFT...
...YOU KISSED ME.

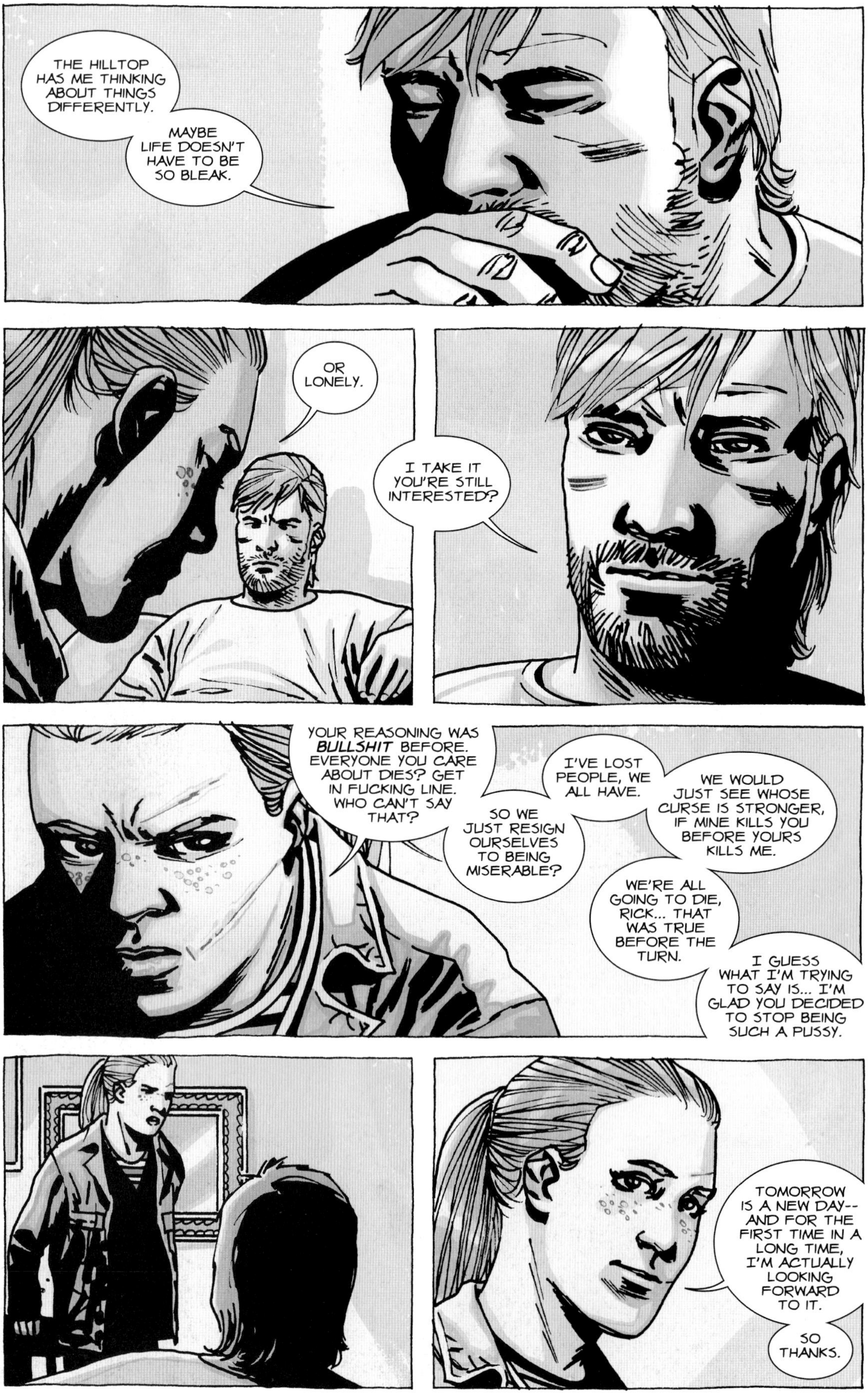
THE HILLTOP HAS ME THINKING ABOUT THINGS DIFFERENTLY.
MAYBE LIFE DOESN'T HAVE TO BE SO BLEAK.
OR LONELY.
I TAKE IT YOU'RE STILL INTERESTED?
YOUR REASONING WAS **BULLSHIT** BEFORE. EVERYONE YOU CARE ABOUT DIES? GET IN FUCKING LINE. WHO CAN'T SAY THAT?
SO WE JUST RESIGN OURSELVES TO BEING MISERABLE?
I'VE LOST PEOPLE, WE ALL HAVE.
WE WOULD JUST SEE WHOSE CURSE IS STRONGER, IF MINE KILLS YOU BEFORE YOURS KILLS ME.
WE'RE ALL GOING TO DIE, RICK... THAT WAS TRUE BEFORE THE TURN.
I GUESS WHAT I'M TRYING TO SAY IS... I'M GLAD YOU DECIDED TO STOP BEING SUCH A PUSSY.
TOMORROW IS A NEW DAY-- AND FOR THE FIRST TIME IN A LONG TIME, I'M ACTUALLY LOOKING FORWARD TO IT.
SO THANKS.

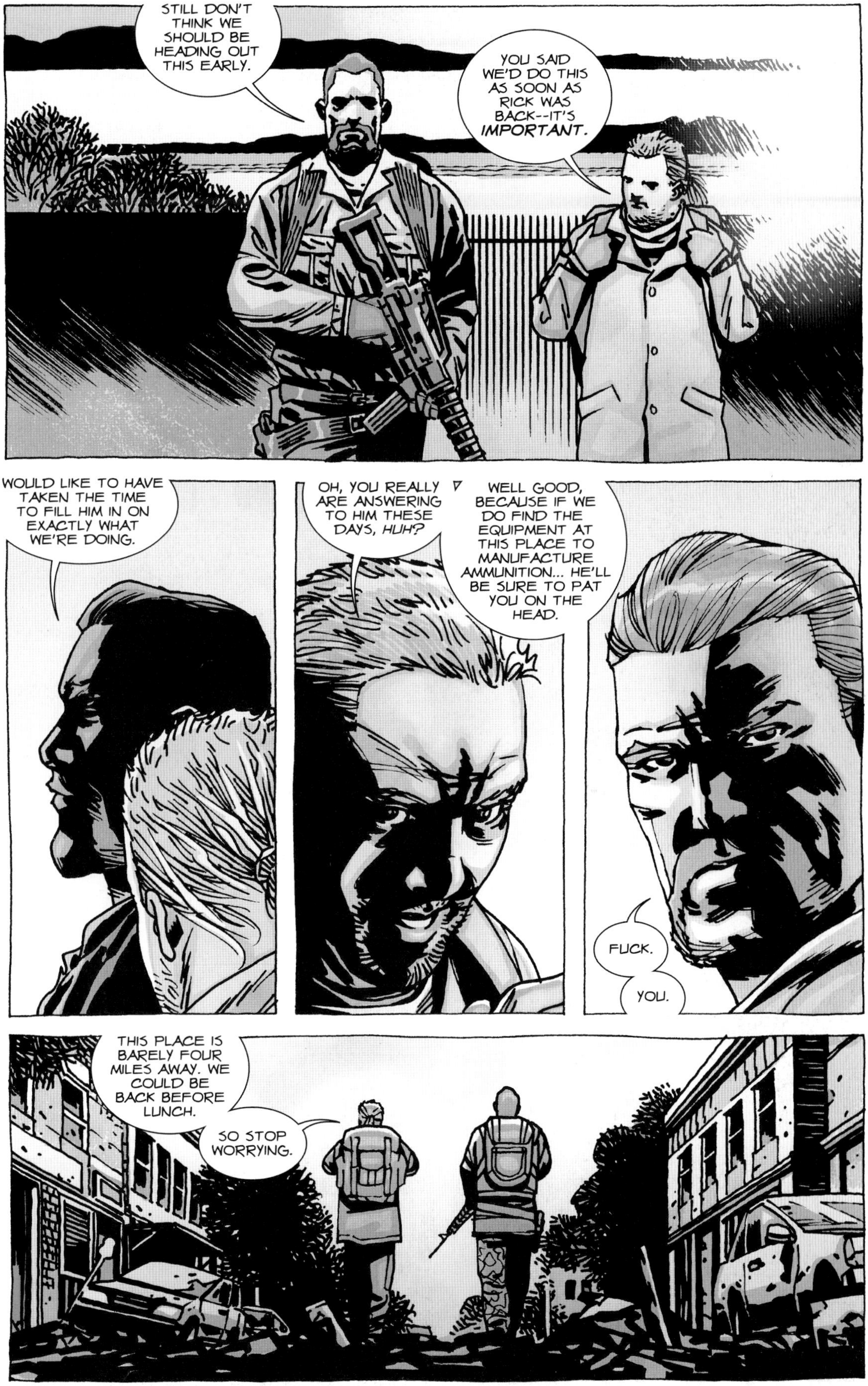
STILL DON'T THINK WE SHOULD BE HEADING OUT THIS EARLY.
YOU SAID WE'D DO THIS AS SOON AS RICK WAS BACK--IT'S *IMPORTANT*.
WOULD LIKE TO HAVE TAKEN THE TIME TO FILL HIM IN ON EXACTLY WHAT WE'RE DOING.
OH, YOU REALLY ARE ANSWERING TO HIM THESE DAYS, *HUH?*
WELL GOOD, BECAUSE IF WE DO FIND THE EQUIPMENT AT THIS PLACE TO MANUFACTURE AMMUNITION... HE'LL BE SURE TO PAT YOU ON THE HEAD.
FUCK.
YOU.
THIS PLACE IS BARELY FOUR MILES AWAY. WE COULD BE BACK BEFORE LUNCH.
SO STOP WORRYING.

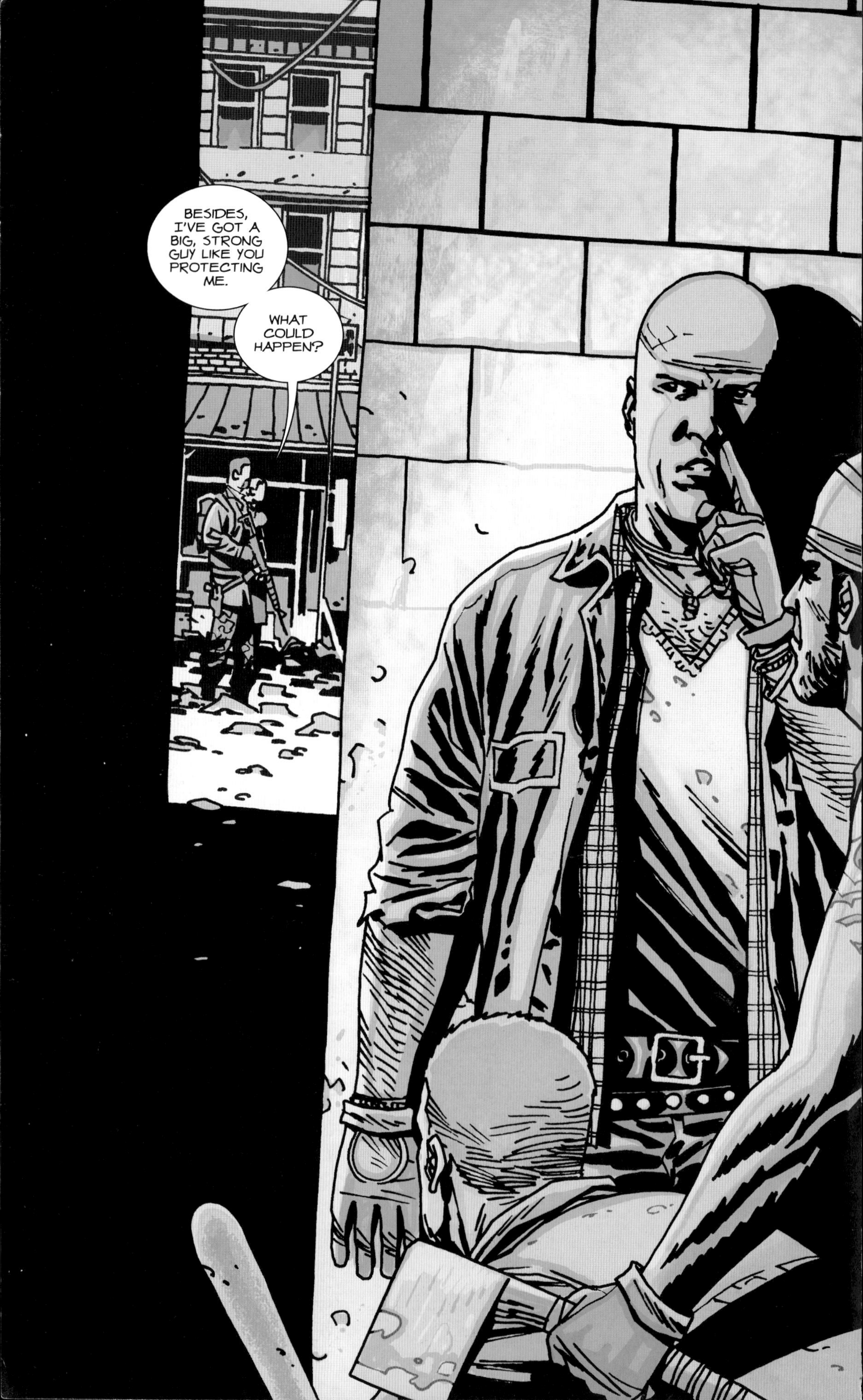
BESIDES, I'VE GOT A BIG, STRONG GUY LIKE YOU PROTECTING ME.
WHAT COULD HAPPEN?

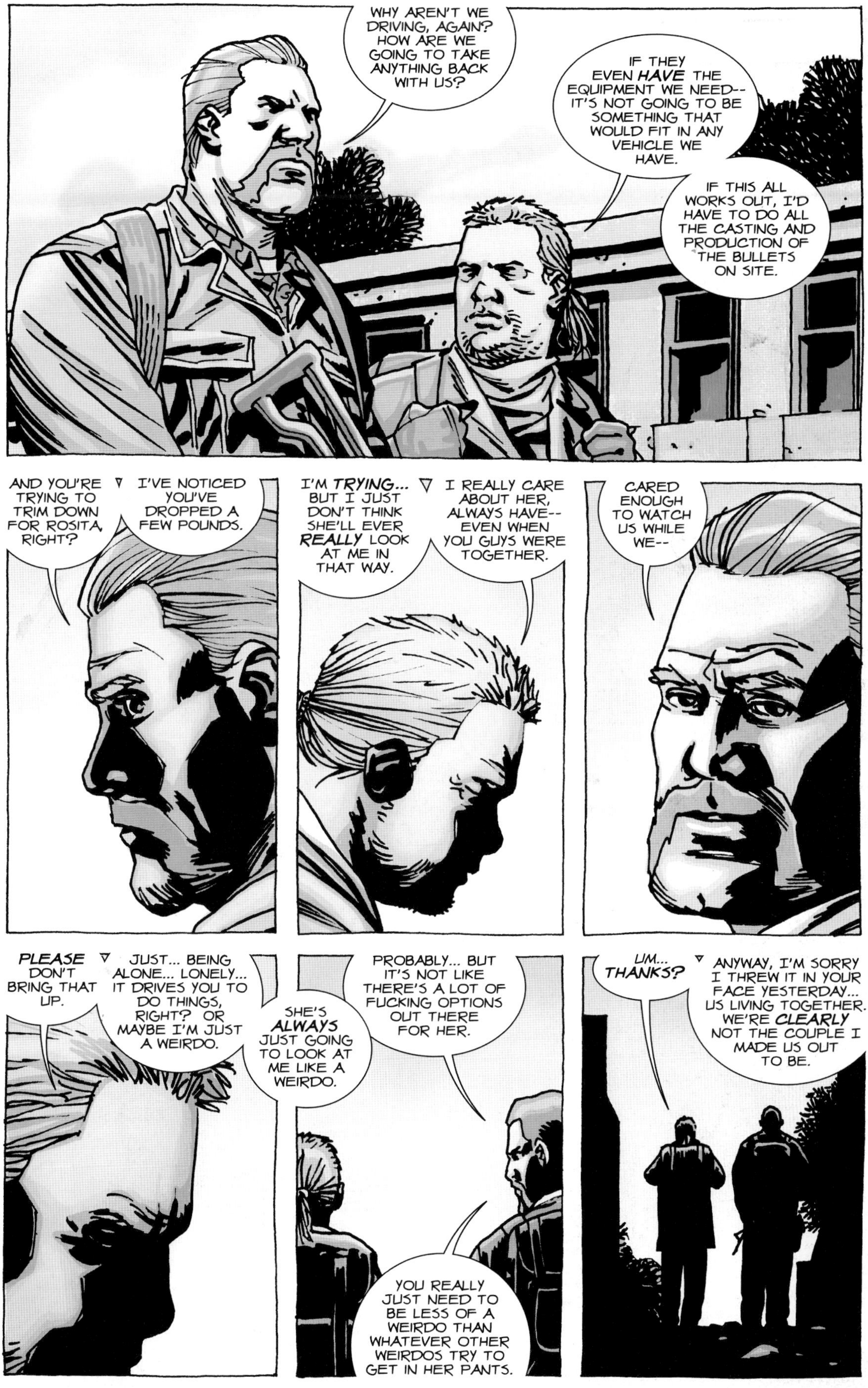
WHY AREN'T WE DRIVING, AGAIN? HOW ARE WE GOING TO TAKE ANYTHING BACK WITH US?
IF THEY EVEN HAVE THE EQUIPMENT WE NEED-- IT'S NOT GOING TO BE SOMETHING THAT WOULD FIT IN ANY VEHICLE WE HAVE.
IF THIS ALL WORKS OUT, I'D HAVE TO DO ALL THE CASTING AND PRODUCTION OF THE BULLETS ON SITE.
AND YOU'RE TRYING TO TRIM DOWN FOR ROSITA, RIGHT?
I'VE NOTICED YOU'VE DROPPED A FEW POUNDS.
I'M TRYING... BUT I JUST DON'T THINK SHE'LL EVER REALLY LOOK AT ME IN THAT WAY.
I REALLY CARE ABOUT HER, ALWAYS HAVE-- EVEN WHEN YOU GUYS WERE TOGETHER.
CARED ENOUGH TO WATCH US WHILE WE--
PLEASE DON'T BRING THAT UP.
JUST... BEING ALONE... LONELY... IT DRIVES YOU TO DO THINGS, RIGHT? OR MAYBE I'M JUST A WEIRDO.
SHE'S ALWAYS JUST GOING TO LOOK AT ME LIKE A WEIRDO.
PROBABLY... BUT IT'S NOT LIKE THERE'S A LOT OF FUCKING OPTIONS OUT THERE FOR HER.
YOU REALLY JUST NEED TO BE LESS OF A WEIRDO THAN WHATEVER OTHER WEIRDOS TRY TO GET IN HER PANTS.
UM... THANKS?
ANYWAY, I'M SORRY I THREW IT IN YOUR FACE YESTERDAY... US LIVING TOGETHER. WE'RE CLEARLY NOT THE COUPLE I MADE US OUT TO BE.

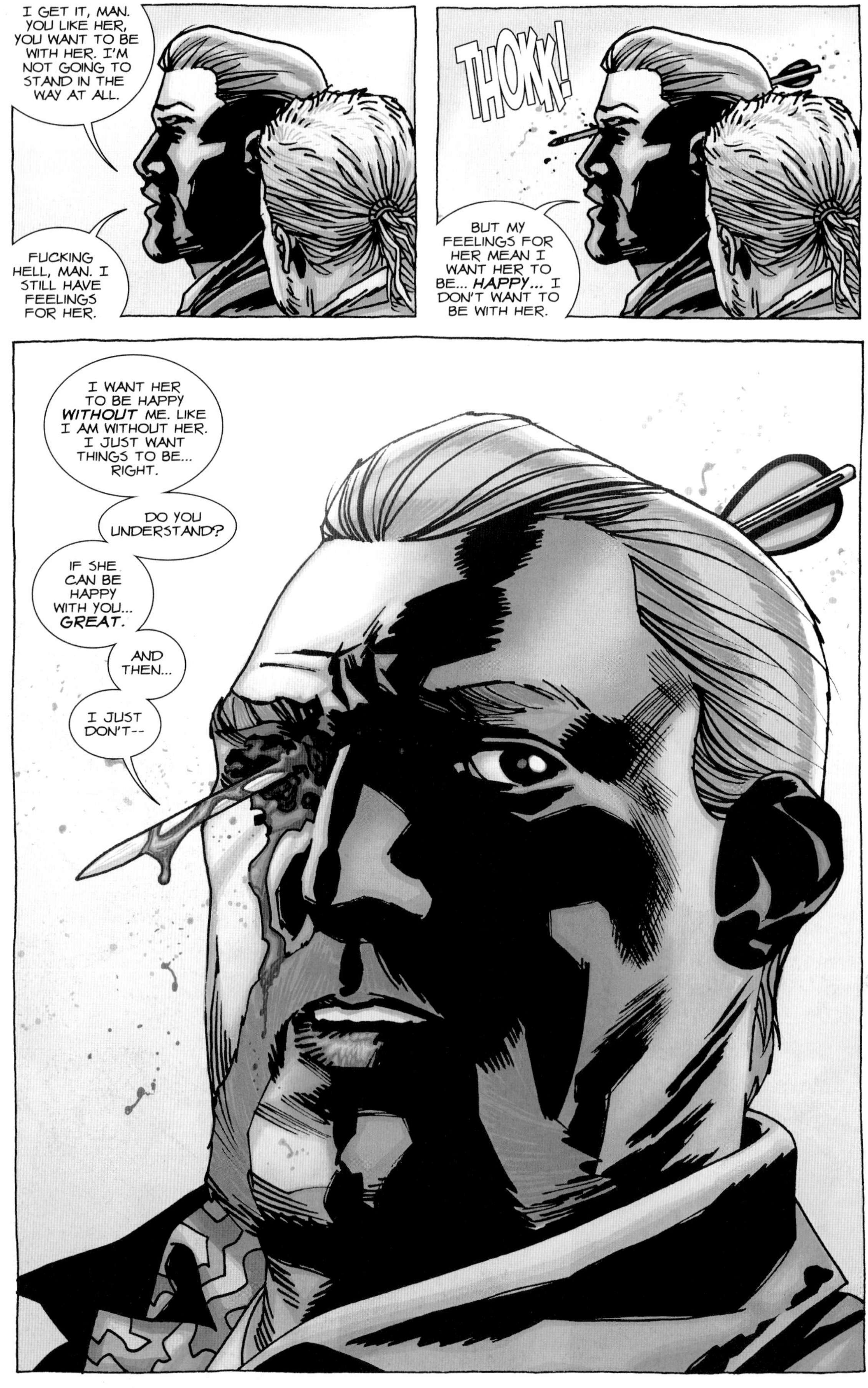
I GET IT, MAN. YOU LIKE HER, YOU WANT TO BE WITH HER. I'M NOT GOING TO STAND IN THE WAY AT ALL.
FUCKING HELL, MAN. I STILL HAVE FEELINGS FOR HER.
THOKK!
BUT MY FEELINGS FOR HER MEAN I WANT HER TO BE... HAPPY... I DON'T WANT TO BE WITH HER.
I WANT HER TO BE HAPPY WITHOUT ME. LIKE I AM WITHOUT HER. I JUST WANT THINGS TO BE... RIGHT.
DO YOU UNDERSTAND?
IF SHE CAN BE HAPPY WITH YOU... GREAT.
AND THEN...
I JUST DON'T--

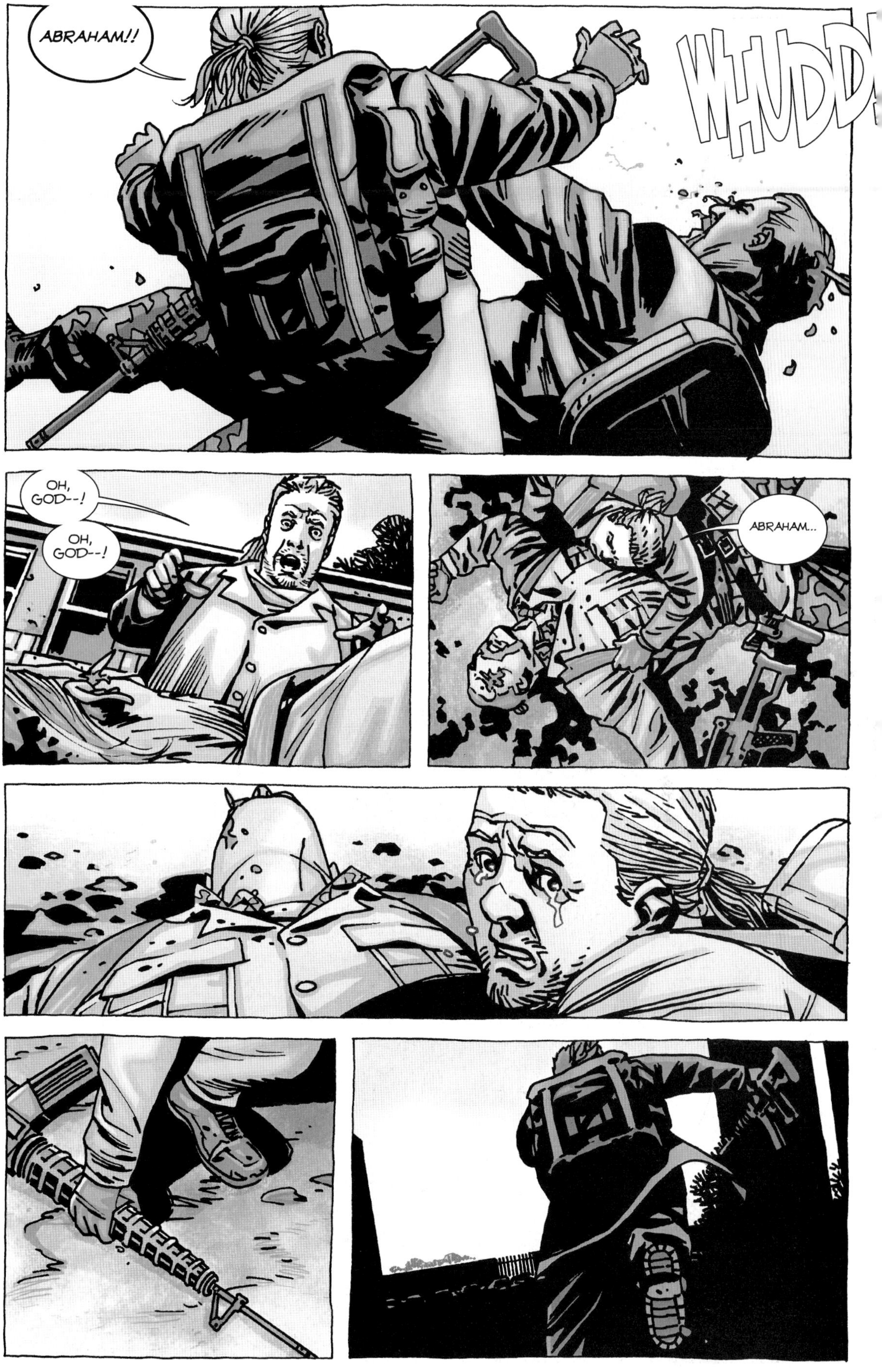
ABRAHAM!!
WHUDD
OH, GOD--!
OH, GOD--!
ABRAHAM...

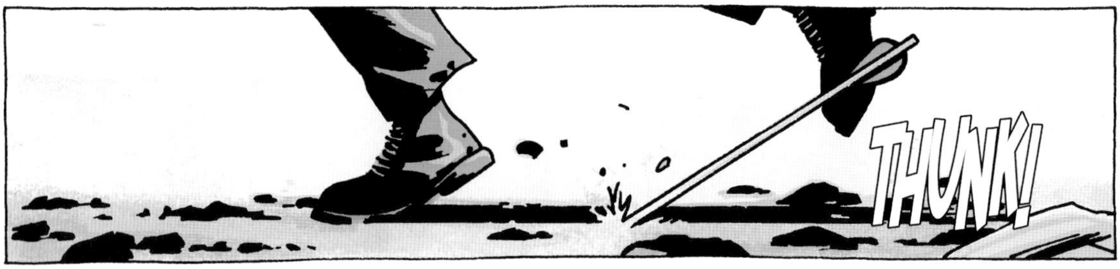
THUNK!

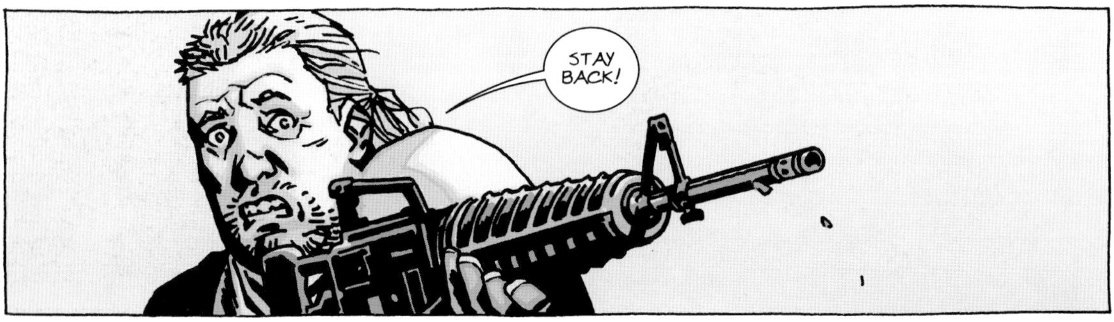
STAY BACK!

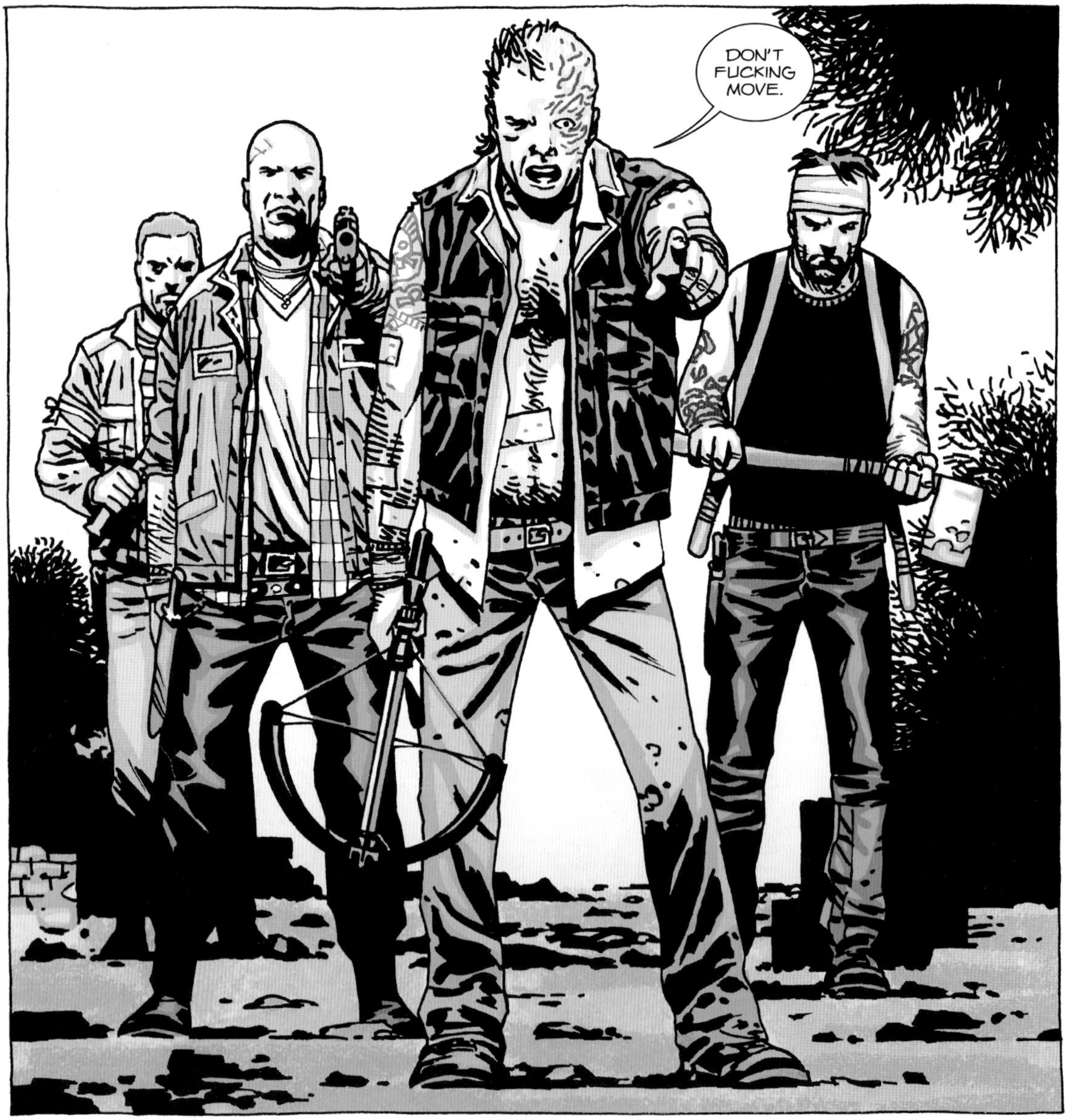
DON'T FUCKING MOVE.

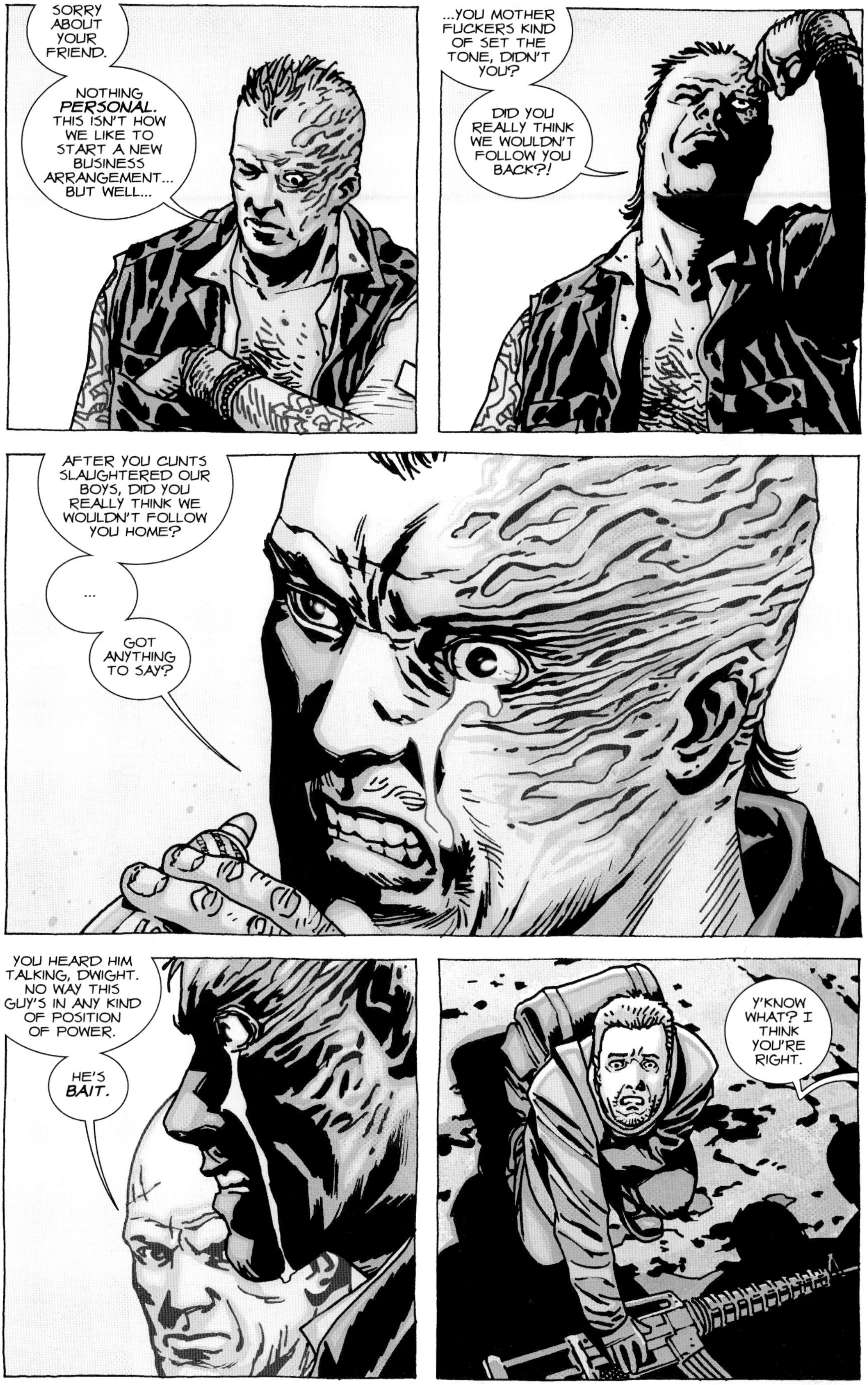
SORRY ABOUT YOUR FRIEND.
NOTHING PERSONAL. THIS ISN'T HOW WE LIKE TO START A NEW BUSINESS ARRANGEMENT... BUT WELL...
...YOU MOTHER FUCKERS KIND OF SET THE TONE, DIDN'T YOU?
DID YOU REALLY THINK WE WOULDN'T FOLLOW YOU BACK?!
AFTER YOU CUNTS SLAUGHTERED OUR BOYS, DID YOU REALLY THINK WE WOULDN'T FOLLOW YOU HOME?
...
GOT ANYTHING TO SAY?
YOU HEARD HIM TALKING, DWIGHT. NO WAY THIS GUY'S IN ANY KIND OF POSITION OF POWER.
HE'S BAIT.
Y'KNOW WHAT? I THINK YOU'RE RIGHT.

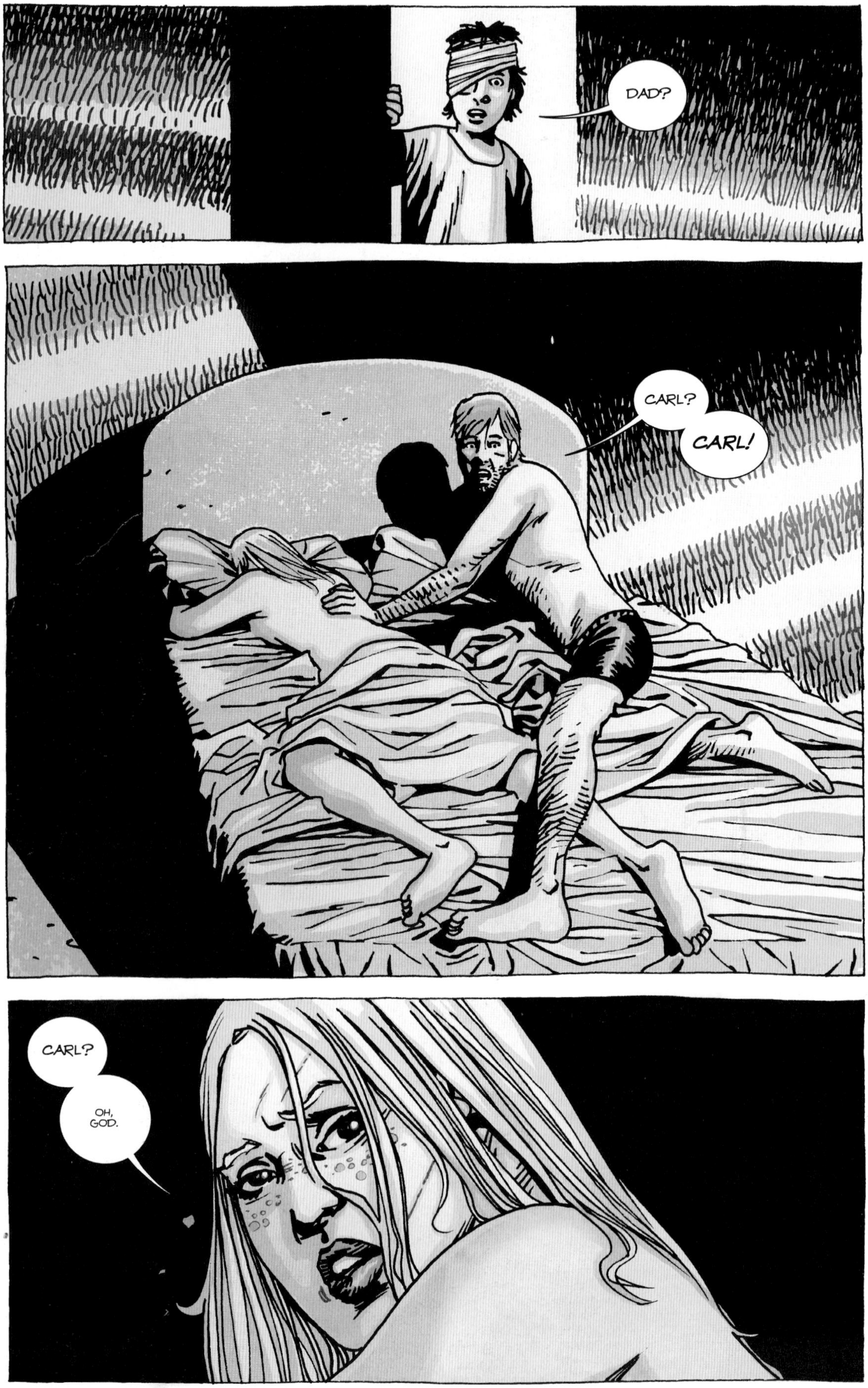
DAD?
CARL?
CARL!
CARL?
OH, GOD.

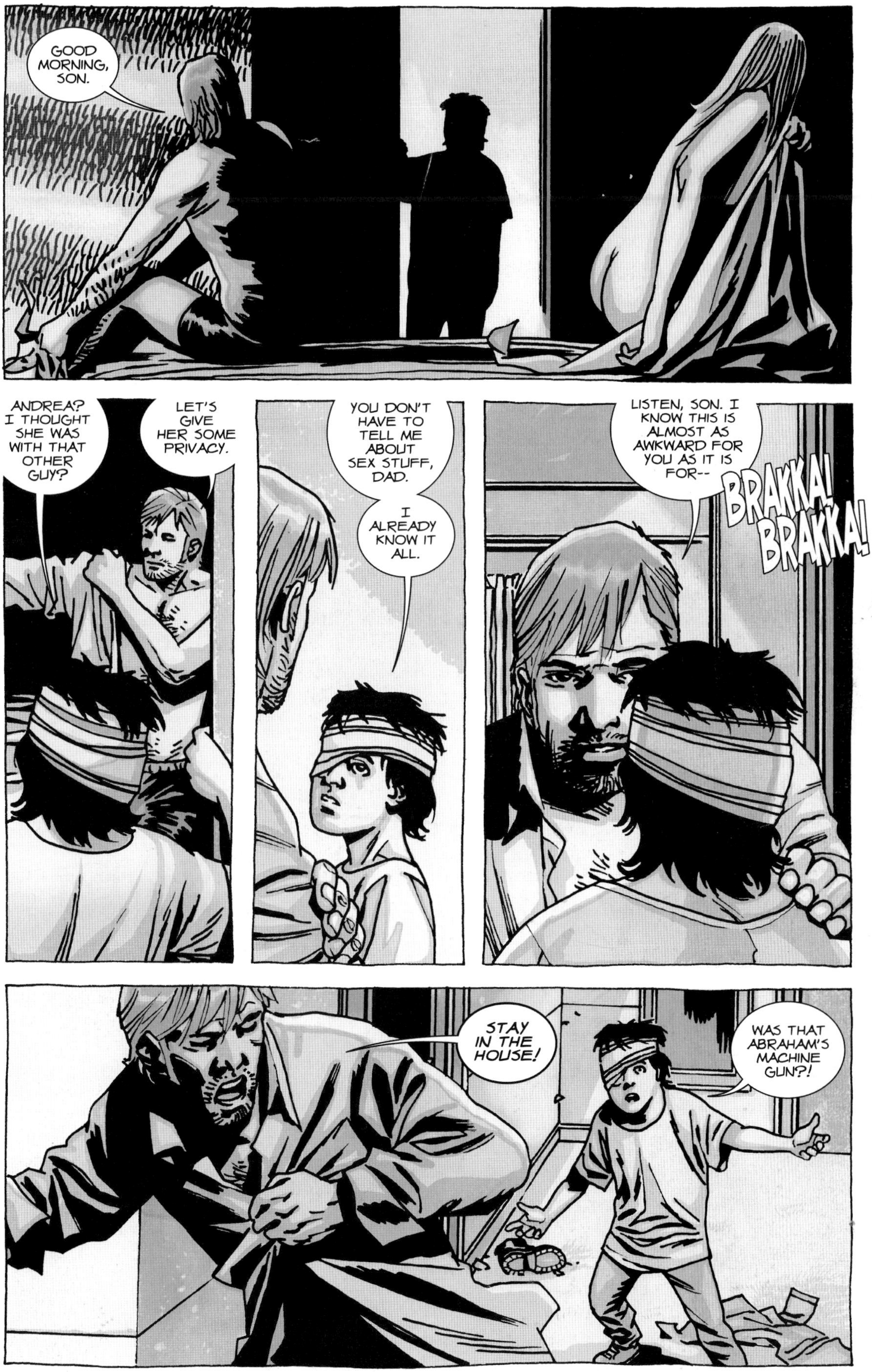
GOOD MORNING, SON.
ANDREA? I THOUGHT SHE WAS WITH THAT OTHER GUY?
LET'S GIVE HER SOME PRIVACY.
YOU DON'T HAVE TO TELL ME ABOUT SEX STUFF, DAD.
I ALREADY KNOW IT ALL.
LISTEN, SON. I KNOW THIS IS ALMOST AS AWKWARD FOR YOU AS IT IS FOR--
BRAKKA! BRAKKA!
STAY IN THE HOUSE!
WAS THAT ABRAHAM'S MACHINE GUN?!

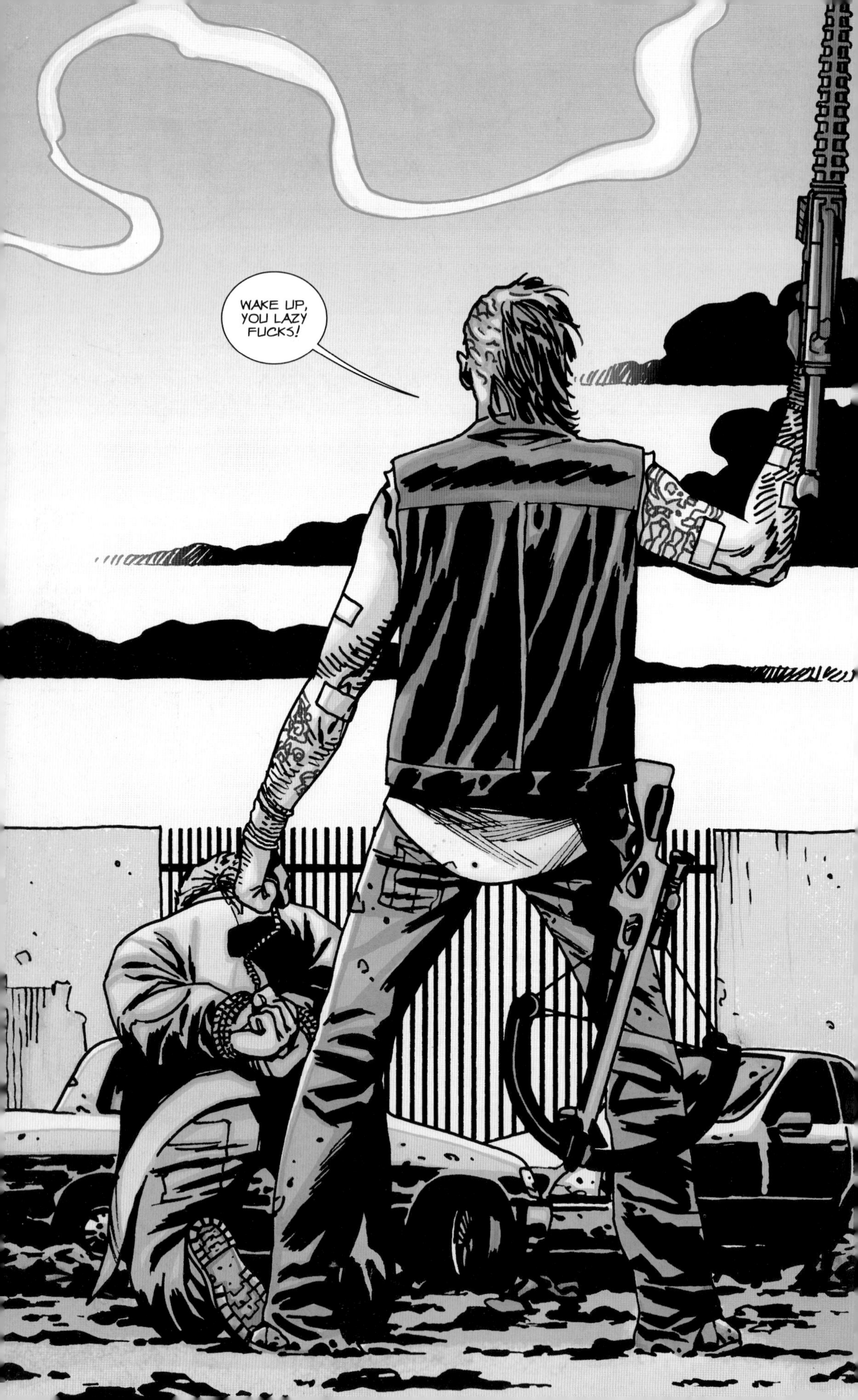
WAKE UP, YOU LAZY FUCKS!

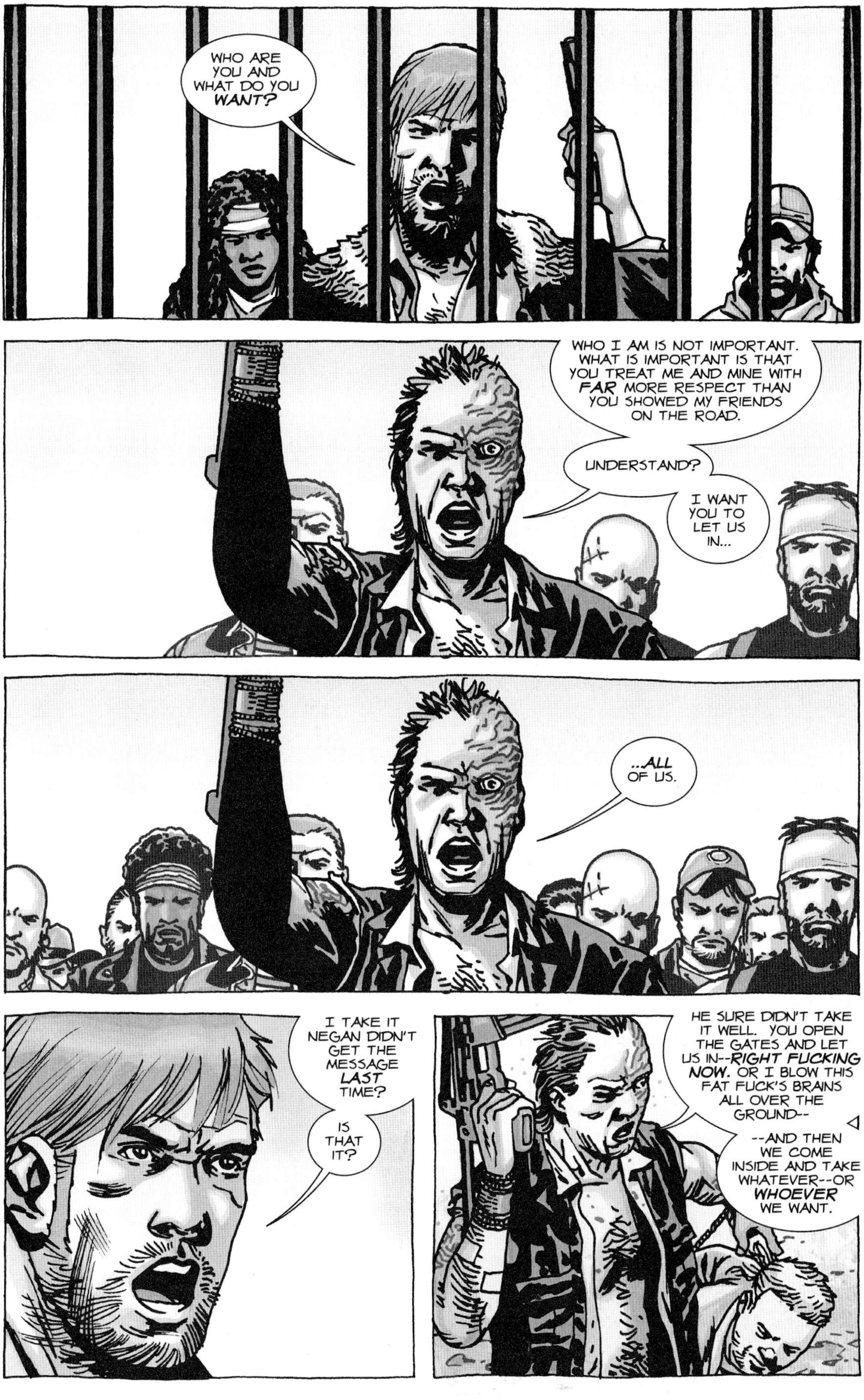

WHO ARE YOU AND WHAT DO YOU WANT?
WHO I AM IS NOT IMPORTANT. WHAT IS IMPORTANT IS THAT YOU TREAT ME AND MINE WITH FAR MORE RESPECT THAN YOU SHOWED MY FRIENDS ON THE ROAD.
UNDERSTAND?
I WANT YOU TO LET US IN...
...ALL OF US.
I TAKE IT NEGAN DIDN'T GET THE MESSAGE LAST TIME?
IS THAT IT?
HE SURE DIDN'T TAKE IT WELL. YOU OPEN THE GATES AND LET US IN--RIGHT FUCKING NOW. OR I BLOW THIS FAT FUCK'S BRAINS ALL OVER THE GROUND--
--AND THEN WE COME INSIDE AND TAKE WHATEVER--OR WHOEVER WE WANT.

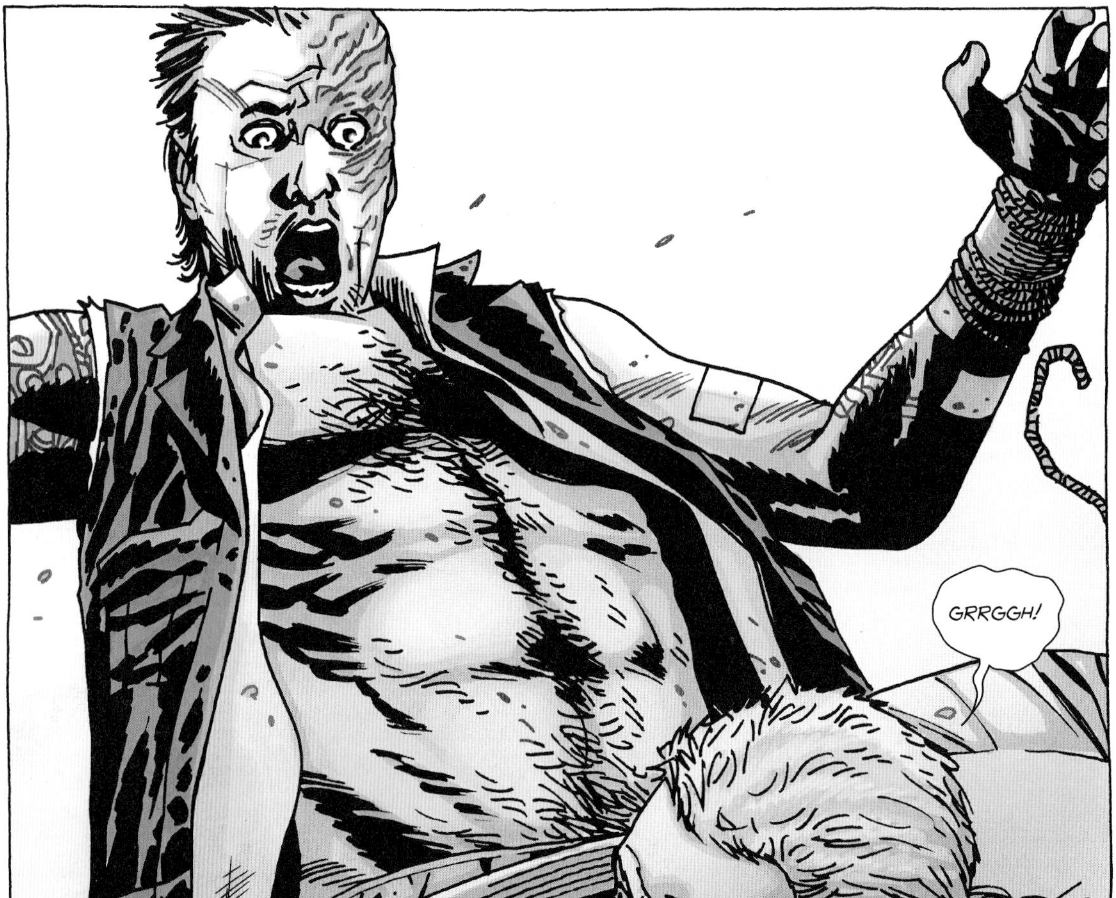
GRRGGH!

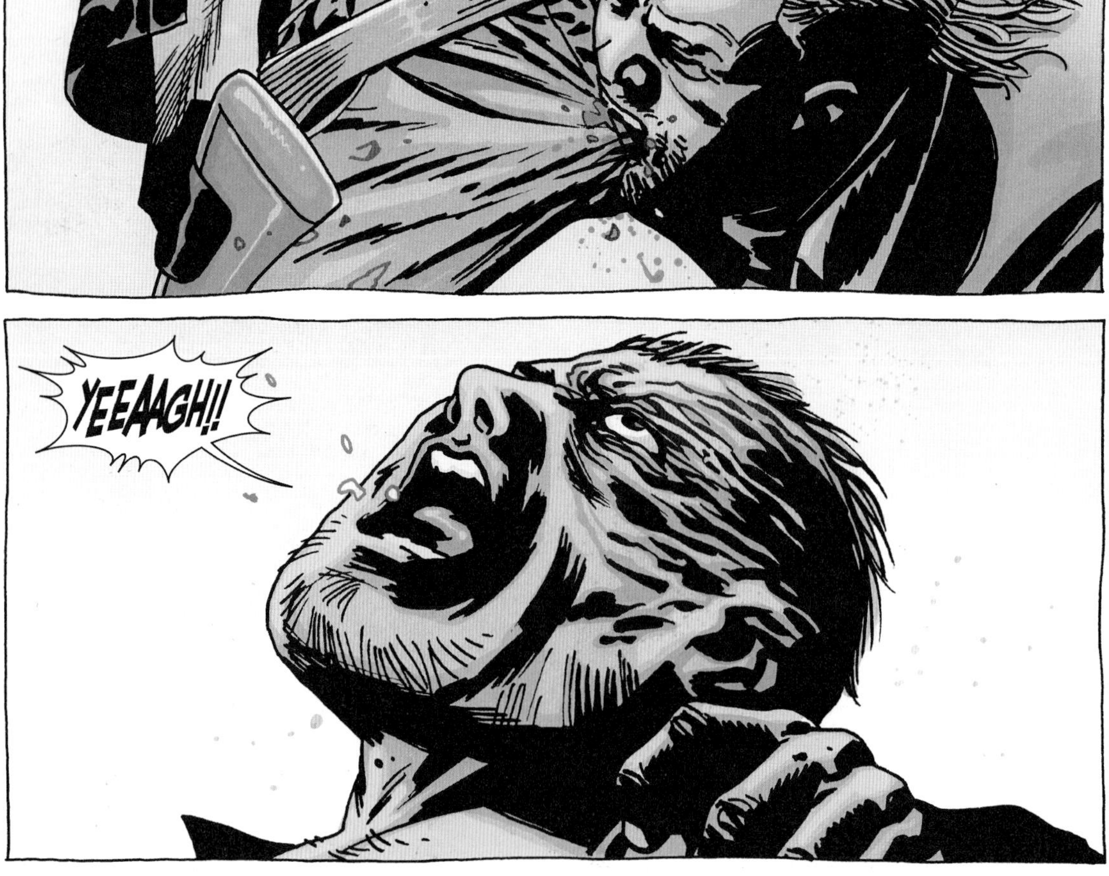
YEEAAGH!!

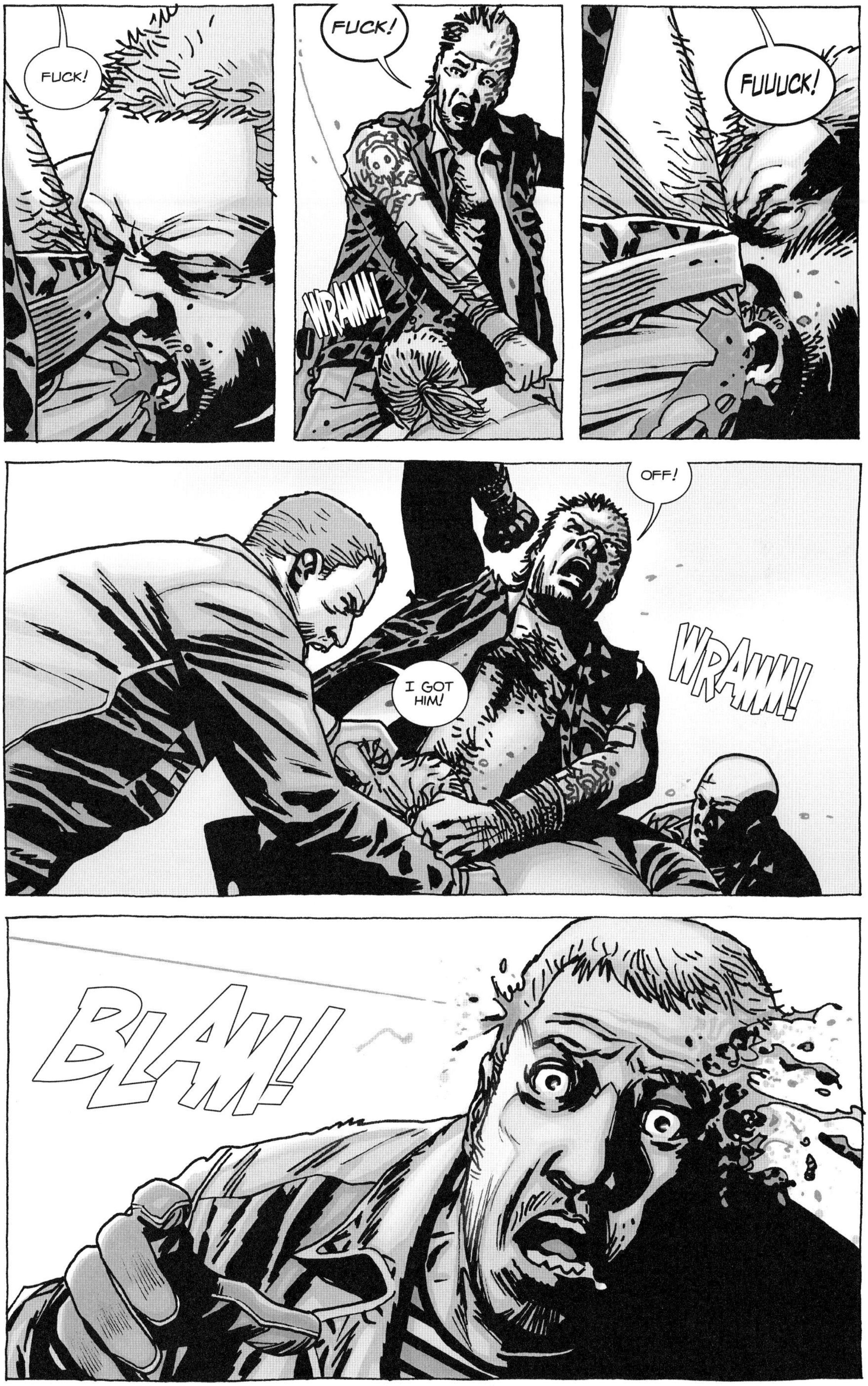
FUCK!
FUCK!
WRAMM!
FUUUCK!
OFF!
I GOT HIM!
WRAMM!
BLAM!

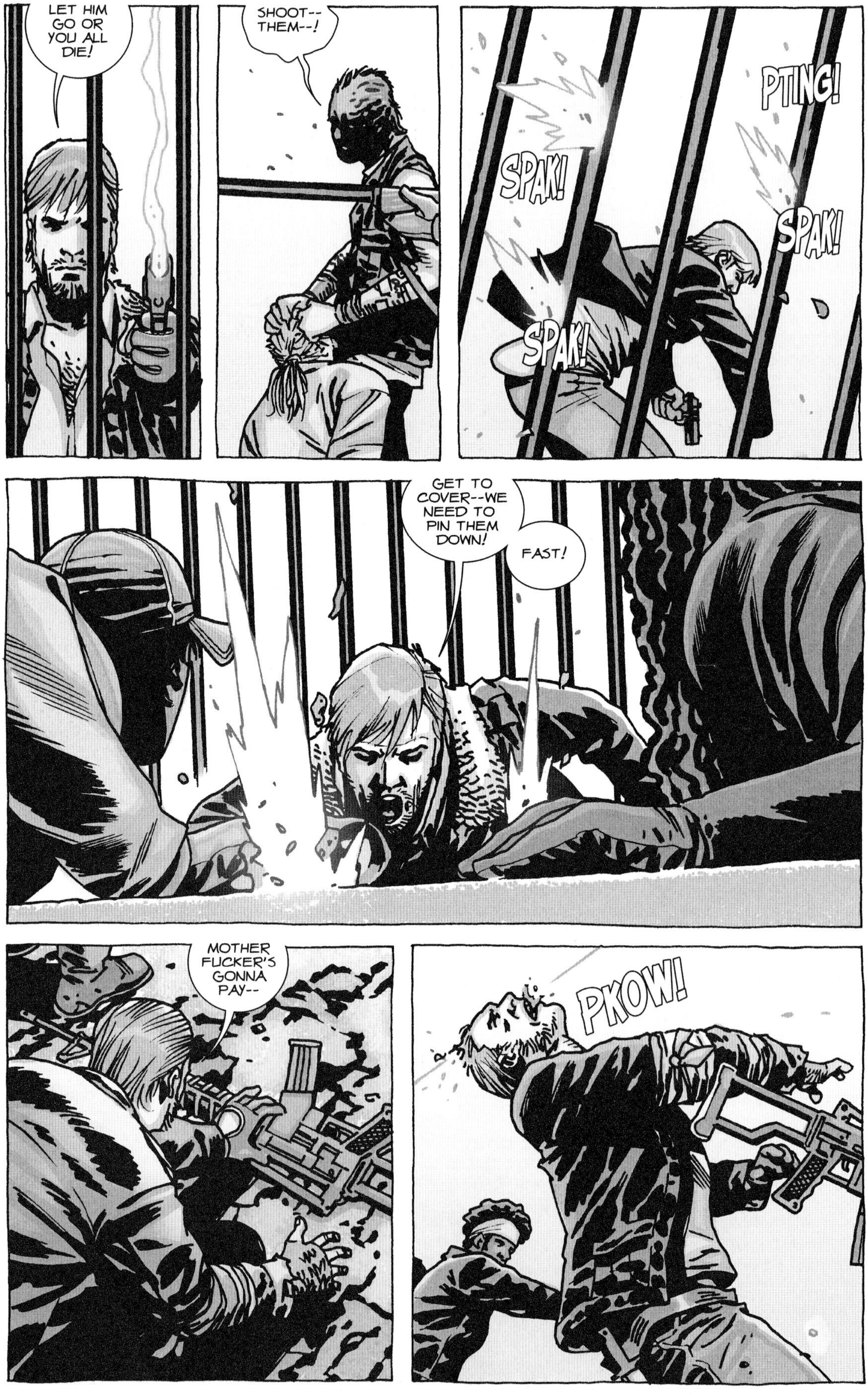
LET HIM GO OR YOU ALL DIE!
SHOOT-- THEM--!
PTING!
SPAK!
SPAK!
SPAK!
GET TO COVER--WE NEED TO PIN THEM DOWN!
FAST!
MOTHER FUCKER'S GONNA PAY--
PKOW!

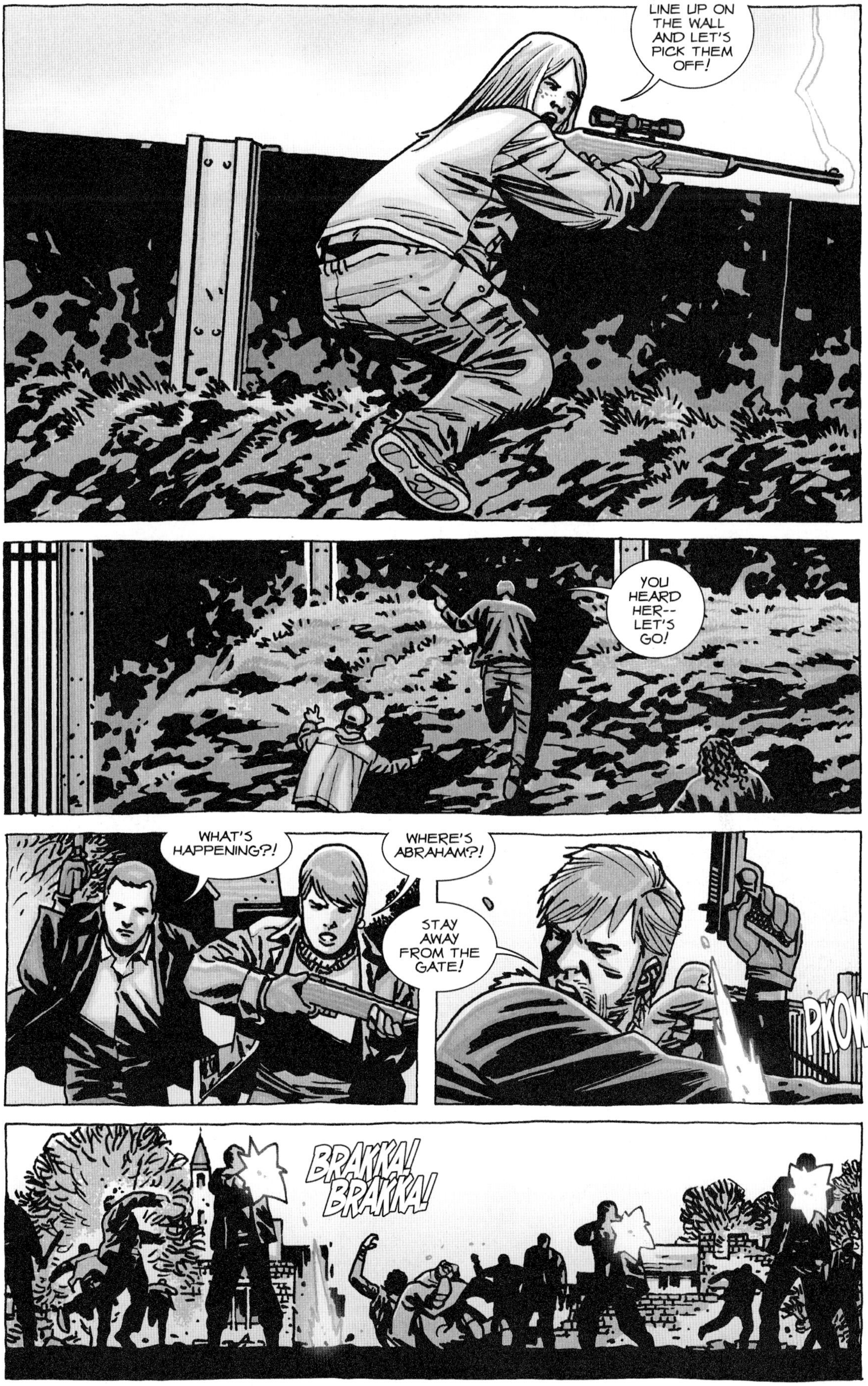
LINE UP ON THE WALL AND LET'S PICK THEM OFF!
YOU HEARD HER-- LET'S GO!
WHAT'S HAPPENING?!
WHERE'S ABRAHAM?!
STAY AWAY FROM THE GATE!
PKOW!
BRAKKA! BRAKKA!

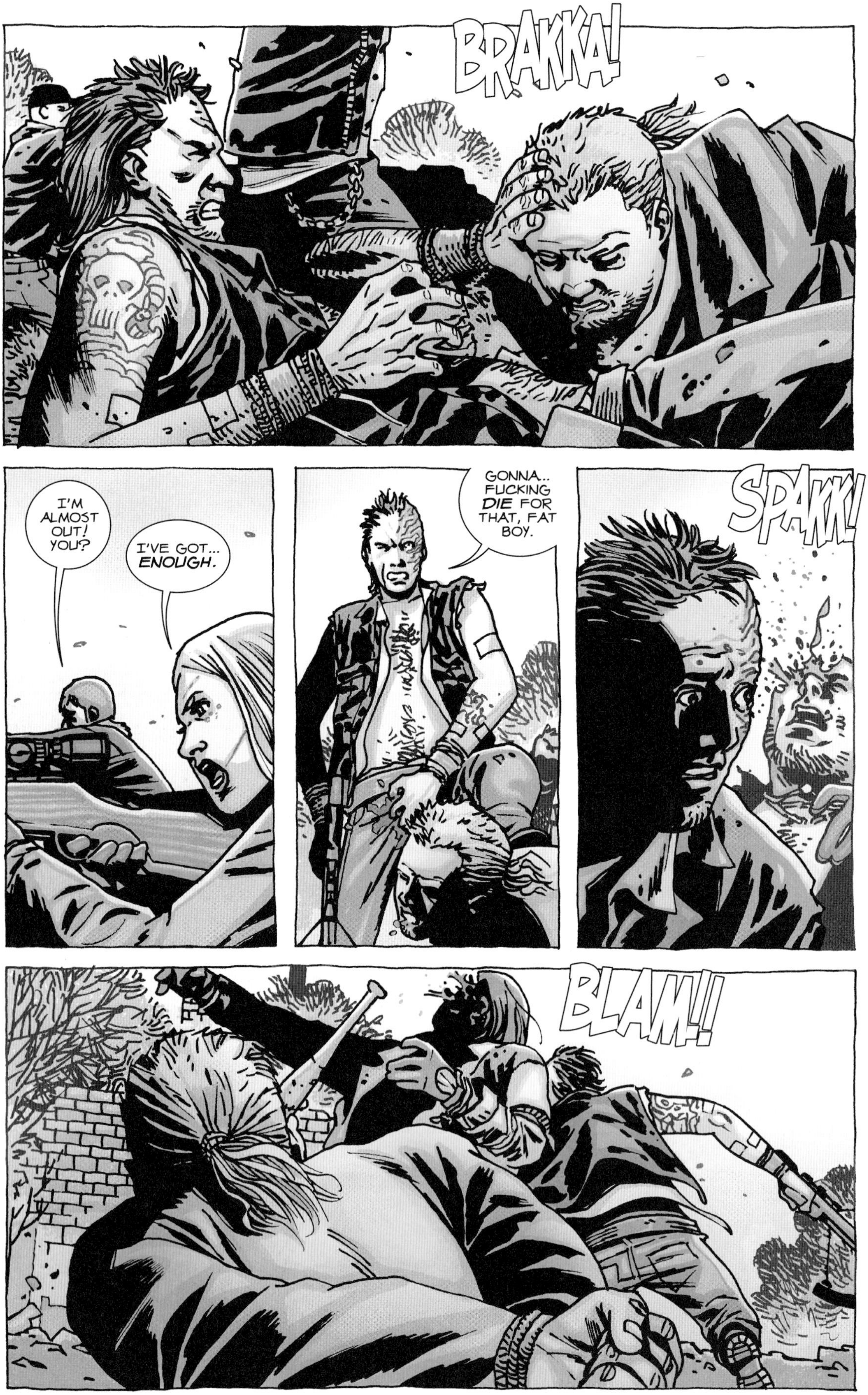
BRAKKA!
I'M ALMOST OUT! YOU?
I'VE GOT... ENOUGH.
GONNA.. FUCKING DIE FOR THAT, FAT BOY.
SPAKK!
BLAM!!

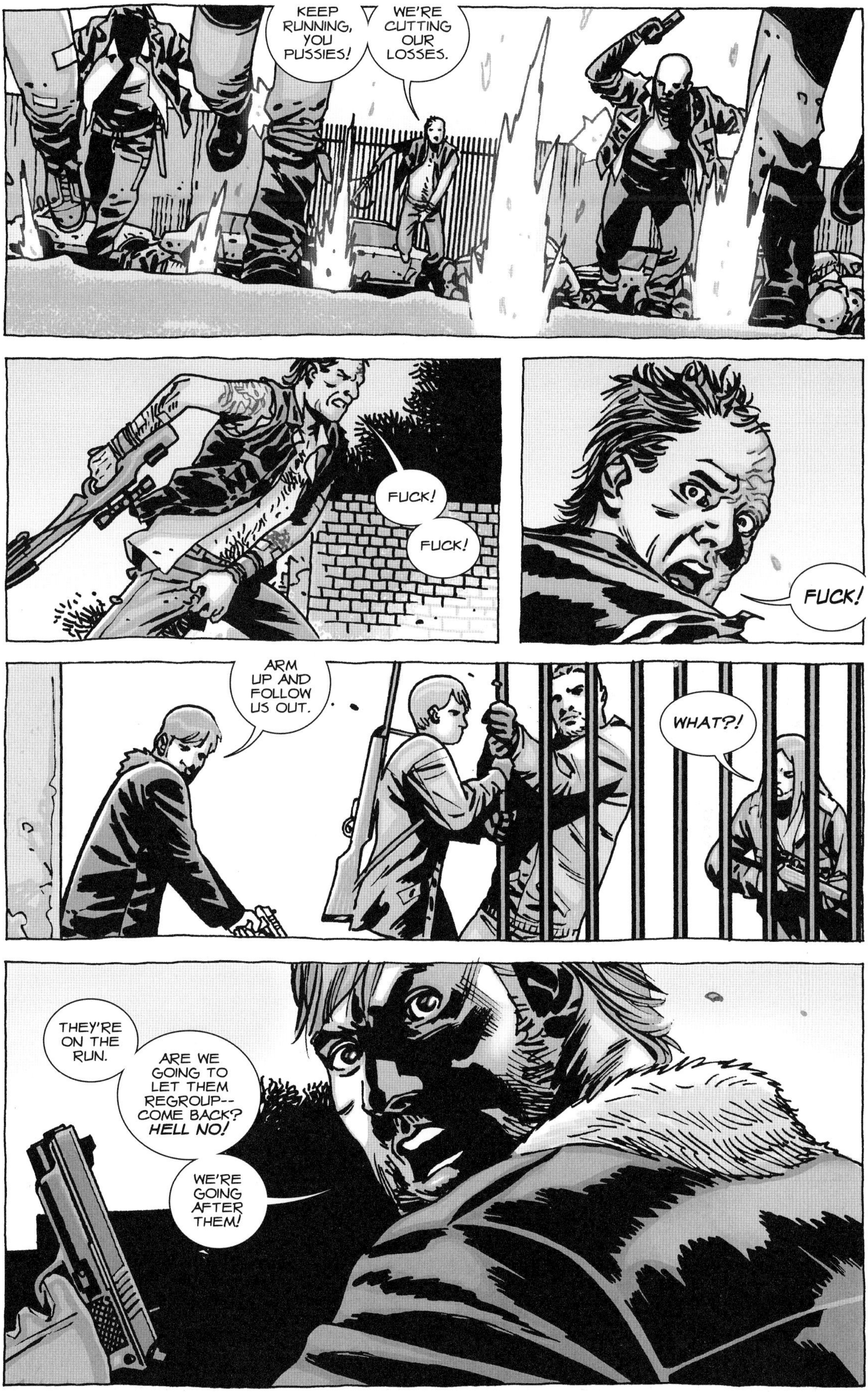
KEEP RUNNING, YOU PUSSIES!
WE'RE CUTTING OUR LOSSES.
FUCK!
FUCK!
FUCK!
ARM UP AND FOLLOW US OUT.
WHAT?!
THEY'RE ON THE RUN.
ARE WE GOING TO LET THEM REGROUP-- COME BACK? HELL NO!
WE'RE GOING AFTER THEM!

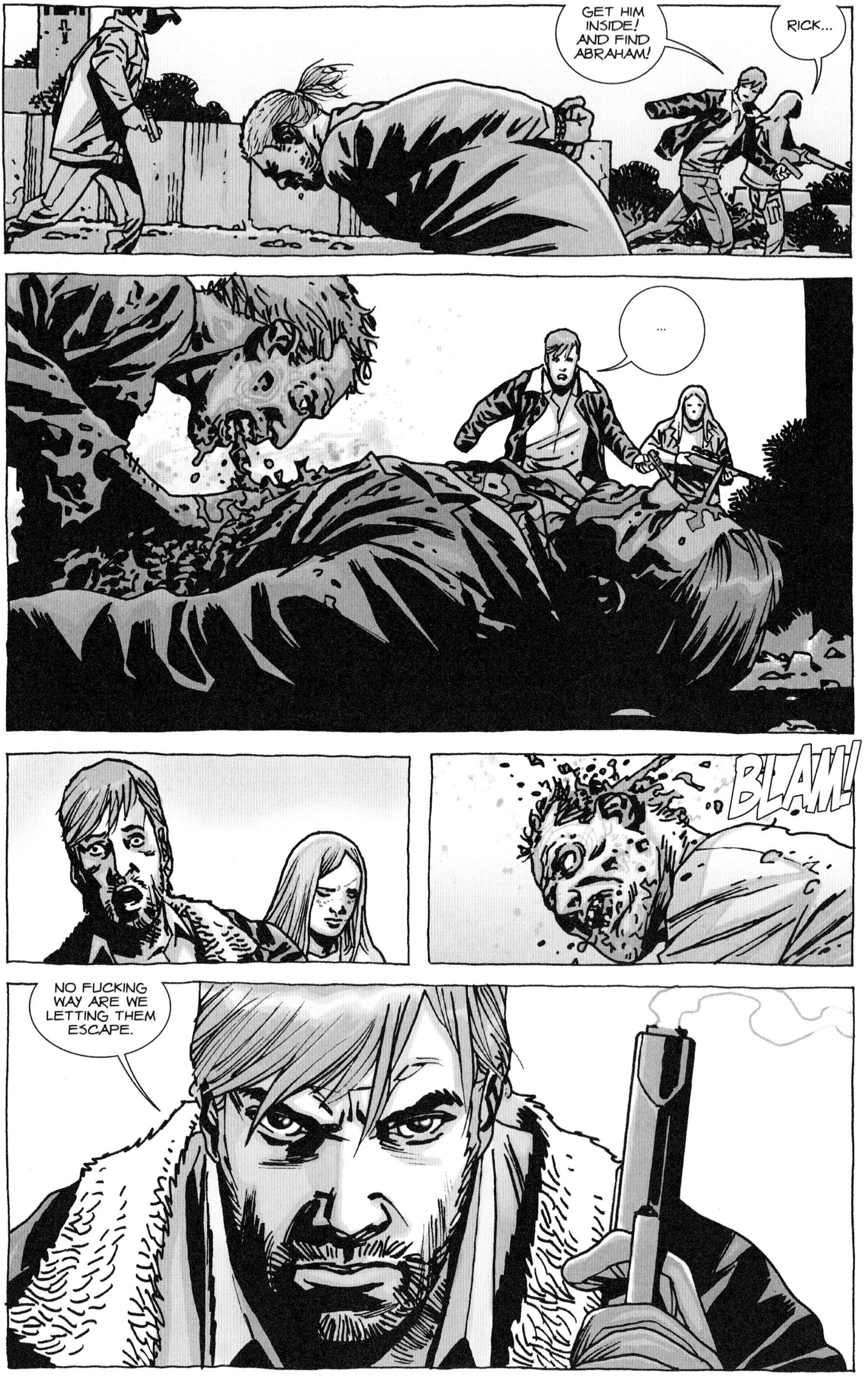

GET HIM INSIDE! AND FIND ABRAHAM!
RICK...
...
BLAM!
NO FUCKING WAY ARE WE LETTING THEM ESCAPE.

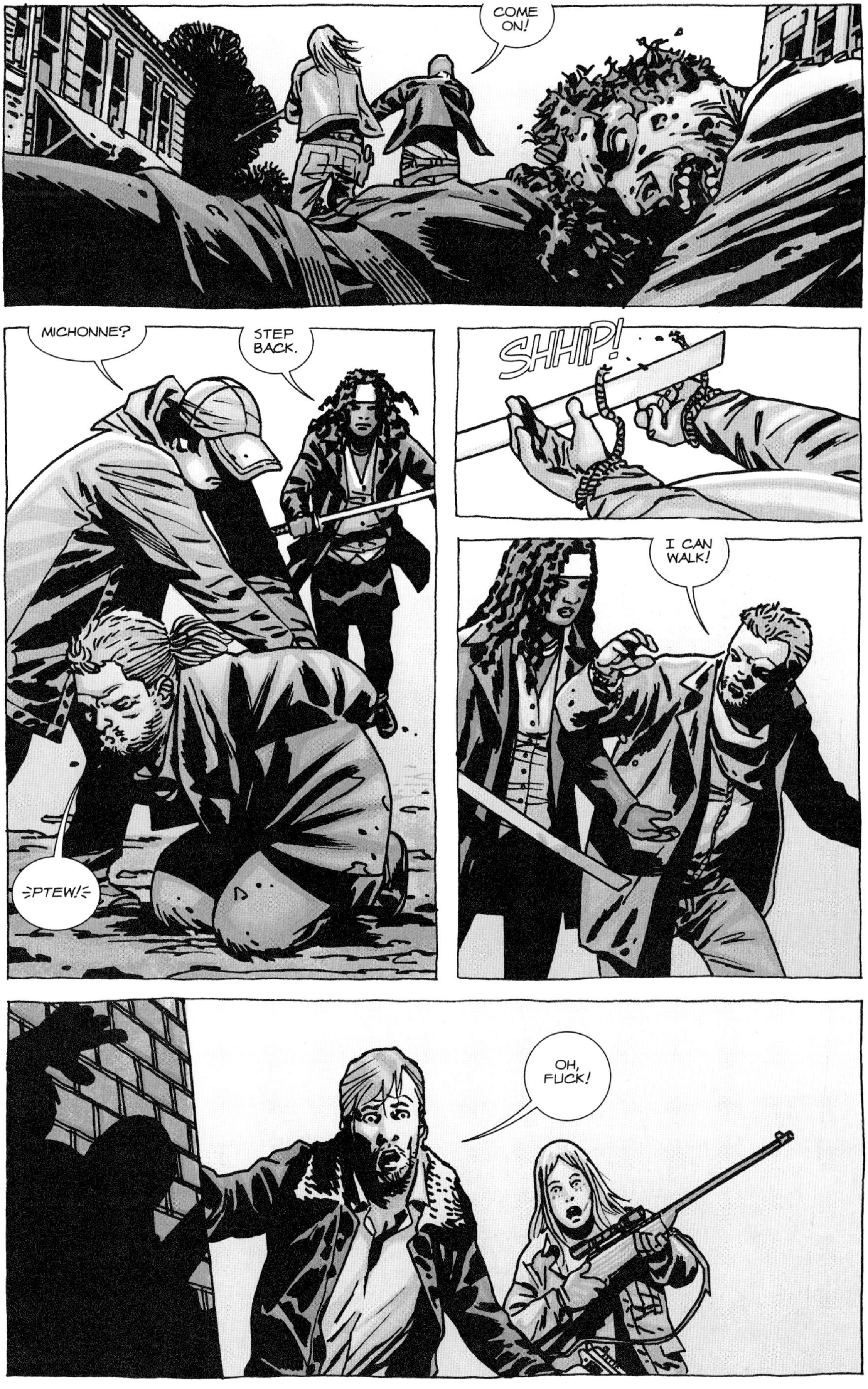
COME ON!
MICHONNE?
STEP BACK.
PTEW!
SHHIP!
I CAN WALK!
OH, FUCK!

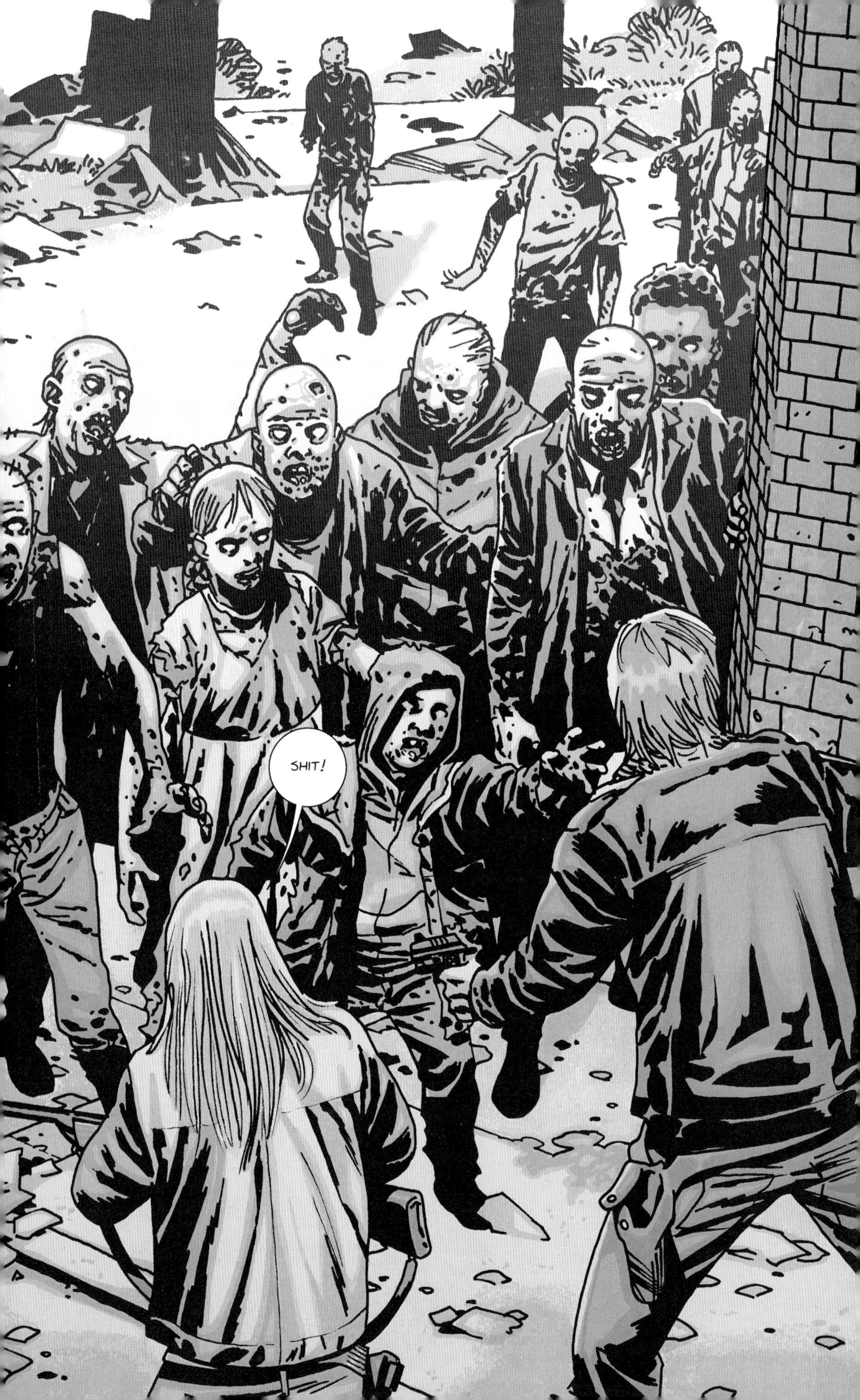
SHIT!

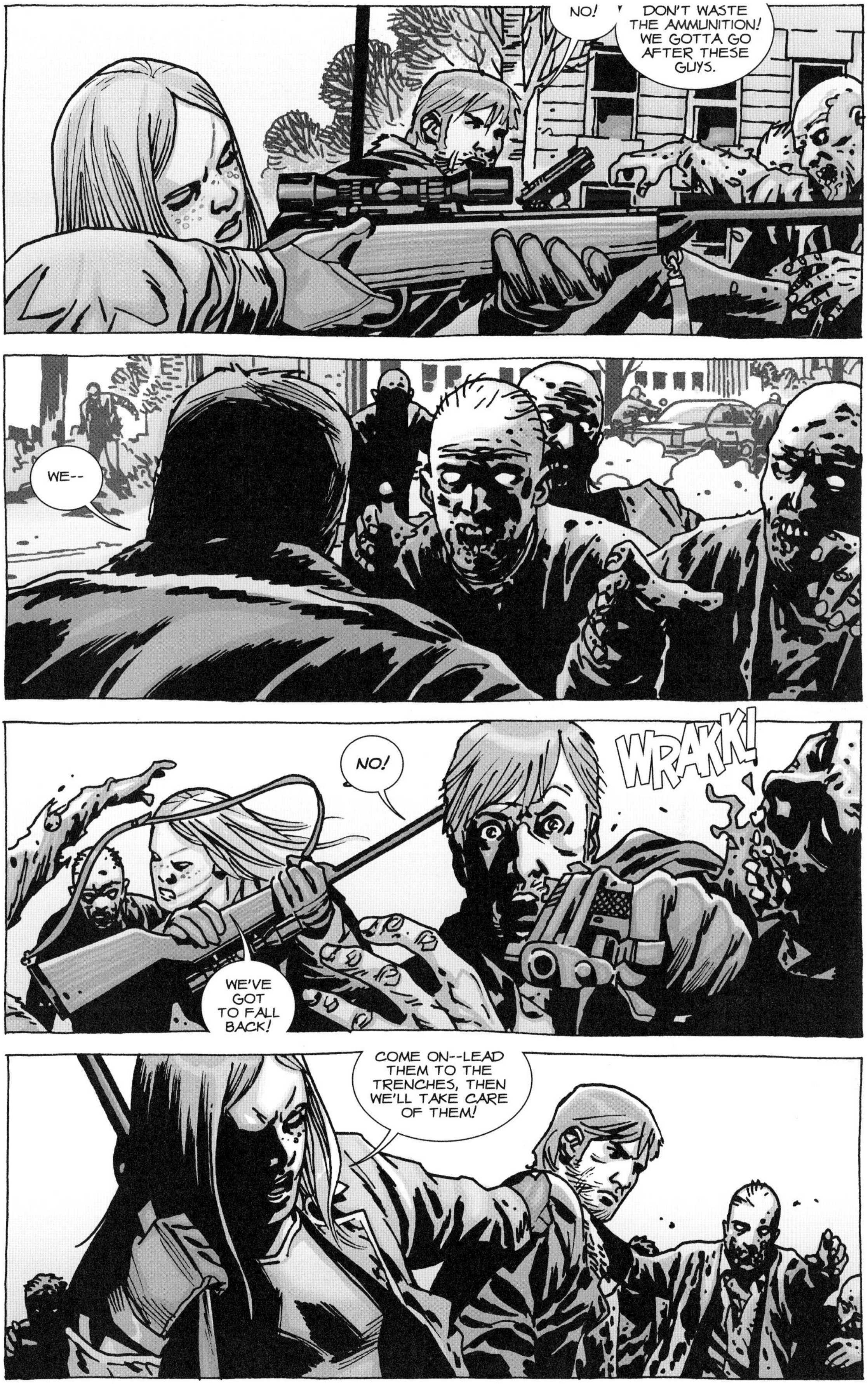
NO!
DON'T WASTE THE AMMUNITION! WE GOTTA GO AFTER THESE GUYS.
WE--
NO!
WRAKK!
WE'VE GOT TO FALL BACK!
COME ON--LEAD THEM TO THE TRENCHES, THEN WE'LL TAKE CARE OF THEM!

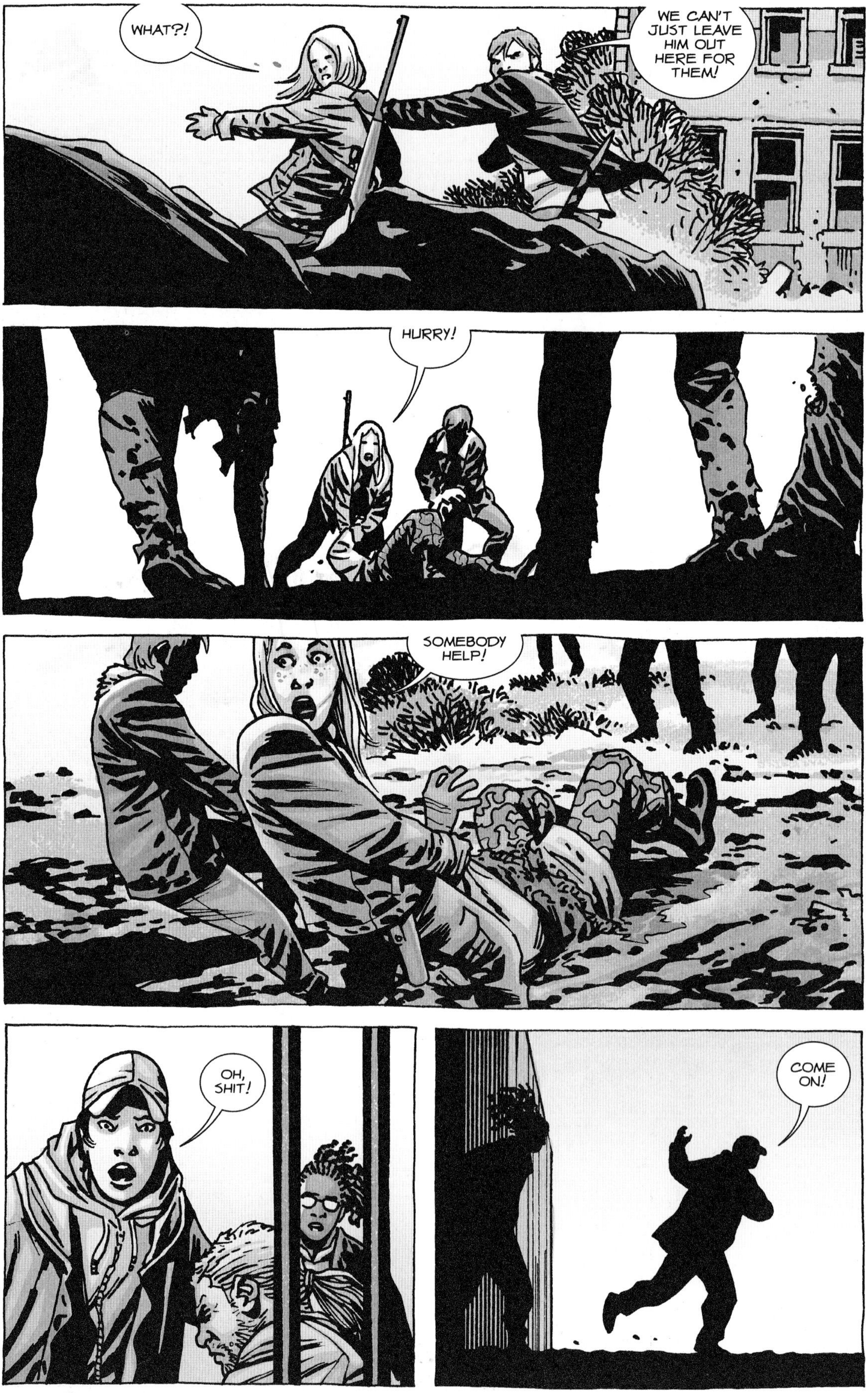
WHAT?!
WE CAN'T JUST LEAVE HIM OUT HERE FOR THEM!
HURRY!
SOMEBODY HELP!
OH, SHIT!
COME ON!

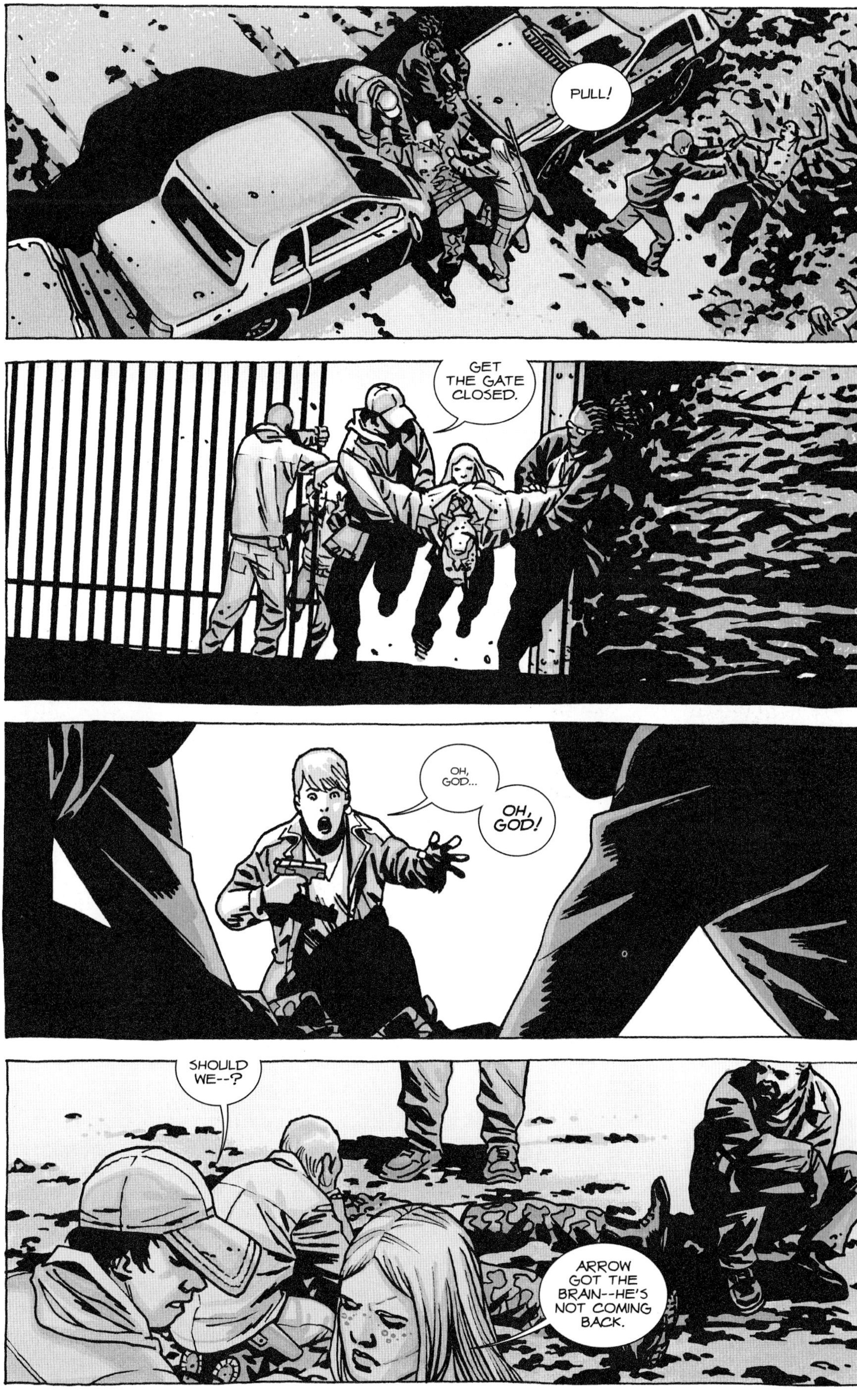
PULL!
GET THE GATE CLOSED.
OH, GOD...
OH, GOD!
SHOULD WE--?
ARROW GOT THE BRAIN--HE'S NOT COMING BACK.

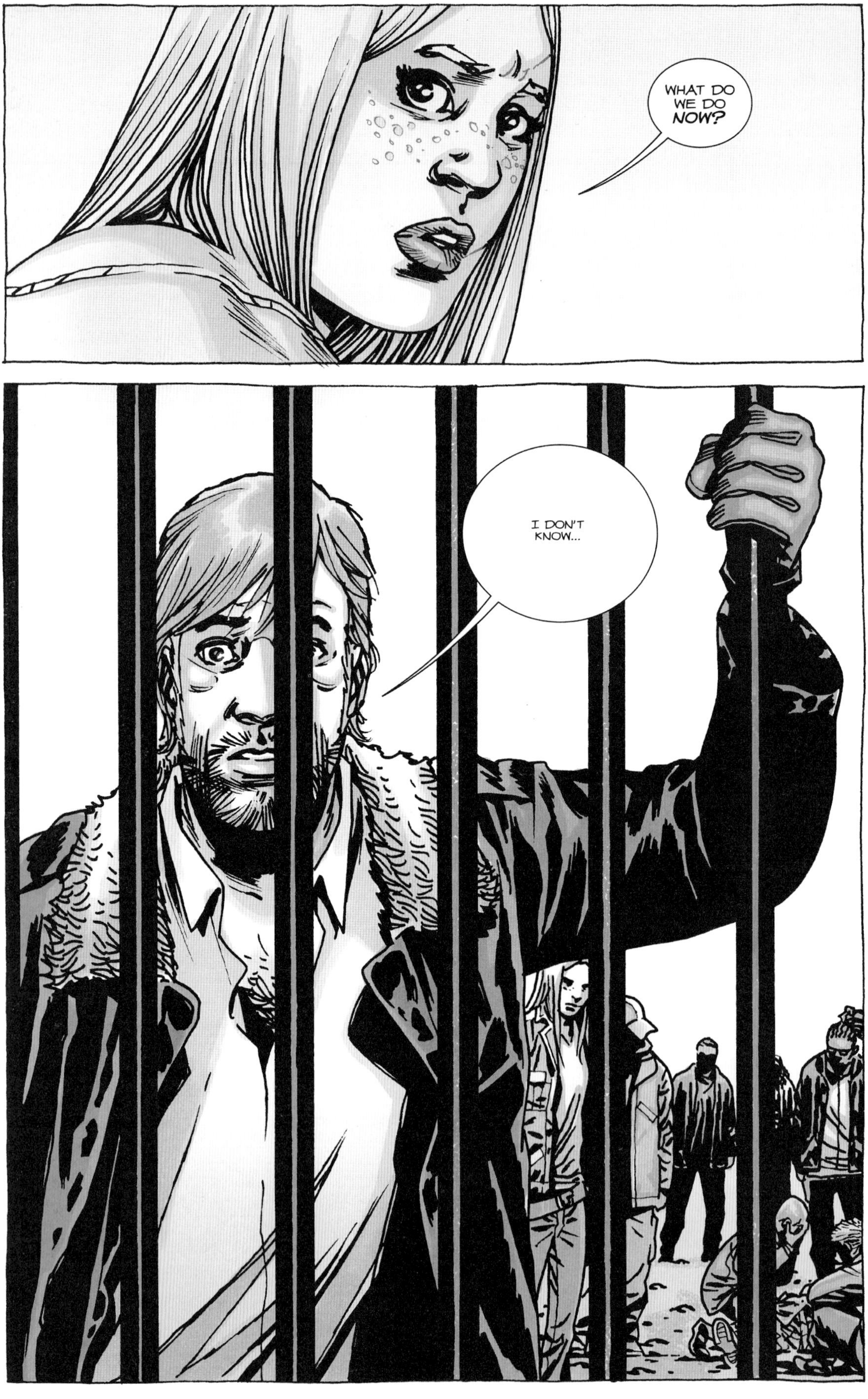
WHAT DO WE DO NOW?
I DON'T KNOW...

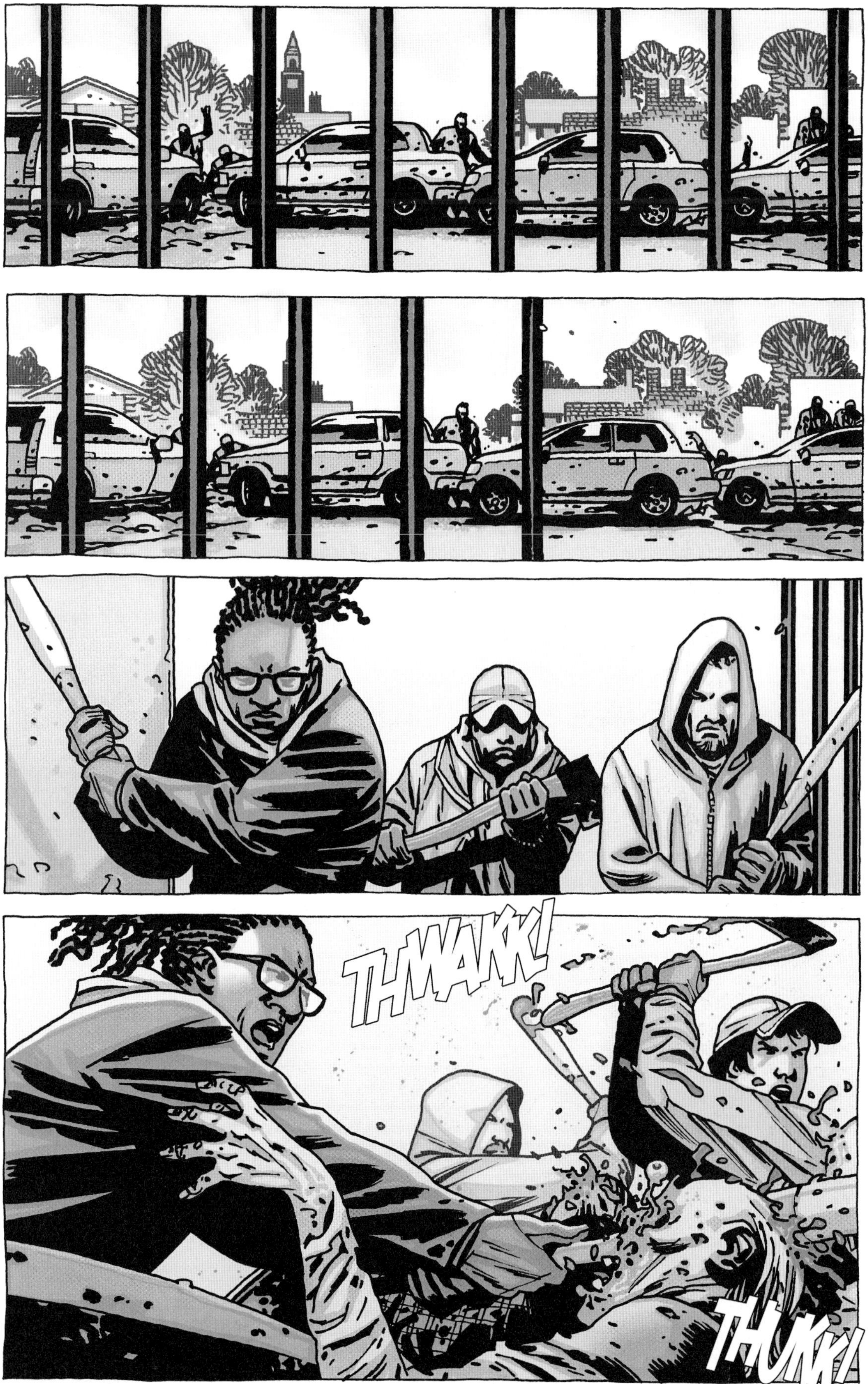
THWAKK!
THUKK!

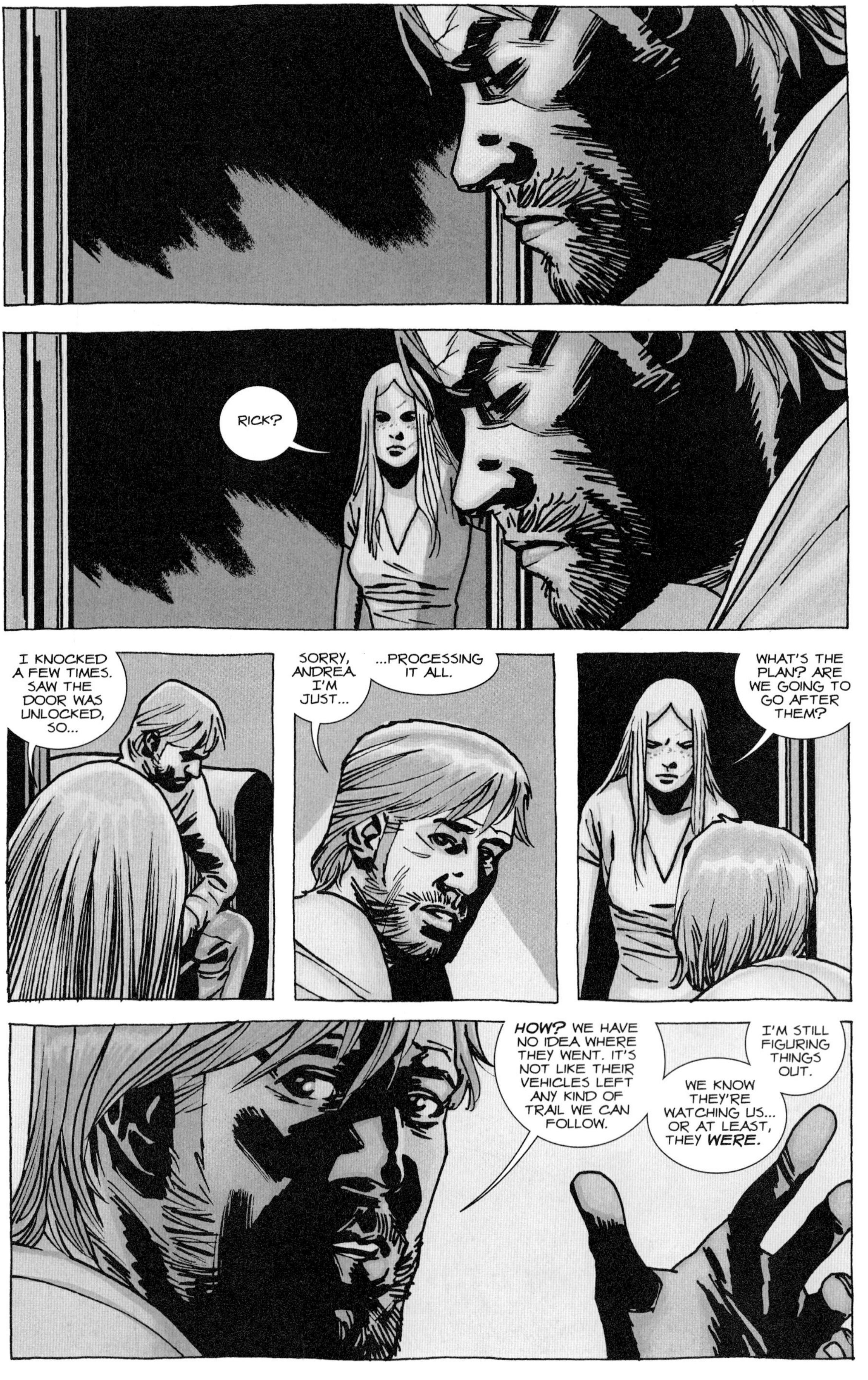
RICK?
I KNOCKED A FEW TIMES. SAW THE DOOR WAS UNLOCKED, SO...
SORRY, ANDREA. I'M JUST...
...PROCESSING IT ALL.
WHAT'S THE PLAN? ARE WE GOING TO GO AFTER THEM?
HOW? WE HAVE NO IDEA WHERE THEY WENT. IT'S NOT LIKE THEIR VEHICLES LEFT ANY KIND OF TRAIL WE CAN FOLLOW.
I'M STILL FIGURING THINGS OUT.
WE KNOW THEY'RE WATCHING US... OR AT LEAST, THEY WERE.

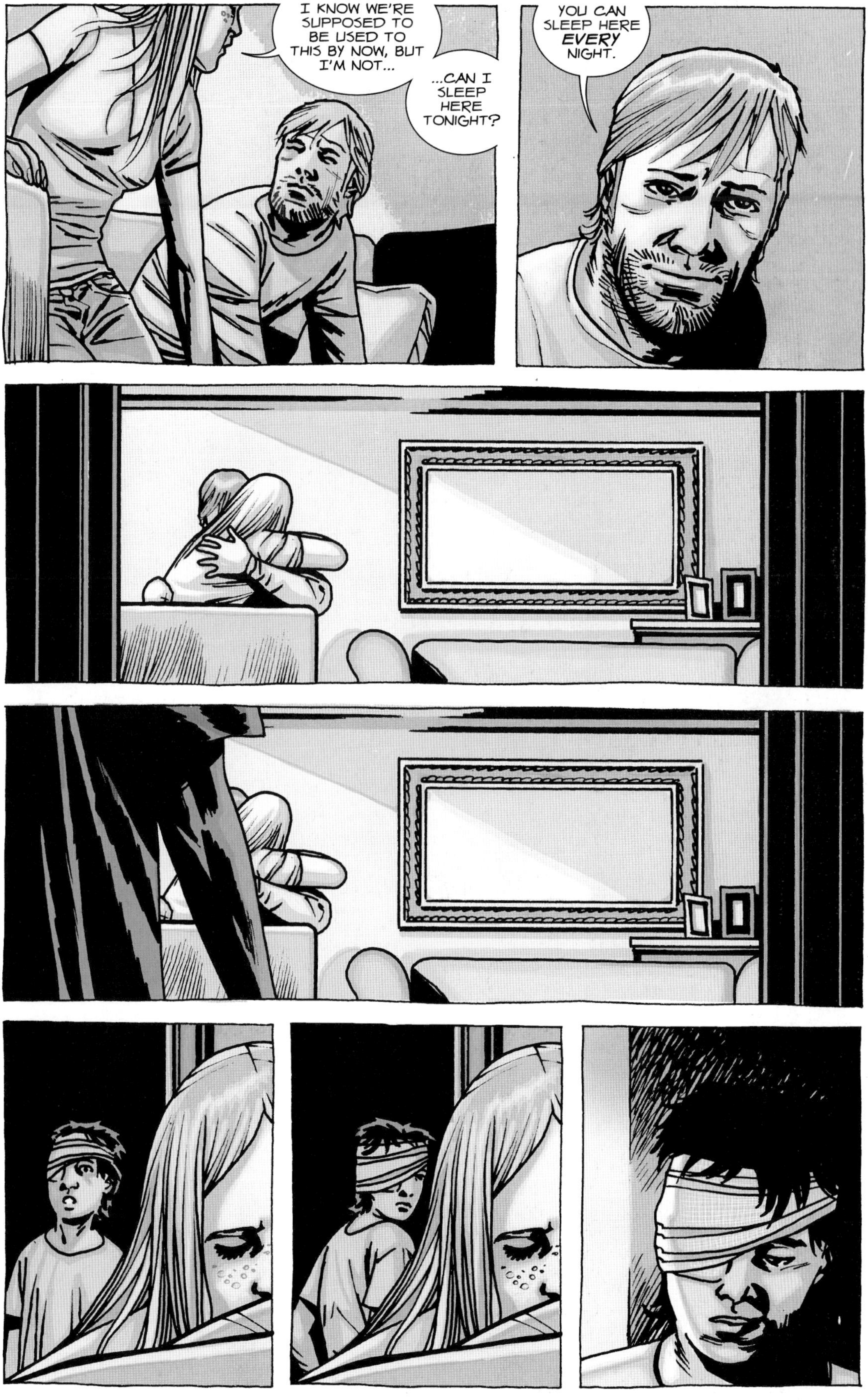
I KNOW WE'RE SUPPOSED TO BE USED TO THIS BY NOW, BUT I'M NOT...
...CAN I SLEEP HERE TONIGHT?
YOU CAN SLEEP HERE EVERY NIGHT.

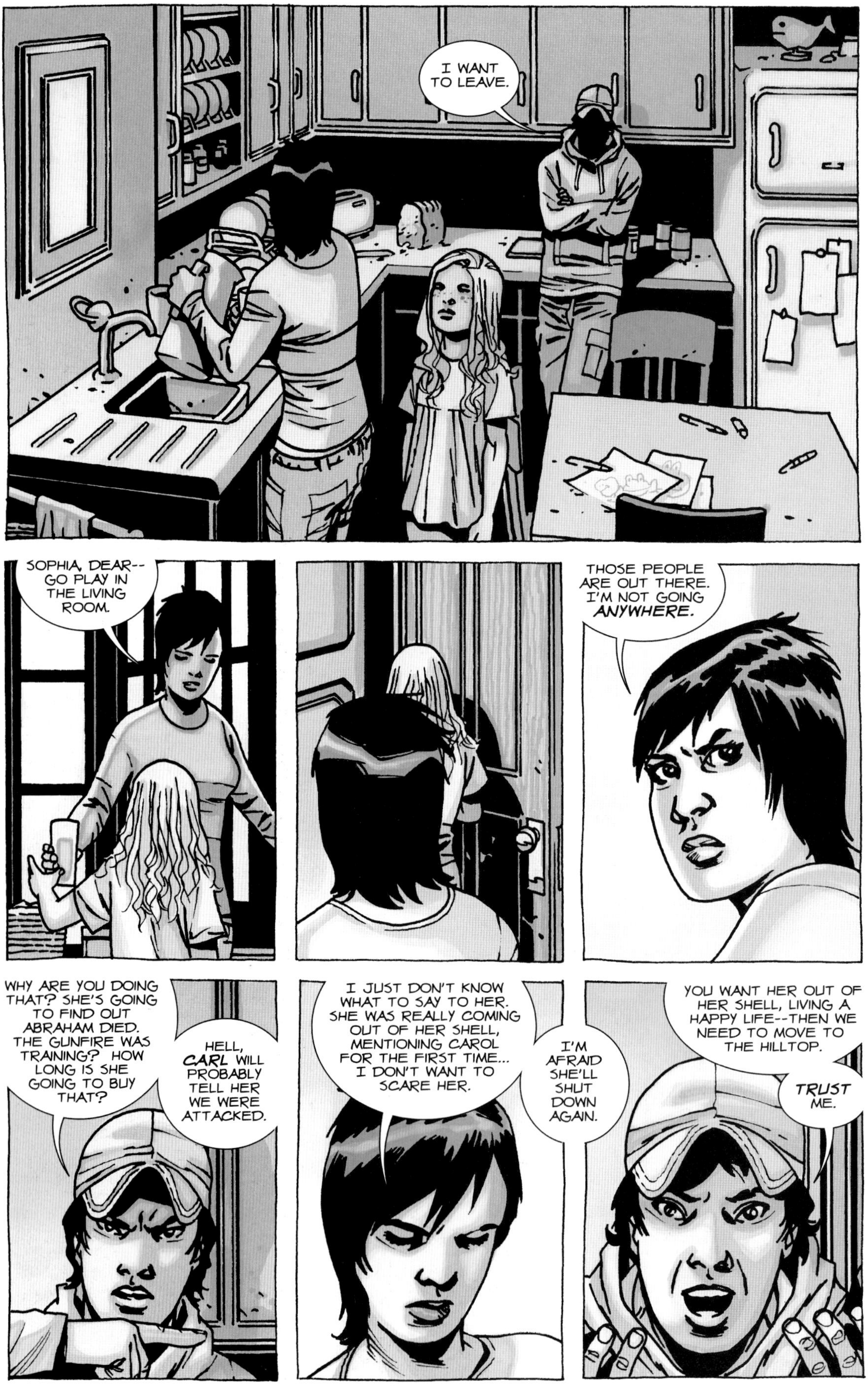
I WANT TO LEAVE.
SOPHIA, DEAR-- GO PLAY IN THE LIVING ROOM.
THOSE PEOPLE ARE OUT THERE. I'M NOT GOING *ANYWHERE.*
WHY ARE YOU DOING THAT? SHE'S GOING TO FIND OUT ABRAHAM DIED. THE GUNFIRE WAS TRAINING? HOW LONG IS SHE GOING TO BUY THAT?
HELL, *CARL* WILL PROBABLY TELL HER WE WERE ATTACKED.
I JUST DON'T KNOW WHAT TO SAY TO HER. SHE WAS REALLY COMING OUT OF HER SHELL, MENTIONING CAROL FOR THE FIRST TIME... I DON'T WANT TO SCARE HER.
I'M AFRAID SHE'LL SHUT DOWN AGAIN.
YOU WANT HER OUT OF HER SHELL, LIVING A HAPPY LIFE--THEN WE NEED TO MOVE TO THE HILLTOP.
TRUST ME.

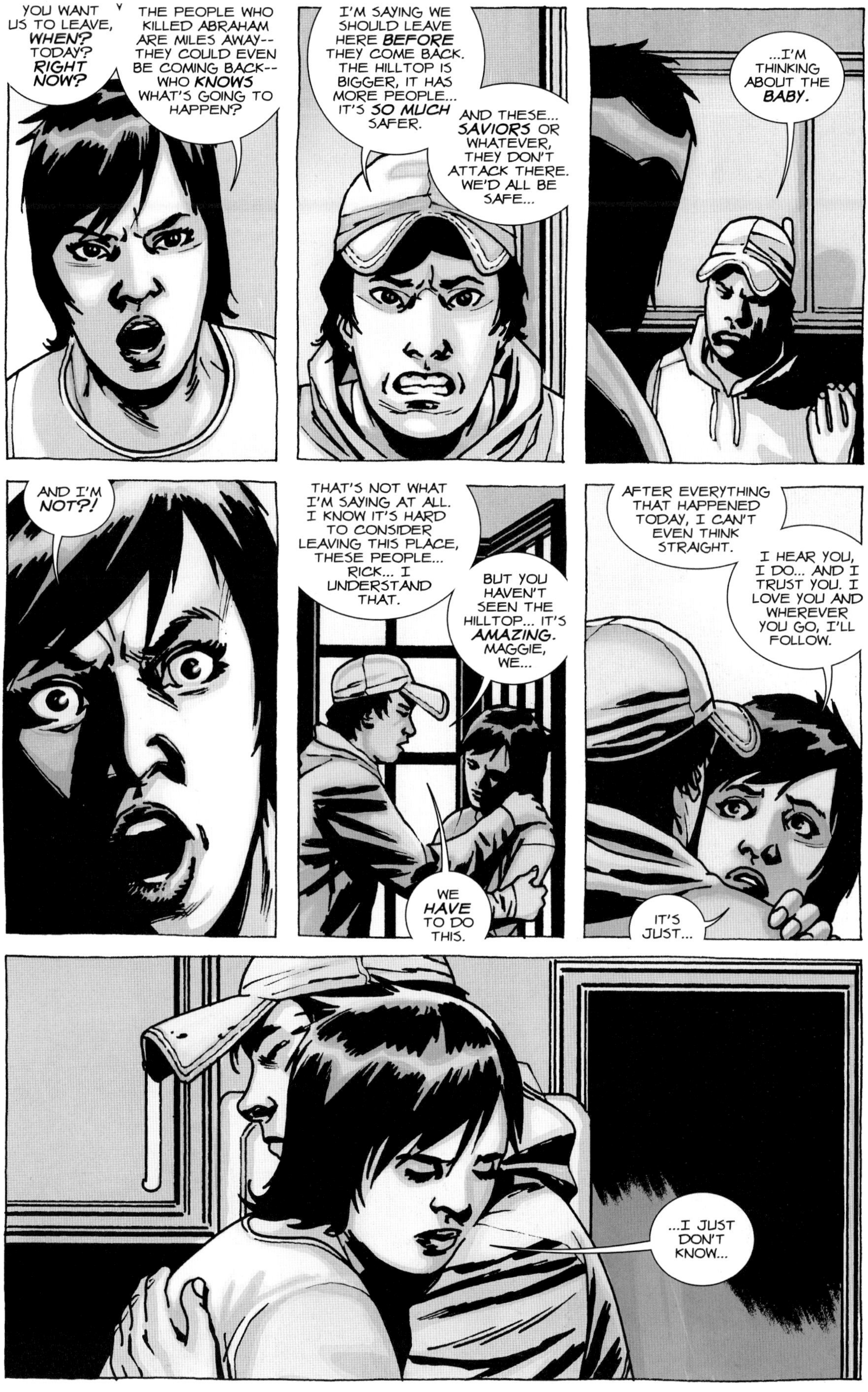
YOU WANT US TO LEAVE, WHEN? TODAY? RIGHT NOW?
THE PEOPLE WHO KILLED ABRAHAM ARE MILES AWAY-- THEY COULD EVEN BE COMING BACK-- WHO KNOWS WHAT'S GOING TO HAPPEN?
I'M SAYING WE SHOULD LEAVE HERE BEFORE THEY COME BACK. THE HILLTOP IS BIGGER, IT HAS MORE PEOPLE... IT'S SO MUCH SAFER.
AND THESE... SAVIORS OR WHATEVER, THEY DON'T ATTACK THERE. WE'D ALL BE SAFE...
...I'M THINKING ABOUT THE BABY.
AND I'M NOT?!
THAT'S NOT WHAT I'M SAYING AT ALL. I KNOW IT'S HARD TO CONSIDER LEAVING THIS PLACE, THESE PEOPLE... RICK... I UNDERSTAND THAT.
BUT YOU HAVEN'T SEEN THE HILLTOP... IT'S AMAZING. MAGGIE, WE...
WE HAVE TO DO THIS.
AFTER EVERYTHING THAT HAPPENED TODAY, I CAN'T EVEN THINK STRAIGHT.
I HEAR YOU, I DO... AND I TRUST YOU. I LOVE YOU AND WHEREVER YOU GO, I'LL FOLLOW.
IT'S JUST...
...I JUST DON'T KNOW...

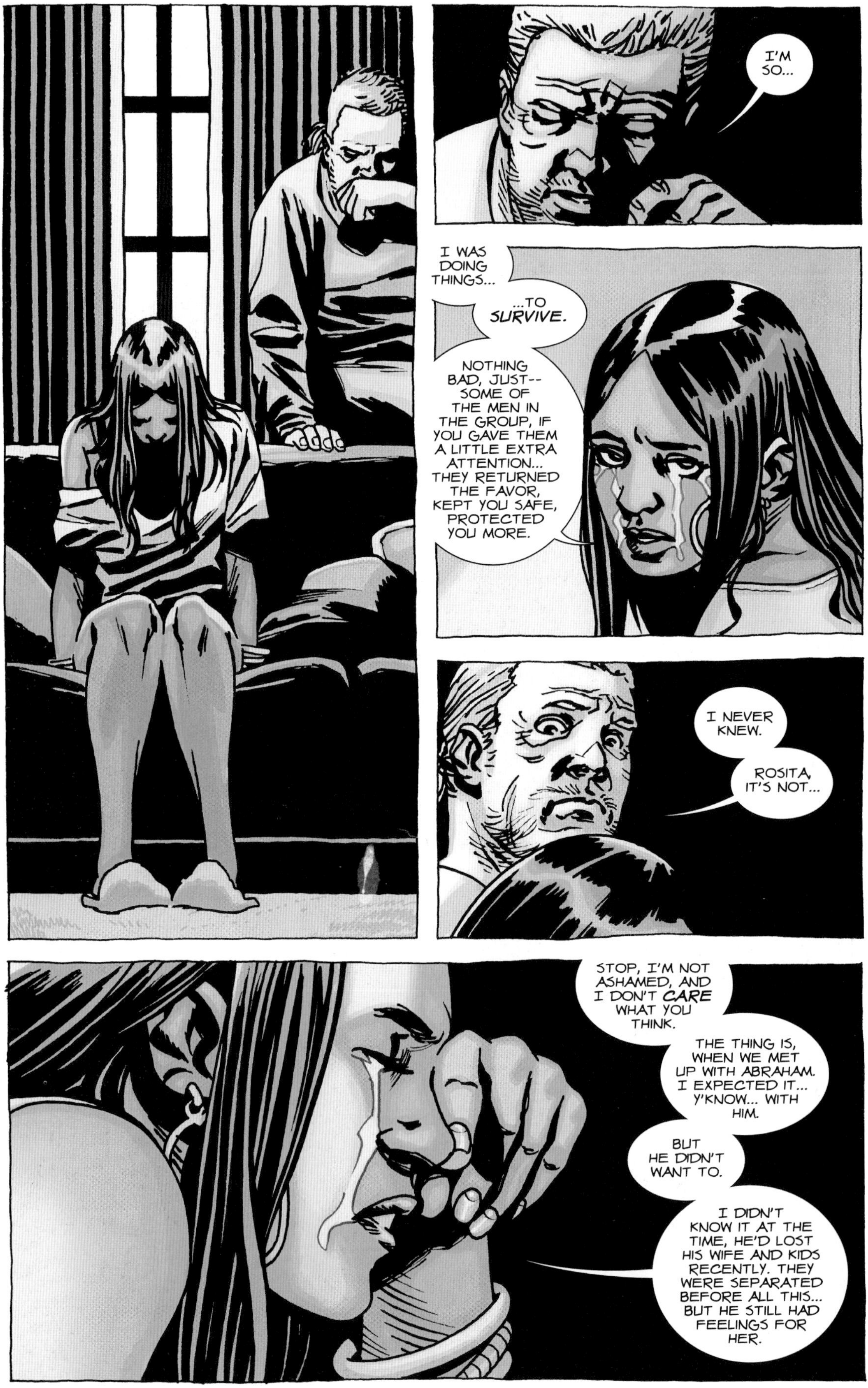
I'M SO...
I WAS DOING THINGS...
...TO SURVIVE.
NOTHING BAD, JUST-- SOME OF THE MEN IN THE GROUP, IF YOU GAVE THEM A LITTLE EXTRA ATTENTION... THEY RETURNED THE FAVOR, KEPT YOU SAFE, PROTECTED YOU MORE.
I NEVER KNEW.
ROSITA, IT'S NOT...
STOP, I'M NOT ASHAMED, AND I DON'T CARE WHAT YOU THINK.
THE THING IS, WHEN WE MET UP WITH ABRAHAM. I EXPECTED IT... Y'KNOW... WITH HIM.
BUT HE DIDN'T WANT TO.
I DIDN'T KNOW IT AT THE TIME, HE'D LOST HIS WIFE AND KIDS RECENTLY. THEY WERE SEPARATED BEFORE ALL THIS... BUT HE STILL HAD FEELINGS FOR HER.

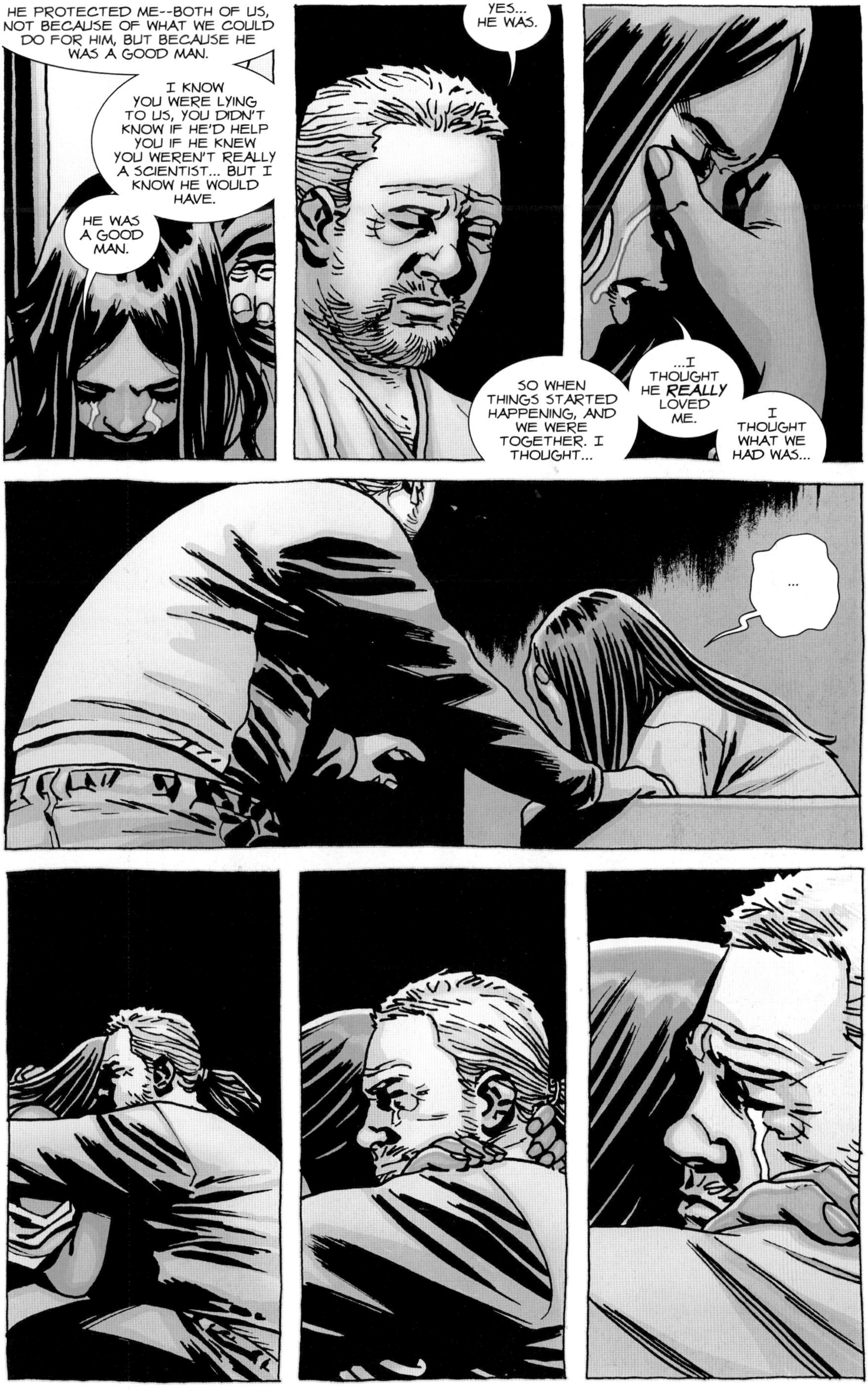
HE PROTECTED ME--BOTH OF US, NOT BECAUSE OF WHAT WE COULD DO FOR HIM, BUT BECAUSE HE WAS A GOOD MAN.
I KNOW YOU WERE LYING TO US, YOU DIDN'T KNOW IF HE'D HELP YOU IF HE KNEW YOU WEREN'T REALLY A SCIENTIST... BUT I KNOW HE WOULD HAVE.
HE WAS A GOOD MAN.
YES... HE WAS.
SO WHEN THINGS STARTED HAPPENING, AND WE WERE TOGETHER. I THOUGHT...
...I THOUGHT HE *REALLY* LOVED ME.
I THOUGHT WHAT WE HAD WAS...
...

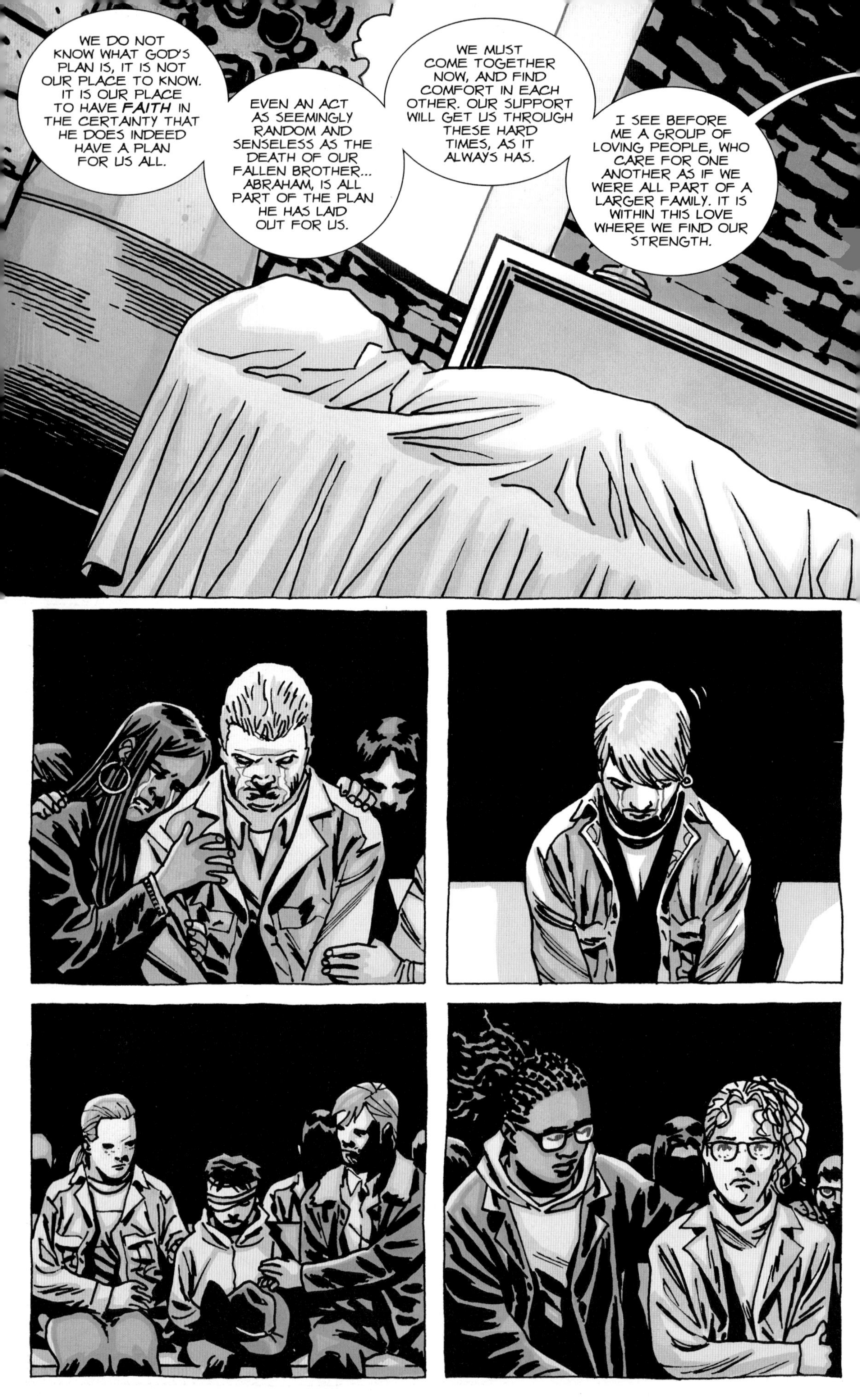
WE DO NOT KNOW WHAT GOD'S PLAN IS, IT IS NOT OUR PLACE TO KNOW. IT IS OUR PLACE TO HAVE FAITH IN THE CERTAINTY THAT HE DOES INDEED HAVE A PLAN FOR US ALL.
EVEN AN ACT AS SEEMINGLY RANDOM AND SENSELESS AS THE DEATH OF OUR FALLEN BROTHER... ABRAHAM, IS ALL PART OF THE PLAN HE HAS LAID OUT FOR US.
WE MUST COME TOGETHER NOW, AND FIND COMFORT IN EACH OTHER. OUR SUPPORT WILL GET US THROUGH THESE HARD TIMES, AS IT ALWAYS HAS.
I SEE BEFORE ME A GROUP OF LOVING PEOPLE, WHO CARE FOR ONE ANOTHER AS IF WE WERE ALL PART OF A LARGER FAMILY. IT IS WITHIN THIS LOVE WHERE WE FIND OUR STRENGTH.

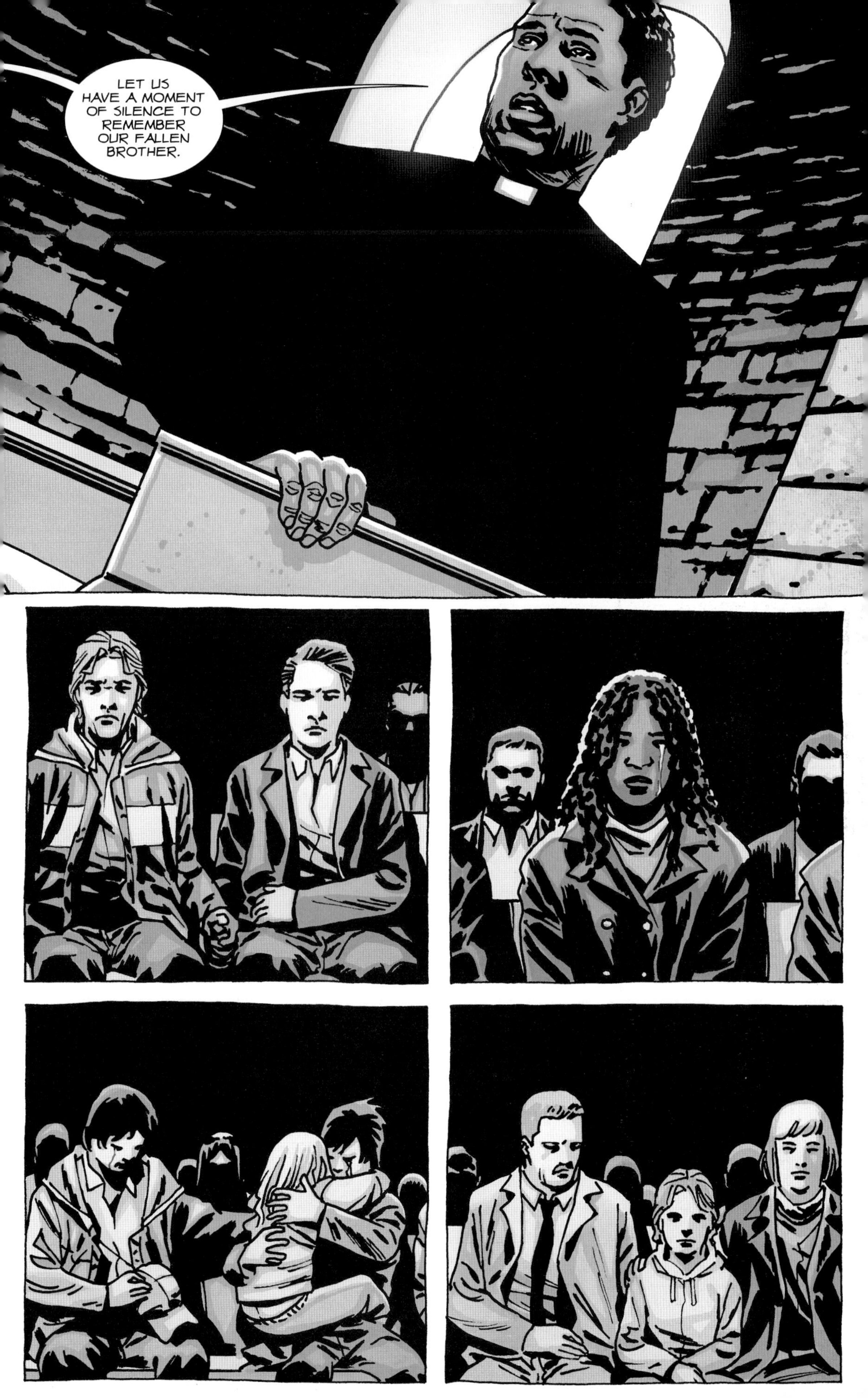
LET US HAVE A MOMENT OF SILENCE TO REMEMBER OUR FALLEN BROTHER.

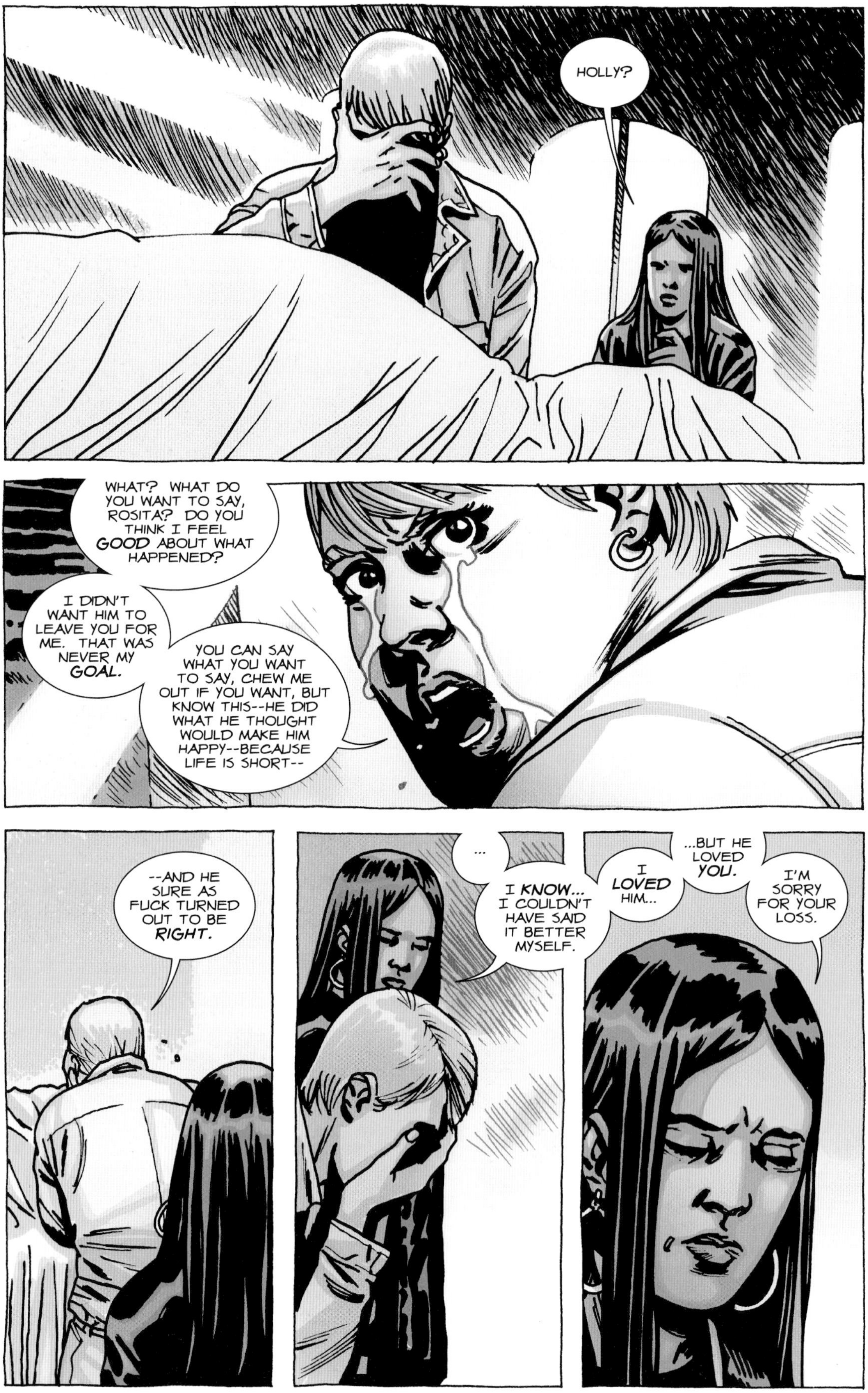
HOLLY?
WHAT? WHAT DO YOU WANT TO SAY, ROSITA? DO YOU THINK I FEEL GOOD ABOUT WHAT HAPPENED?
I DIDN'T WANT HIM TO LEAVE YOU FOR ME. THAT WAS NEVER MY GOAL.
YOU CAN SAY WHAT YOU WANT TO SAY, CHEW ME OUT IF YOU WANT, BUT KNOW THIS--HE DID WHAT HE THOUGHT WOULD MAKE HIM HAPPY--BECAUSE LIFE IS SHORT--
--AND HE SURE AS FUCK TURNED OUT TO BE RIGHT.
...
I KNOW... I COULDN'T HAVE SAID IT BETTER MYSELF.
I LOVED HIM...
...BUT HE LOVED YOU.
I'M SORRY FOR YOUR LOSS.

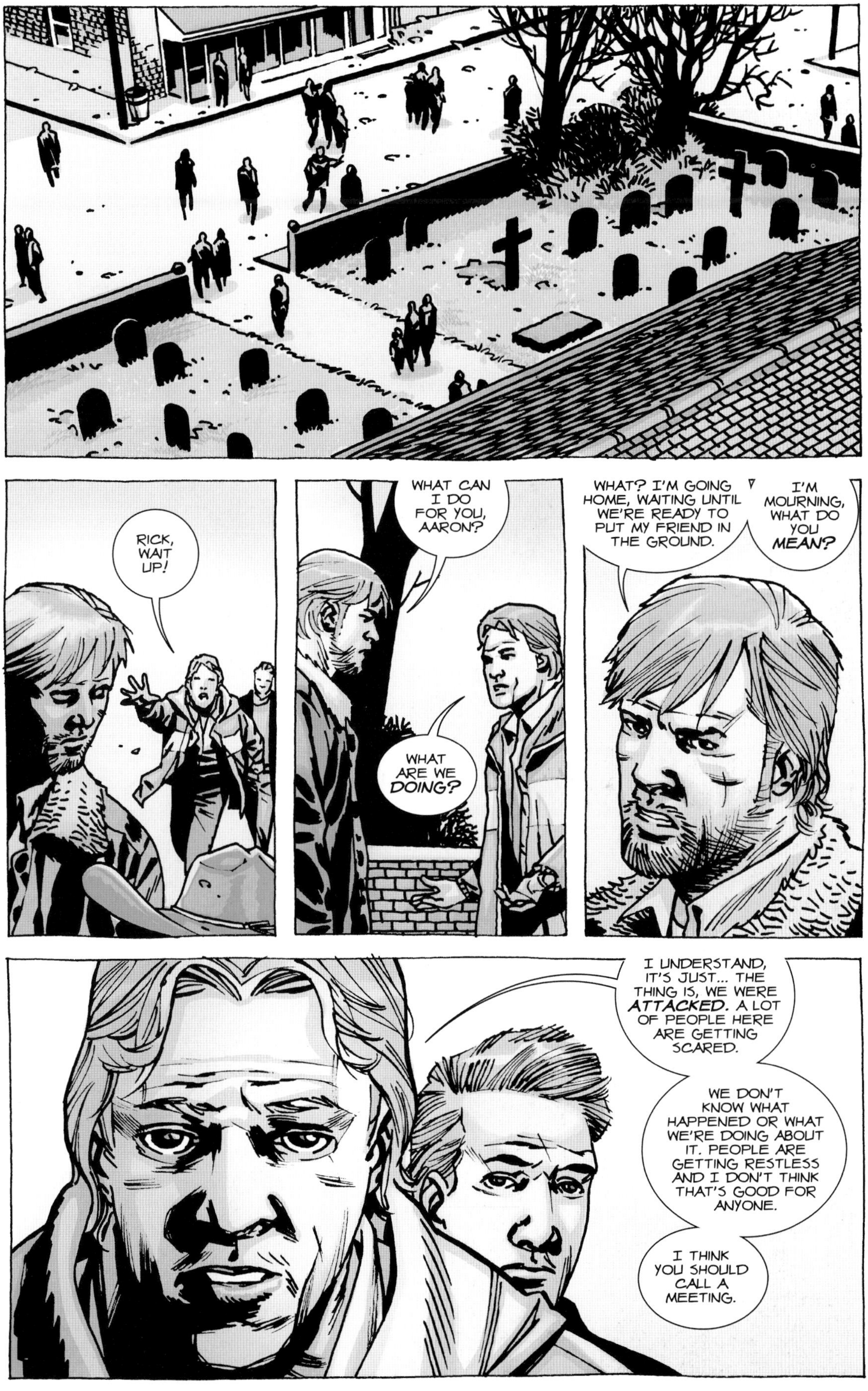
RICK, WAIT UP!
WHAT CAN I DO FOR YOU, AARON?
WHAT ARE WE DOING?
WHAT? I'M GOING HOME, WAITING UNTIL WE'RE READY TO PUT MY FRIEND IN THE GROUND.
I'M MOURNING, WHAT DO YOU MEAN?
I UNDERSTAND, IT'S JUST... THE THING IS, WE WERE ATTACKED. A LOT OF PEOPLE HERE ARE GETTING SCARED.
WE DON'T KNOW WHAT HAPPENED OR WHAT WE'RE DOING ABOUT IT. PEOPLE ARE GETTING RESTLESS AND I DON'T THINK THAT'S GOOD FOR ANYONE.
I THINK YOU SHOULD CALL A MEETING.

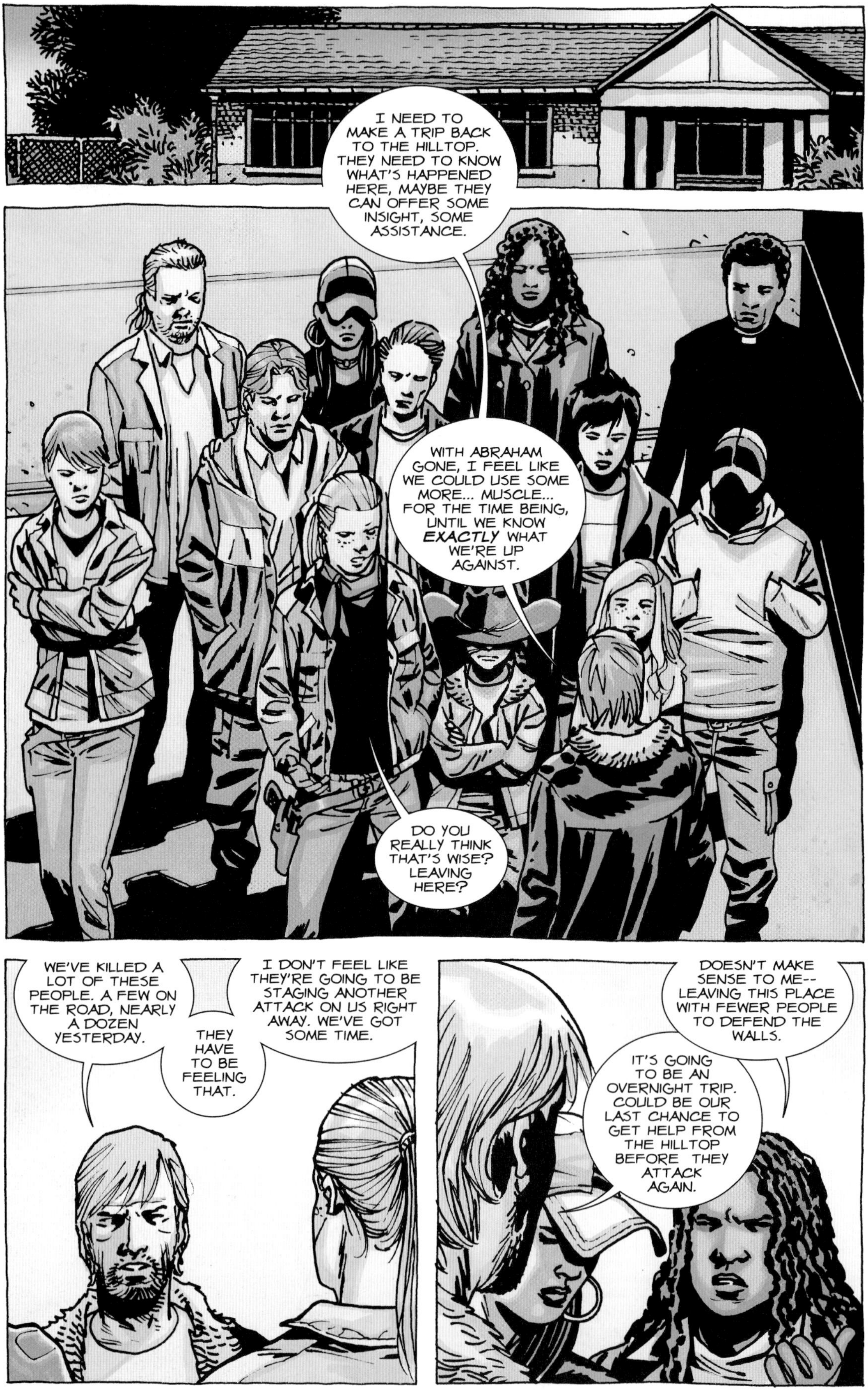
I NEED TO MAKE A TRIP BACK TO THE HILLTOP. THEY NEED TO KNOW WHAT'S HAPPENED HERE, MAYBE THEY CAN OFFER SOME INSIGHT, SOME ASSISTANCE.
WITH ABRAHAM GONE, I FEEL LIKE WE COULD USE SOME MORE... MUSCLE... FOR THE TIME BEING, UNTIL WE KNOW EXACTLY WHAT WE'RE UP AGAINST.
DO YOU REALLY THINK THAT'S WISE? LEAVING HERE?
WE'VE KILLED A LOT OF THESE PEOPLE. A FEW ON THE ROAD, NEARLY A DOZEN YESTERDAY.
THEY HAVE TO BE FEELING THAT.
I DON'T FEEL LIKE THEY'RE GOING TO BE STAGING ANOTHER ATTACK ON US RIGHT AWAY. WE'VE GOT SOME TIME.
DOESN'T MAKE SENSE TO ME-- LEAVING THIS PLACE WITH FEWER PEOPLE TO DEFEND THE WALLS.
IT'S GOING TO BE AN OVERNIGHT TRIP. COULD BE OUR LAST CHANCE TO GET HELP FROM THE HILLTOP BEFORE THEY ATTACK AGAIN.

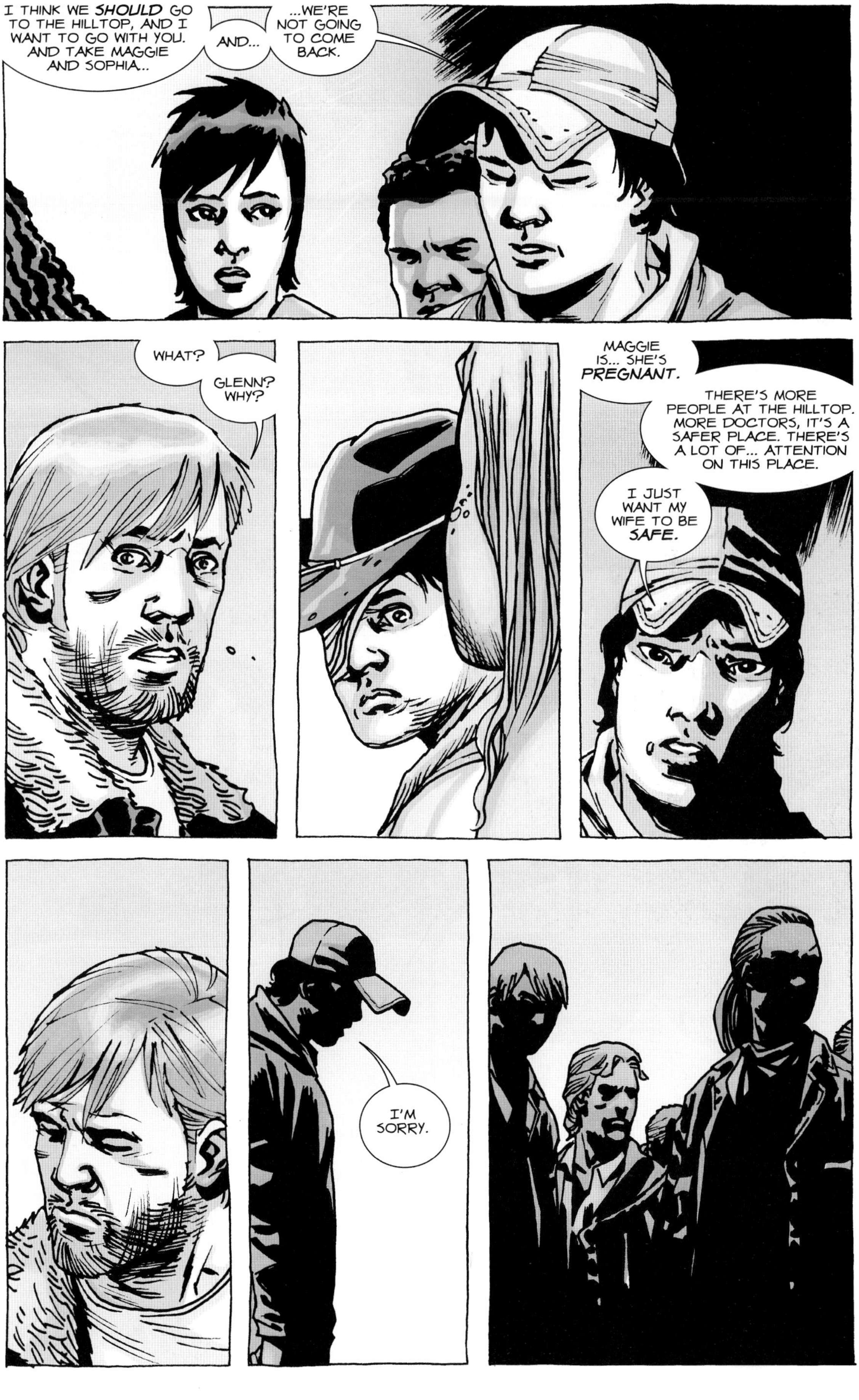
I THINK WE SHOULD GO TO THE HILLTOP, AND I WANT TO GO WITH YOU. AND TAKE MAGGIE AND SOPHIA...
AND...
...WE'RE NOT GOING TO COME BACK.
WHAT?
GLENN? WHY?
MAGGIE IS... SHE'S PREGNANT.
THERE'S MORE PEOPLE AT THE HILLTOP. MORE DOCTORS, IT'S A SAFER PLACE. THERE'S A LOT OF... ATTENTION ON THIS PLACE.
I JUST WANT MY WIFE TO BE SAFE.
I'M SORRY.

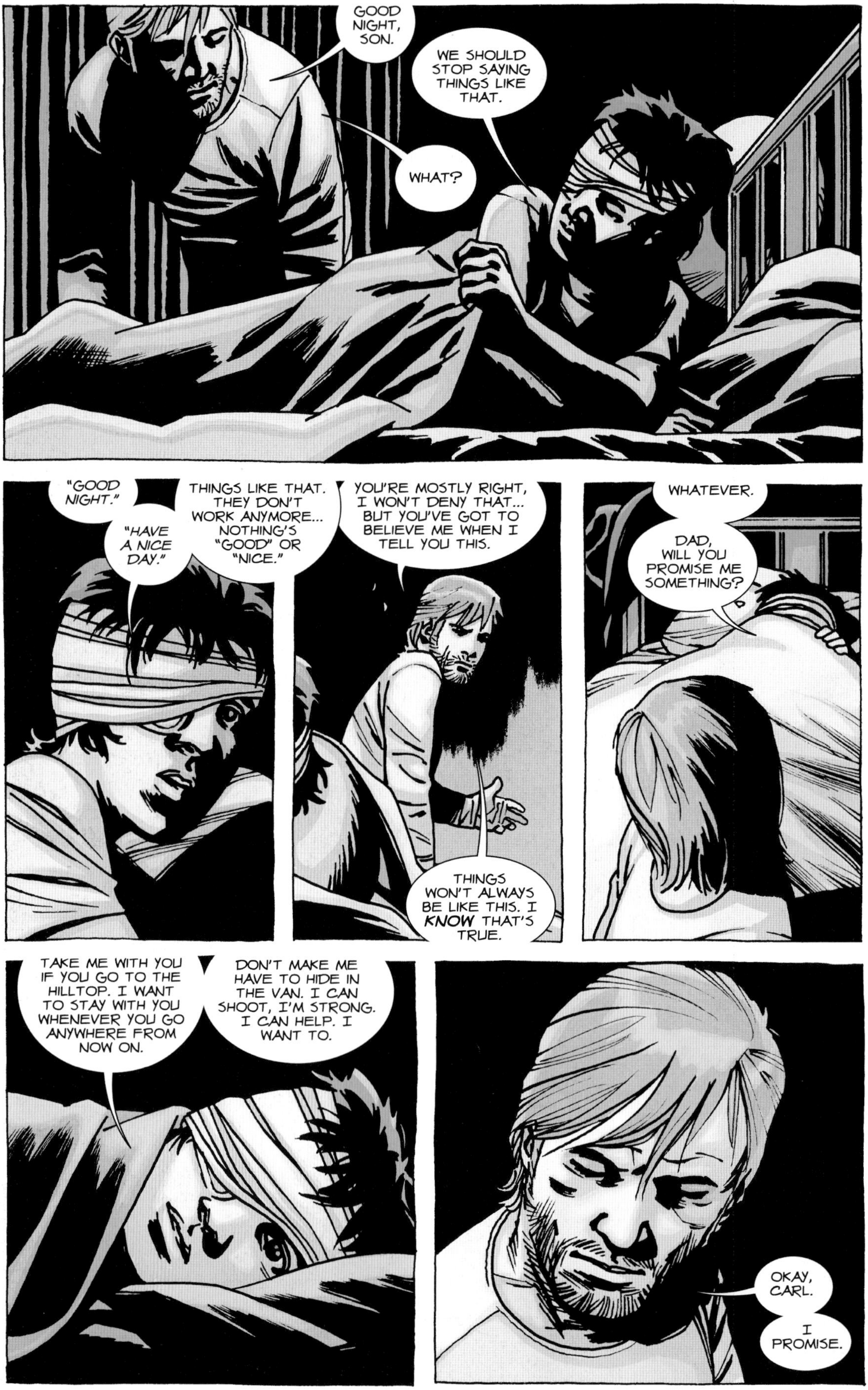
GOOD NIGHT, SON.
WE SHOULD STOP SAYING THINGS LIKE THAT.
WHAT?
"GOOD NIGHT."
"HAVE A NICE DAY."
THINGS LIKE THAT. THEY DON'T WORK ANYMORE... NOTHING'S "GOOD" OR "NICE."
YOU'RE MOSTLY RIGHT, I WON'T DENY THAT... BUT YOU'VE GOT TO BELIEVE ME WHEN I TELL YOU THIS.
THINGS WON'T ALWAYS BE LIKE THIS. I KNOW THAT'S TRUE.
WHATEVER.
DAD, WILL YOU PROMISE ME SOMETHING?
TAKE ME WITH YOU IF YOU GO TO THE HILLTOP. I WANT TO STAY WITH YOU WHENEVER YOU GO ANYWHERE FROM NOW ON.
DON'T MAKE ME HAVE TO HIDE IN THE VAN. I CAN SHOOT, I'M STRONG. I CAN HELP. I WANT TO.
OKAY, CARL.
I PROMISE.

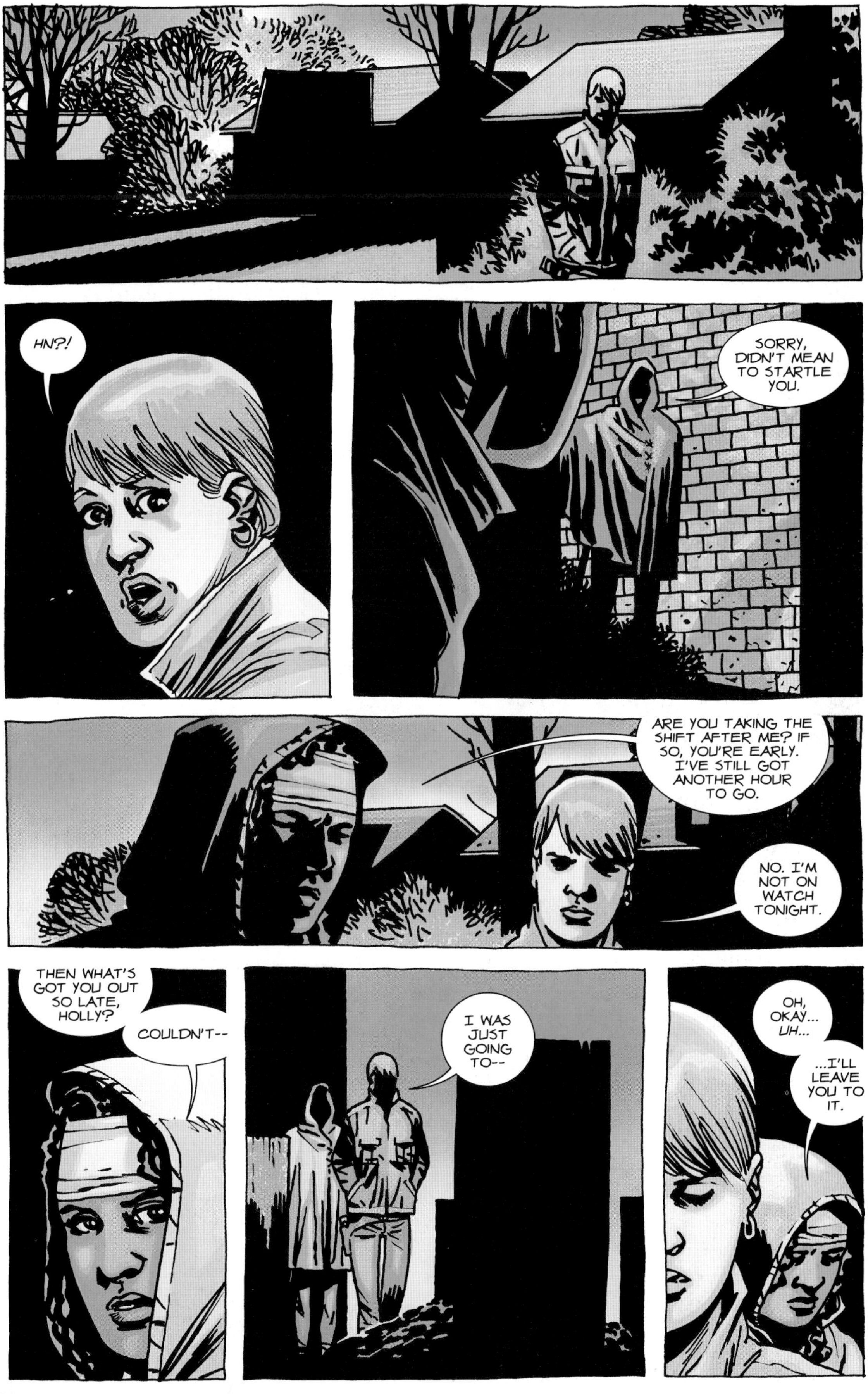
HN?!
SORRY, DIDN'T MEAN TO STARTLE YOU.
ARE YOU TAKING THE SHIFT AFTER ME? IF SO, YOU'RE EARLY. I'VE STILL GOT ANOTHER HOUR TO GO.
NO. I'M NOT ON WATCH TONIGHT.
THEN WHAT'S GOT YOU OUT SO LATE, HOLLY?
COULDN'T--
I WAS JUST GOING TO--
OH, OKAY... UH...
...I'LL LEAVE YOU TO IT.

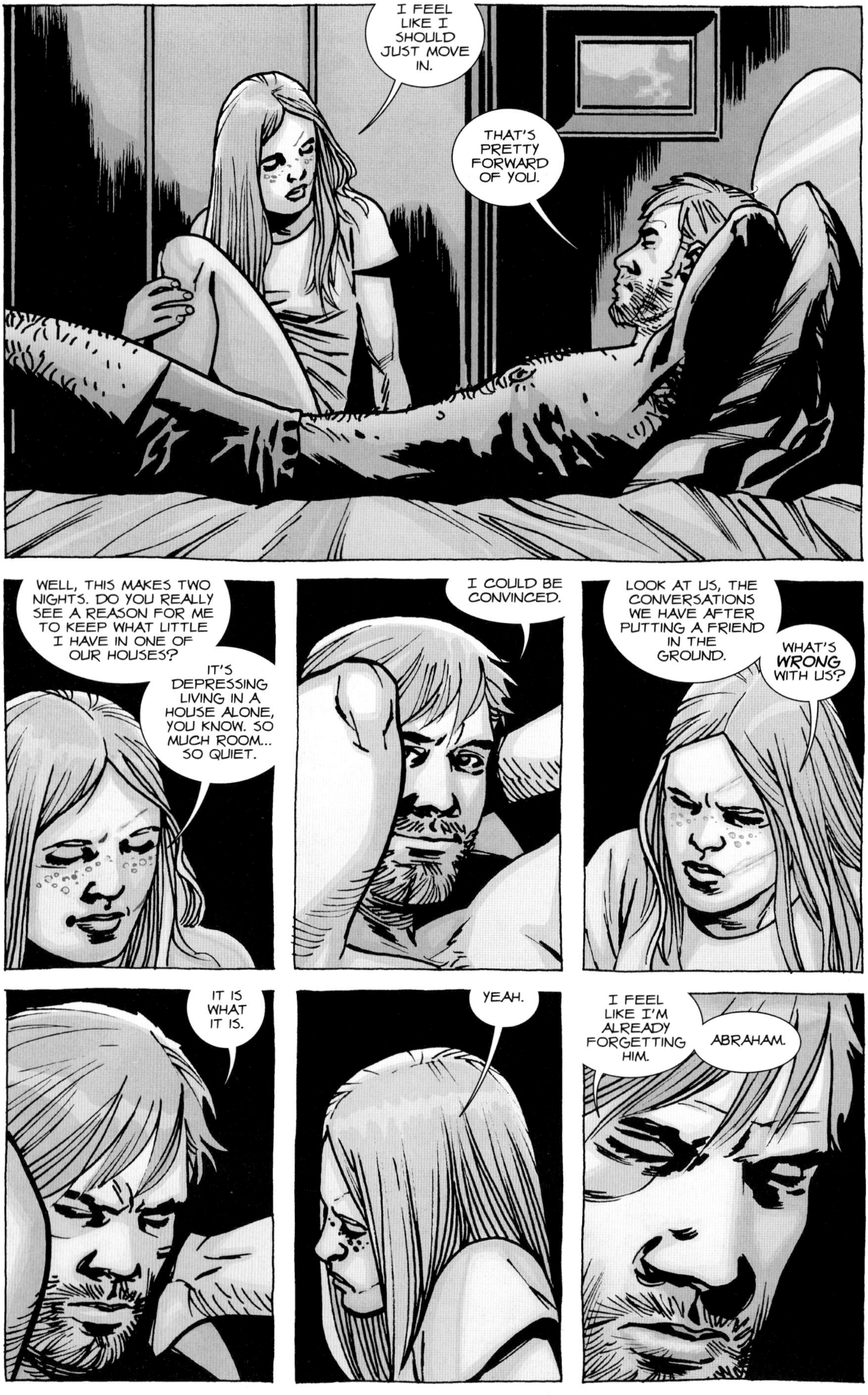
I FEEL LIKE I SHOULD JUST MOVE IN.
THAT'S PRETTY FORWARD OF YOU.
WELL, THIS MAKES TWO NIGHTS. DO YOU REALLY SEE A REASON FOR ME TO KEEP WHAT LITTLE I HAVE IN ONE OF OUR HOUSES?
IT'S DEPRESSING LIVING IN A HOUSE ALONE, YOU KNOW. SO MUCH ROOM... SO QUIET.
I COULD BE CONVINCED.
LOOK AT US, THE CONVERSATIONS WE HAVE AFTER PUTTING A FRIEND IN THE GROUND.
WHAT'S **WRONG** WITH US?
IT IS WHAT IT IS.
YEAH.
I FEEL LIKE I'M ALREADY FORGETTING HIM.
ABRAHAM.

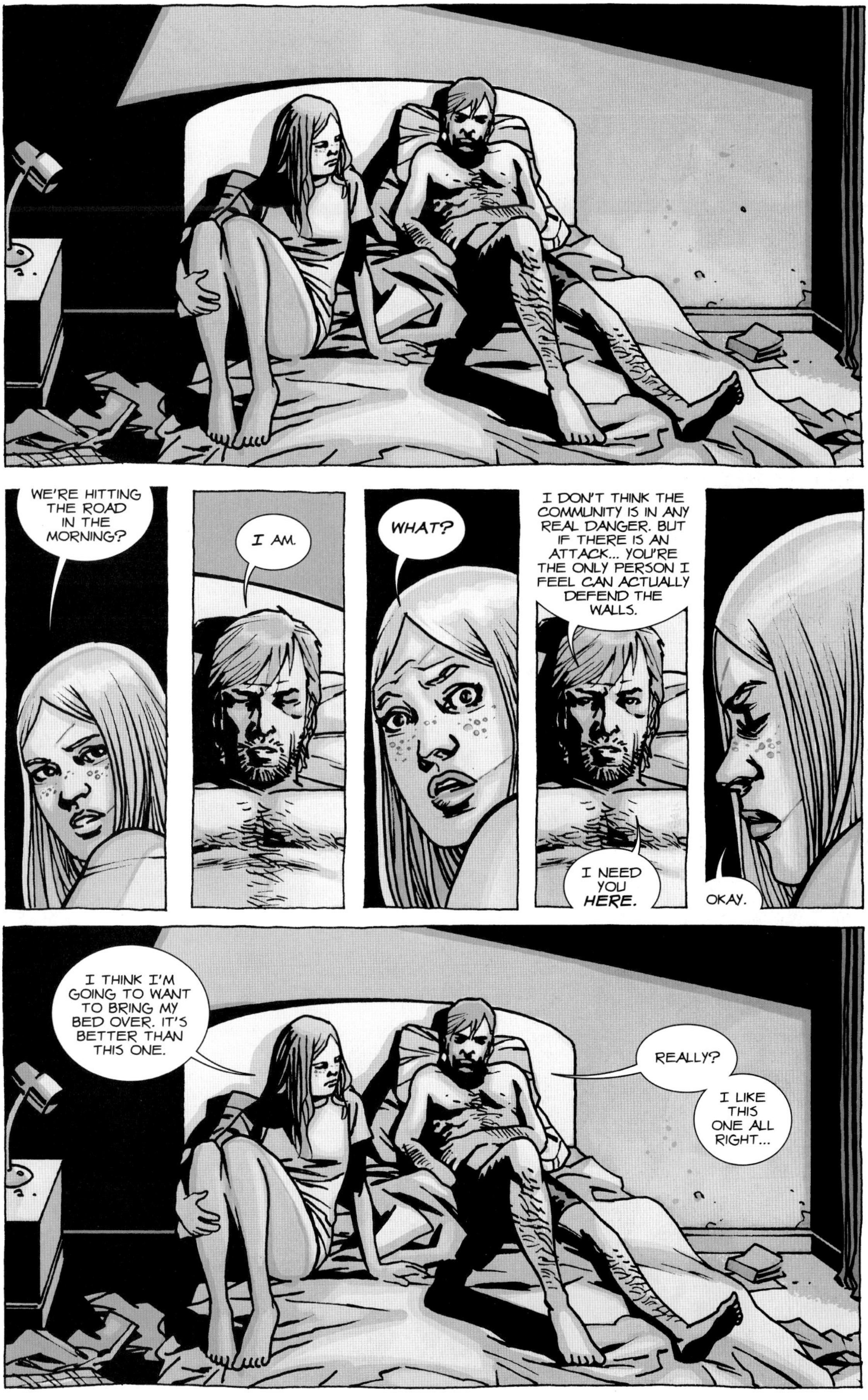

WE'RE HITTING THE ROAD IN THE MORNING?
I AM.
WHAT?
I DON'T THINK THE COMMUNITY IS IN ANY REAL DANGER. BUT IF THERE IS AN ATTACK... YOU'RE THE ONLY PERSON I FEEL CAN ACTUALLY DEFEND THE WALLS.
I NEED YOU HERE.
OKAY.
I THINK I'M GOING TO WANT TO BRING MY BED OVER. IT'S BETTER THAN THIS ONE.
REALLY?
I LIKE THIS ONE ALL RIGHT...

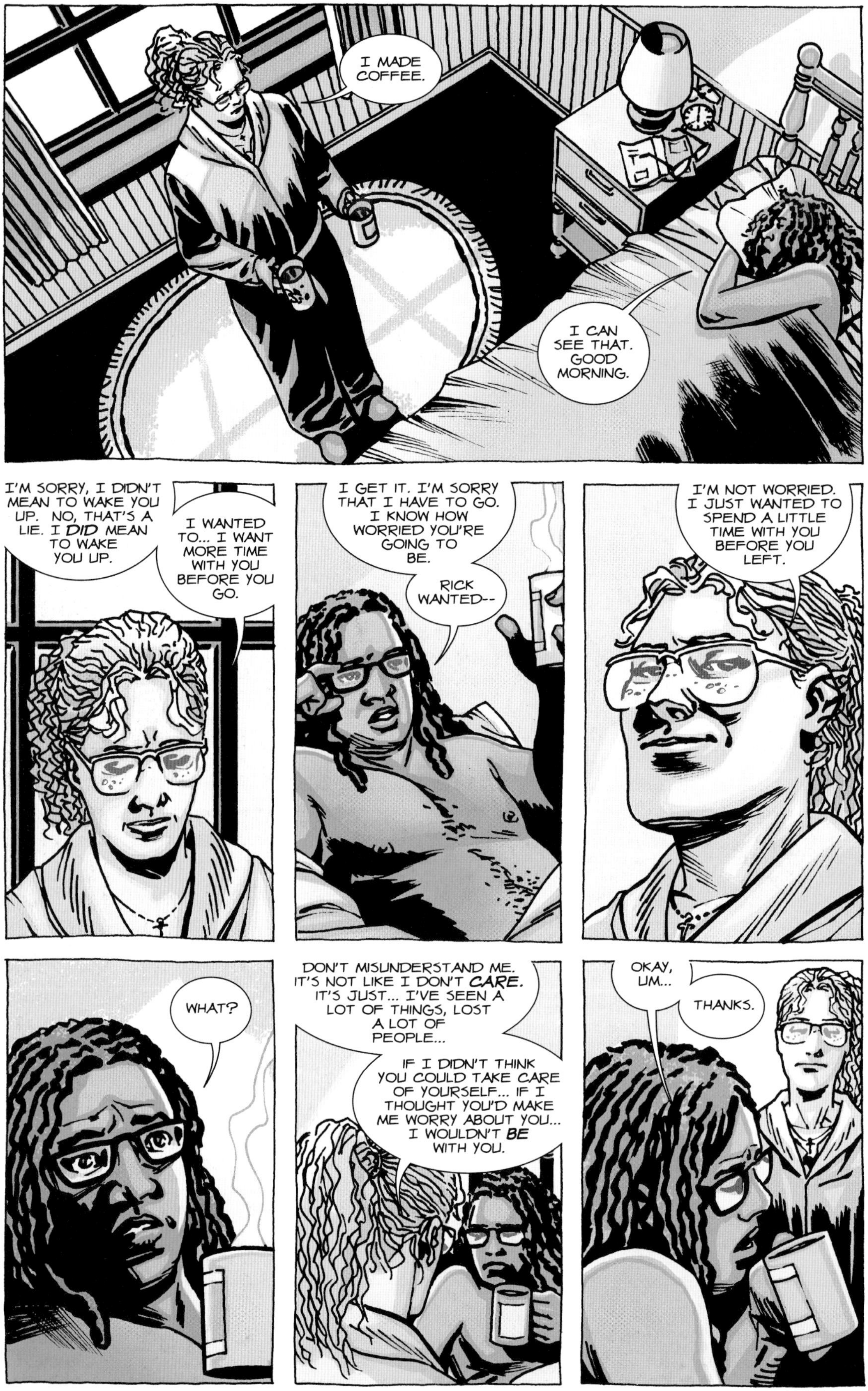
I MADE COFFEE.
I CAN SEE THAT. GOOD MORNING.
I'M SORRY, I DIDN'T MEAN TO WAKE YOU UP. NO, THAT'S A LIE. I *DID* MEAN TO WAKE YOU UP.
I WANTED TO... I WANT MORE TIME WITH YOU BEFORE YOU GO.
I GET IT. I'M SORRY THAT I HAVE TO GO. I KNOW HOW WORRIED YOU'RE GOING TO BE.
RICK WANTED--
I'M NOT WORRIED. I JUST WANTED TO SPEND A LITTLE TIME WITH YOU BEFORE YOU LEFT.
WHAT?
DON'T MISUNDERSTAND ME. IT'S NOT LIKE I DON'T *CARE.* IT'S JUST... I'VE SEEN A LOT OF THINGS, LOST A LOT OF PEOPLE...
IF I DIDN'T THINK YOU COULD TAKE CARE OF YOURSELF... IF I THOUGHT YOU'D MAKE ME WORRY ABOUT YOU... I WOULDN'T *BE* WITH YOU.
OKAY, UM...
THANKS.

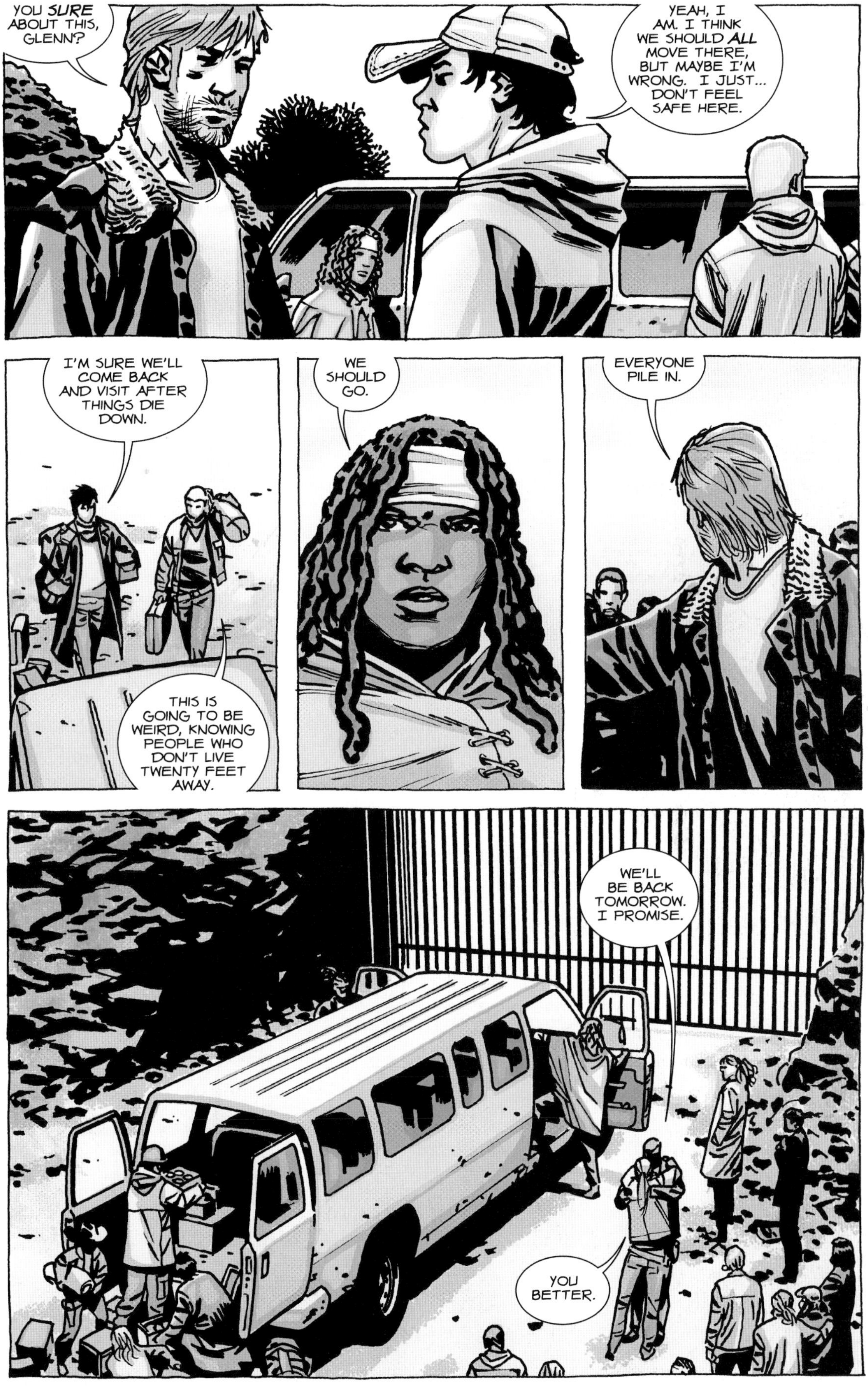
YOU SURE ABOUT THIS, GLENN?
YEAH, I AM. I THINK WE SHOULD ALL MOVE THERE, BUT MAYBE I'M WRONG. I JUST... DON'T FEEL SAFE HERE.
I'M SURE WE'LL COME BACK AND VISIT AFTER THINGS DIE DOWN.
THIS IS GOING TO BE WEIRD, KNOWING PEOPLE WHO DON'T LIVE TWENTY FEET AWAY.
WE SHOULD GO.
EVERYONE PILE IN.
WE'LL BE BACK TOMORROW. I PROMISE.
YOU BETTER.

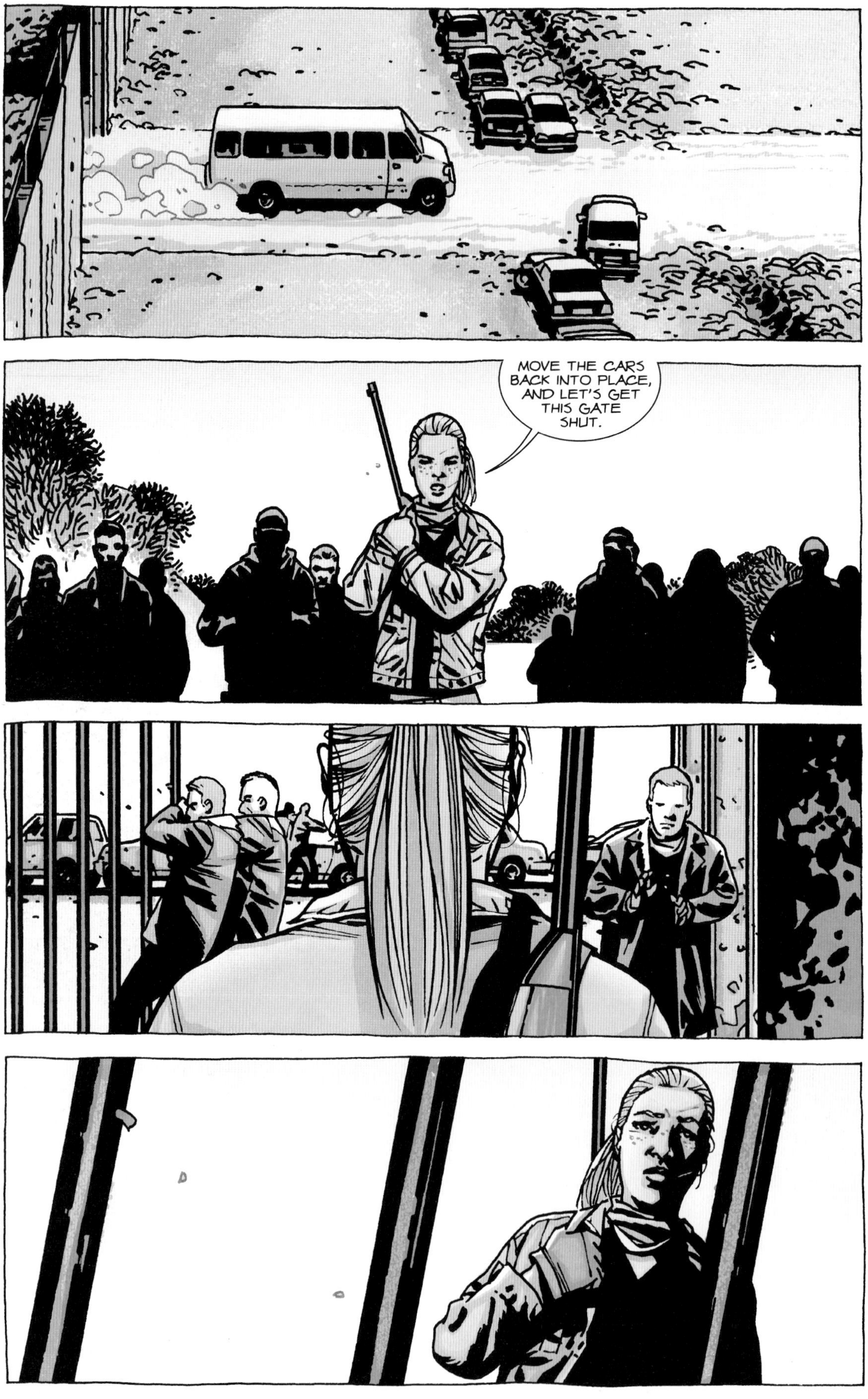
MOVE THE CARS BACK INTO PLACE, AND LET'S GET THIS GATE SHUT.

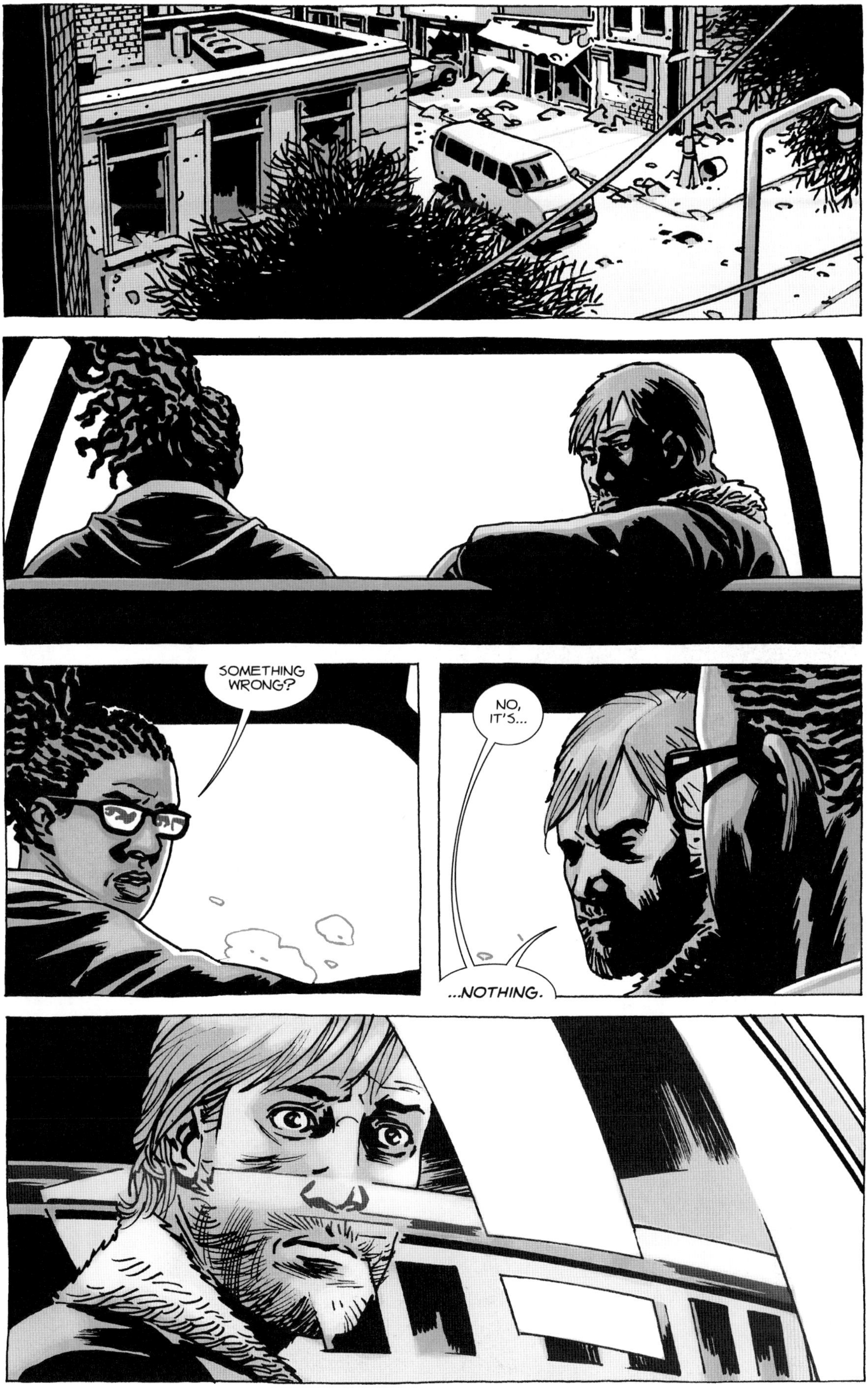
SOMETHING WRONG?
NO, IT'S...
...NOTHING.

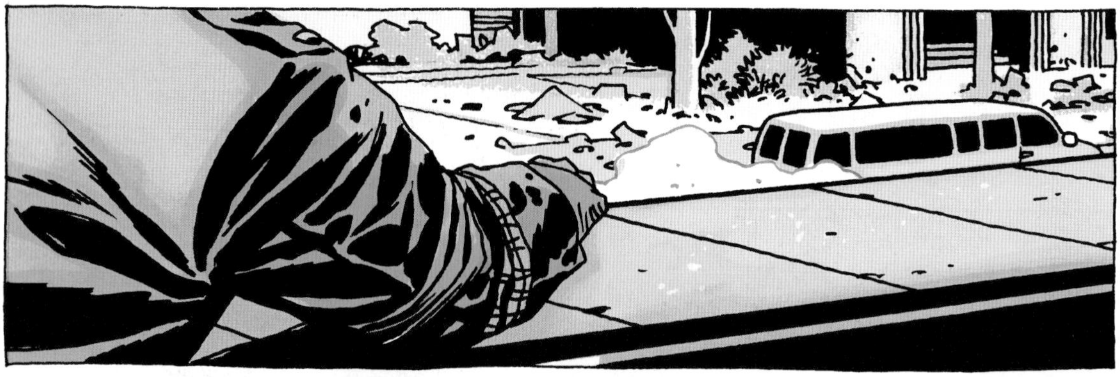

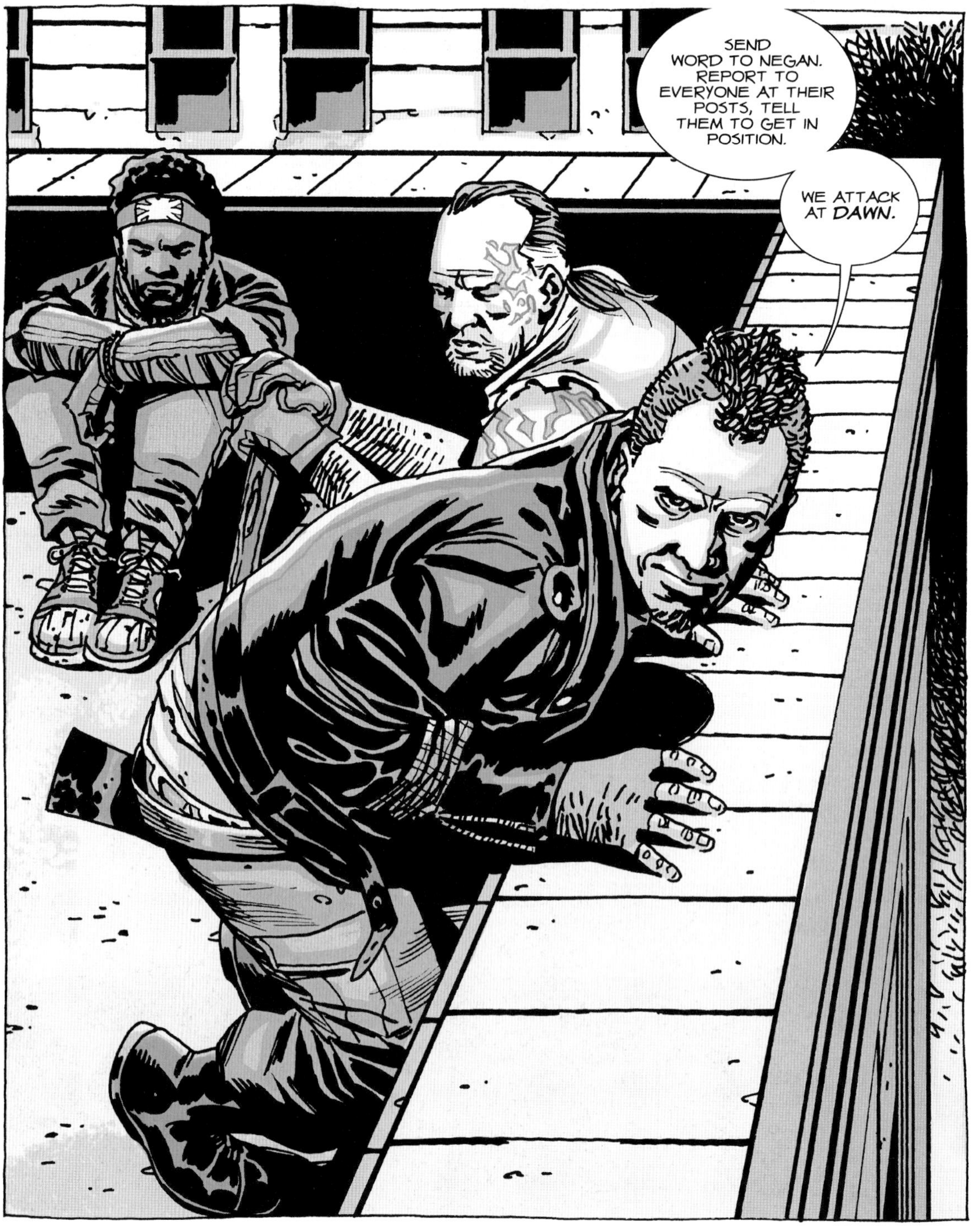
SEND WORD TO NEGAN. REPORT TO EVERYONE AT THEIR POSTS, TELL THEM TO GET IN POSITION.
WE ATTACK AT DAWN.

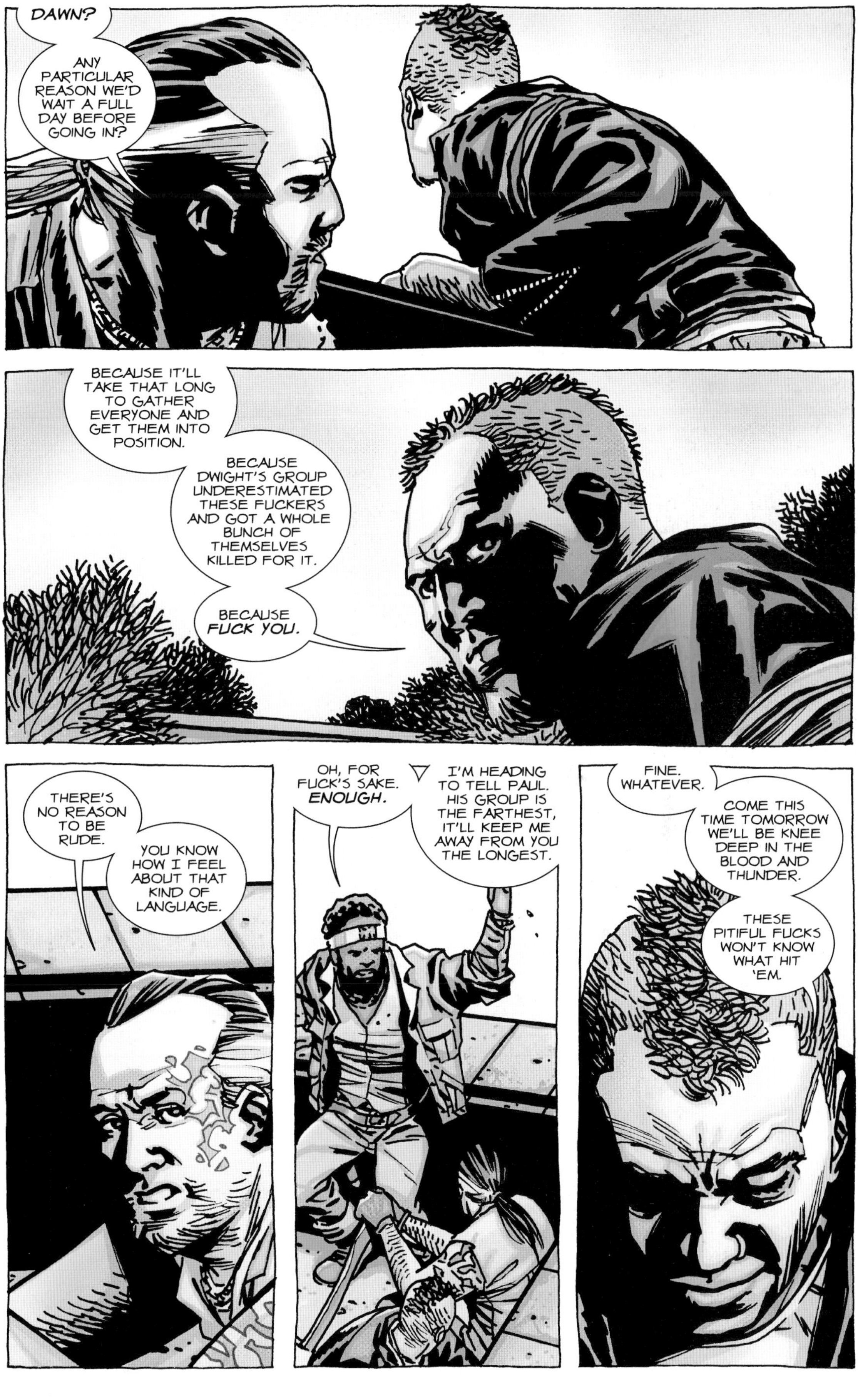
DAWN?
ANY PARTICULAR REASON WE'D WAIT A FULL DAY BEFORE GOING IN?
BECAUSE IT'LL TAKE THAT LONG TO GATHER EVERYONE AND GET THEM INTO POSITION.
BECAUSE DWIGHT'S GROUP UNDERESTIMATED THESE FUCKERS AND GOT A WHOLE BUNCH OF THEMSELVES KILLED FOR IT.
BECAUSE *FUCK YOU.*
THERE'S NO REASON TO BE RUDE.
YOU KNOW HOW I FEEL ABOUT THAT KIND OF LANGUAGE.
OH, FOR FUCK'S SAKE. *ENOUGH.*
I'M HEADING TO TELL PAUL. HIS GROUP IS THE FARTHEST, IT'LL KEEP ME AWAY FROM YOU THE LONGEST.
FINE. WHATEVER.
COME THIS TIME TOMORROW WE'LL BE KNEE DEEP IN THE BLOOD AND THUNDER.
THESE PITIFUL FUCKS WON'T KNOW WHAT HIT 'EM.

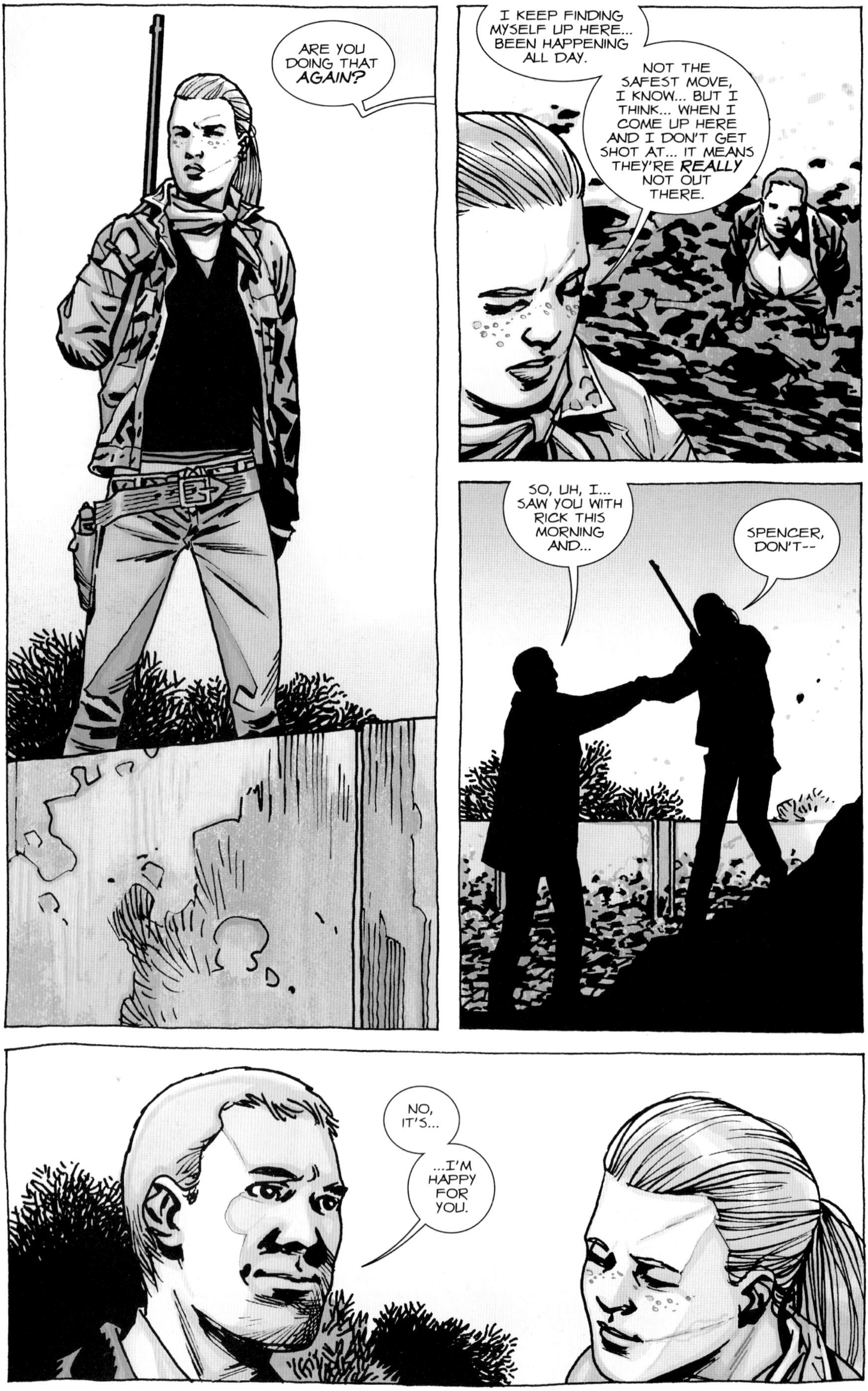
ARE YOU DOING THAT *AGAIN?*
I KEEP FINDING MYSELF UP HERE... BEEN HAPPENING ALL DAY.
NOT THE SAFEST MOVE, I KNOW... BUT I THINK... WHEN I COME UP HERE AND I DON'T GET SHOT AT... IT MEANS THEY'RE *REALLY* NOT OUT THERE.
SO, UH, I... SAW YOU WITH RICK THIS MORNING AND...
SPENCER, DON'T--
NO, IT'S...
...I'M HAPPY FOR YOU.

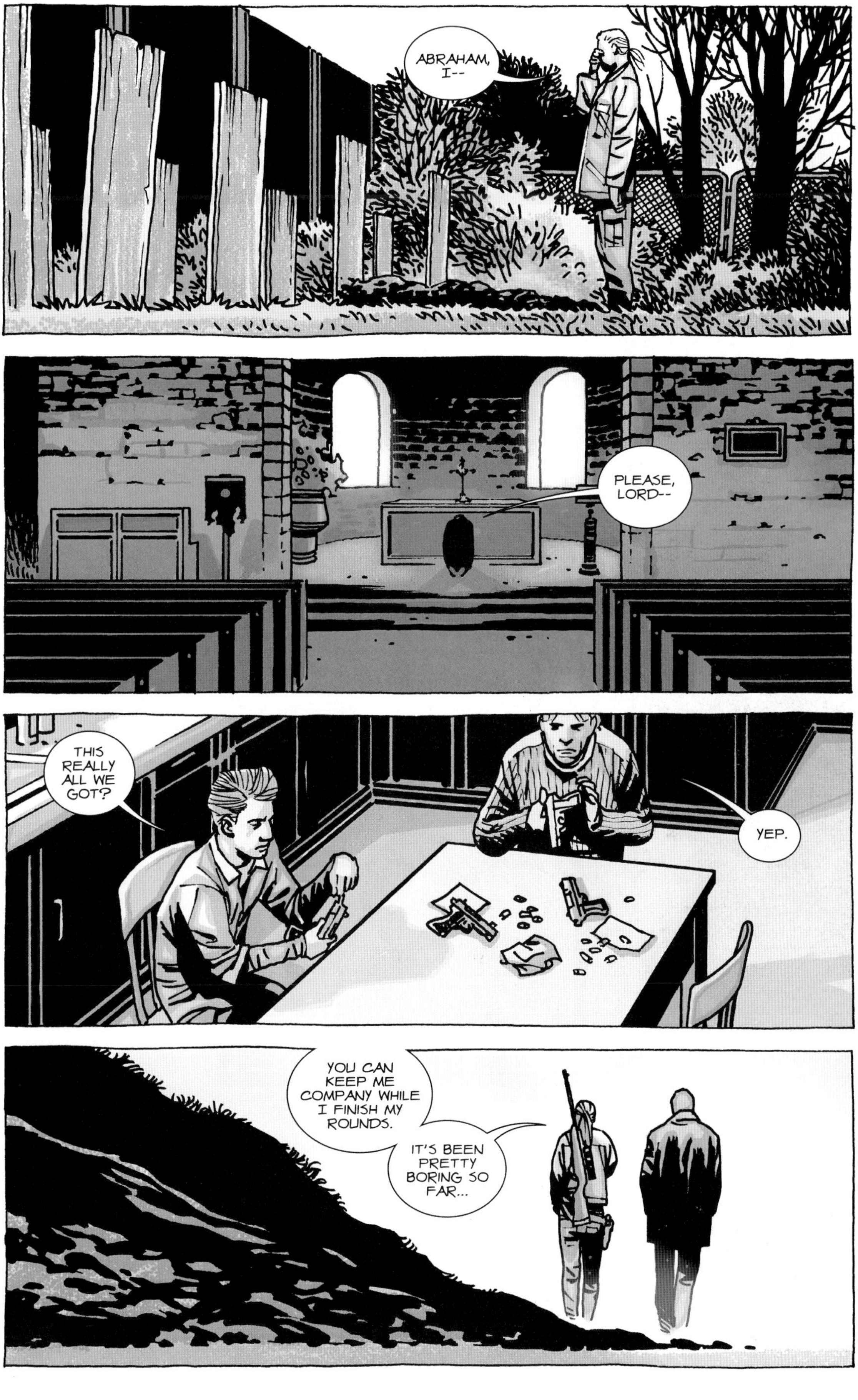
ABRAHAM, I--
PLEASE, LORD--
THIS REALLY ALL WE GOT?
YEP.
YOU CAN KEEP ME COMPANY WHILE I FINISH MY ROUNDS.
IT'S BEEN PRETTY BORING SO FAR...

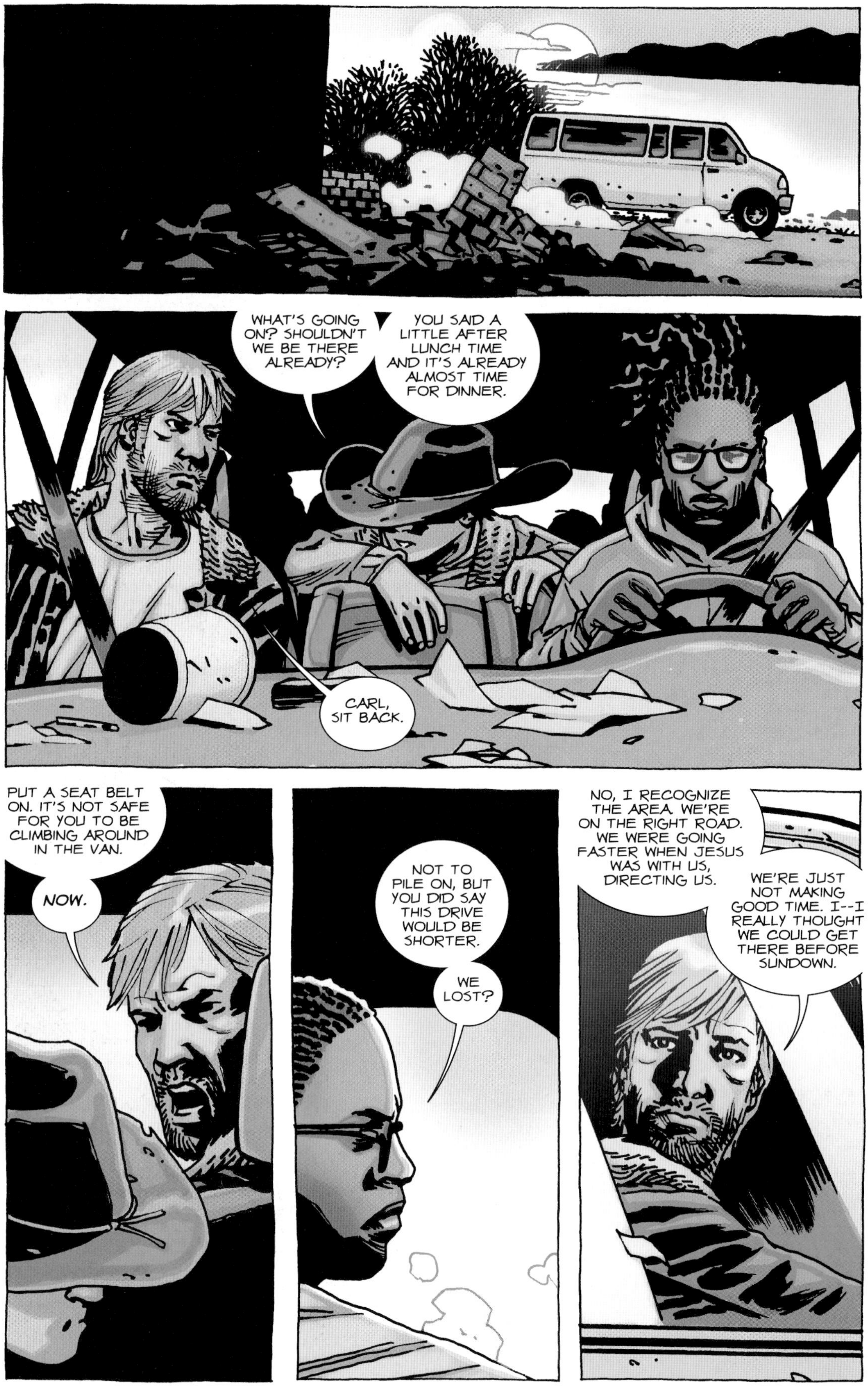
WHAT'S GOING ON? SHOULDN'T WE BE THERE ALREADY?
YOU SAID A LITTLE AFTER LUNCH TIME AND IT'S ALREADY ALMOST TIME FOR DINNER.
CARL, SIT BACK.
PUT A SEAT BELT ON. IT'S NOT SAFE FOR YOU TO BE CLIMBING AROUND IN THE VAN.
NOW.
NOT TO PILE ON, BUT YOU DID SAY THIS DRIVE WOULD BE SHORTER.
WE LOST?
NO, I RECOGNIZE THE AREA. WE'RE ON THE RIGHT ROAD. WE WERE GOING FASTER WHEN JESUS WAS WITH US, DIRECTING US.
WE'RE JUST NOT MAKING GOOD TIME. I--I REALLY THOUGHT WE COULD GET THERE BEFORE SUNDOWN.

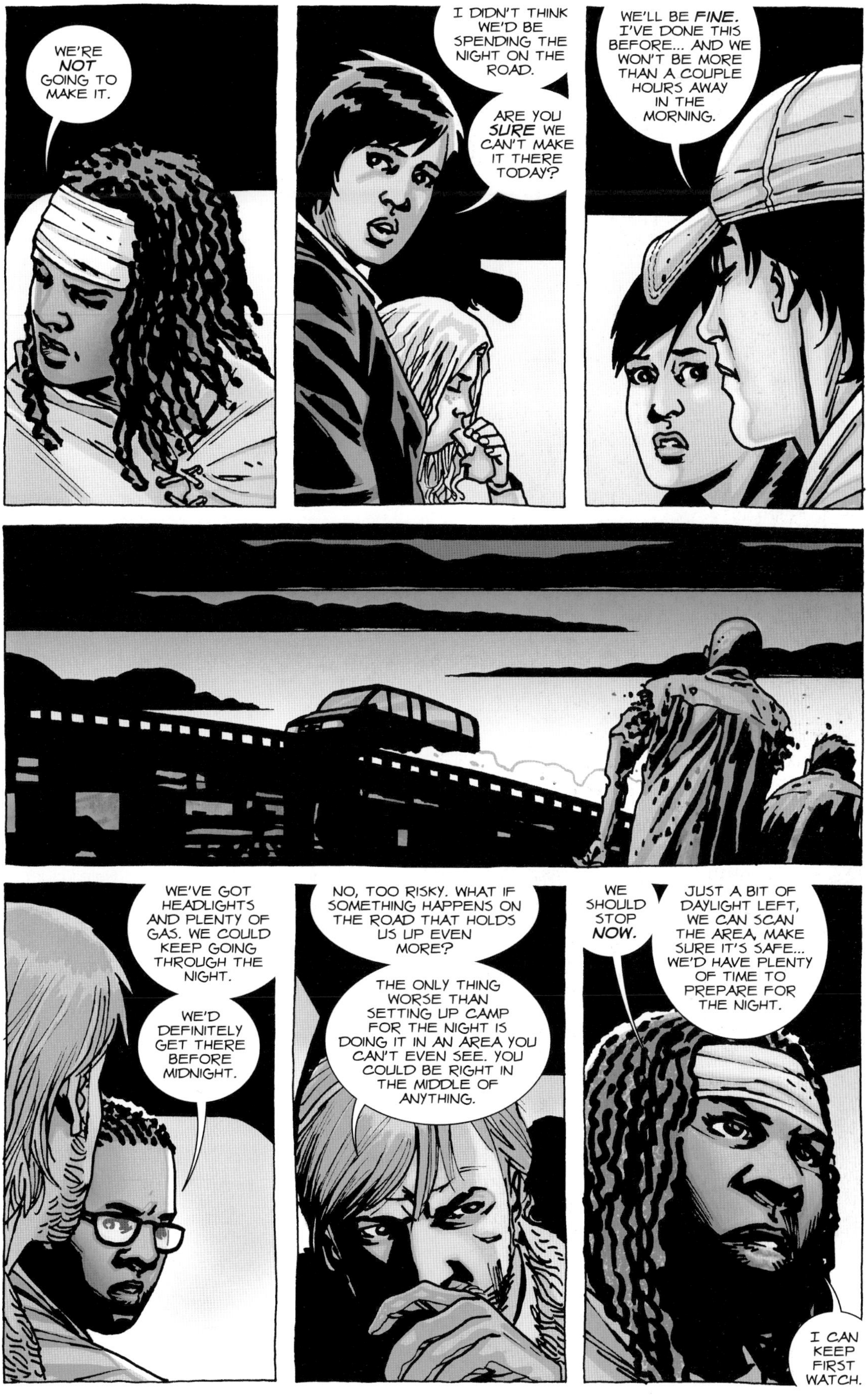
WE'RE NOT GOING TO MAKE IT.
I DIDN'T THINK WE'D BE SPENDING THE NIGHT ON THE ROAD.
ARE YOU SURE WE CAN'T MAKE IT THERE TODAY?
WE'LL BE FINE. I'VE DONE THIS BEFORE... AND WE WON'T BE MORE THAN A COUPLE HOURS AWAY IN THE MORNING.
WE'VE GOT HEADLIGHTS AND PLENTY OF GAS. WE COULD KEEP GOING THROUGH THE NIGHT.
WE'D DEFINITELY GET THERE BEFORE MIDNIGHT.
NO, TOO RISKY. WHAT IF SOMETHING HAPPENS ON THE ROAD THAT HOLDS US UP EVEN MORE?
THE ONLY THING WORSE THAN SETTING UP CAMP FOR THE NIGHT IS DOING IT IN AN AREA YOU CAN'T EVEN SEE. YOU COULD BE RIGHT IN THE MIDDLE OF ANYTHING.
WE SHOULD STOP NOW.
JUST A BIT OF DAYLIGHT LEFT, WE CAN SCAN THE AREA, MAKE SURE IT'S SAFE... WE'D HAVE PLENTY OF TIME TO PREPARE FOR THE NIGHT.
I CAN KEEP FIRST WATCH.

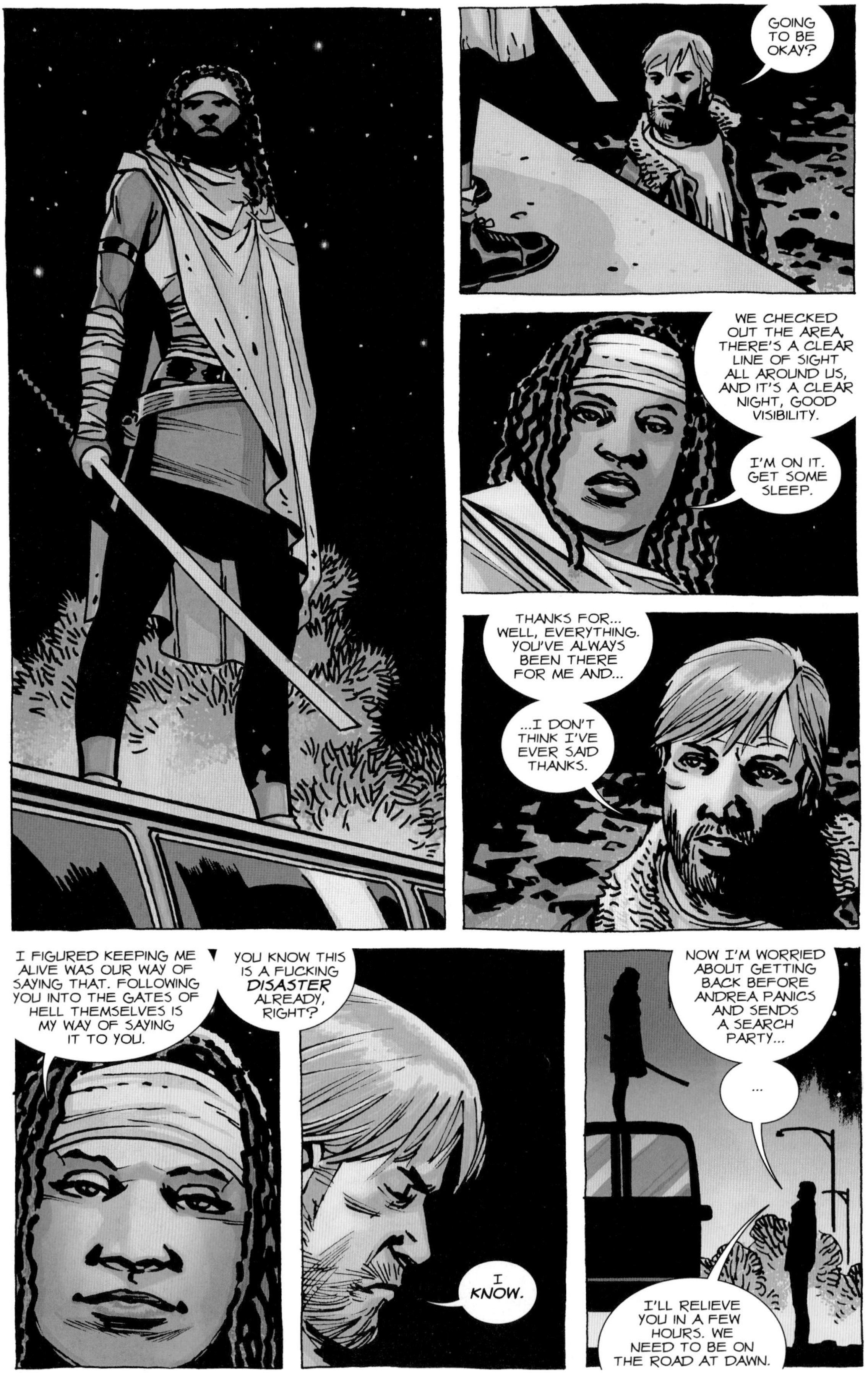
GOING TO BE OKAY?
WE CHECKED OUT THE AREA, THERE'S A CLEAR LINE OF SIGHT ALL AROUND US, AND IT'S A CLEAR NIGHT, GOOD VISIBILITY.
I'M ON IT. GET SOME SLEEP.
THANKS FOR... WELL, EVERYTHING. YOU'VE ALWAYS BEEN THERE FOR ME AND...
...I DON'T THINK I'VE EVER SAID THANKS.
I FIGURED KEEPING ME ALIVE WAS OUR WAY OF SAYING THAT. FOLLOWING YOU INTO THE GATES OF HELL THEMSELVES IS MY WAY OF SAYING IT TO YOU.
YOU KNOW THIS IS A FUCKING *DISASTER* ALREADY, RIGHT?
I *KNOW.*
NOW I'M WORRIED ABOUT GETTING BACK BEFORE ANDREA PANICS AND SENDS A SEARCH PARTY...
...
I'LL RELIEVE YOU IN A FEW HOURS. WE NEED TO BE ON THE ROAD AT DAWN.

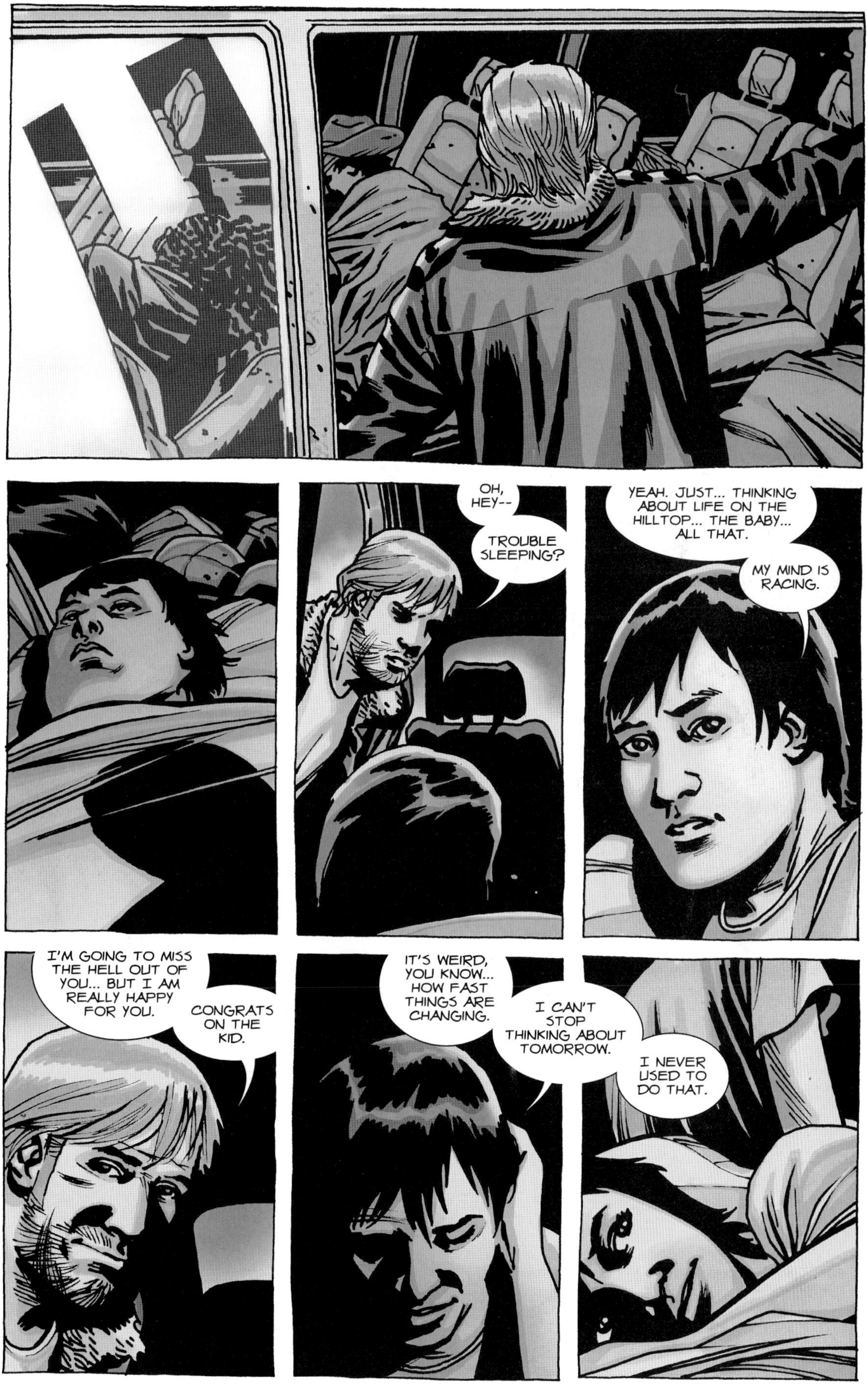
OH, HEY--
TROUBLE SLEEPING?
YEAH. JUST... THINKING ABOUT LIFE ON THE HILLTOP... THE BABY... ALL THAT.
MY MIND IS RACING.
I'M GOING TO MISS THE HELL OUT OF YOU... BUT I AM REALLY HAPPY FOR YOU.
CONGRATS ON THE KID.
IT'S WEIRD, YOU KNOW... HOW FAST THINGS ARE CHANGING.
I CAN'T STOP THINKING ABOUT TOMORROW.
I NEVER USED TO DO THAT.

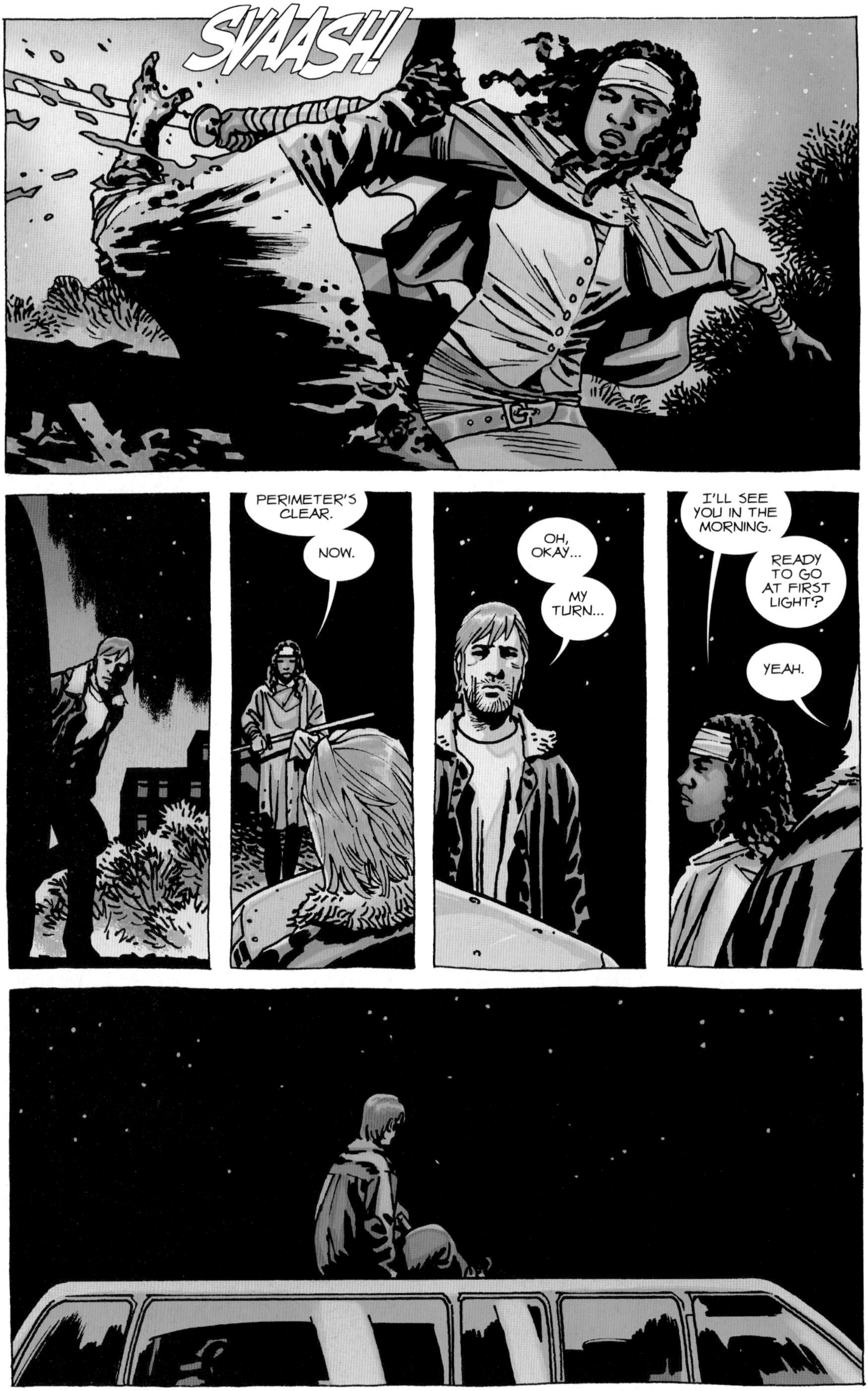
SVAASH!
PERIMETER'S CLEAR.
NOW.
OH, OKAY...
MY TURN...
I'LL SEE YOU IN THE MORNING.
READY TO GO AT FIRST LIGHT?
YEAH.

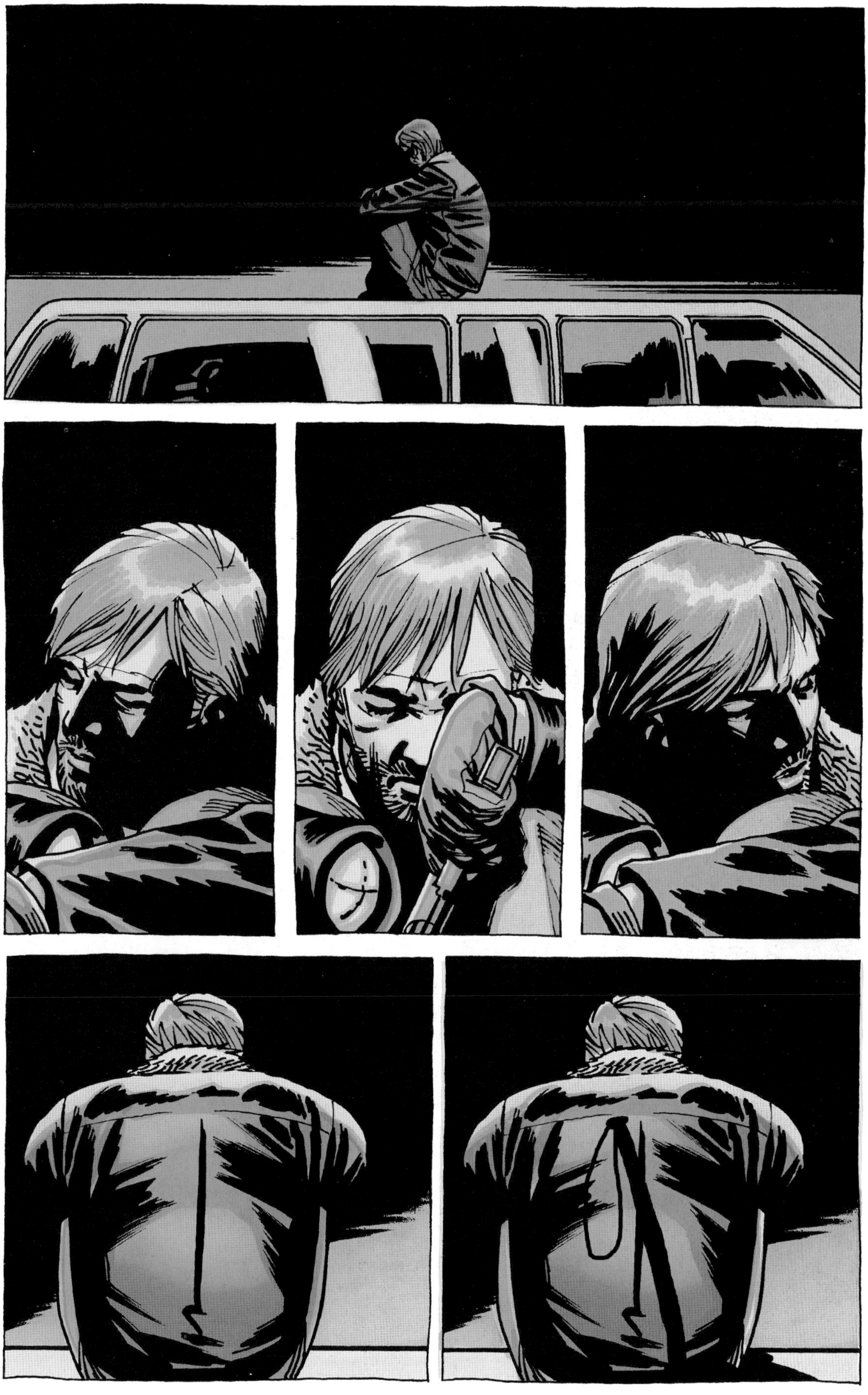

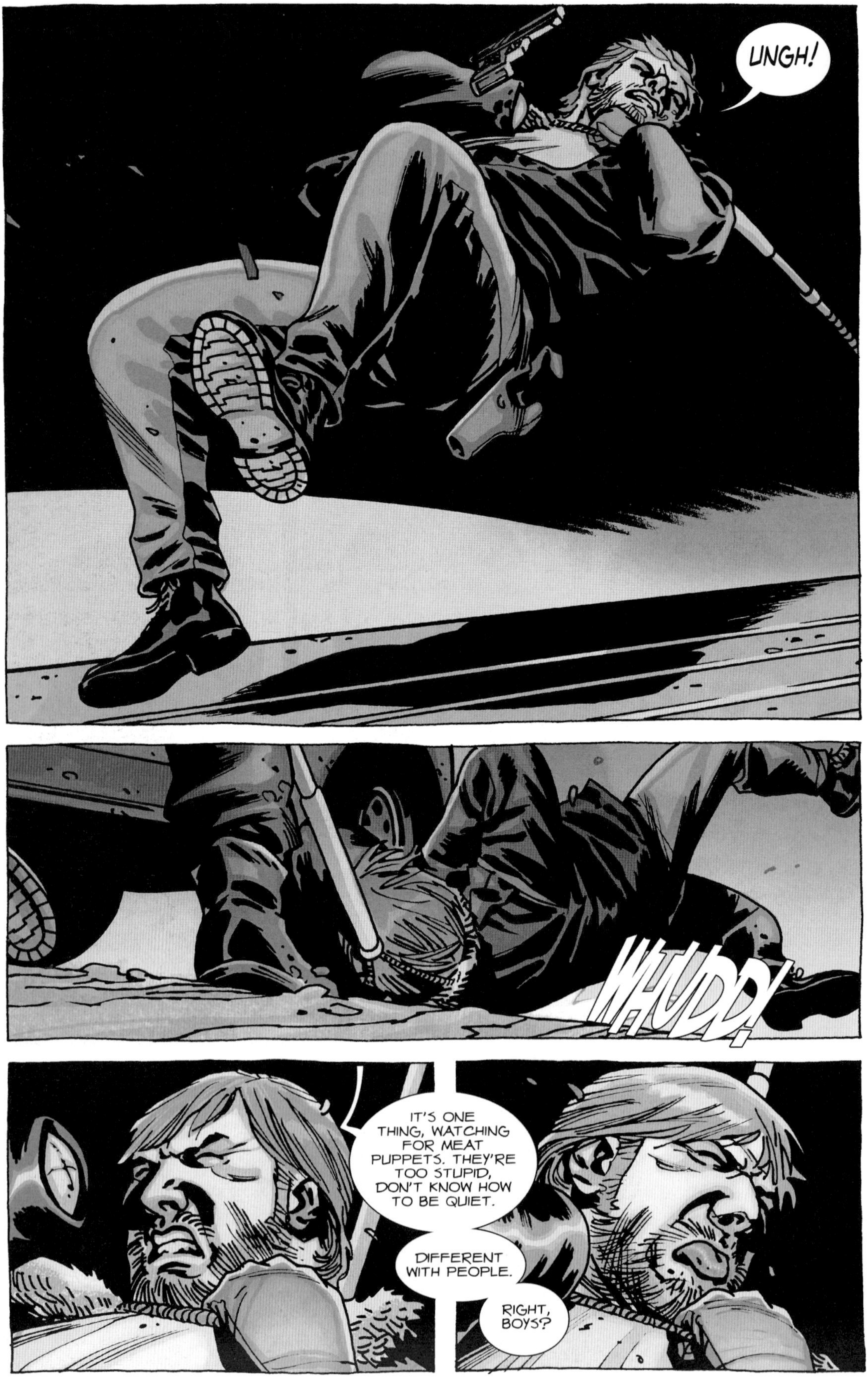
UNGH!
WHUDD!
IT'S ONE THING, WATCHING FOR MEAT PUPPETS. THEY'RE TOO STUPID, DON'T KNOW HOW TO BE QUIET.
DIFFERENT WITH PEOPLE.
RIGHT, BOYS?

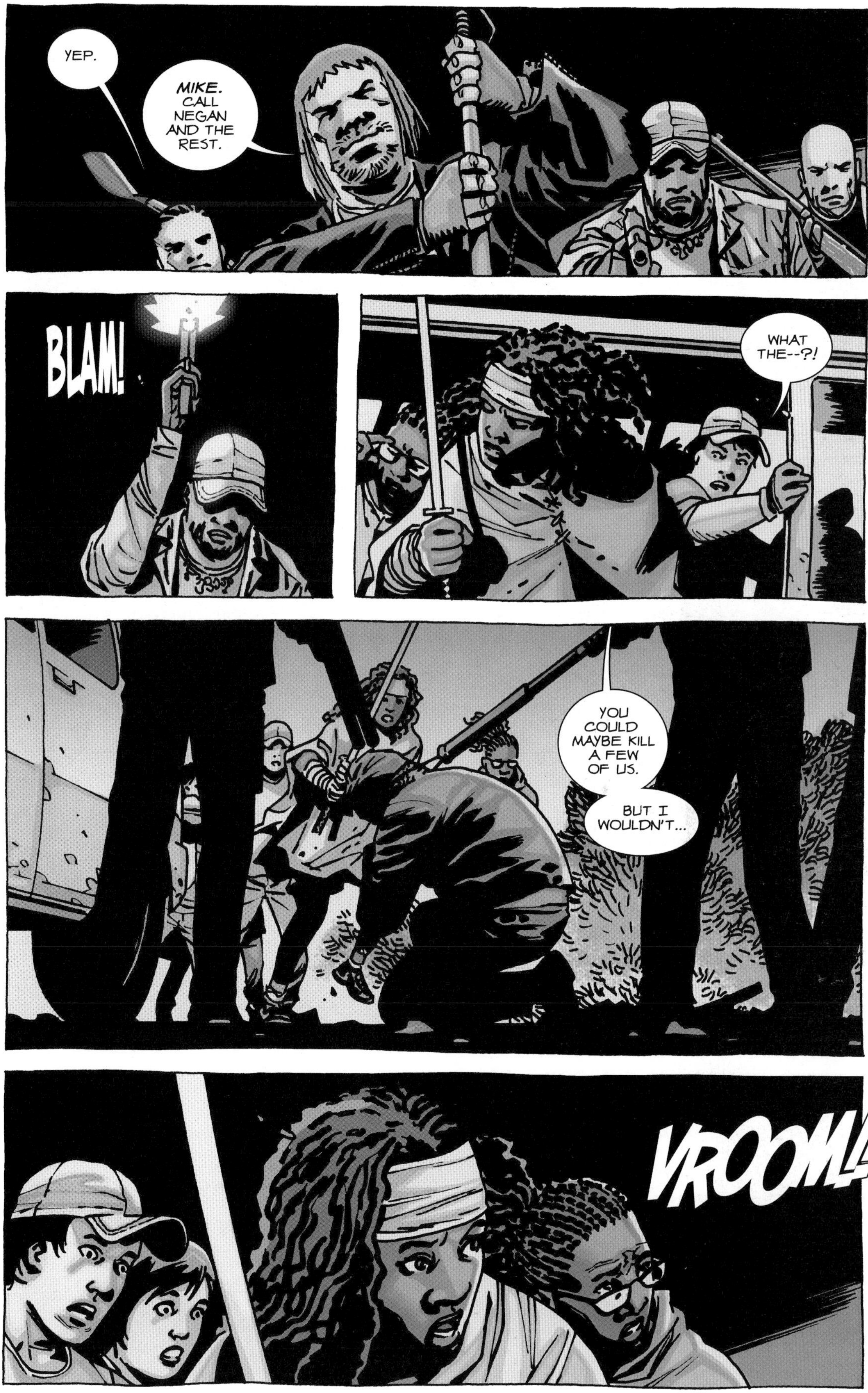
YEP.
MIKE. CALL NEGAN AND THE REST.
BLAM!
WHAT THE--?!
YOU COULD MAYBE KILL A FEW OF US.
BUT I WOULDN'T...
VROOM!!

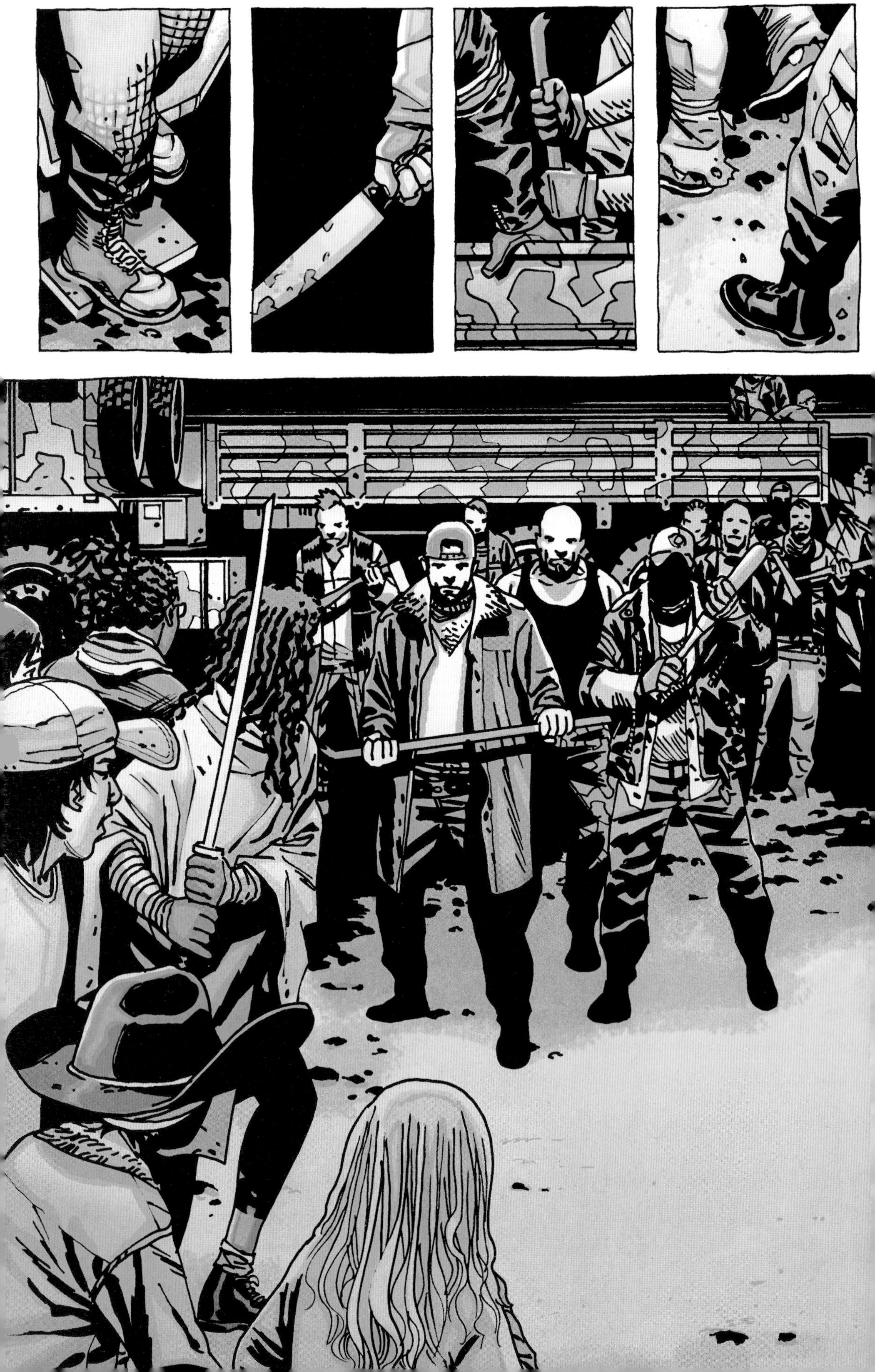

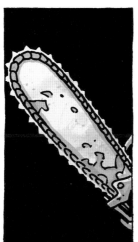

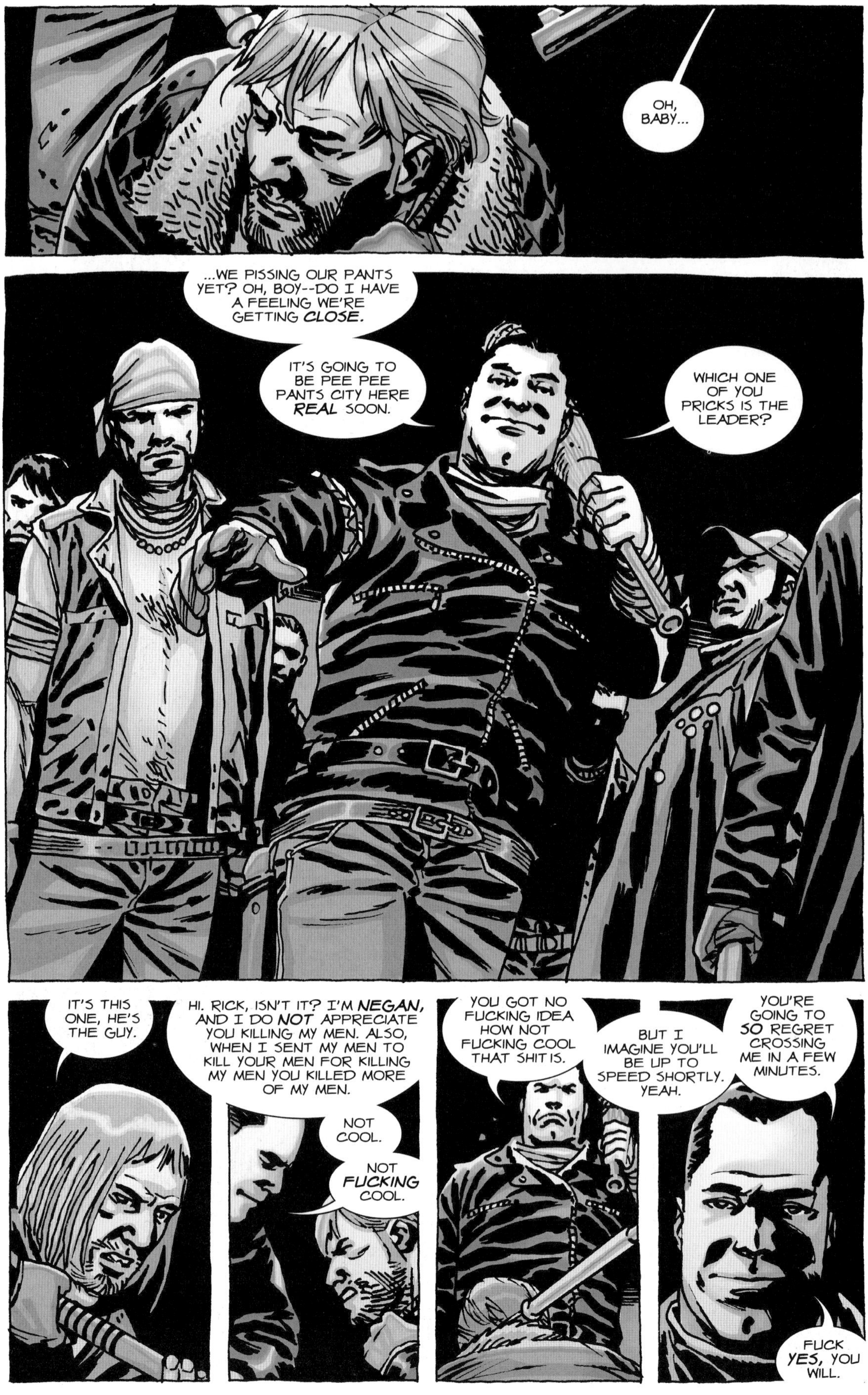
OH, BABY...
...WE PISSING OUR PANTS YET? OH, BOY--DO I HAVE A FEELING WE'RE GETTING CLOSE.
IT'S GOING TO BE PEE PEE PANTS CITY HERE REAL SOON.
WHICH ONE OF YOU PRICKS IS THE LEADER?
IT'S THIS ONE, HE'S THE GUY.
HI. RICK, ISN'T IT? I'M NEGAN, AND I DO NOT APPRECIATE YOU KILLING MY MEN. ALSO, WHEN I SENT MY MEN TO KILL YOUR MEN FOR KILLING MY MEN YOU KILLED MORE OF MY MEN.
NOT COOL.
NOT FUCKING COOL.
YOU GOT NO FUCKING IDEA HOW NOT FUCKING COOL THAT SHIT IS.
BUT I IMAGINE YOU'LL BE UP TO SPEED SHORTLY. YEAH.
YOU'RE GOING TO SO REGRET CROSSING ME IN A FEW MINUTES.
FUCK YES, YOU WILL.

YOU SEE, RICK. WHATEVER YOU DO... NO MATTER FUCKING WHAT... YOU **DO NOT** MESS WITH THE NEW WORLD ORDER.

THE NEW WORLD ORDER IS THIS, AND IT'S **VERY** SIMPLE, SO EVEN IF YOU'RE FUCKING STUPID... WHICH YOU MAY VERY WELL BE... YOU CAN UNDERSTAND IT.

READY? HERE GOES... PAY ATTENTION.

GIVE ME **YOUR SHIT** OR I WILL KILL YOU.

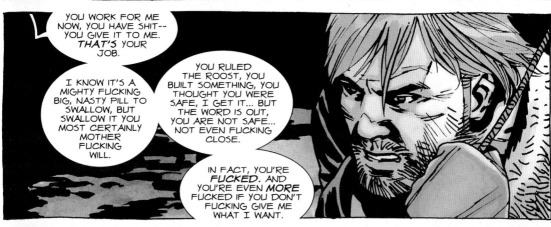

YOU WORK FOR ME NOW, YOU HAVE SHIT-- YOU GIVE IT TO ME. **THAT'S** YOUR JOB.

I KNOW IT'S A MIGHTY FUCKING BIG, NASTY PILL TO SWALLOW, BUT SWALLOW IT YOU MOST CERTAINLY MOTHER FUCKING WILL.

YOU RULED THE ROOST, YOU BUILT SOMETHING, YOU THOUGHT YOU WERE SAFE, I GET IT... BUT THE WORD IS OUT, YOU ARE NOT SAFE... NOT EVEN FUCKING CLOSE.

IN FACT, YOU'RE **FUCKED.** AND YOU'RE EVEN **MORE** FUCKED IF YOU DON'T FUCKING GIVE ME WHAT I WANT.

AND WHAT I WANT IS HALF YOUR SHIT--IF THAT'S TOO MUCH, JUST MAKE, FIND OR STEAL MORE AND IT'LL ALL EVEN OUT EVENTUALLY.

THIS IS YOUR WAY OF LIFE NOW. THE MORE YOU FIGHT BACK, THE HARDER IT'S GOING TO BE.

NEXT TIME SOMEONE COMES TO YOUR DOOR... YOU FUCKING **LET US IN.** WE OWN THAT DOOR. YOU TRY TO STOP US-- WE'LL FUCKING KNOCK IT THE FUCK DOWN.

UNDERSTAND?

NO ANSWER?

WELL, YOU DIDN'T REALLY THINK YOU WERE GOING TO GET THROUGH THIS WITHOUT GETTING **PUNISHED,** NOW DID YOU?

LINE THEM UP.

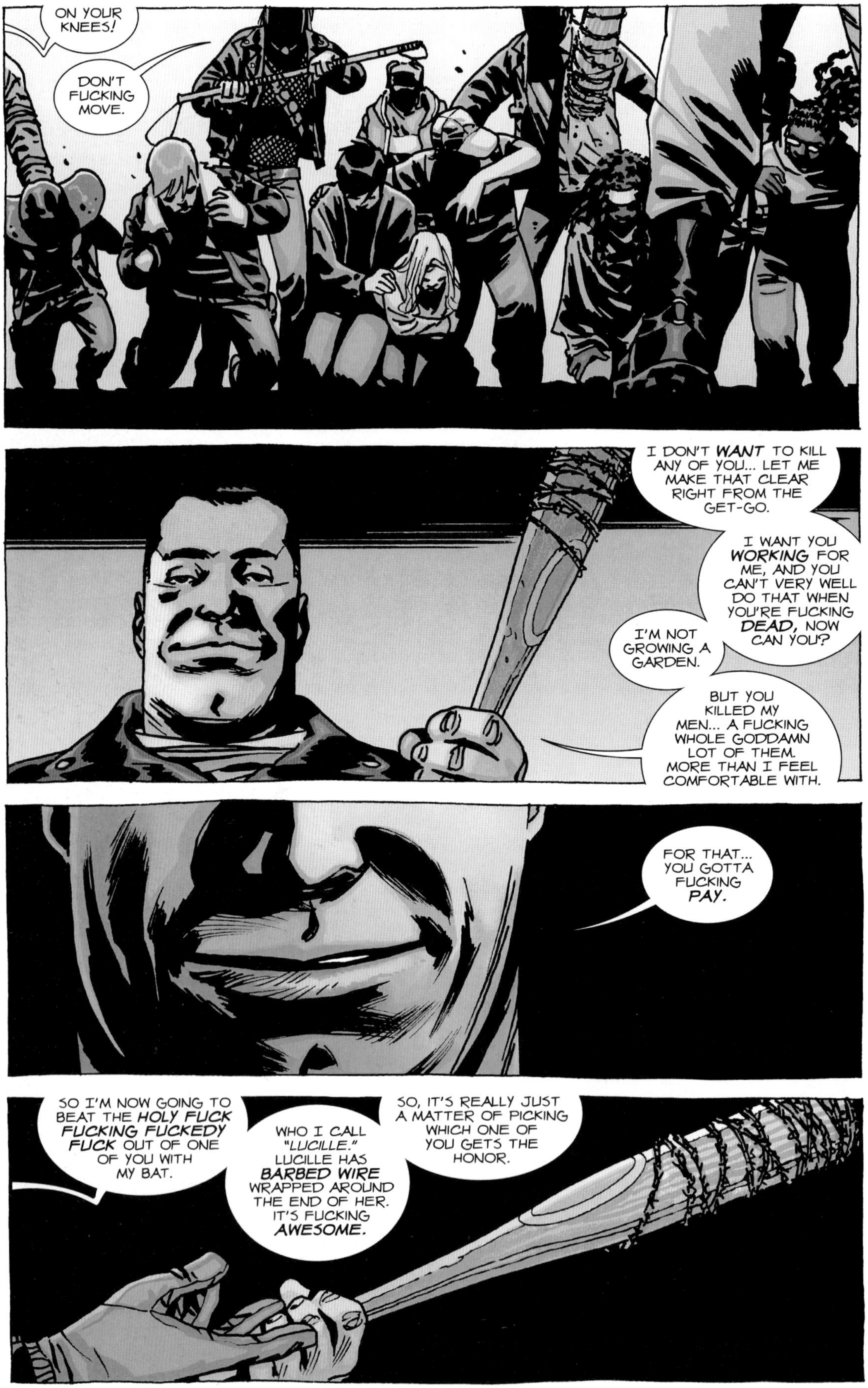

ON YOUR KNEES!
DON'T FUCKING MOVE.
I DON'T WANT TO KILL ANY OF YOU... LET ME MAKE THAT CLEAR RIGHT FROM THE GET-GO.
I WANT YOU WORKING FOR ME, AND YOU CAN'T VERY WELL DO THAT WHEN YOU'RE FUCKING DEAD, NOW CAN YOU?
I'M NOT GROWING A GARDEN.
BUT YOU KILLED MY MEN... A FUCKING WHOLE GODDAMN LOT OF THEM. MORE THAN I FEEL COMFORTABLE WITH.
FOR THAT... YOU GOTTA FUCKING PAY.
SO I'M NOW GOING TO BEAT THE HOLY FUCK FUCKING FUCKEDY FUCK OUT OF ONE OF YOU WITH MY BAT.
WHO I CALL "LUCILLE." LUCILLE HAS BARBED WIRE WRAPPED AROUND THE END OF HER. IT'S FUCKING AWESOME.
SO, IT'S REALLY JUST A MATTER OF PICKING WHICH ONE OF YOU GETS THE HONOR.

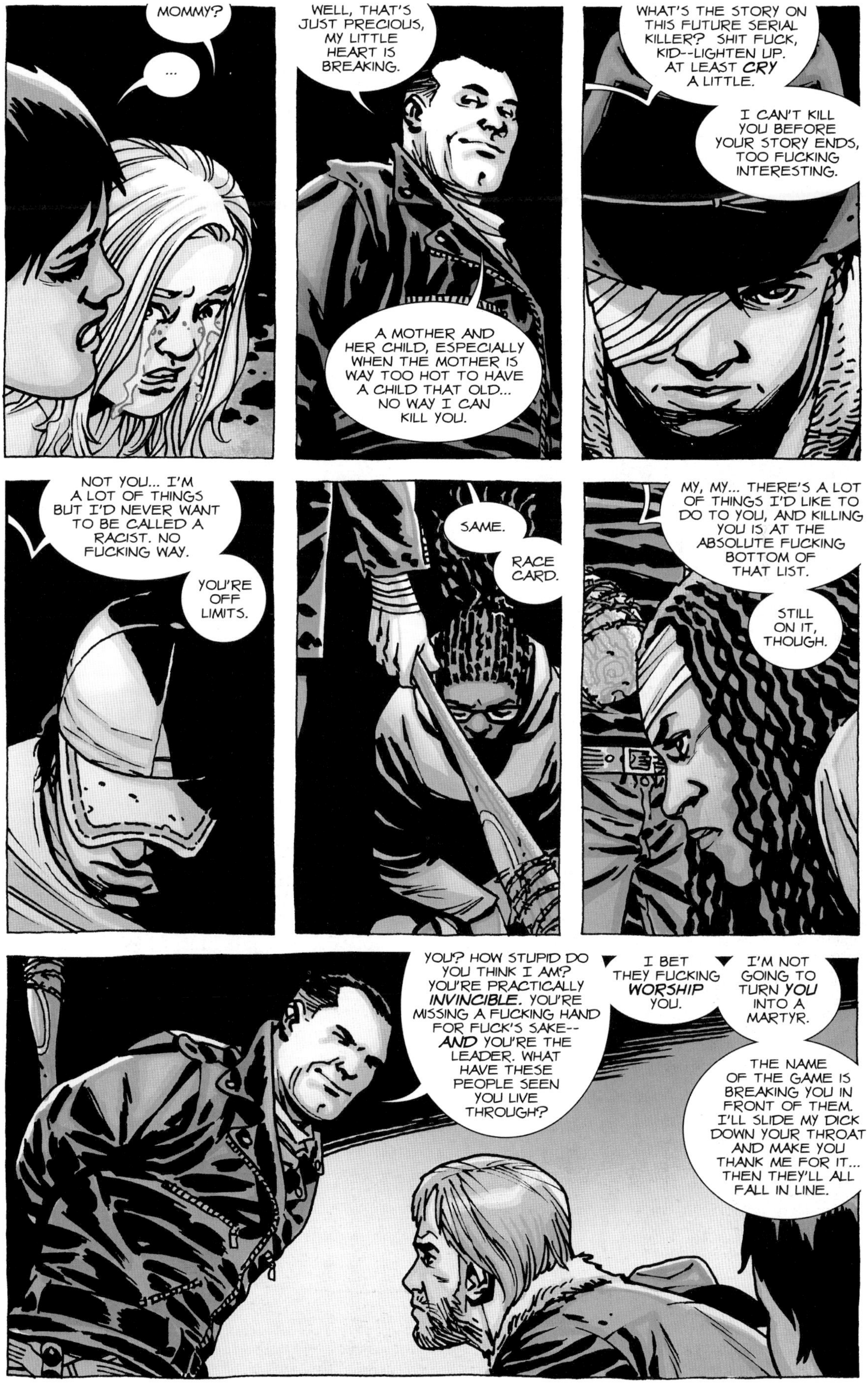
MOMMY?
...
WELL, THAT'S JUST PRECIOUS, MY LITTLE HEART IS BREAKING.
A MOTHER AND HER CHILD, ESPECIALLY WHEN THE MOTHER IS WAY TOO HOT TO HAVE A CHILD THAT OLD... NO WAY I CAN KILL YOU.
WHAT'S THE STORY ON THIS FUTURE SERIAL KILLER? SHIT FUCK, KID--LIGHTEN UP. AT LEAST CRY A LITTLE.
I CAN'T KILL YOU BEFORE YOUR STORY ENDS, TOO FUCKING INTERESTING.
NOT YOU... I'M A LOT OF THINGS BUT I'D NEVER WANT TO BE CALLED A RACIST. NO FUCKING WAY.
YOU'RE OFF LIMITS.
SAME.
RACE CARD.
MY, MY... THERE'S A LOT OF THINGS I'D LIKE TO DO TO YOU, AND KILLING YOU IS AT THE ABSOLUTE FUCKING BOTTOM OF THAT LIST.
STILL ON IT, THOUGH.
YOU? HOW STUPID DO YOU THINK I AM? YOU'RE PRACTICALLY INVINCIBLE. YOU'RE MISSING A FUCKING HAND FOR FUCK'S SAKE-- AND YOU'RE THE LEADER. WHAT HAVE THESE PEOPLE SEEN YOU LIVE THROUGH?
I BET THEY FUCKING WORSHIP YOU.
I'M NOT GOING TO TURN YOU INTO A MARTYR.
THE NAME OF THE GAME IS BREAKING YOU IN FRONT OF THEM. I'LL SLIDE MY DICK DOWN YOUR THROAT AND MAKE YOU THANK ME FOR IT... THEN THEY'LL ALL FALL IN LINE.

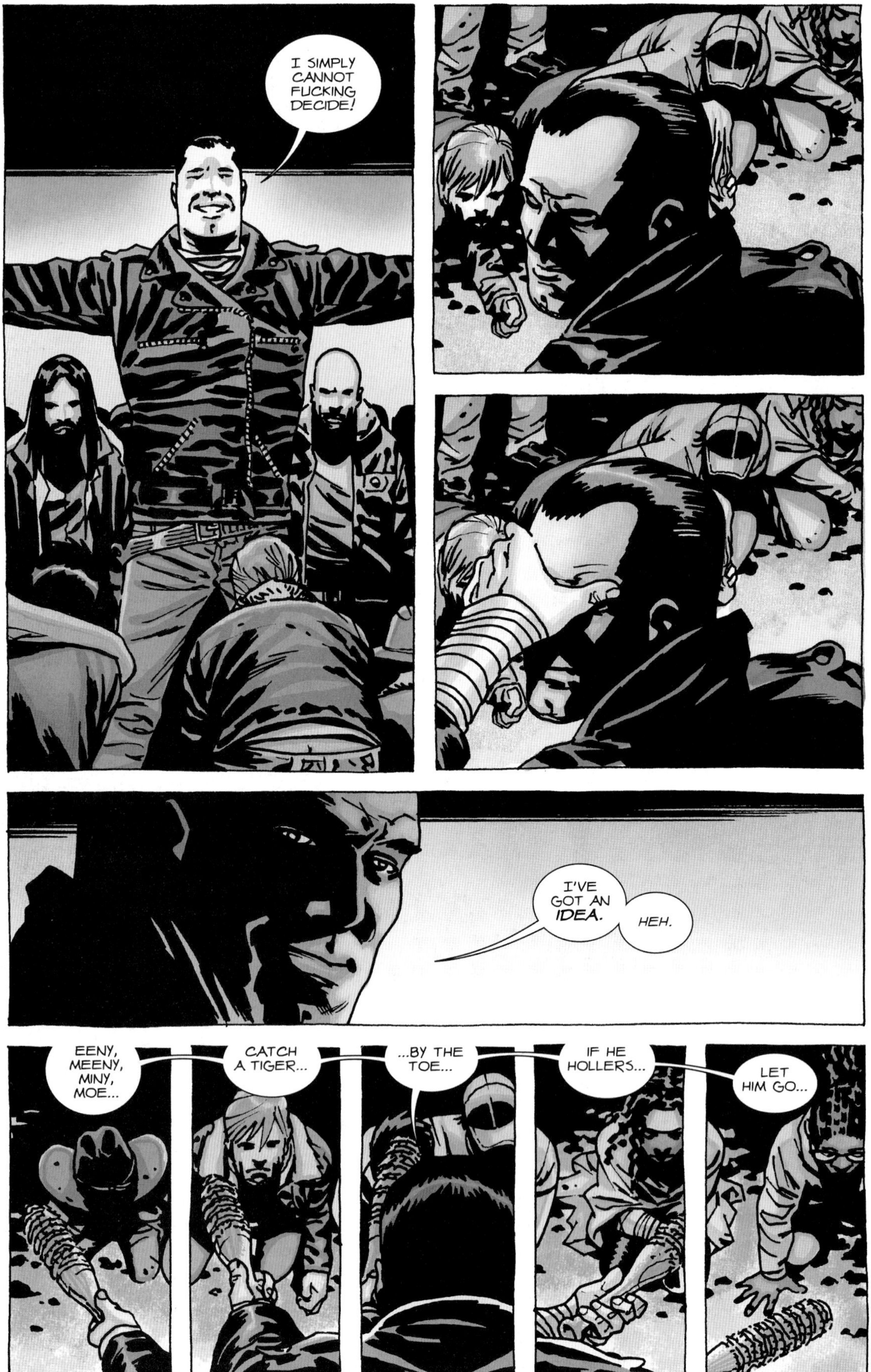
I SIMPLY CANNOT FUCKING DECIDE!
I'VE GOT AN IDEA.
HEH.
EENY, MEENY, MINY, MOE...
CATCH A TIGER...
...BY THE TOE...
IF HE HOLLERS...
LET HIM GO...

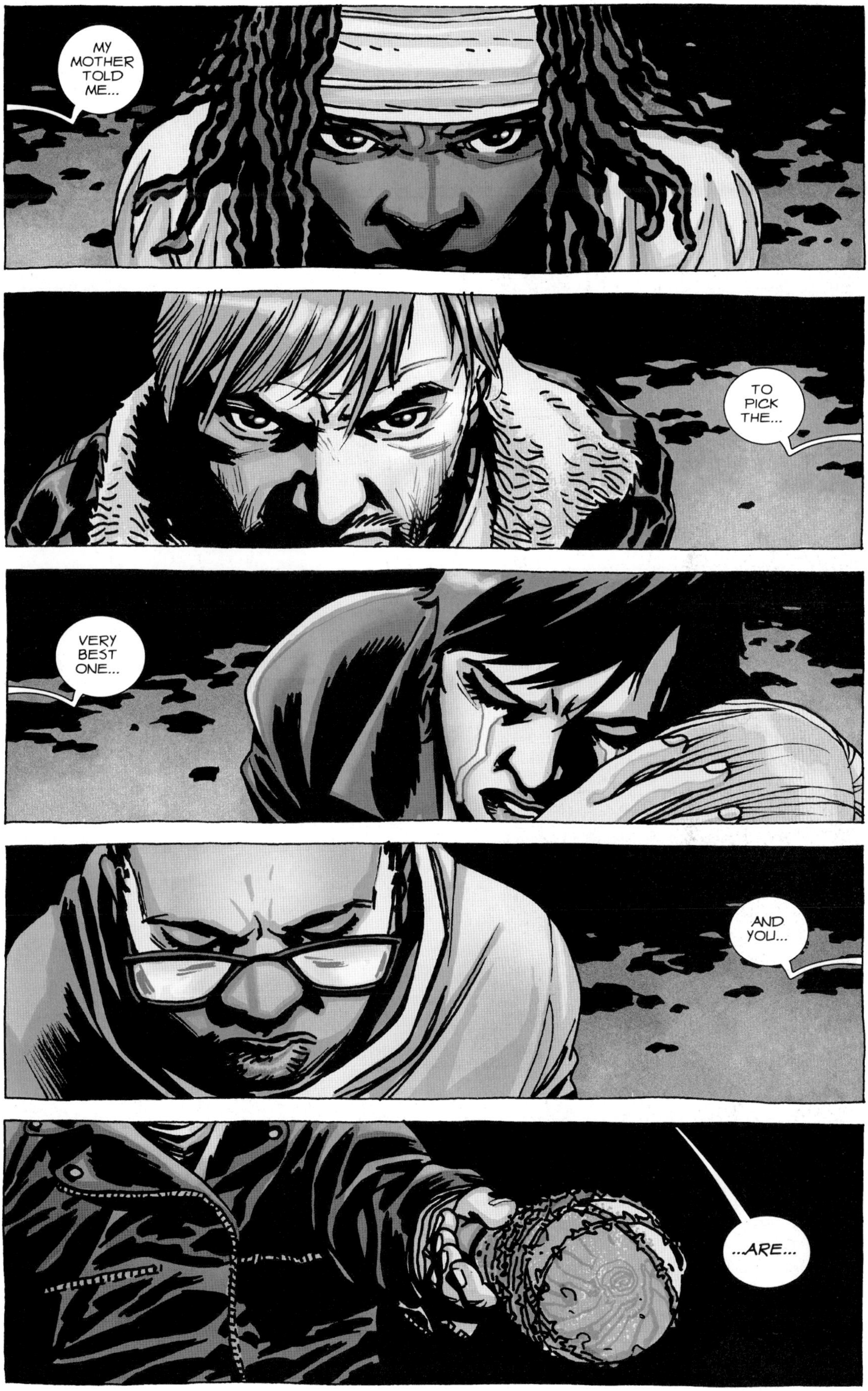
MY MOTHER TOLD ME...
TO PICK THE...
VERY BEST ONE...
AND YOU...
...ARE...

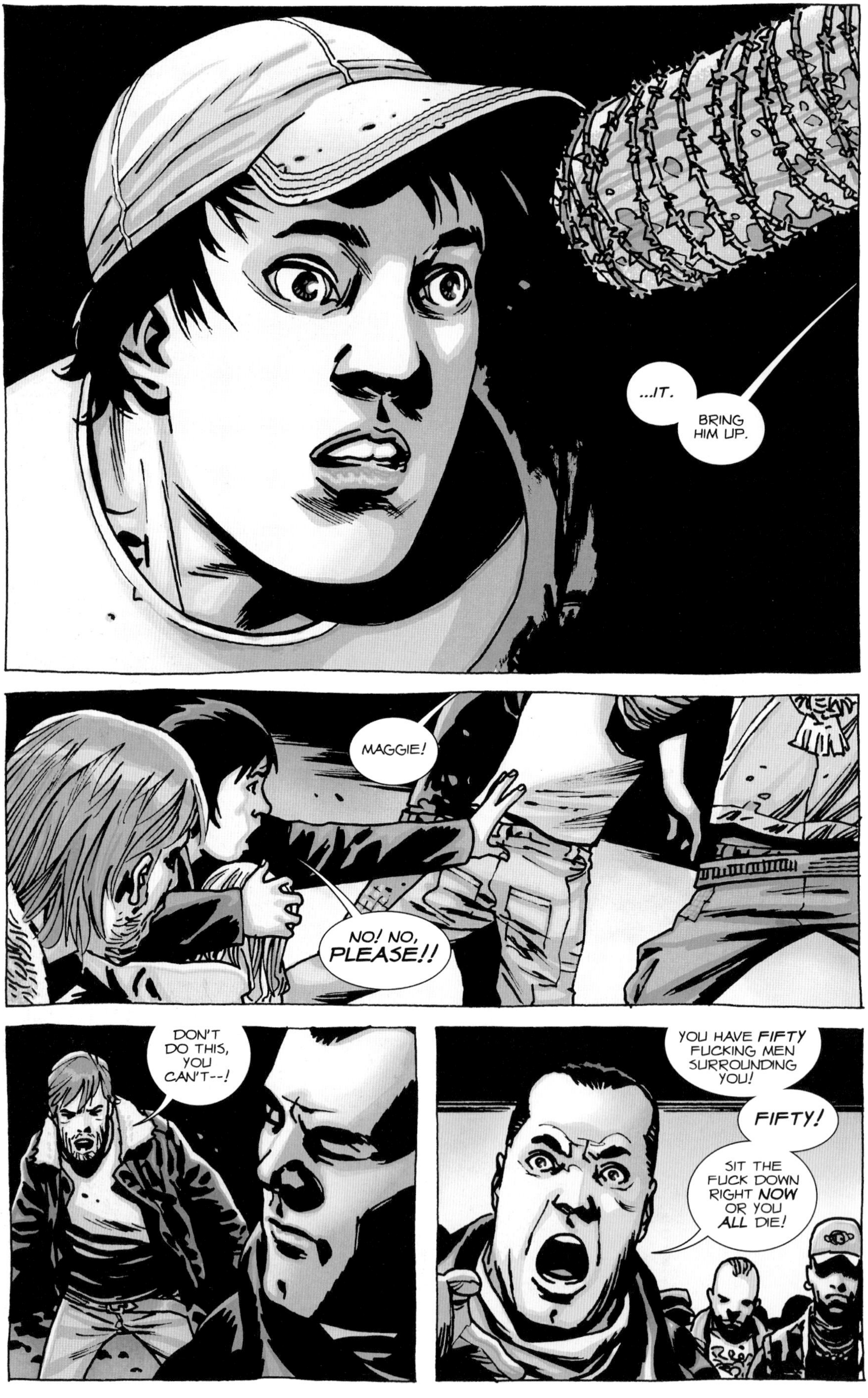
...IT.
BRING HIM UP.
MAGGIE!
NO! NO, PLEASE!!
DON'T DO THIS, YOU CAN'T--!
YOU HAVE FIFTY FUCKING MEN SURROUNDING YOU!
FIFTY!
SIT THE FUCK DOWN RIGHT NOW OR YOU ALL DIE!

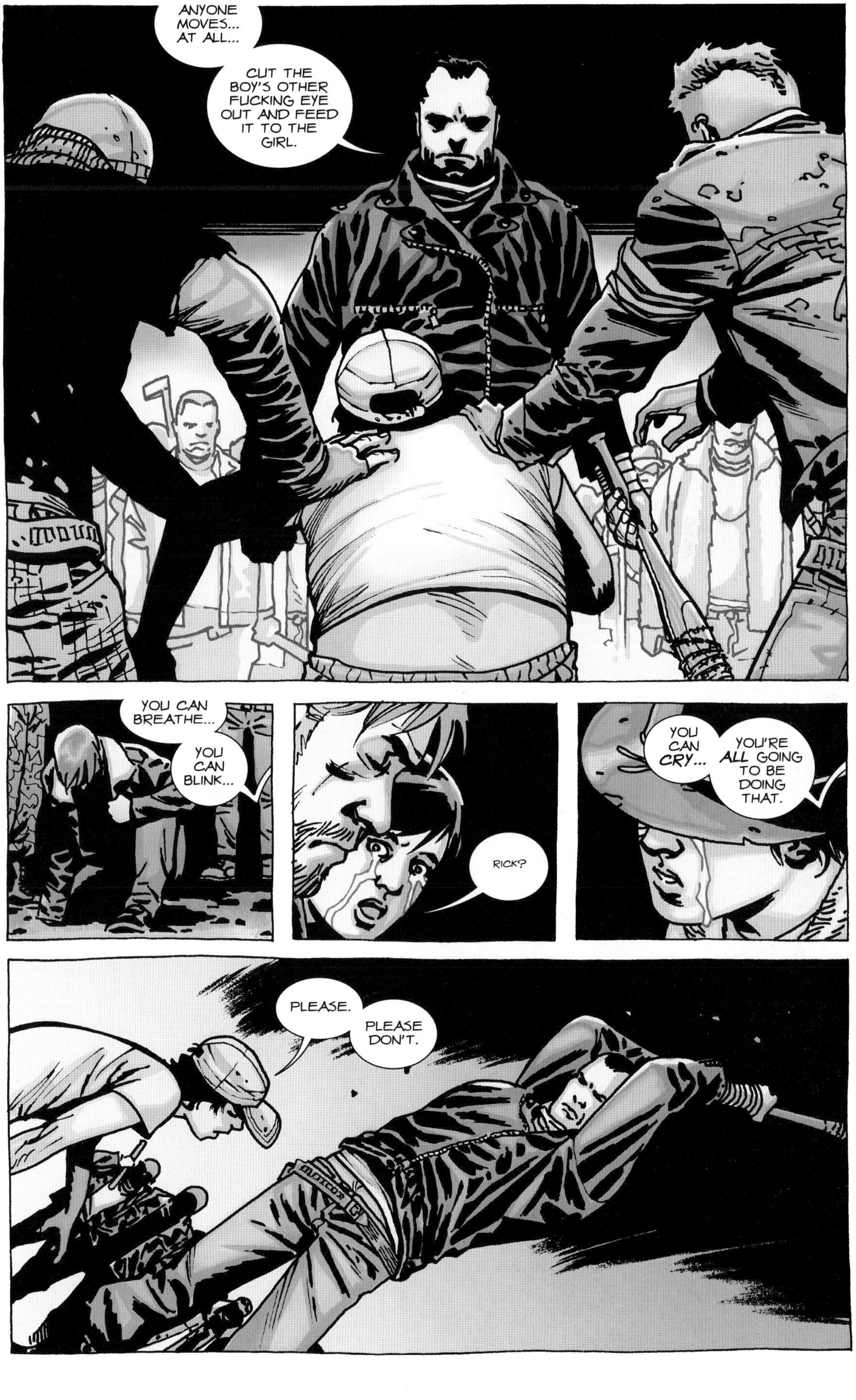
ANYONE MOVES... AT ALL...
CUT THE BOY'S OTHER FUCKING EYE OUT AND FEED IT TO THE GIRL.
YOU CAN BREATHE...
YOU CAN BLINK...
RICK?
YOU CAN CRY...
YOU'RE ALL GOING TO BE DOING THAT.
PLEASE.
PLEASE DON'T.

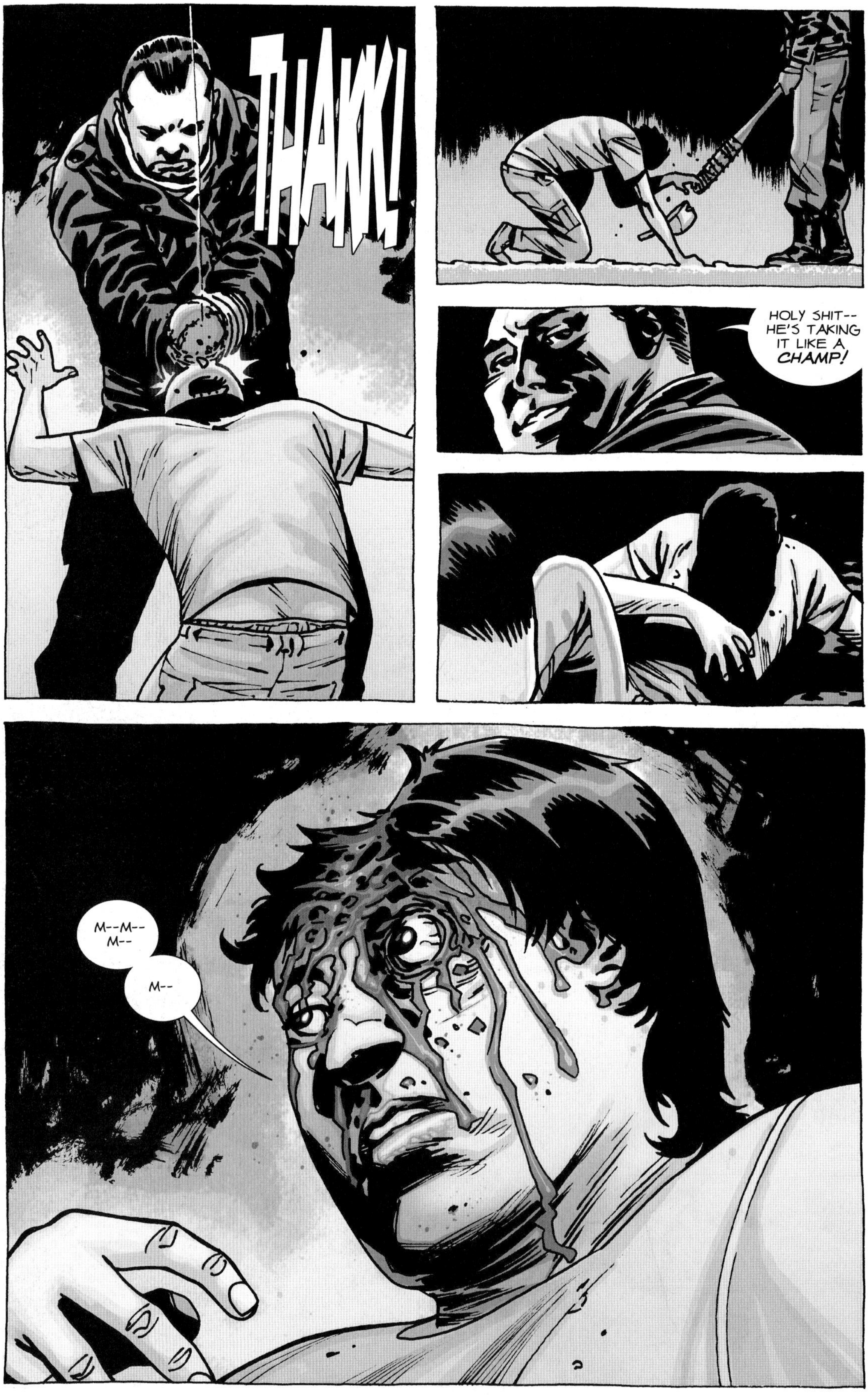
THAKK!
HOLY SHIT-- HE'S TAKING IT LIKE A CHAMP!
M--M-- M--
M--

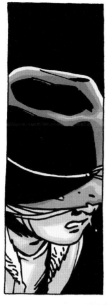

YOU IN THERE, BUDDY? I JUST DON'T KNOW. SEEMS LIKE YOU'RE TRYING TO SPEAK, BUT YOU JUST TOOK A *HELL* OF A HIT.

I CRACKED YOUR SKULL SO MUCH THAT YOUR FUCKING *EYE* POPPED OUT. IT'S GROSS AS SHIT.

I DON'T THINK--

MAG--!

MAGGIE!

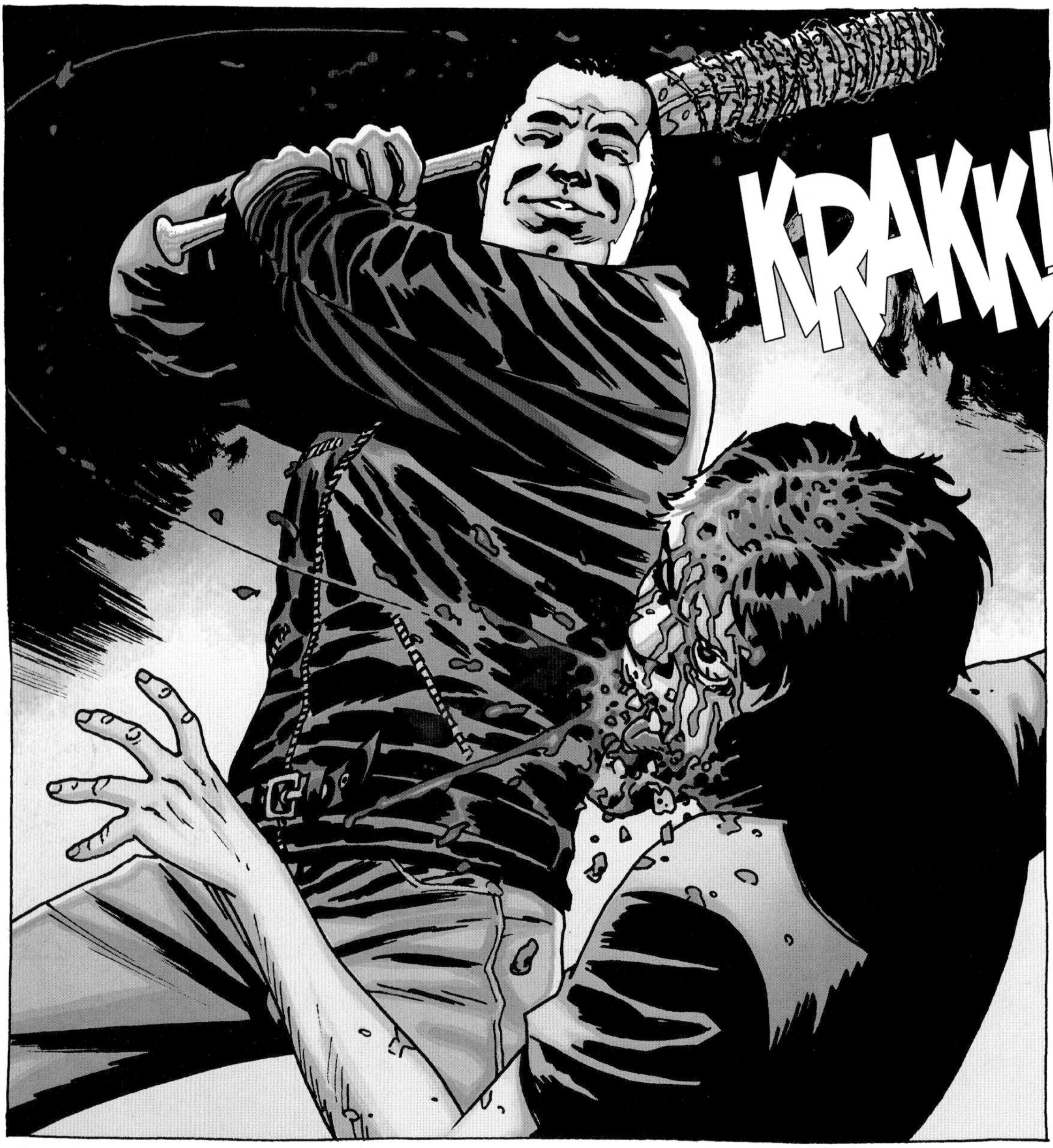
KRAKK!
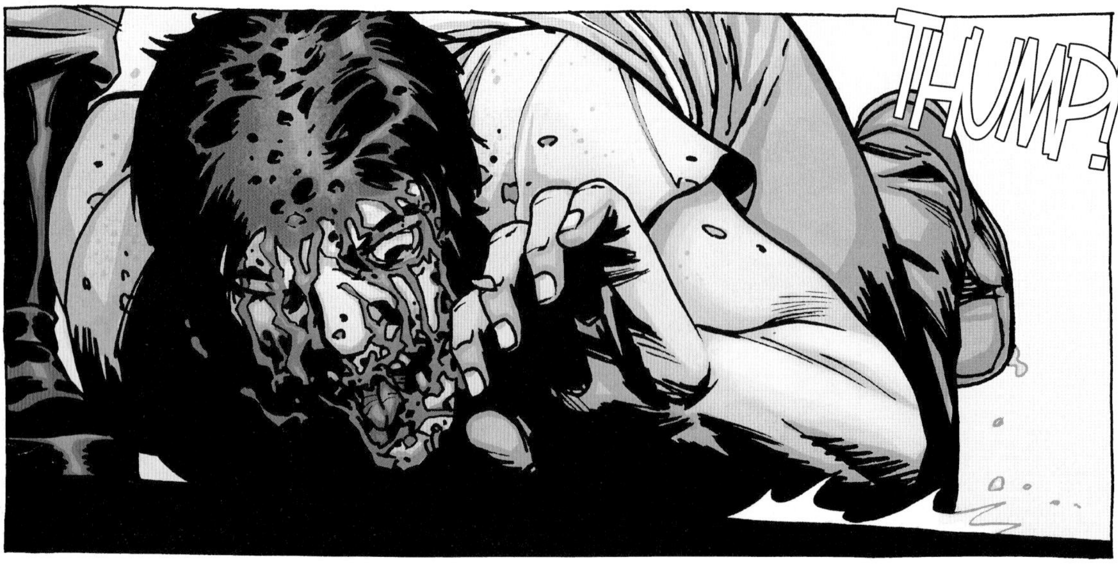
THUMP!

YOU BUNCH OF PUSSIES... I'M JUST GETTING STARTED.

LUCILLE IS *THIRSTY.*

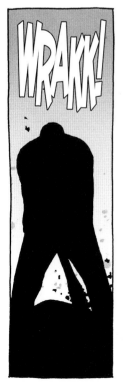

WRAKK!

SPUKK!

SPLAUGG!

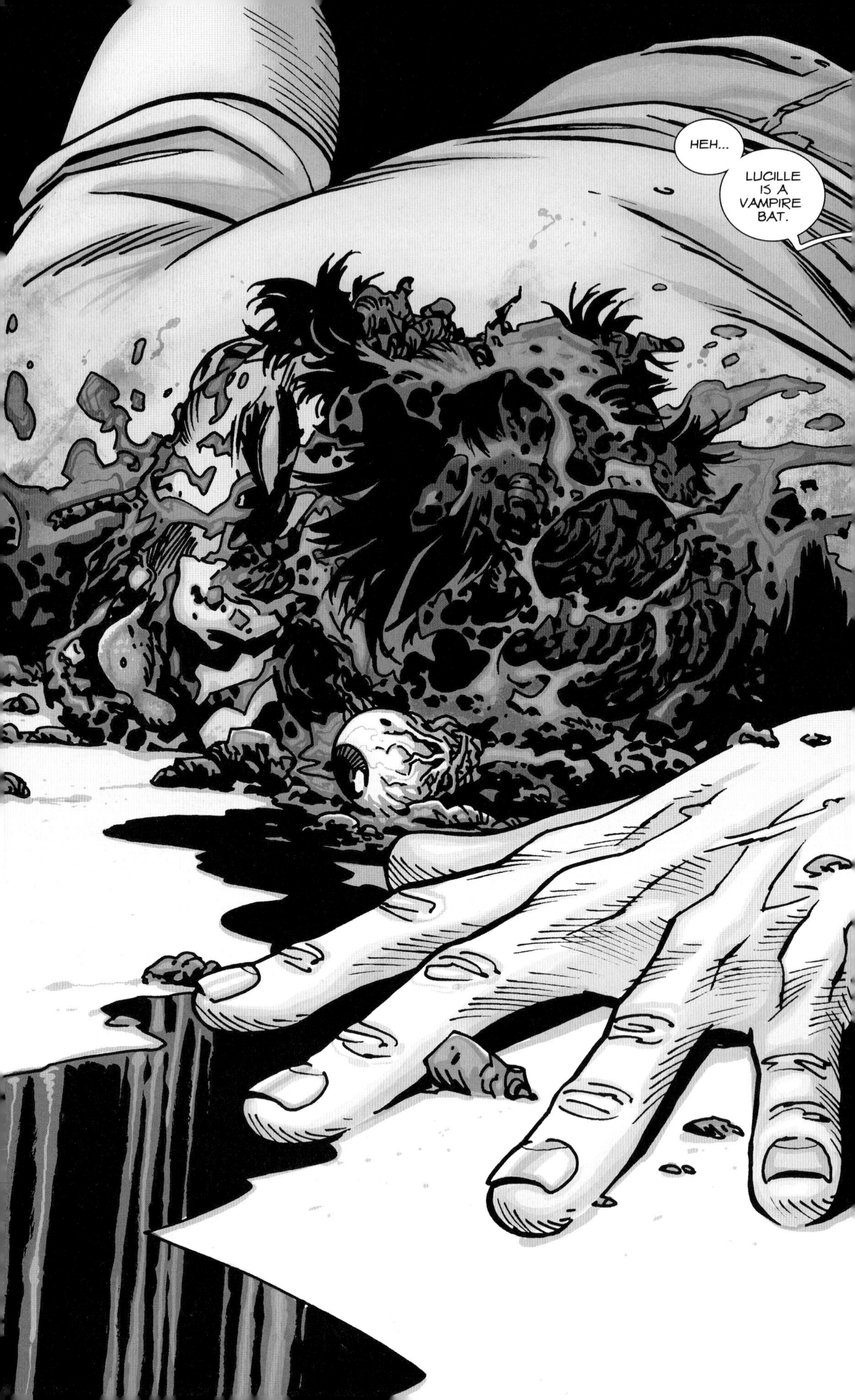
HEH...
LUCILLE IS A VAMPIRE BAT.

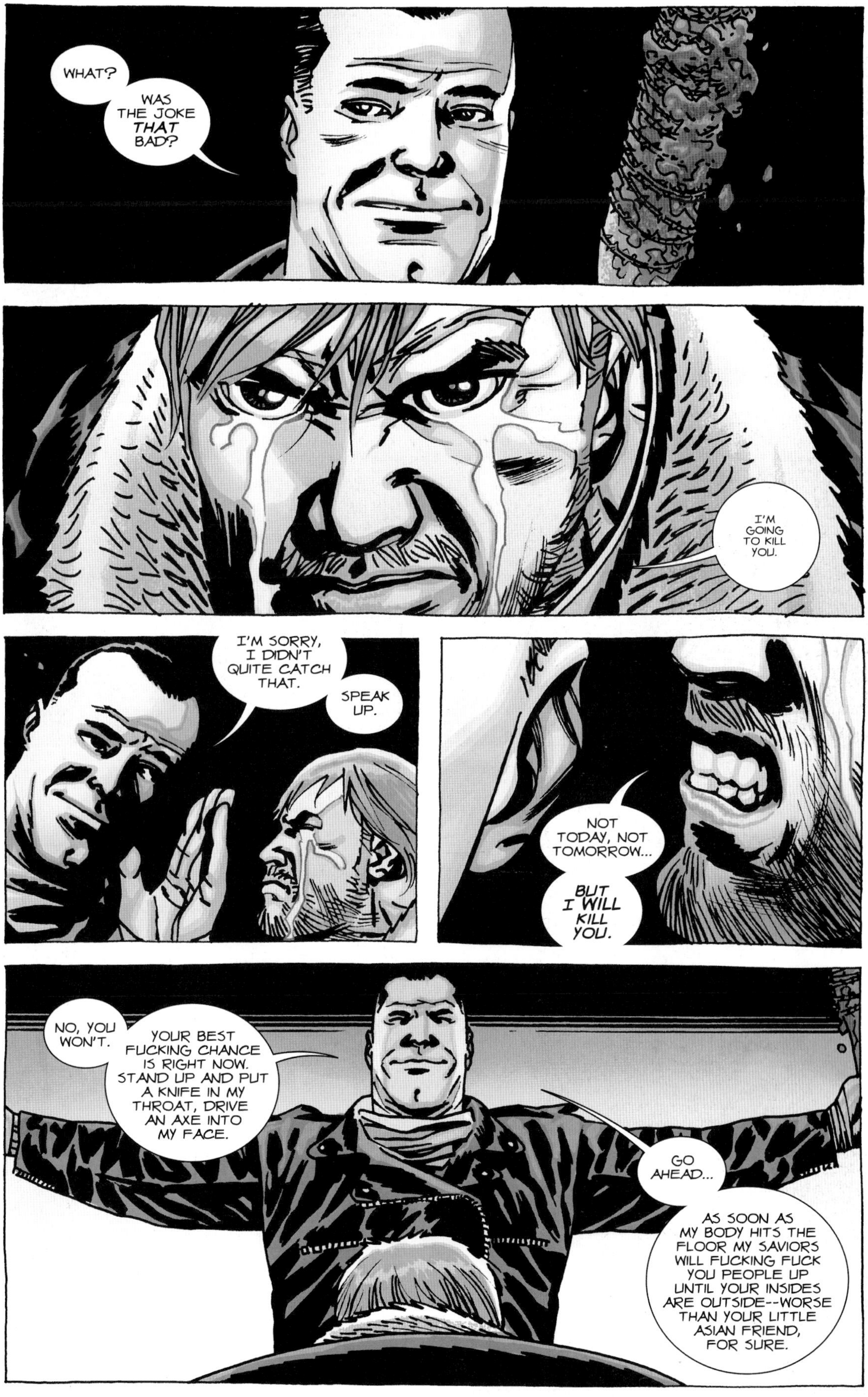
WHAT?
WAS THE JOKE THAT BAD?
I'M GOING TO KILL YOU.
I'M SORRY, I DIDN'T QUITE CATCH THAT.
SPEAK UP.
NOT TODAY, NOT TOMORROW...
BUT I WILL KILL YOU.
NO, YOU WON'T.
YOUR BEST FUCKING CHANCE IS RIGHT NOW. STAND UP AND PUT A KNIFE IN MY THROAT, DRIVE AN AXE INTO MY FACE.
GO AHEAD...
AS SOON AS MY BODY HITS THE FLOOR MY SAVIORS WILL FUCKING FUCK YOU PEOPLE UP UNTIL YOUR INSIDES ARE OUTSIDE--WORSE THAN YOUR LITTLE ASIAN FRIEND, FOR SURE.

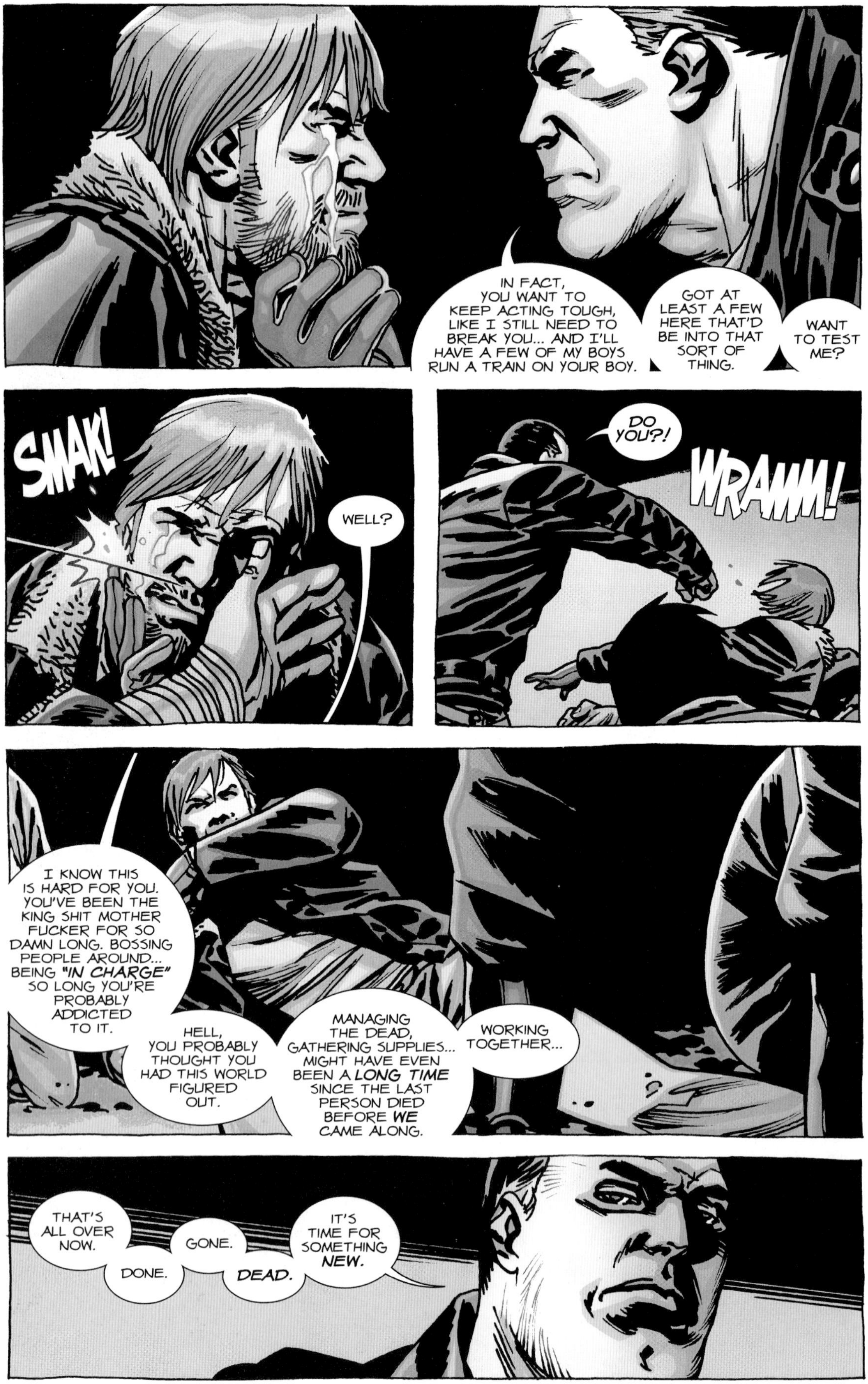
IN FACT, YOU WANT TO KEEP ACTING TOUGH, LIKE I STILL NEED TO BREAK YOU... AND I'LL HAVE A FEW OF MY BOYS RUN A TRAIN ON YOUR BOY.
GOT AT LEAST A FEW HERE THAT'D BE INTO THAT SORT OF THING.
WANT TO TEST ME?
SMAK!
WELL?
DO YOU?!
WRAMM!
I KNOW THIS IS HARD FOR YOU. YOU'VE BEEN THE KING SHIT MOTHER FUCKER FOR SO DAMN LONG. BOSSING PEOPLE AROUND... BEING "IN CHARGE" SO LONG YOU'RE PROBABLY ADDICTED TO IT.
HELL, YOU PROBABLY THOUGHT YOU HAD THIS WORLD FIGURED OUT.
MANAGING THE DEAD, GATHERING SUPPLIES... MIGHT HAVE EVEN BEEN A LONG TIME SINCE THE LAST PERSON DIED BEFORE WE CAME ALONG.
WORKING TOGETHER...
THAT'S ALL OVER NOW.
DONE.
GONE.
DEAD.
IT'S TIME FOR SOMETHING NEW.

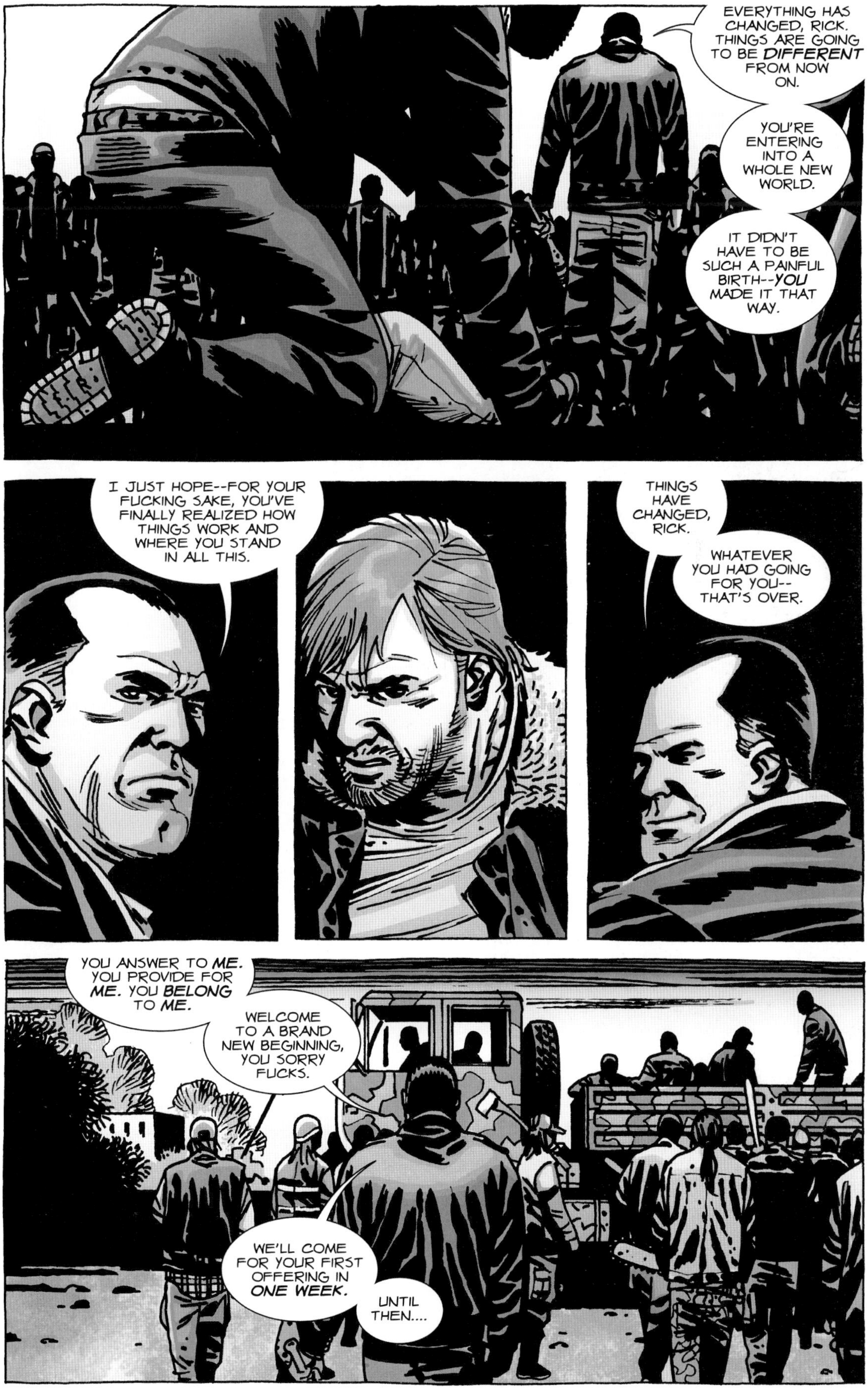
EVERYTHING HAS CHANGED, RICK. THINGS ARE GOING TO BE *DIFFERENT* FROM NOW ON.
YOU'RE ENTERING INTO A WHOLE NEW WORLD.
IT DIDN'T HAVE TO BE SUCH A PAINFUL BIRTH--*YOU* MADE IT THAT WAY.
I JUST HOPE--FOR YOUR FUCKING SAKE, YOU'VE FINALLY REALIZED HOW THINGS WORK AND WHERE YOU STAND IN ALL THIS.
THINGS HAVE CHANGED, RICK.
WHATEVER YOU HAD GOING FOR YOU--THAT'S OVER.
YOU ANSWER TO *ME.* YOU PROVIDE FOR *ME.* YOU *BELONG* TO *ME.*
WELCOME TO A BRAND NEW BEGINNING, YOU SORRY FUCKS.
WE'LL COME FOR YOUR FIRST OFFERING IN *ONE WEEK.*
UNTIL THEN....

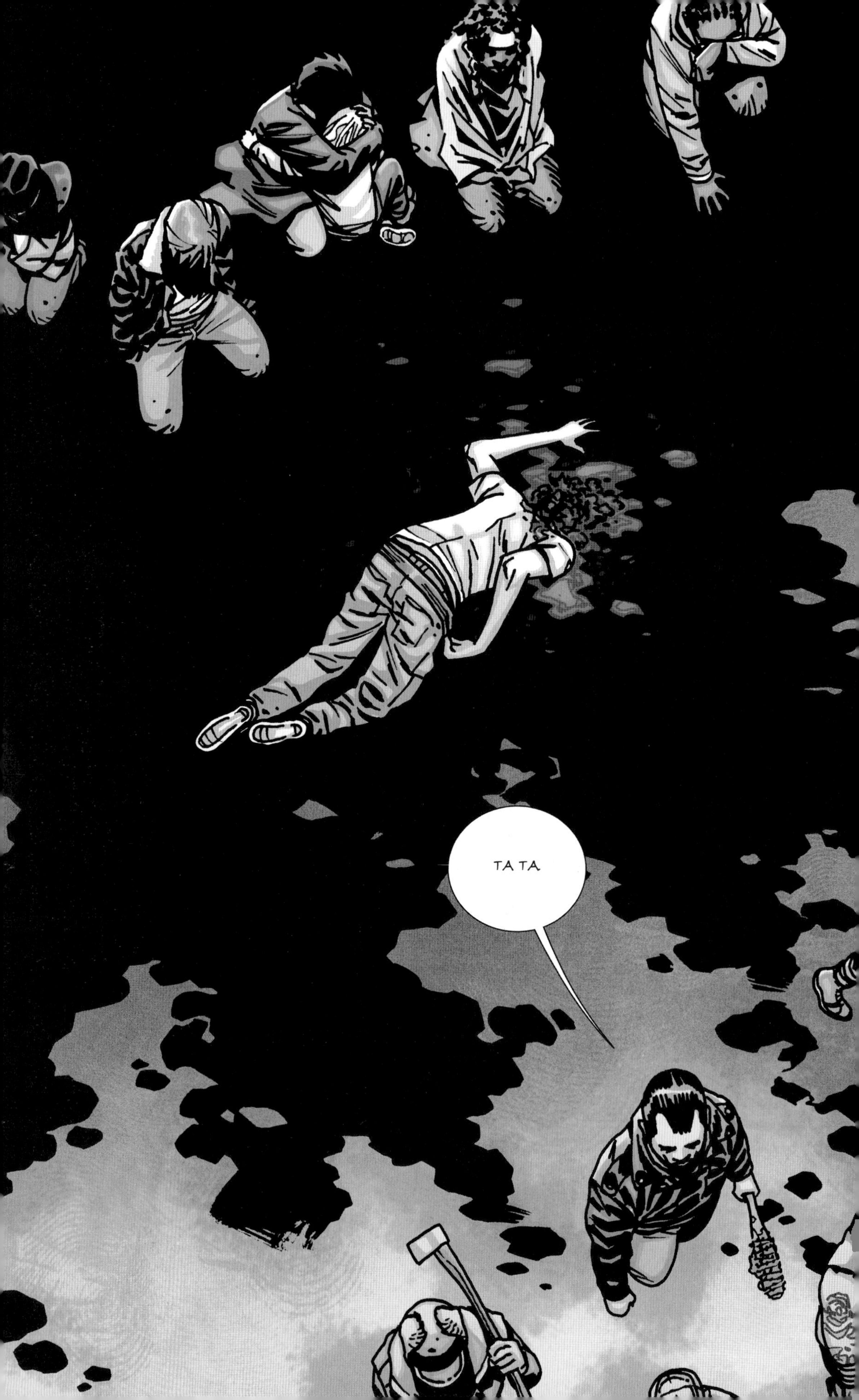
TA TA

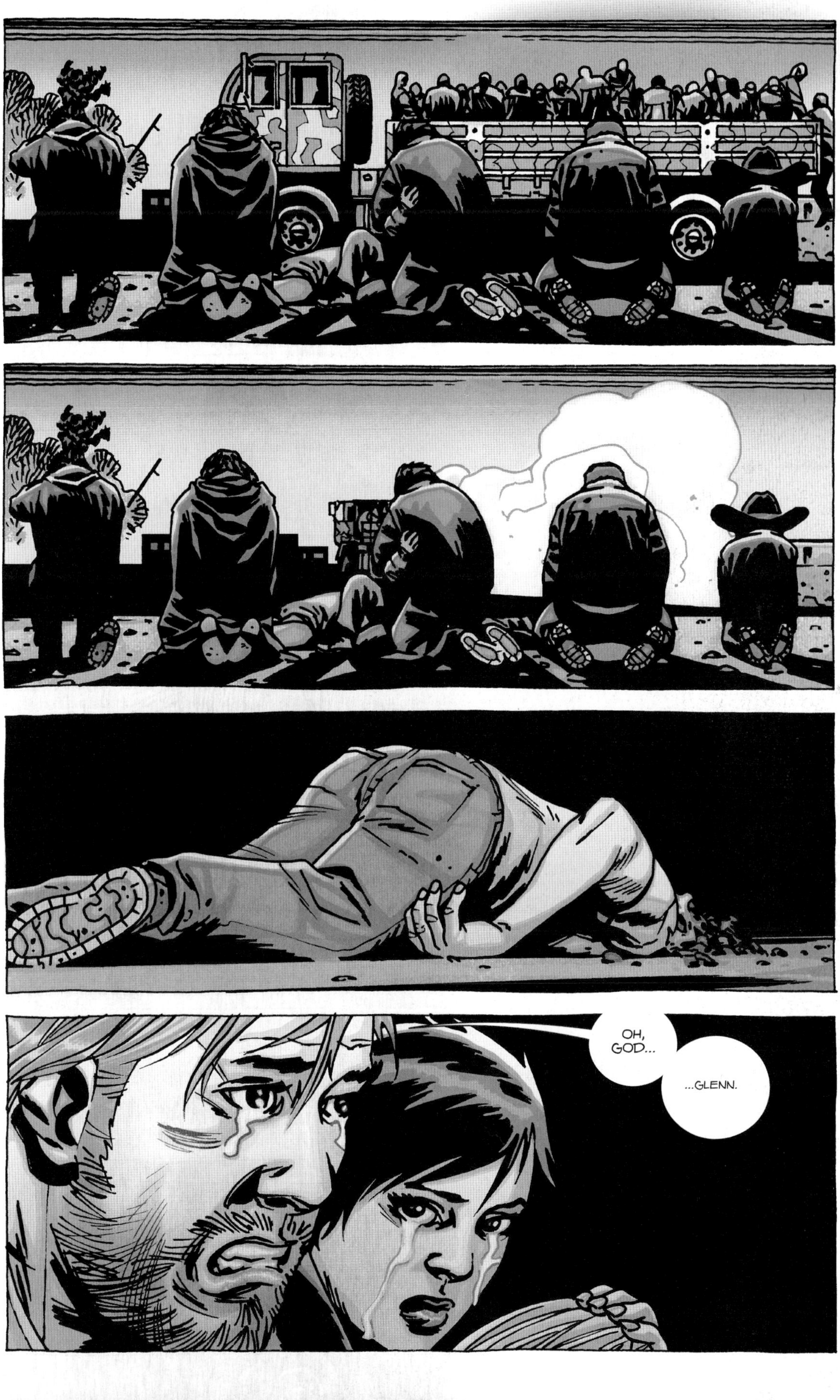
OH, GOD...
...GLENN.

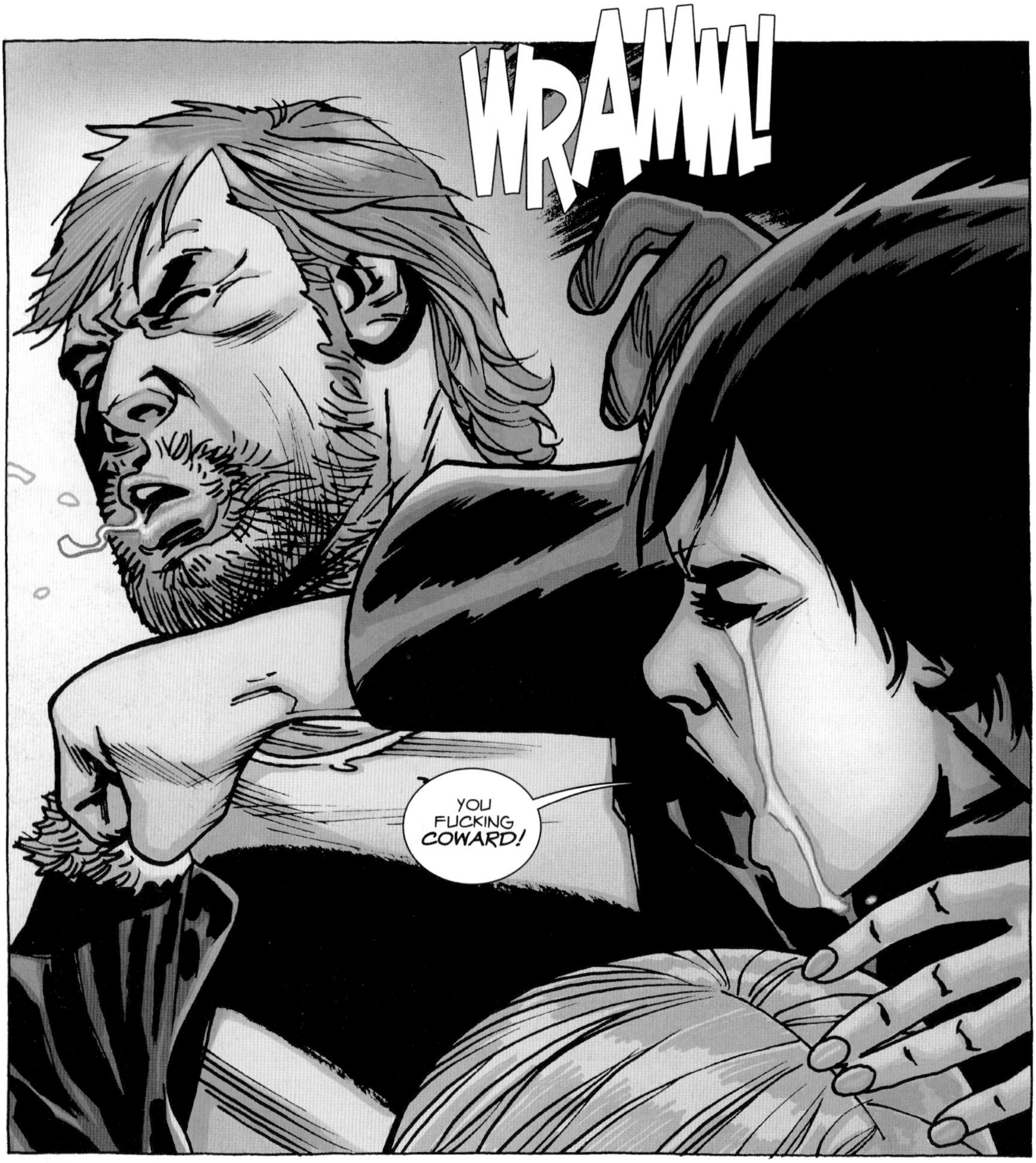
WRAMM!
YOU FUCKING COWARD!

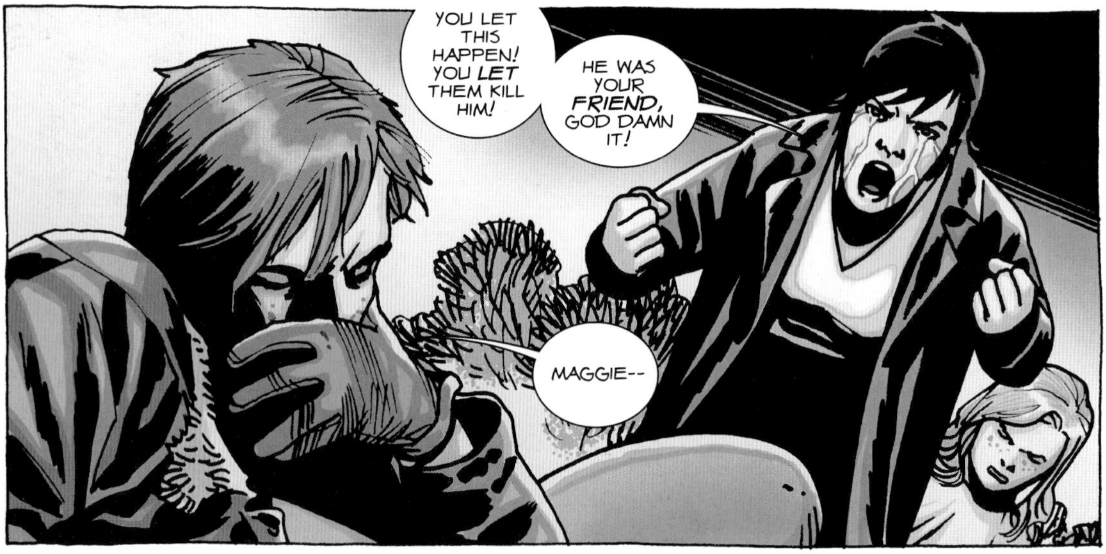
YOU LET THIS HAPPEN! YOU LET THEM KILL HIM!
HE WAS YOUR FRIEND, GOD DAMN IT!
MAGGIE--

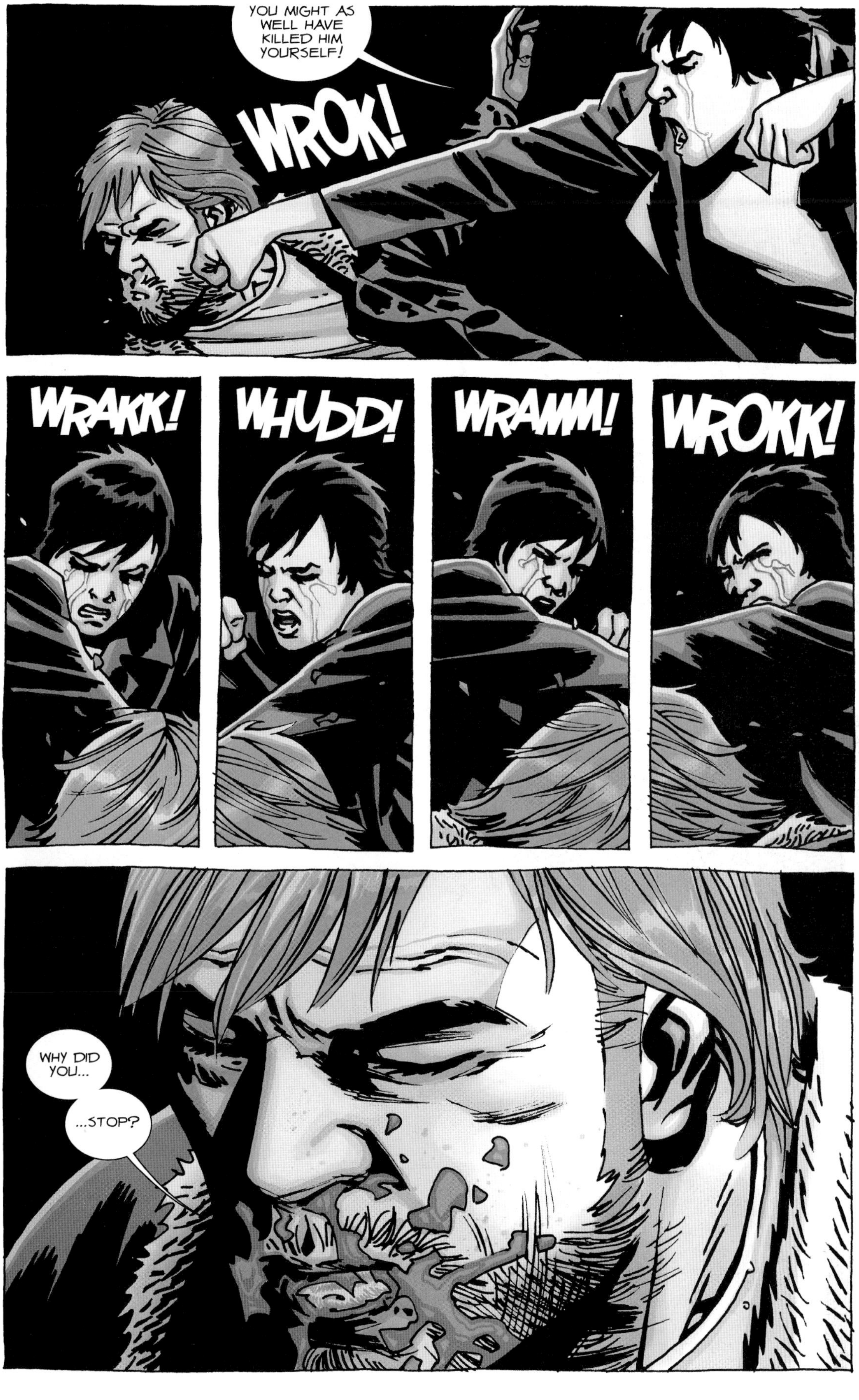
YOU MIGHT AS WELL HAVE KILLED HIM YOURSELF!
WROK!
WRAKK!
WHUDD!
WRAMM!
WROKK!
WHY DID YOU...
...STOP?

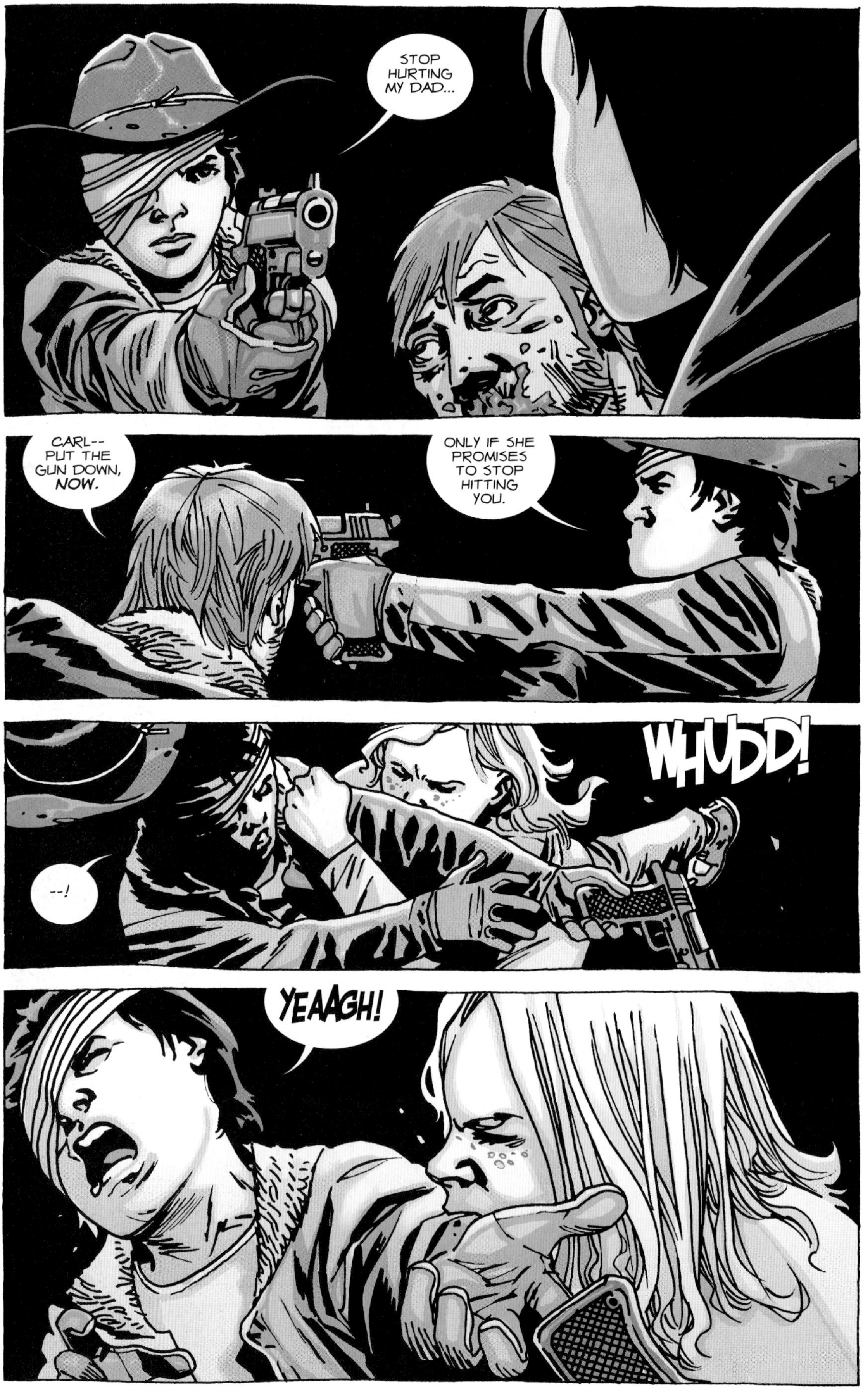
STOP HURTING MY DAD...
CARL-- PUT THE GUN DOWN, **NOW.**
ONLY IF SHE PROMISES TO STOP HITTING YOU.
WHUDD!
--!
YEAAGH!

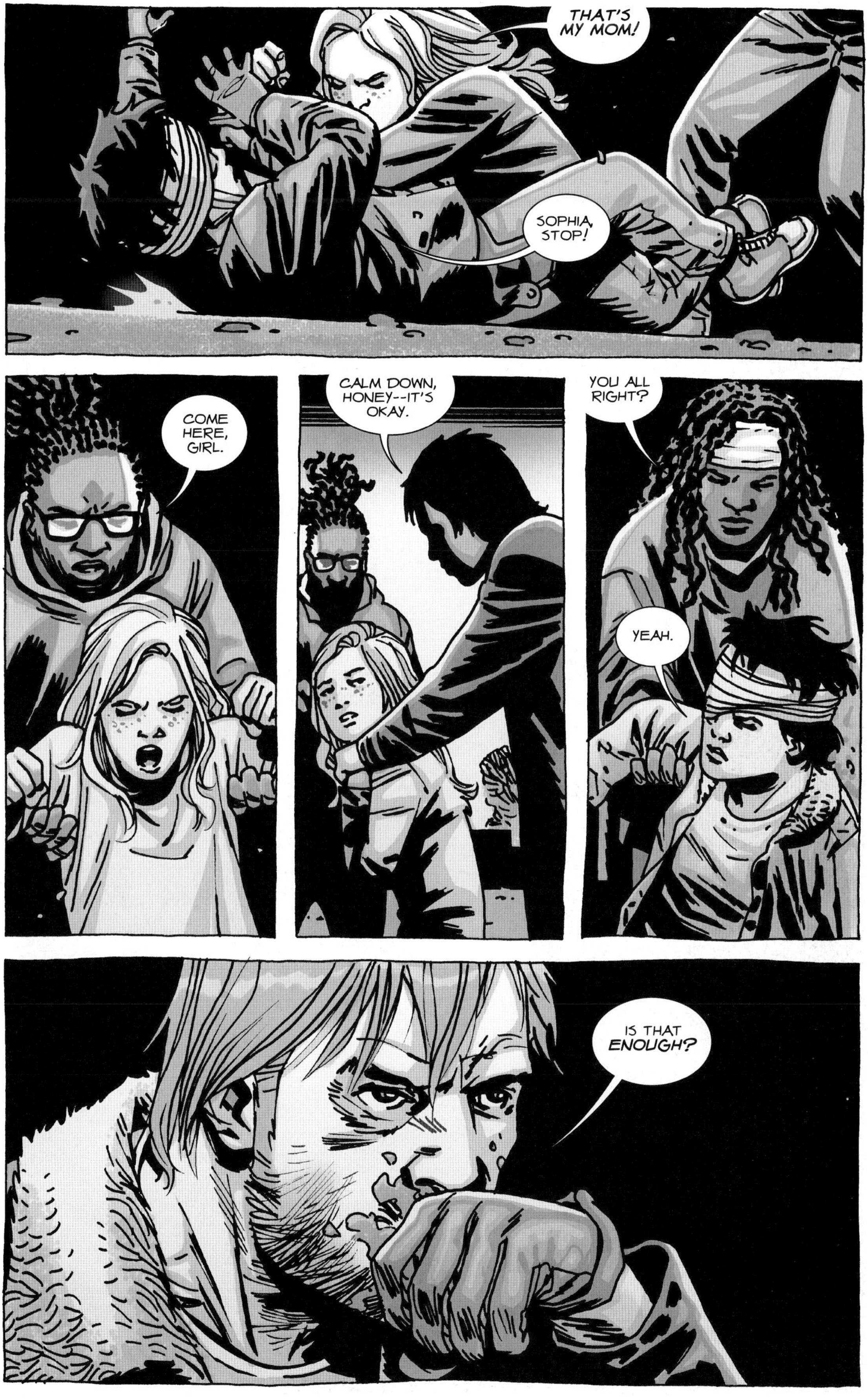
THAT'S MY MOM!
SOPHIA, STOP!
COME HERE, GIRL.
CALM DOWN, HONEY--IT'S OKAY.
YOU ALL RIGHT?
YEAH.
IS THAT ENOUGH?

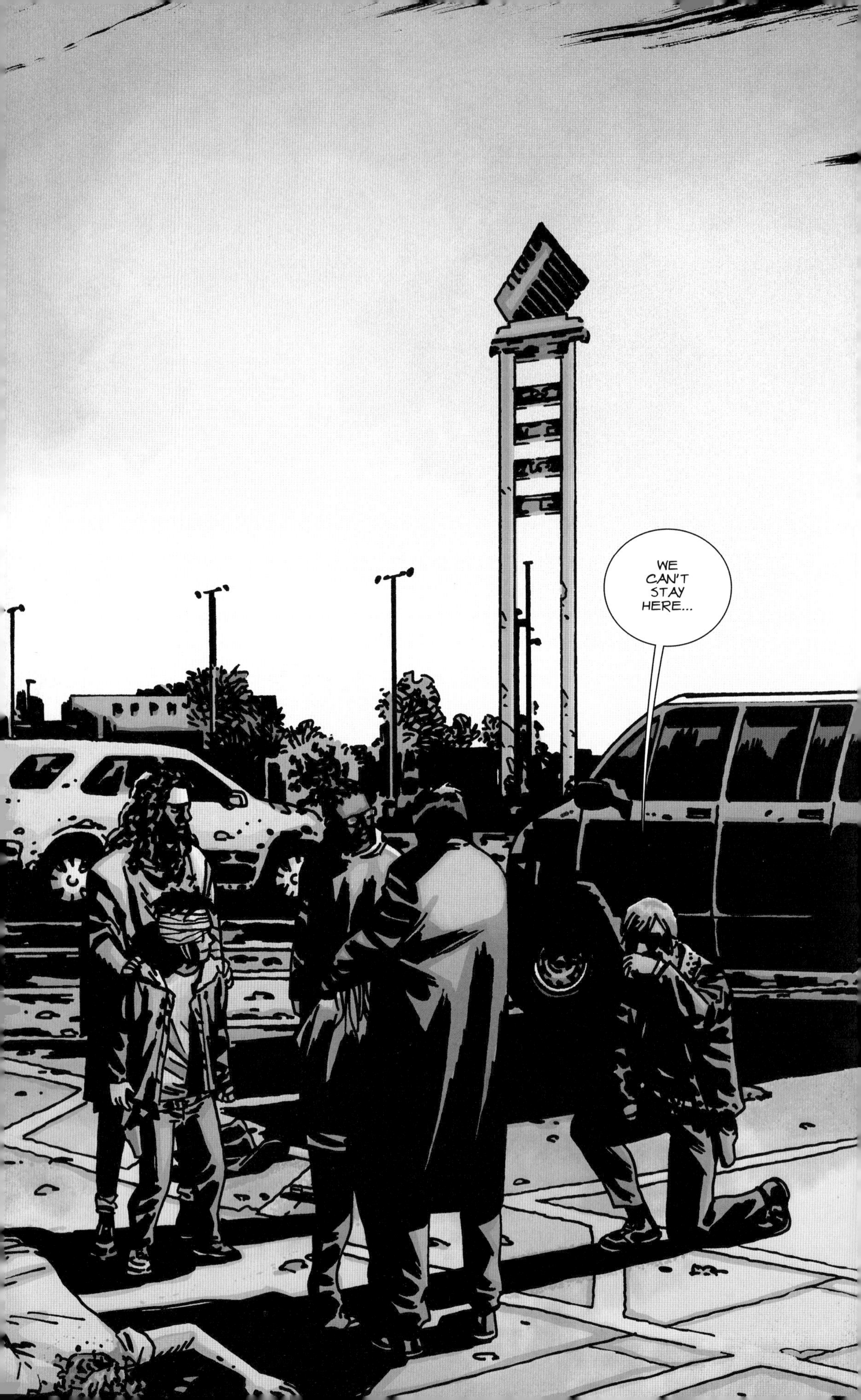
WE CAN'T STAY HERE...

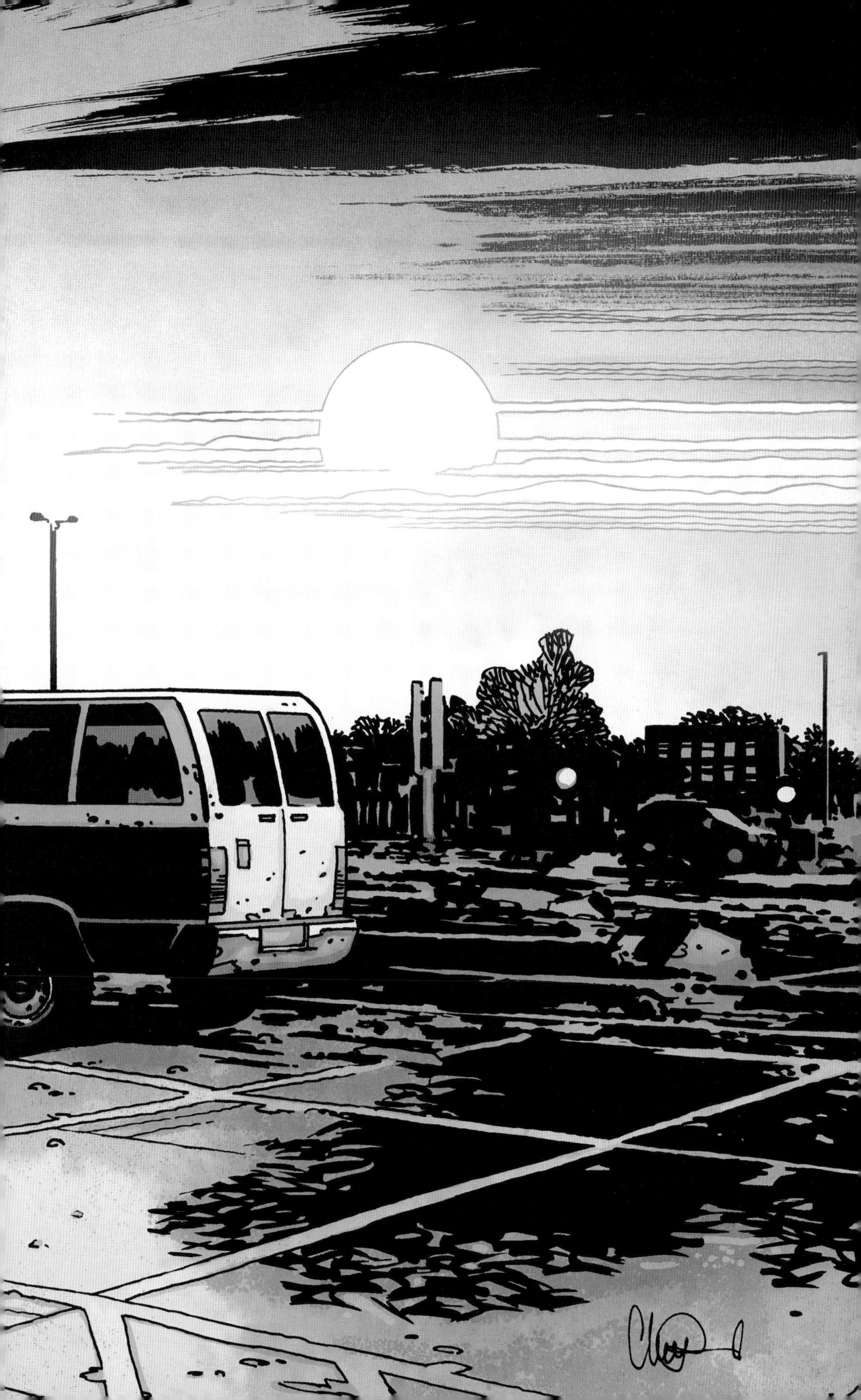

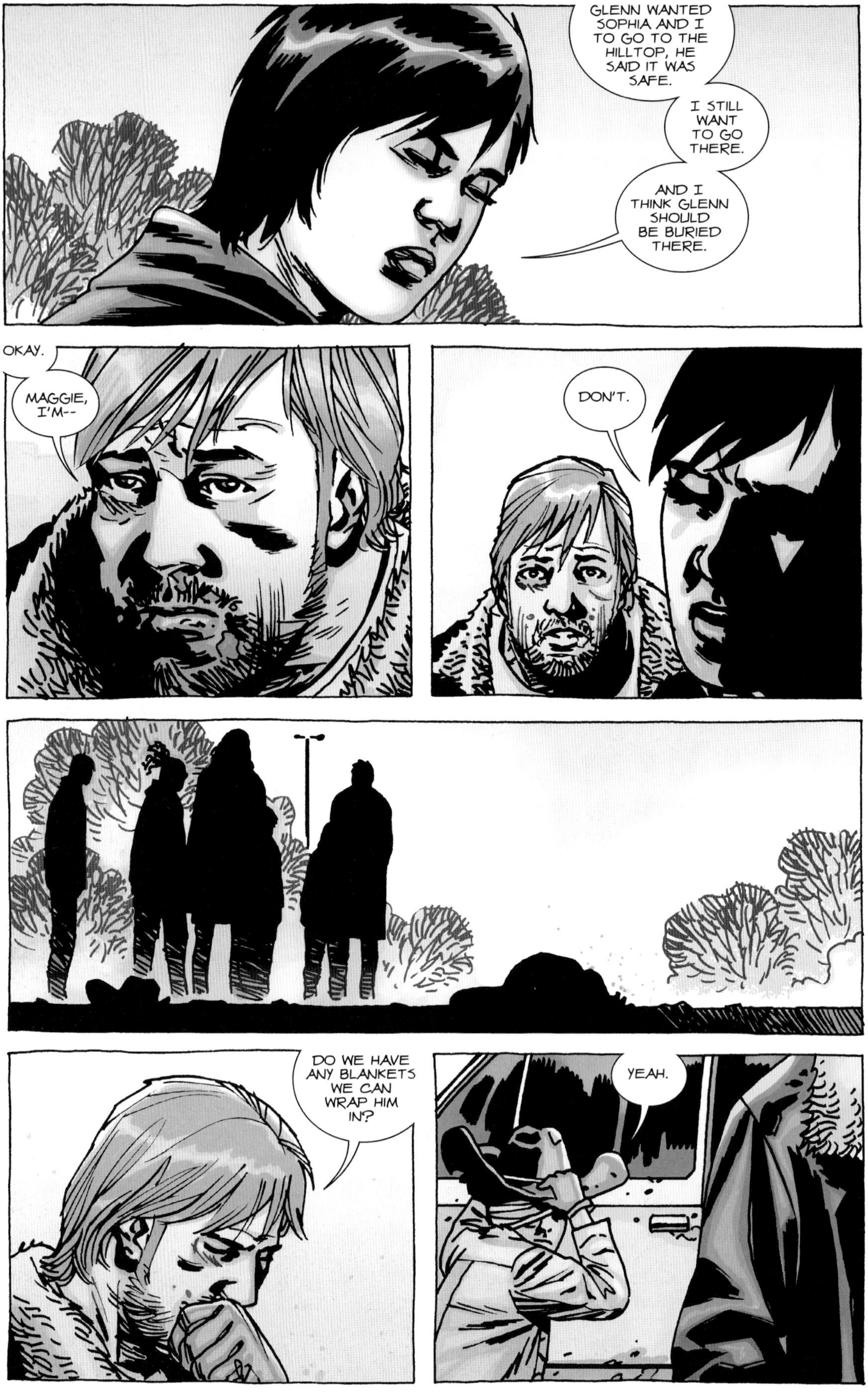
GLENN WANTED SOPHIA AND I TO GO TO THE HILLTOP, HE SAID IT WAS SAFE.
I STILL WANT TO GO THERE.
AND I THINK GLENN SHOULD BE BURIED THERE.
OKAY.
MAGGIE, I'M--
DON'T.
DO WE HAVE ANY BLANKETS WE CAN WRAP HIM IN?
YEAH.

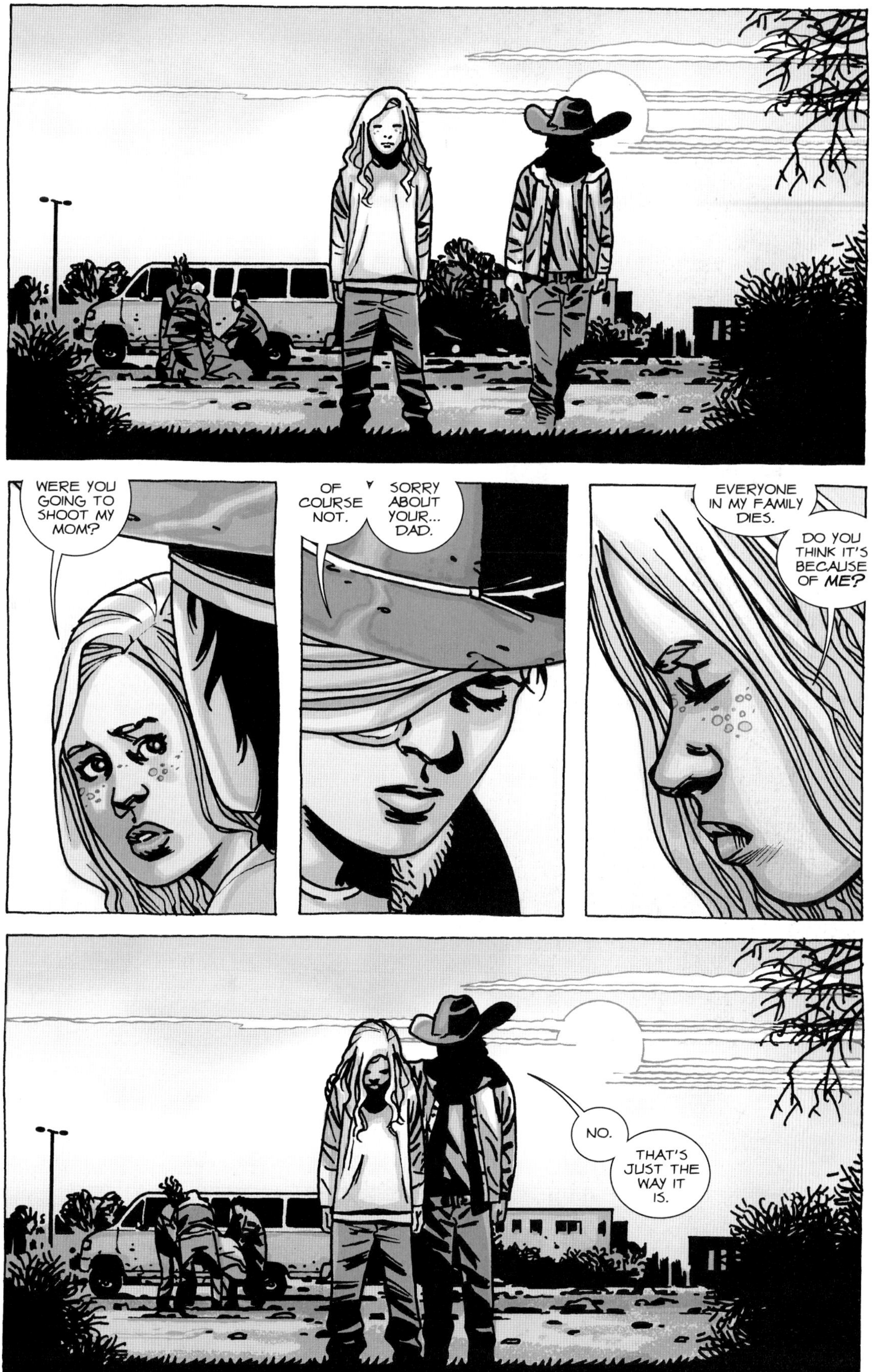
WERE YOU GOING TO SHOOT MY MOM?
OF COURSE NOT.
SORRY ABOUT YOUR... DAD.
EVERYONE IN MY FAMILY DIES.
DO YOU THINK IT'S BECAUSE OF *ME?*
NO.
THAT'S JUST THE WAY IT IS.

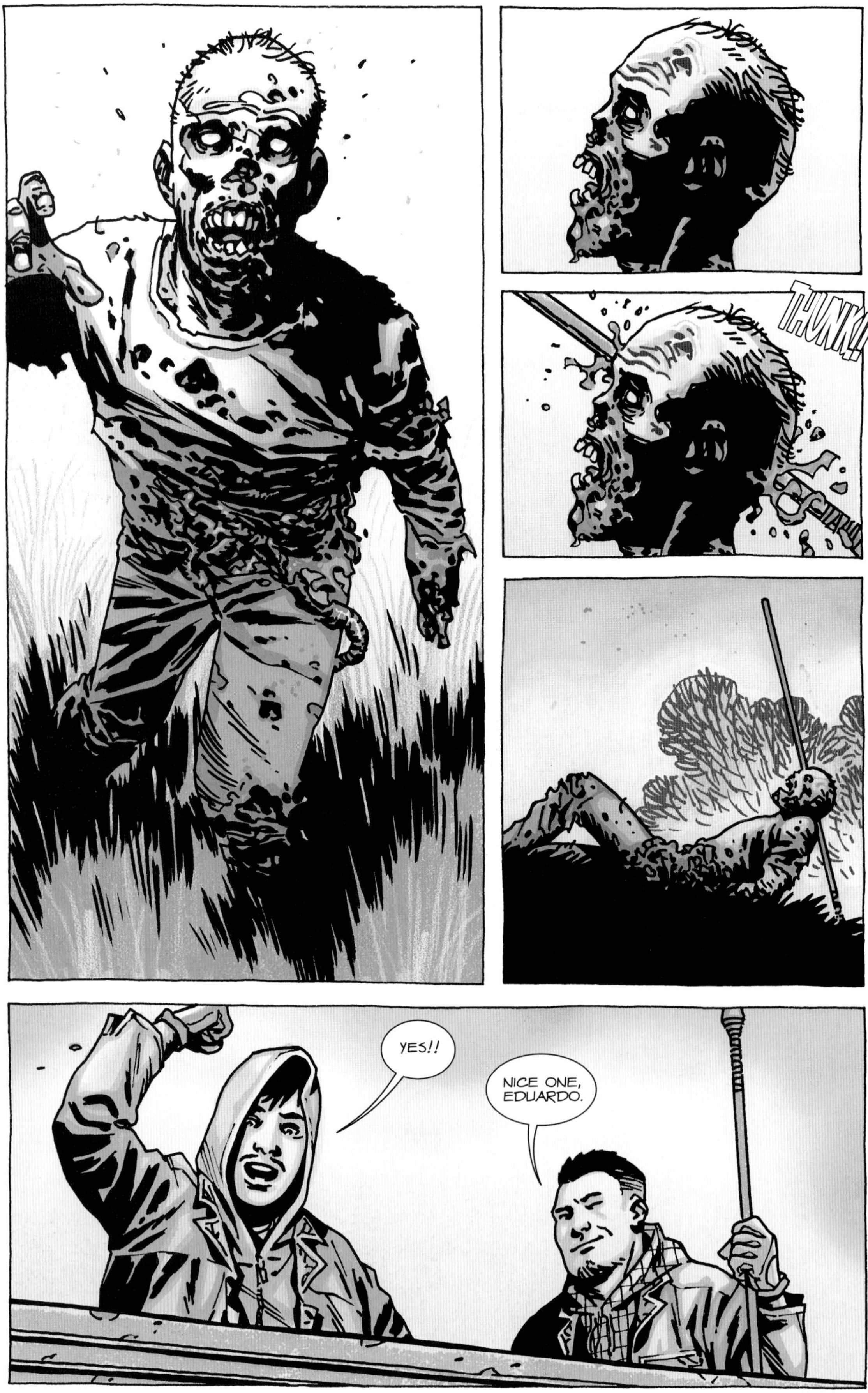
THUNK!!
YES!!
NICE ONE, EDUARDO.

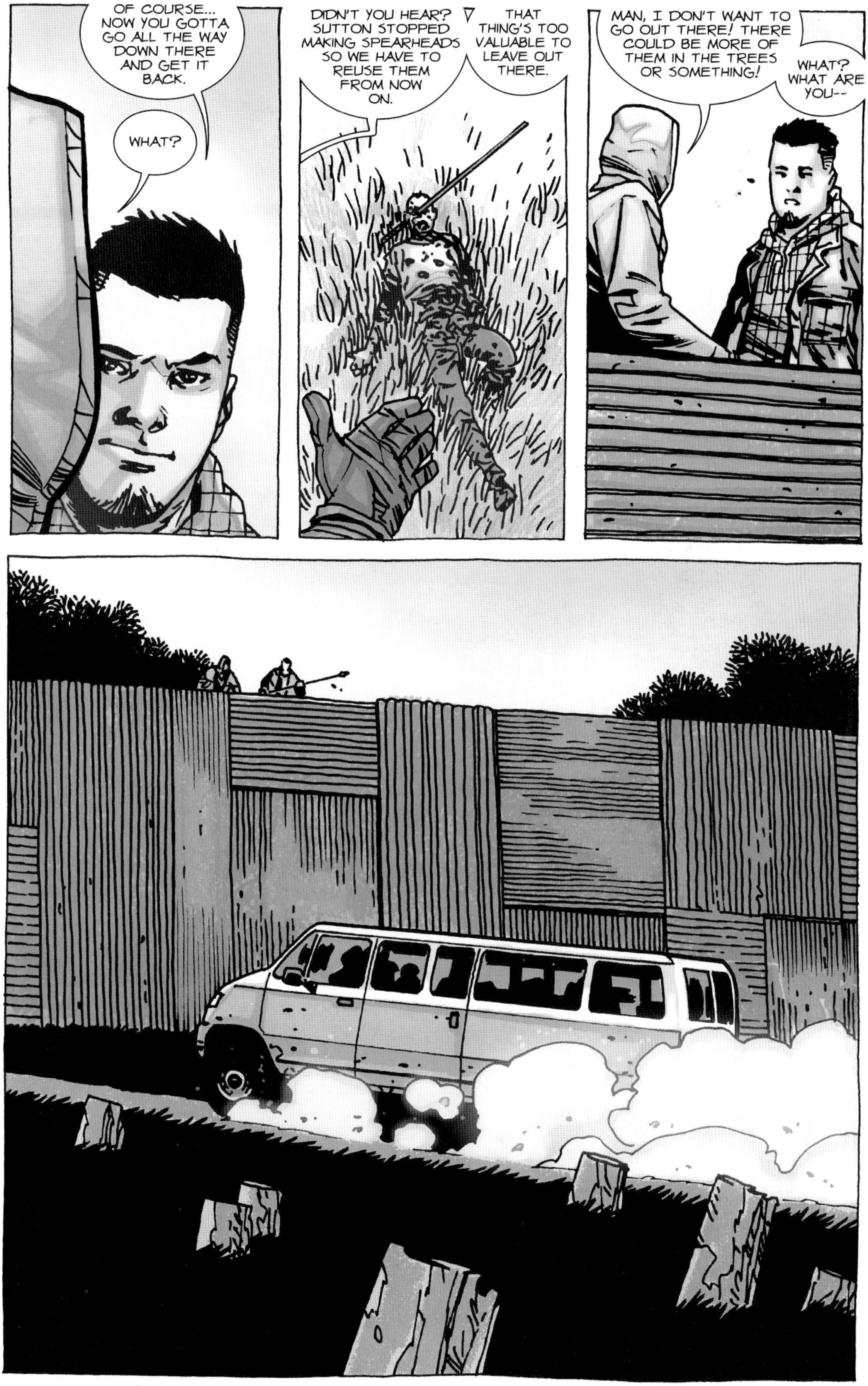
OF COURSE... NOW YOU GOTTA GO ALL THE WAY DOWN THERE AND GET IT BACK.
WHAT?
DIDN'T YOU HEAR? SUTTON STOPPED MAKING SPEARHEADS SO WE HAVE TO REUSE THEM FROM NOW ON.
THAT THING'S TOO VALUABLE TO LEAVE OUT THERE.
MAN, I DON'T WANT TO GO OUT THERE! THERE COULD BE MORE OF THEM IN THE TREES OR SOMETHING!
WHAT? WHAT ARE YOU--

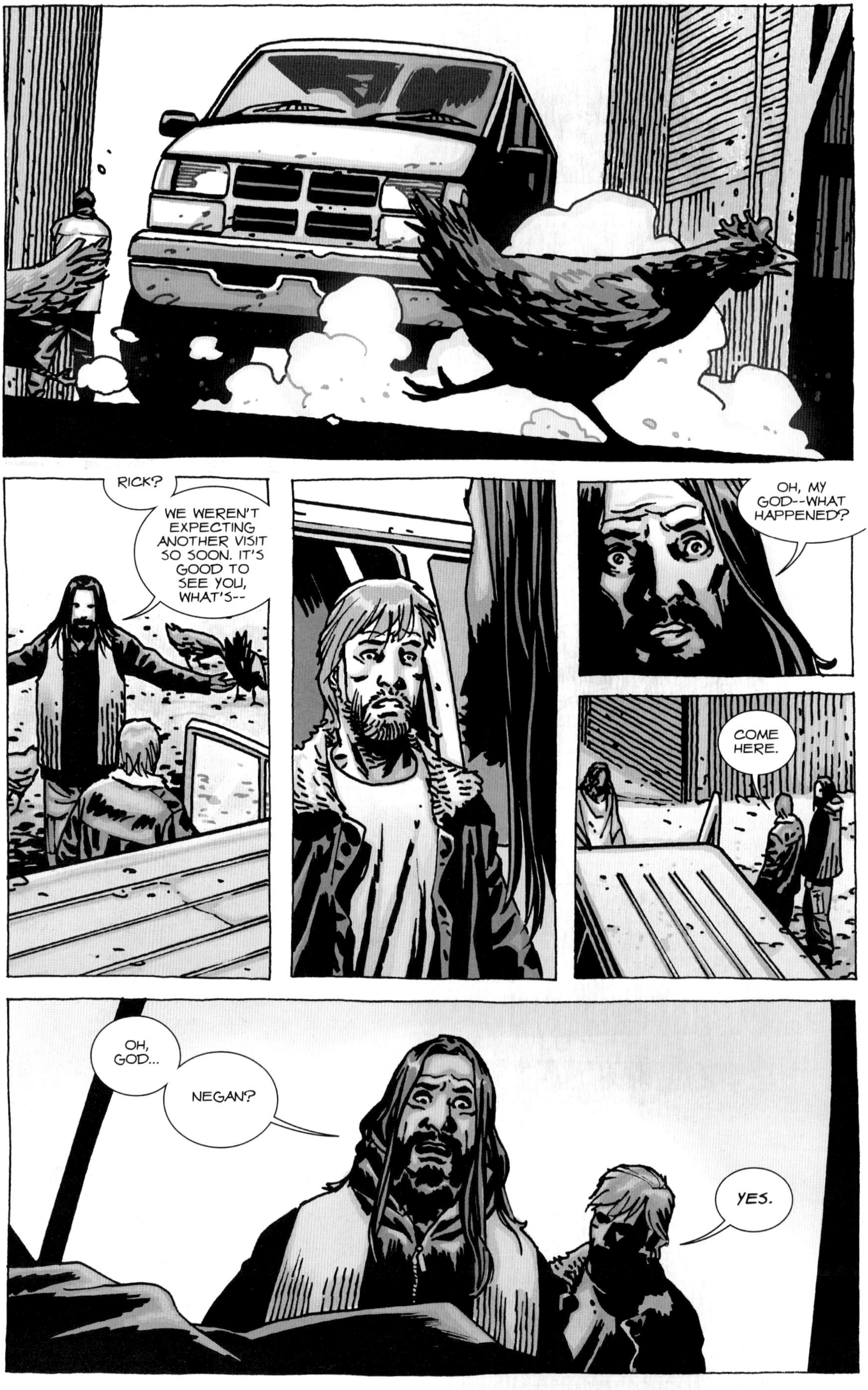
RICK?
WE WEREN'T EXPECTING ANOTHER VISIT SO SOON. IT'S GOOD TO SEE YOU, WHAT'S--
OH, MY GOD--WHAT HAPPENED?
COME HERE.
OH, GOD...
NEGAN?
YES.

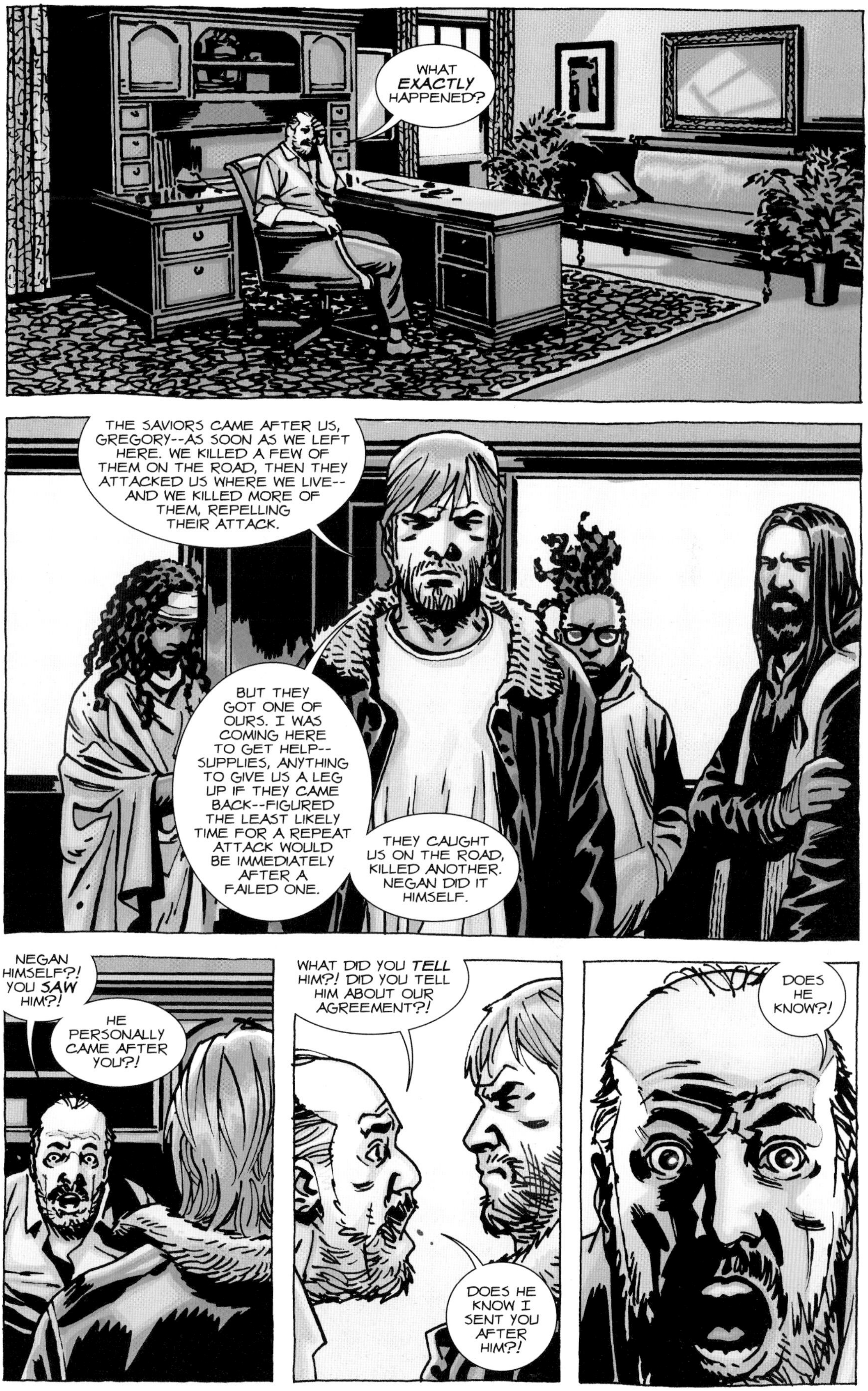
WHAT EXACTLY HAPPENED?
THE SAVIORS CAME AFTER US, GREGORY--AS SOON AS WE LEFT HERE. WE KILLED A FEW OF THEM ON THE ROAD, THEN THEY ATTACKED US WHERE WE LIVE--AND WE KILLED MORE OF THEM, REPELLING THEIR ATTACK.
BUT THEY GOT ONE OF OURS. I WAS COMING HERE TO GET HELP--SUPPLIES, ANYTHING TO GIVE US A LEG UP IF THEY CAME BACK--FIGURED THE LEAST LIKELY TIME FOR A REPEAT ATTACK WOULD BE IMMEDIATELY AFTER A FAILED ONE.
THEY CAUGHT US ON THE ROAD, KILLED ANOTHER. NEGAN DID IT HIMSELF.
NEGAN HIMSELF?! YOU SAW HIM?!
HE PERSONALLY CAME AFTER YOU?!
WHAT DID YOU TELL HIM?! DID YOU TELL HIM ABOUT OUR AGREEMENT?!
DOES HE KNOW I SENT YOU AFTER HIM?!
DOES HE KNOW?!

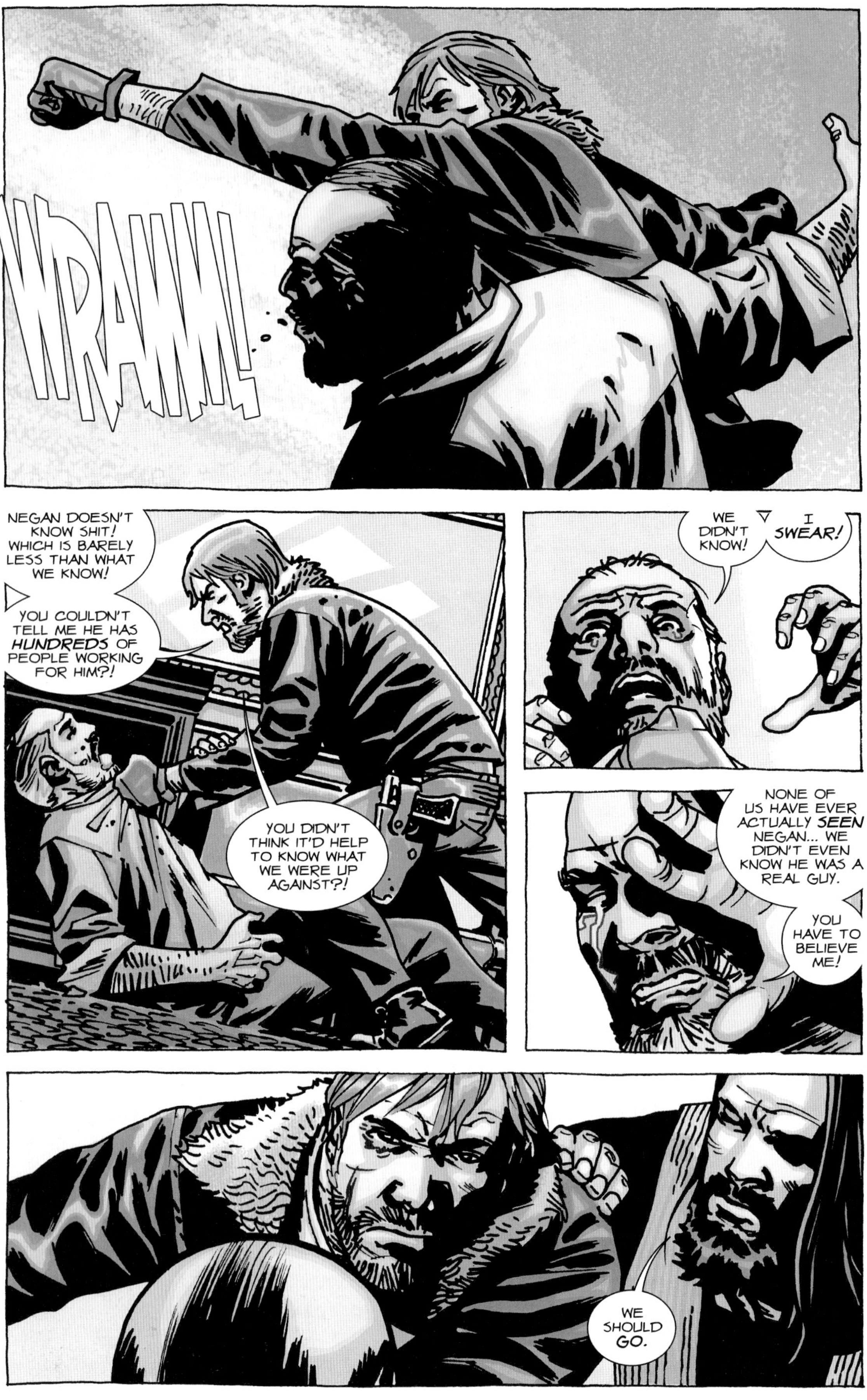
WRAMM!
NEGAN DOESN'T KNOW SHIT! WHICH IS BARELY LESS THAN WHAT WE KNOW!
YOU COULDN'T TELL ME HE HAS HUNDREDS OF PEOPLE WORKING FOR HIM?!
YOU DIDN'T THINK IT'D HELP TO KNOW WHAT WE WERE UP AGAINST?!
WE DIDN'T KNOW!
I SWEAR!
NONE OF US HAVE EVER ACTUALLY SEEN NEGAN... WE DIDN'T EVEN KNOW HE WAS A REAL GUY.
YOU HAVE TO BELIEVE ME!
WE SHOULD GO.

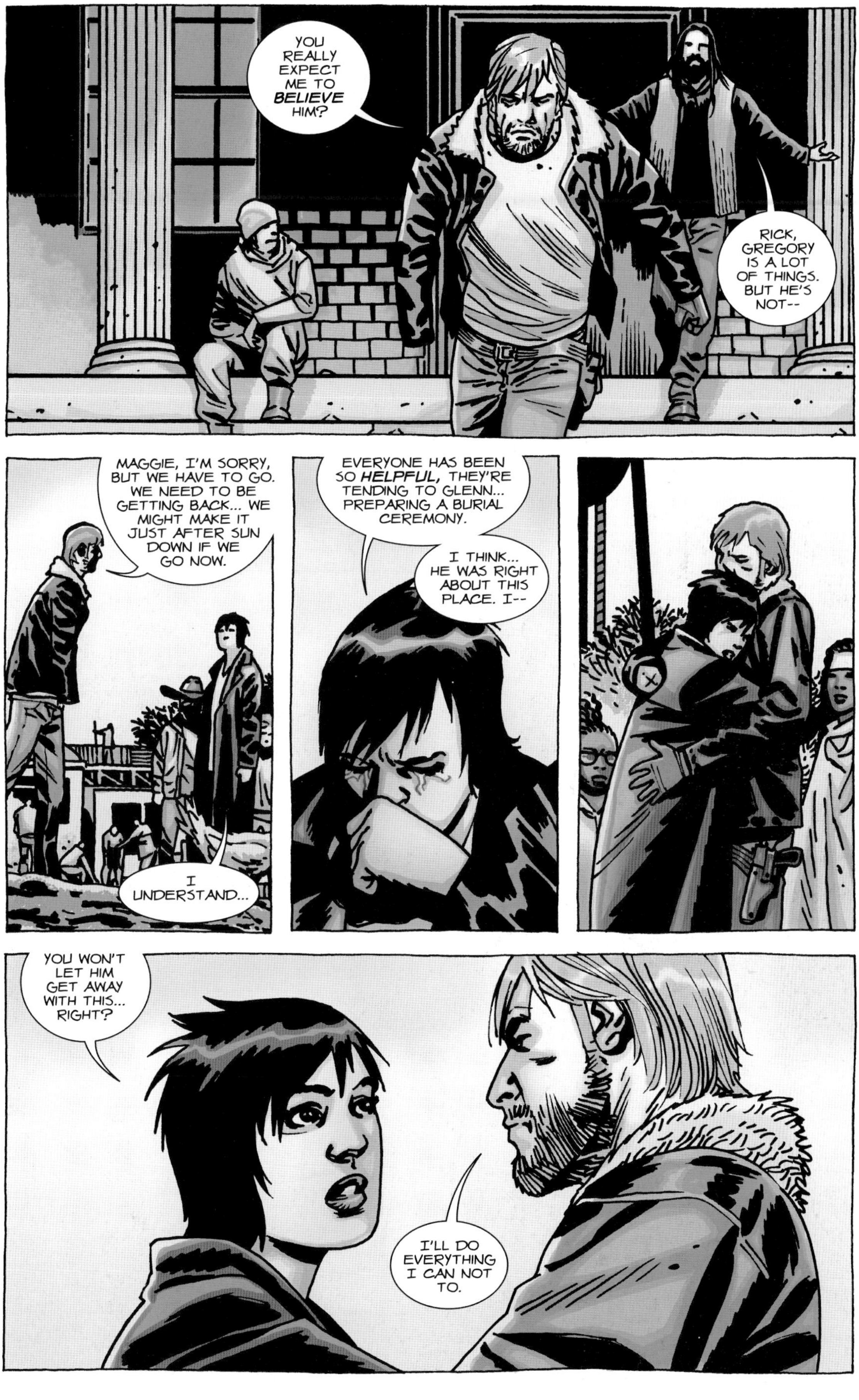
YOU REALLY EXPECT ME TO BELIEVE HIM?
RICK, GREGORY IS A LOT OF THINGS. BUT HE'S NOT--
MAGGIE, I'M SORRY, BUT WE HAVE TO GO. WE NEED TO BE GETTING BACK... WE MIGHT MAKE IT JUST AFTER SUN DOWN IF WE GO NOW.
I UNDERSTAND...
EVERYONE HAS BEEN SO HELPFUL, THEY'RE TENDING TO GLENN... PREPARING A BURIAL CEREMONY.
I THINK... HE WAS RIGHT ABOUT THIS PLACE. I--
YOU WON'T LET HIM GET AWAY WITH THIS... RIGHT?
I'LL DO EVERYTHING I CAN NOT TO.

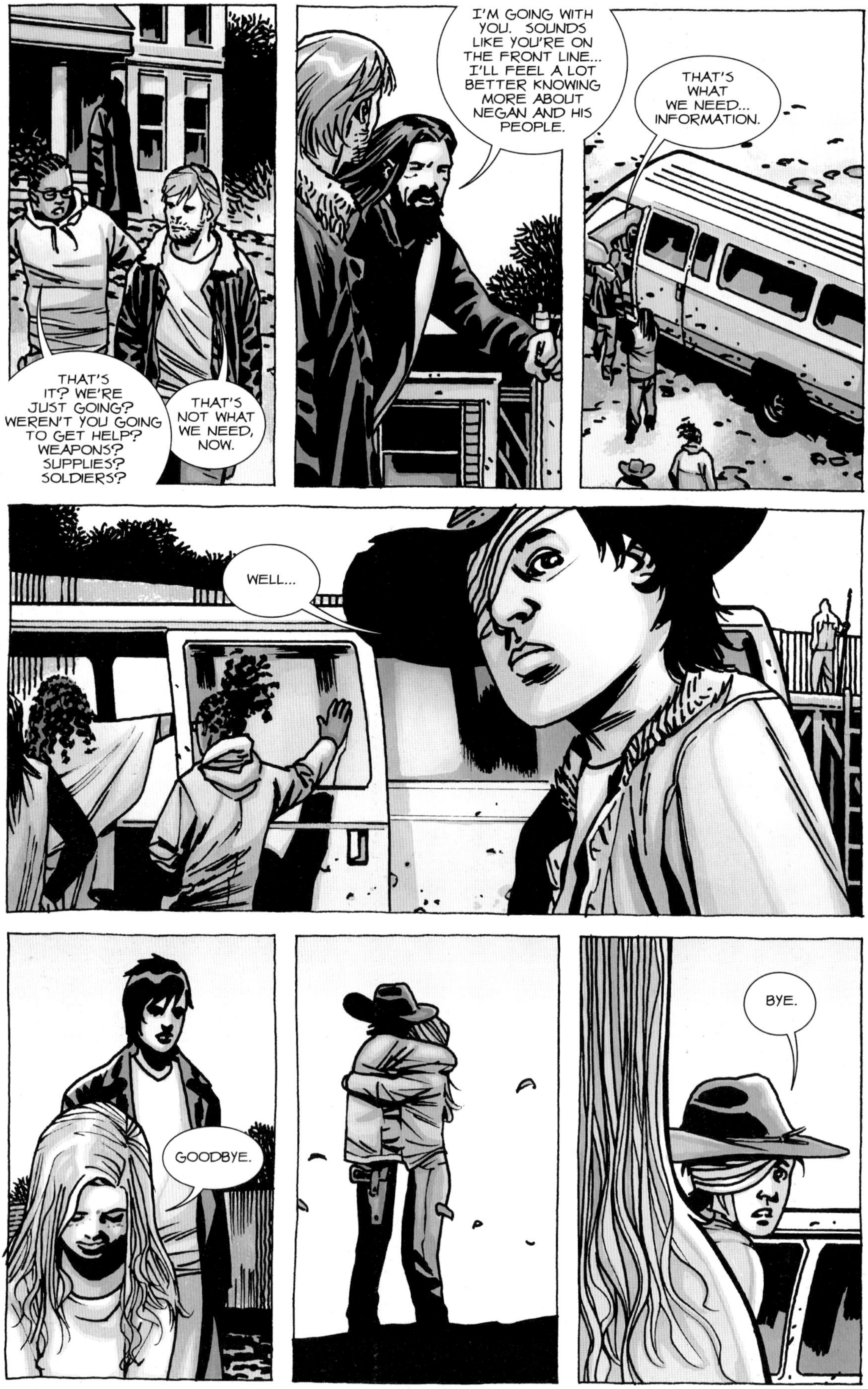
THAT'S IT? WE'RE JUST GOING? WEREN'T YOU GOING TO GET HELP? WEAPONS? SUPPLIES? SOLDIERS?
THAT'S NOT WHAT WE NEED, NOW.
I'M GOING WITH YOU. SOUNDS LIKE YOU'RE ON THE FRONT LINE... I'LL FEEL A LOT BETTER KNOWING MORE ABOUT NEGAN AND HIS PEOPLE.
THAT'S WHAT WE NEED... INFORMATION.
WELL...
GOODBYE.
BYE.

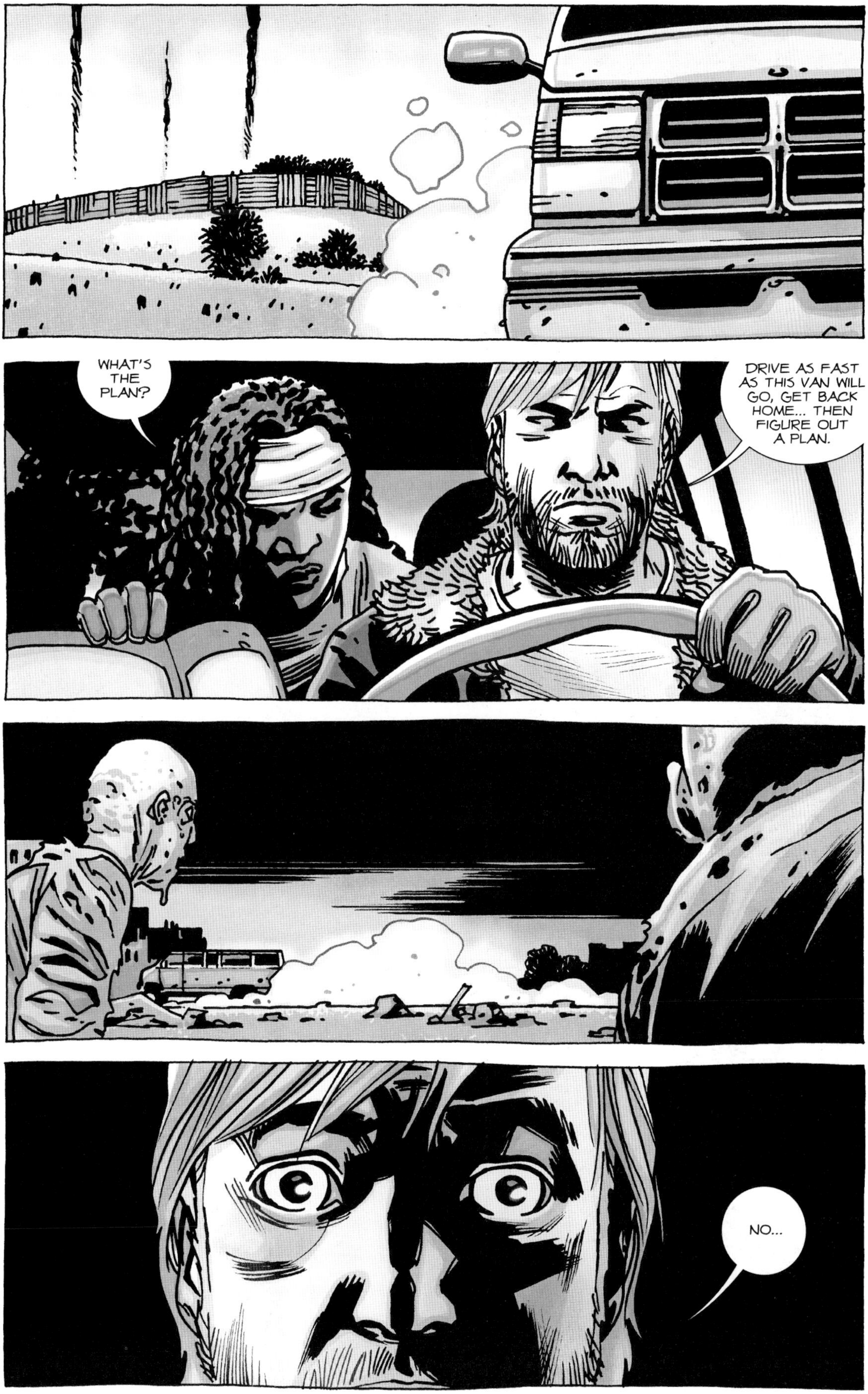
WHAT'S THE PLAN?
DRIVE AS FAST AS THIS VAN WILL GO, GET BACK HOME... THEN FIGURE OUT A PLAN.
NO...

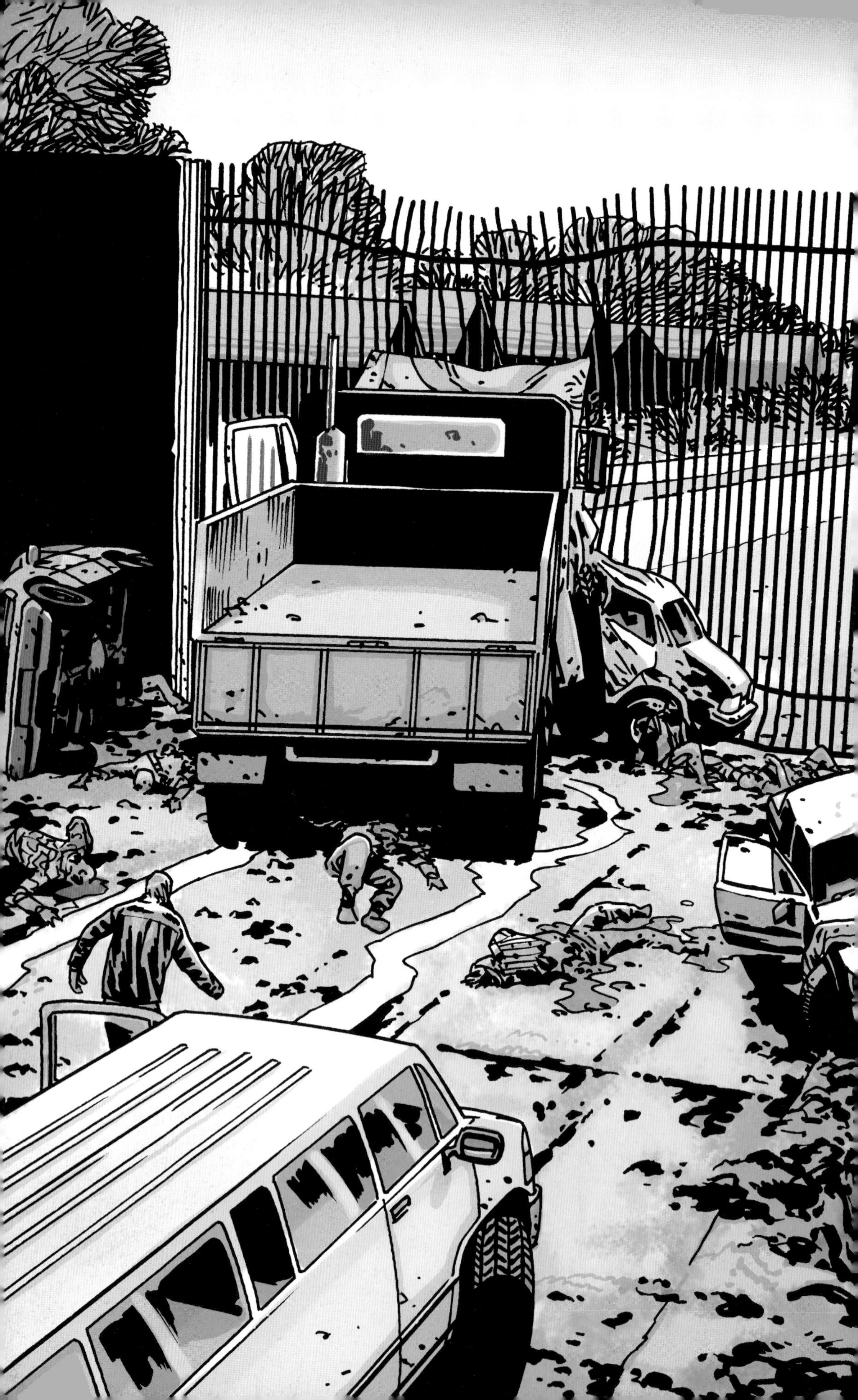

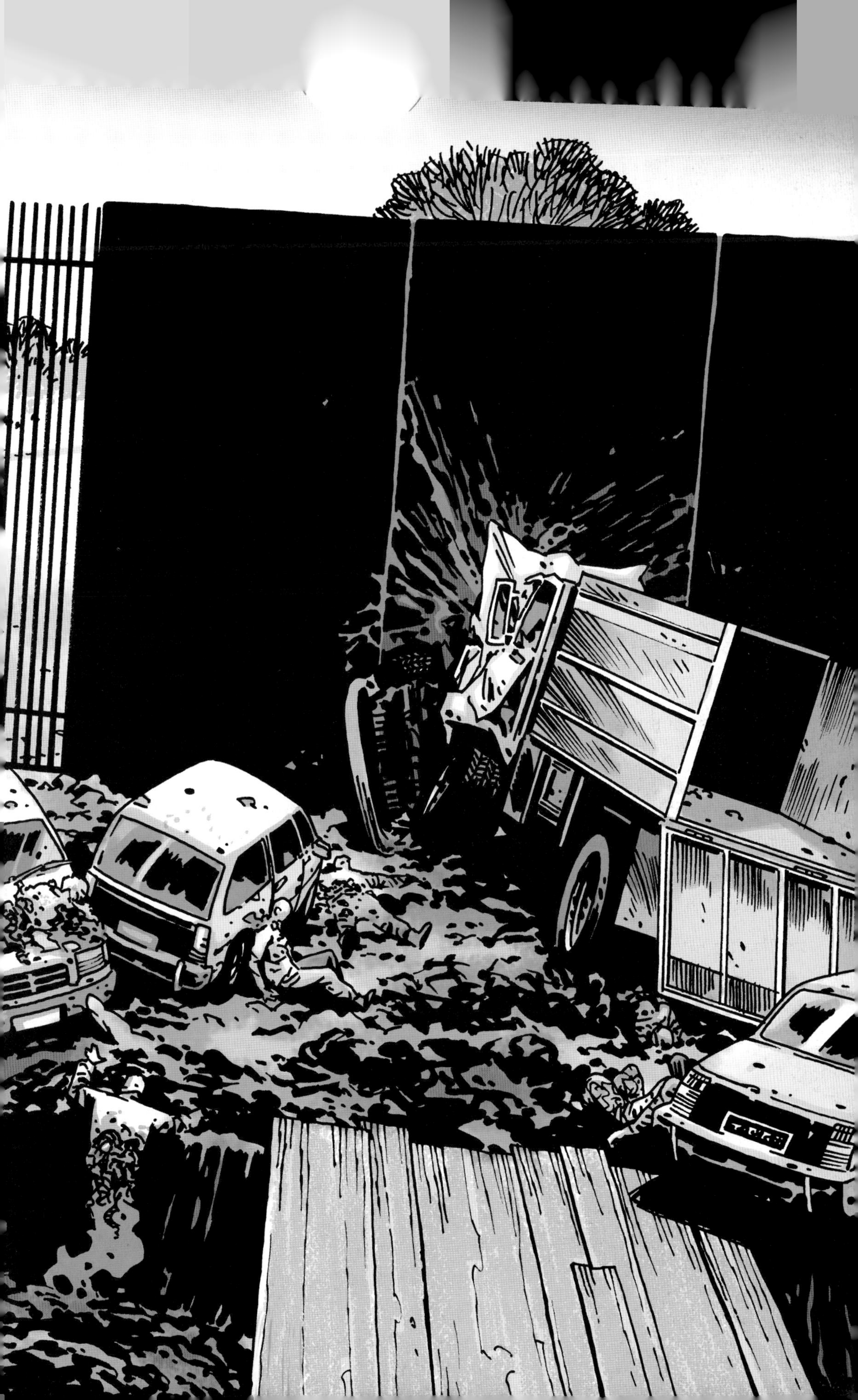

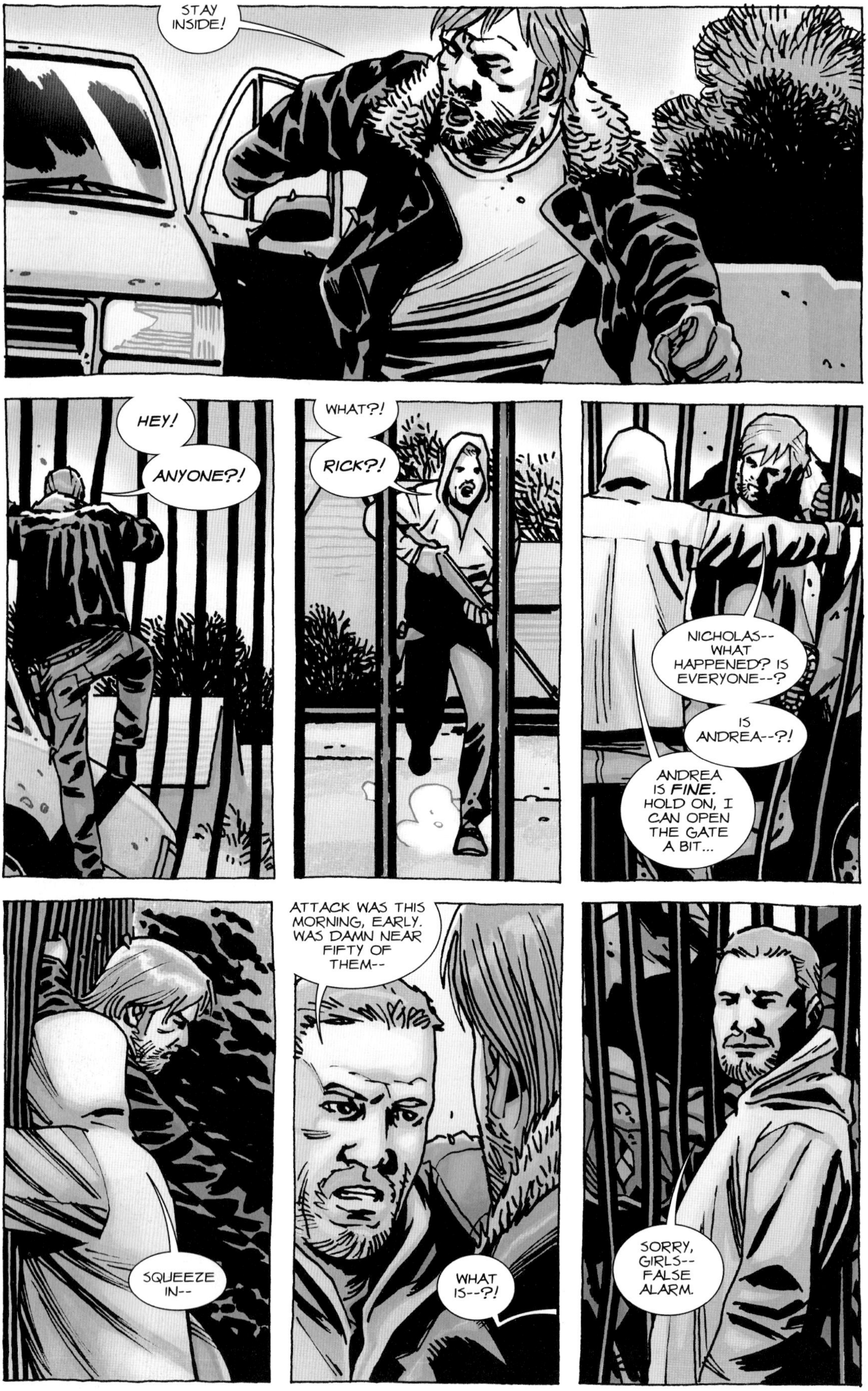
STAY INSIDE!
HEY!
ANYONE?!
WHAT?!
RICK?!
NICHOLAS-- WHAT HAPPENED? IS EVERYONE--?
IS ANDREA--?!
ANDREA IS ***FINE.*** HOLD ON, I CAN OPEN THE GATE A BIT...
SQUEEZE IN--
ATTACK WAS THIS MORNING, EARLY. WAS DAMN NEAR FIFTY OF THEM--
WHAT IS--?!
SORRY, GIRLS-- FALSE ALARM.

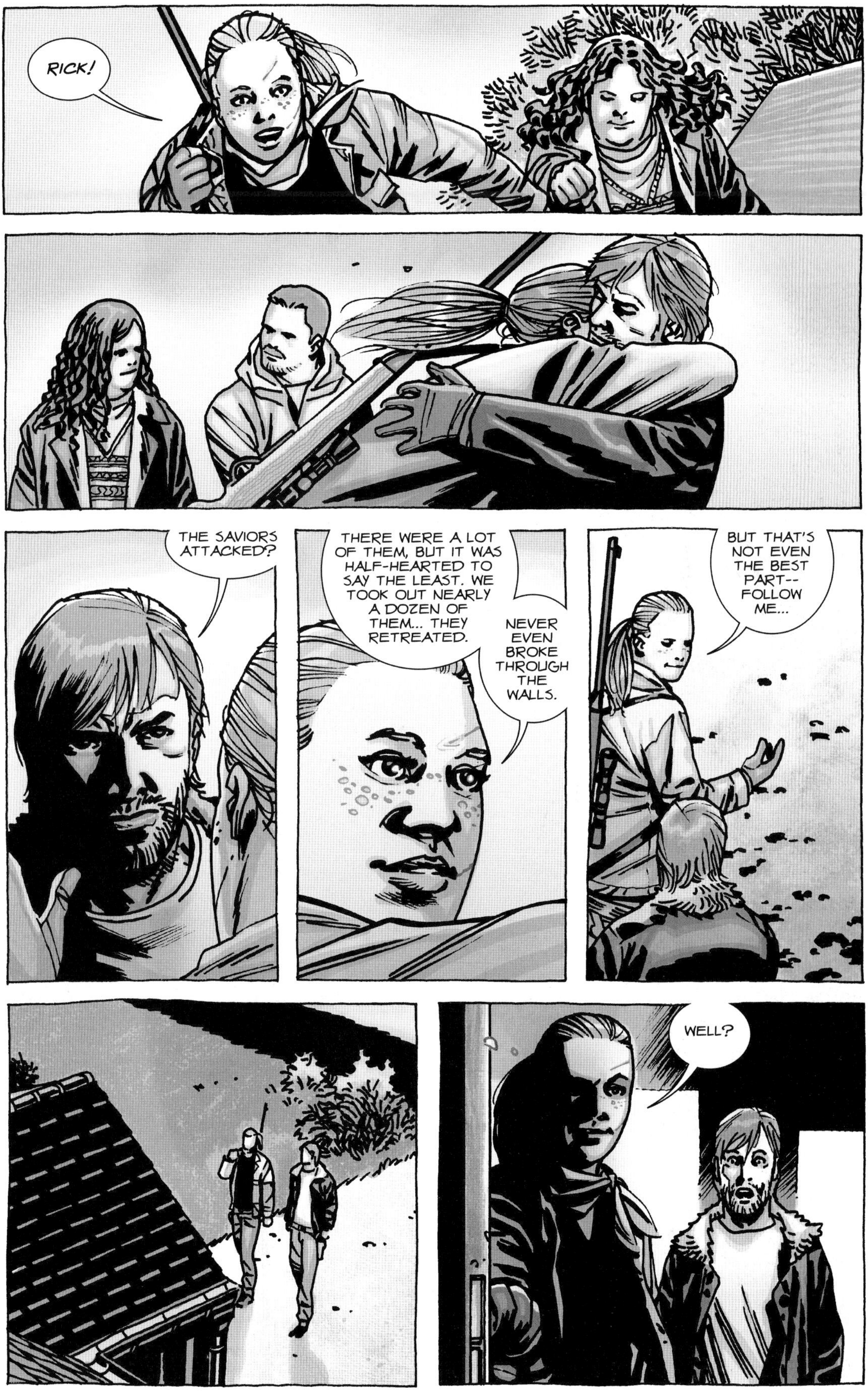
RICK!
THE SAVIORS ATTACKED?
THERE WERE A LOT OF THEM, BUT IT WAS HALF-HEARTED TO SAY THE LEAST. WE TOOK OUT NEARLY A DOZEN OF THEM... THEY RETREATED.
NEVER EVEN BROKE THROUGH THE WALLS.
BUT THAT'S NOT EVEN THE BEST PART-- FOLLOW ME...
WELL?

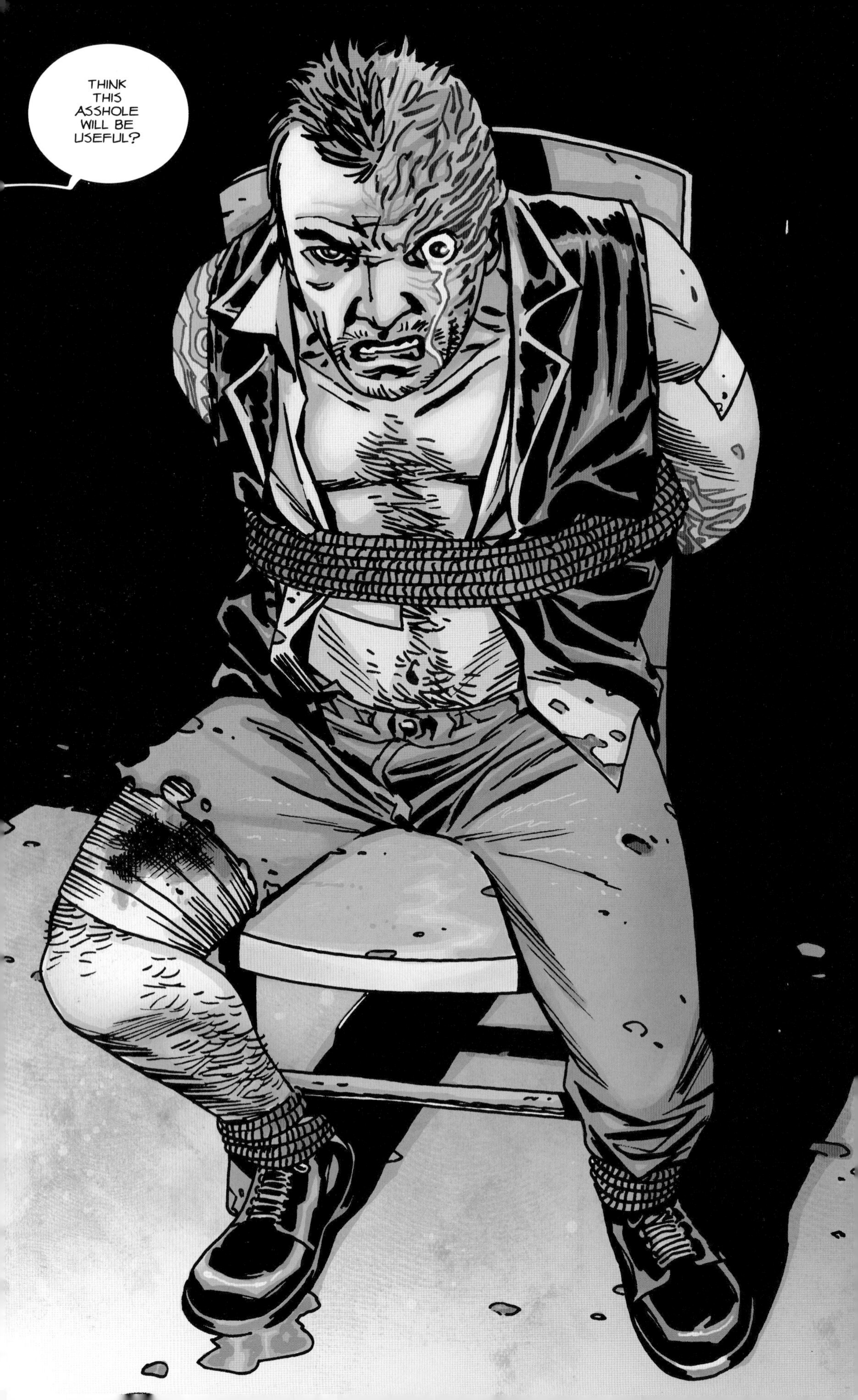
THINK THIS ASSHOLE WILL BE USEFUL?

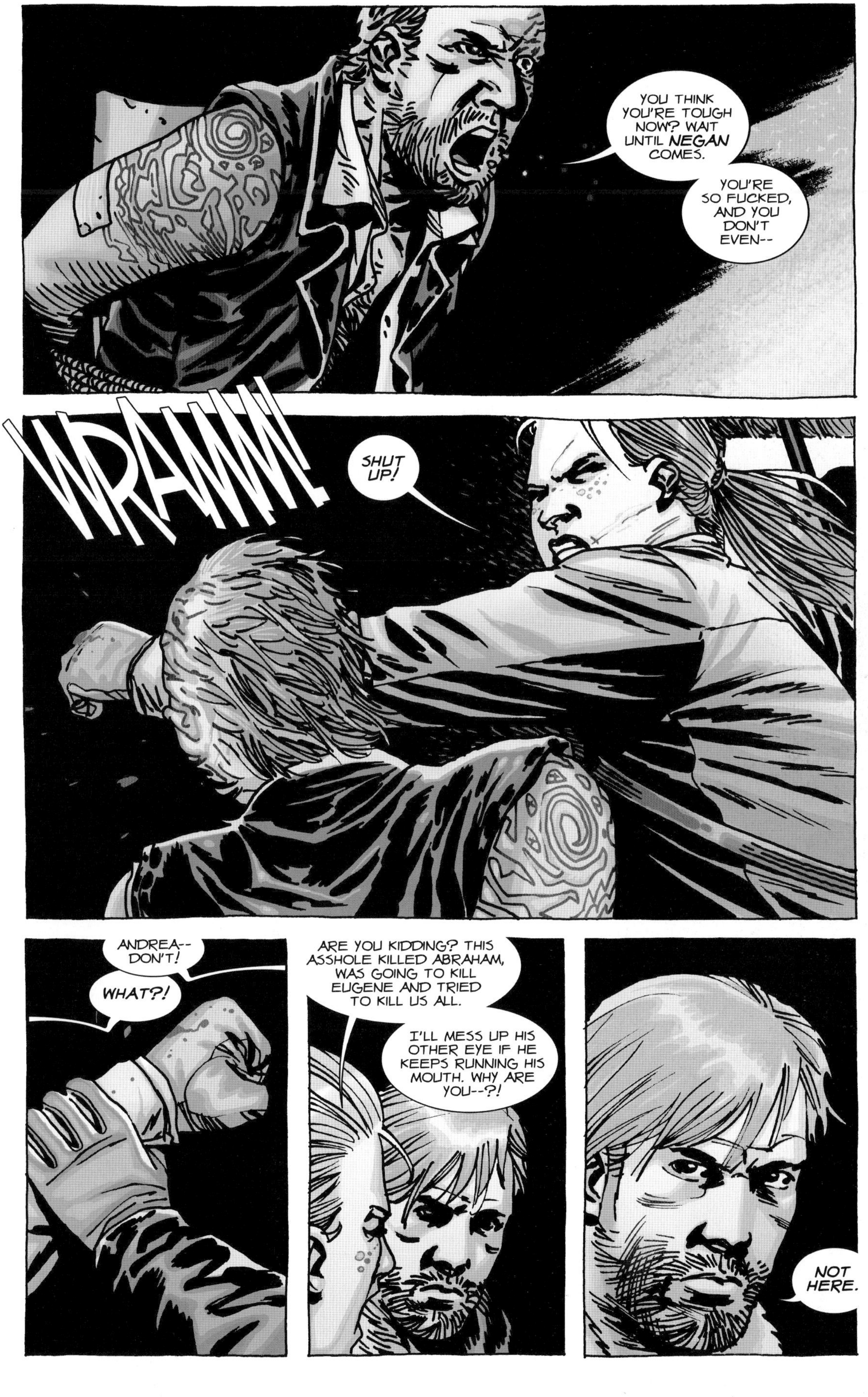

YOU THINK YOU'RE TOUGH NOW? WAIT UNTIL NEGAN COMES.
YOU'RE SO FUCKED, AND YOU DON'T EVEN--
WRAMM!
SHUT UP!
ANDREA-- DON'T!
WHAT?!
ARE YOU KIDDING? THIS ASSHOLE KILLED ABRAHAM, WAS GOING TO KILL EUGENE AND TRIED TO KILL US ALL.
I'LL MESS UP HIS OTHER EYE IF HE KEEPS RUNNING HIS MOUTH. WHY ARE YOU--?!
NOT HERE.

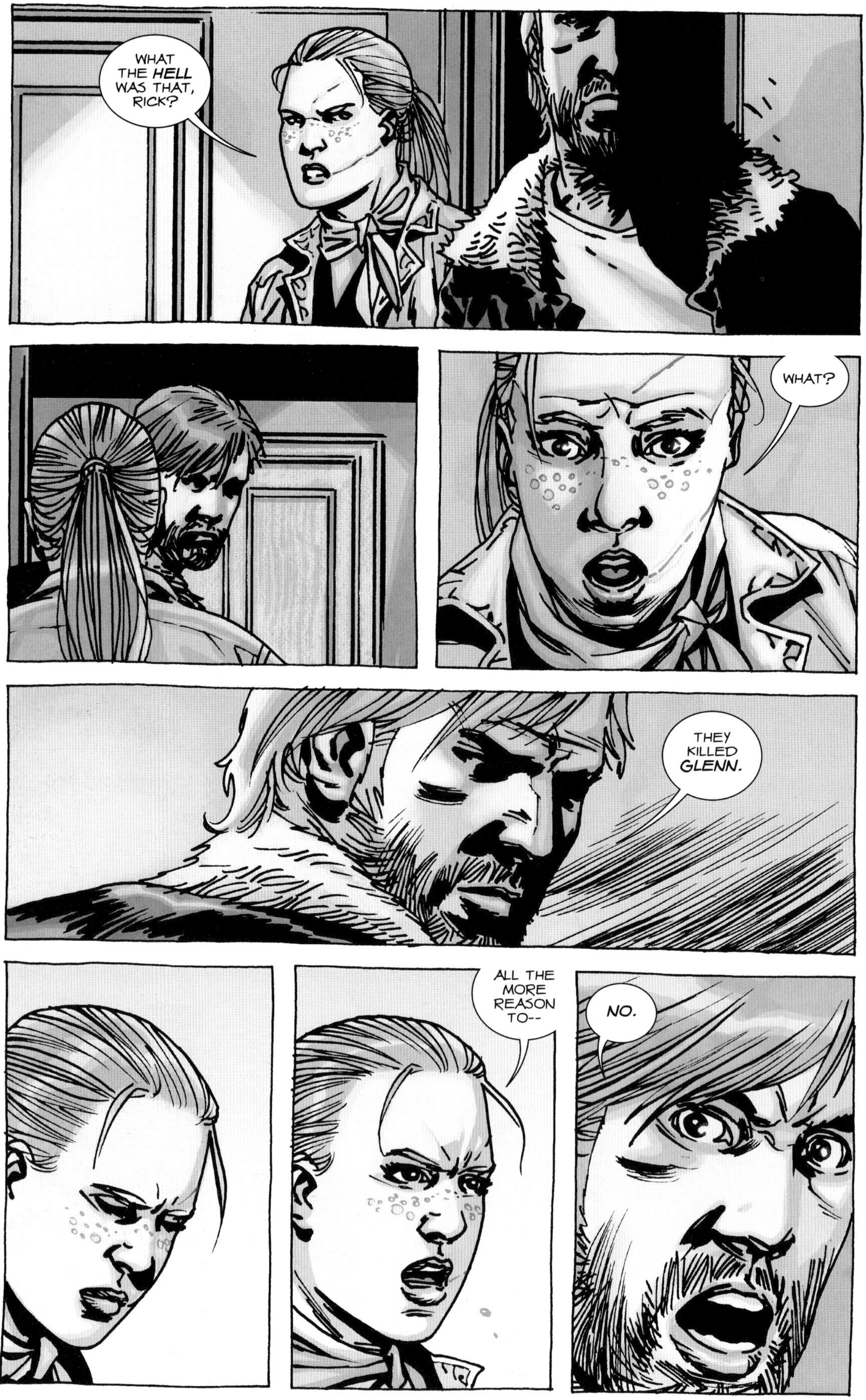
WHAT THE HELL WAS THAT, RICK?
WHAT?
THEY KILLED GLENN.
ALL THE MORE REASON TO--
NO.

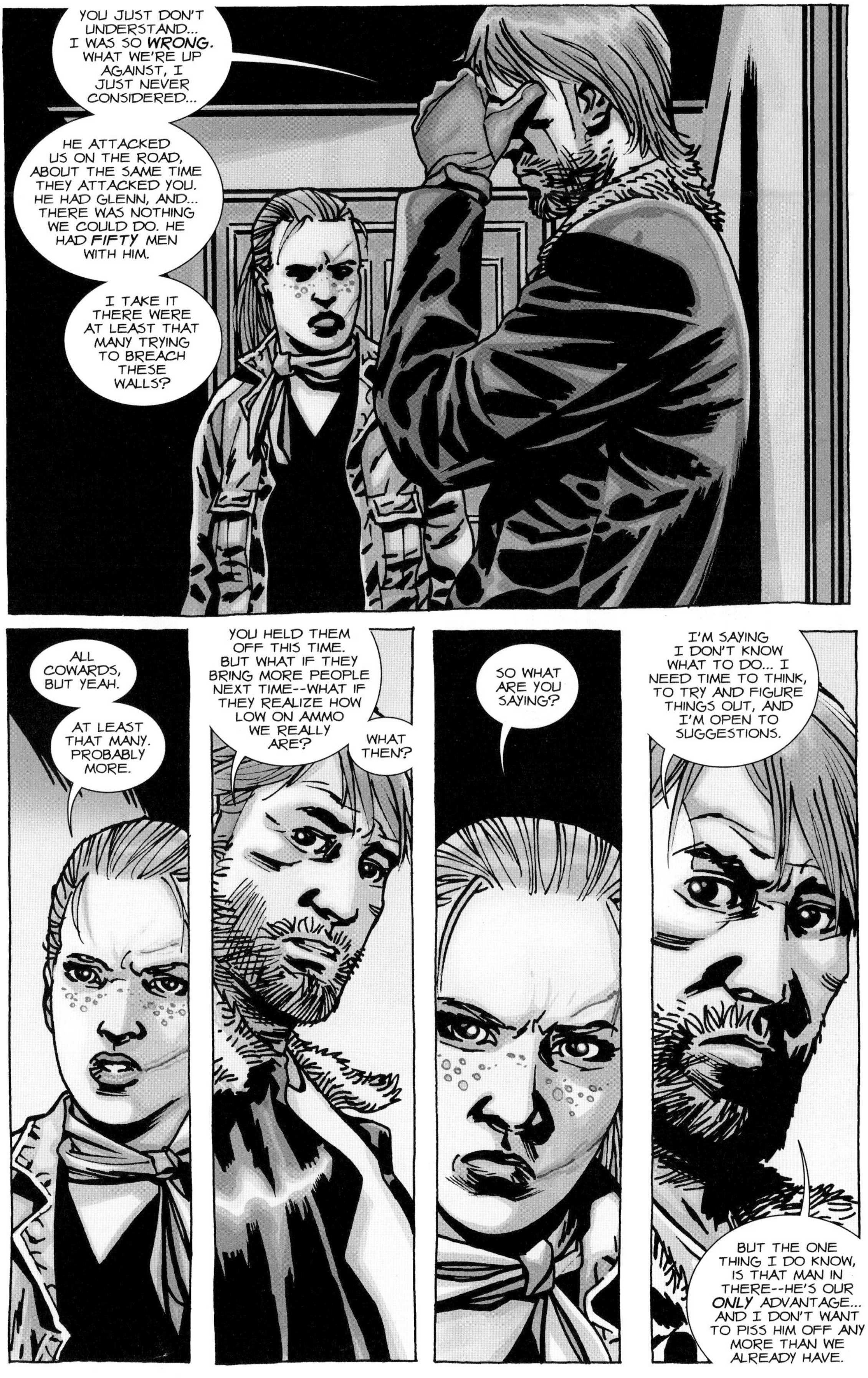
YOU JUST DON'T UNDERSTAND... I WAS SO WRONG. WHAT WE'RE UP AGAINST, I JUST NEVER CONSIDERED...
HE ATTACKED US ON THE ROAD, ABOUT THE SAME TIME THEY ATTACKED YOU. HE HAD GLENN, AND... THERE WAS NOTHING WE COULD DO. HE HAD FIFTY MEN WITH HIM.
I TAKE IT THERE WERE AT LEAST THAT MANY TRYING TO BREACH THESE WALLS?
ALL COWARDS, BUT YEAH.
AT LEAST THAT MANY. PROBABLY MORE.
YOU HELD THEM OFF THIS TIME. BUT WHAT IF THEY BRING MORE PEOPLE NEXT TIME--WHAT IF THEY REALIZE HOW LOW ON AMMO WE REALLY ARE?
WHAT THEN?
SO WHAT ARE YOU SAYING?
I'M SAYING I DON'T KNOW WHAT TO DO... I NEED TIME TO THINK, TO TRY AND FIGURE THINGS OUT, AND I'M OPEN TO SUGGESTIONS.
BUT THE ONE THING I DO KNOW, IS THAT MAN IN THERE--HE'S OUR ONLY ADVANTAGE... AND I DON'T WANT TO PISS HIM OFF ANY MORE THAN WE ALREADY HAVE.

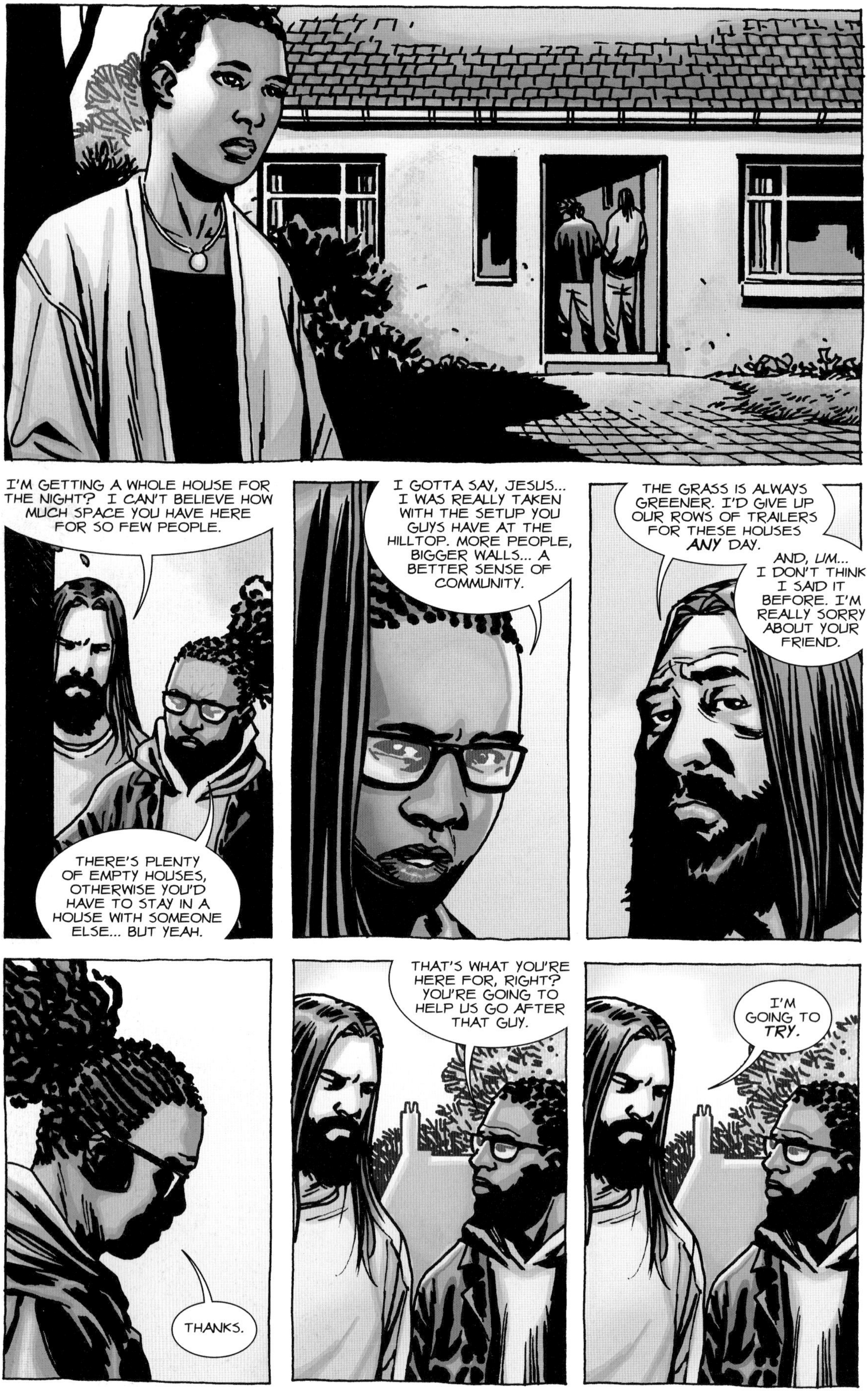
I'M GETTING A WHOLE HOUSE FOR THE NIGHT? I CAN'T BELIEVE HOW MUCH SPACE YOU HAVE HERE FOR SO FEW PEOPLE.
THERE'S PLENTY OF EMPTY HOUSES, OTHERWISE YOU'D HAVE TO STAY IN A HOUSE WITH SOMEONE ELSE... BUT YEAH.
I GOTTA SAY, JESUS... I WAS REALLY TAKEN WITH THE SETUP YOU GUYS HAVE AT THE HILLTOP. MORE PEOPLE, BIGGER WALLS... A BETTER SENSE OF COMMUNITY.
THE GRASS IS ALWAYS GREENER. I'D GIVE UP OUR ROWS OF TRAILERS FOR THESE HOUSES *ANY* DAY.
AND, *UM*... I DON'T THINK I SAID IT BEFORE. I'M REALLY SORRY ABOUT YOUR FRIEND.
THANKS.
THAT'S WHAT YOU'RE HERE FOR, RIGHT? YOU'RE GOING TO HELP US GO AFTER THAT GUY.
I'M GOING TO *TRY*.

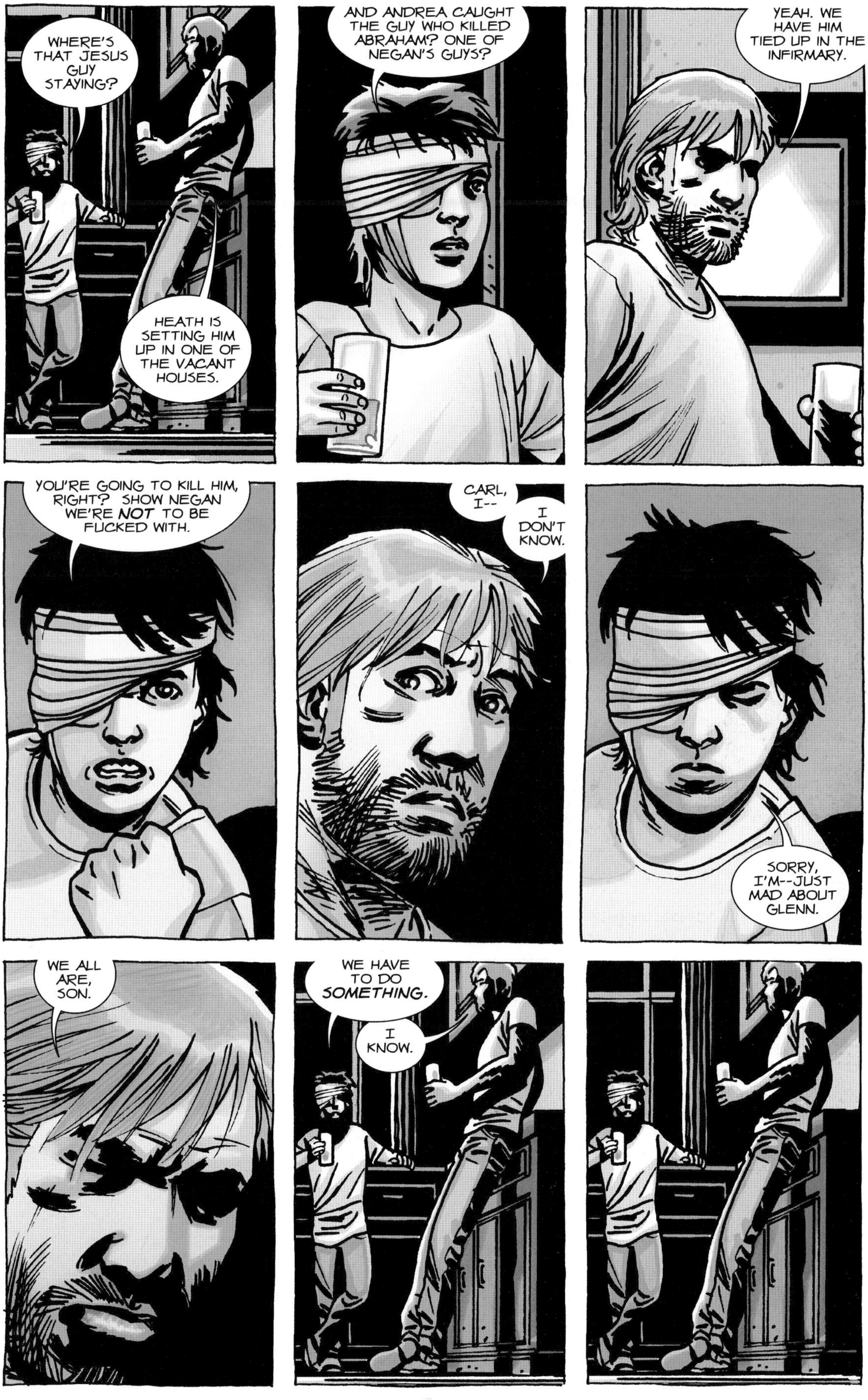
WHERE'S THAT JESUS GUY STAYING?
HEATH IS SETTING HIM UP IN ONE OF THE VACANT HOUSES.
AND ANDREA CAUGHT THE GUY WHO KILLED ABRAHAM? ONE OF NEGAN'S GUYS?
YEAH. WE HAVE HIM TIED UP IN THE INFIRMARY.
YOU'RE GOING TO KILL HIM, RIGHT? SHOW NEGAN WE'RE NOT TO BE FUCKED WITH.
CARL, I--
I DON'T KNOW.
SORRY, I'M--JUST MAD ABOUT GLENN.
WE ALL ARE, SON.
WE HAVE TO DO SOMETHING.
I KNOW.

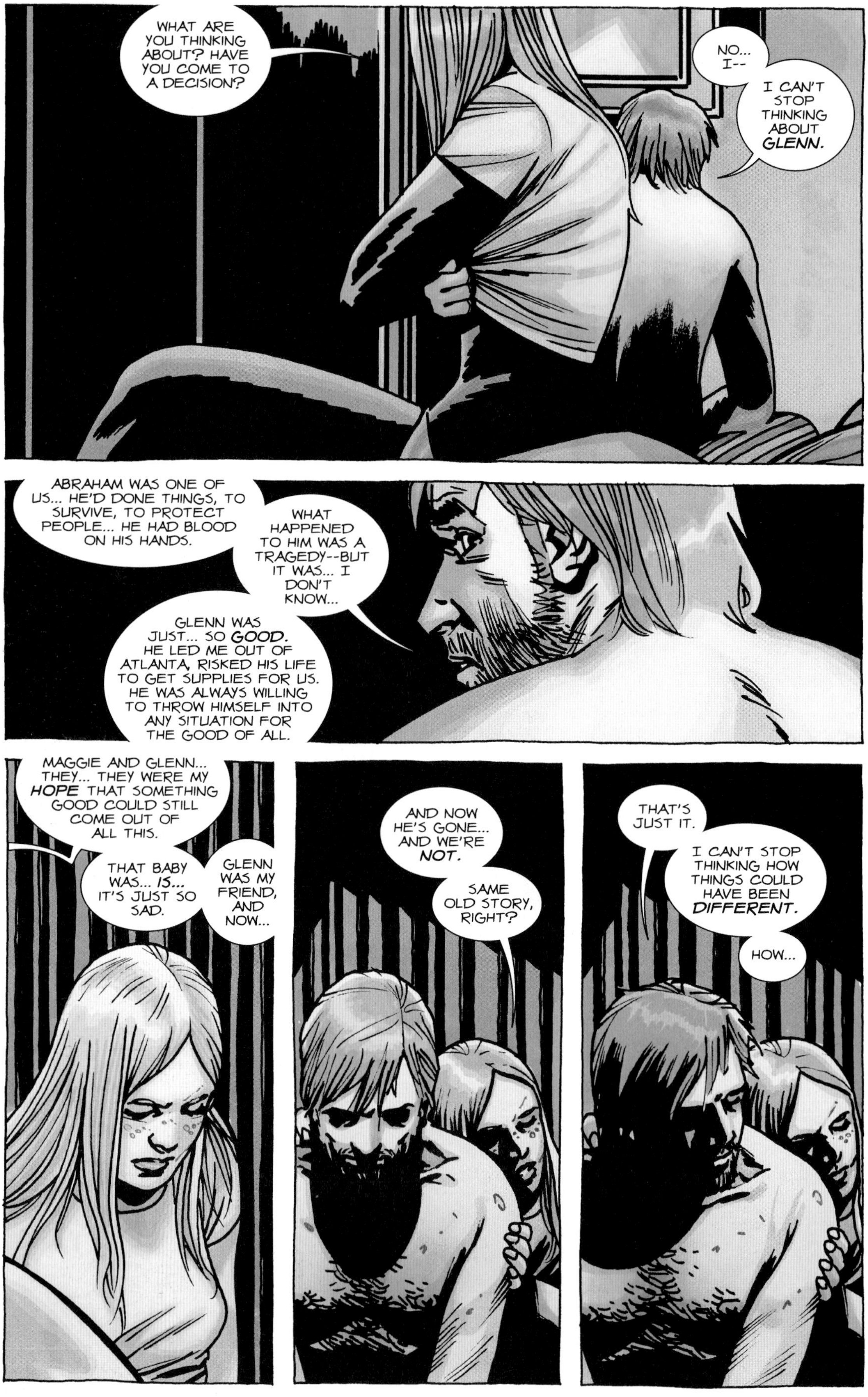
WHAT ARE YOU THINKING ABOUT? HAVE YOU COME TO A DECISION?
NO... I--
I CAN'T STOP THINKING ABOUT GLENN.
ABRAHAM WAS ONE OF US... HE'D DONE THINGS, TO SURVIVE, TO PROTECT PEOPLE... HE HAD BLOOD ON HIS HANDS.
WHAT HAPPENED TO HIM WAS A TRAGEDY--BUT IT WAS... I DON'T KNOW...
GLENN WAS JUST... SO GOOD. HE LED ME OUT OF ATLANTA, RISKED HIS LIFE TO GET SUPPLIES FOR US. HE WAS ALWAYS WILLING TO THROW HIMSELF INTO ANY SITUATION FOR THE GOOD OF ALL.
MAGGIE AND GLENN... THEY... THEY WERE MY HOPE THAT SOMETHING GOOD COULD STILL COME OUT OF ALL THIS.
THAT BABY WAS... IS... IT'S JUST SO SAD.
GLENN WAS MY FRIEND, AND NOW...
AND NOW HE'S GONE... AND WE'RE NOT.
SAME OLD STORY, RIGHT?
THAT'S JUST IT.
I CAN'T STOP THINKING HOW THINGS COULD HAVE BEEN DIFFERENT.
HOW...

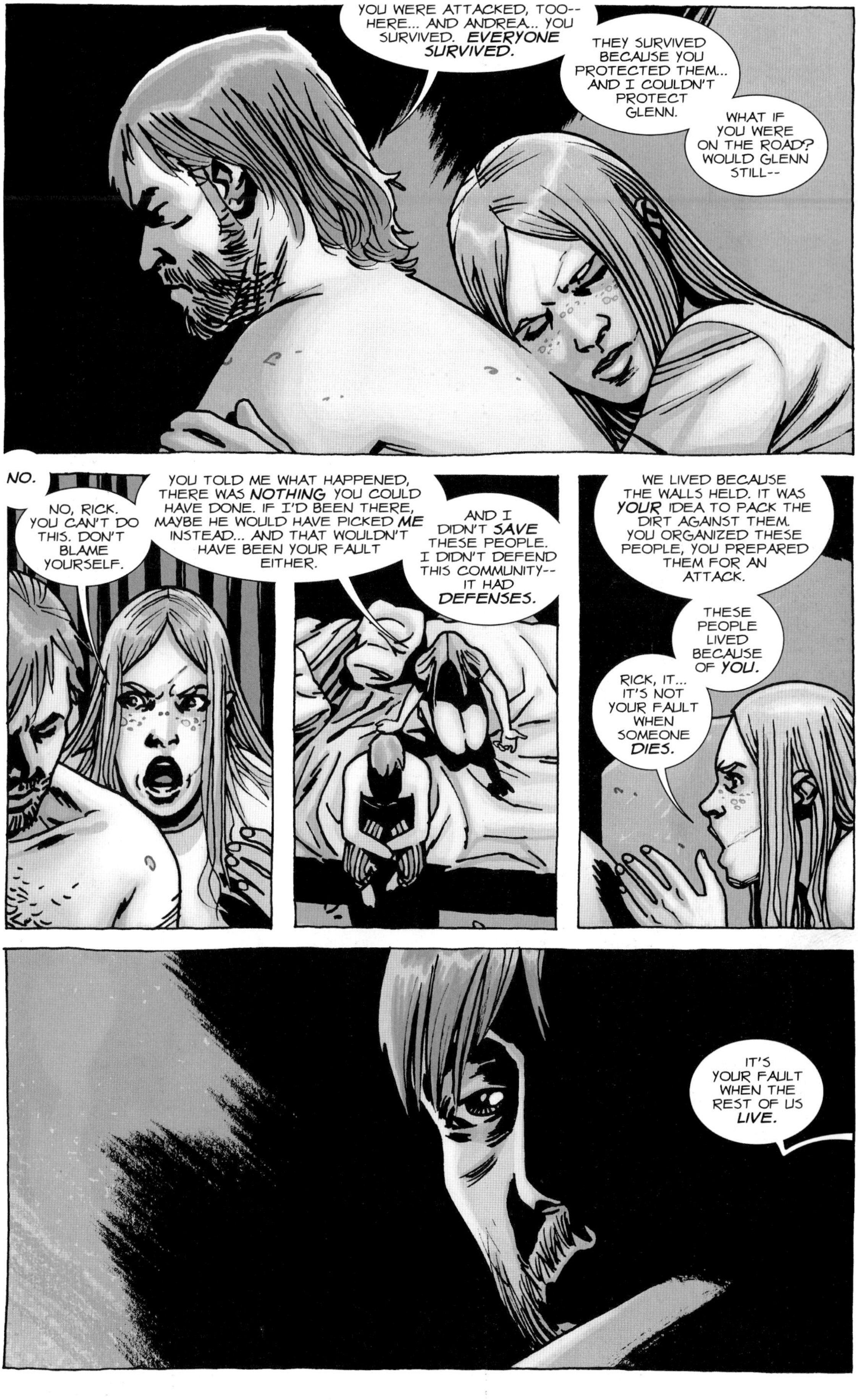

YOU WERE ATTACKED, TOO-- HERE... AND ANDREA... YOU SURVIVED. EVERYONE SURVIVED.
THEY SURVIVED BECAUSE YOU PROTECTED THEM... AND I COULDN'T PROTECT GLENN.
WHAT IF YOU WERE ON THE ROAD? WOULD GLENN STILL--
NO.
NO, RICK. YOU CAN'T DO THIS. DON'T BLAME YOURSELF.
YOU TOLD ME WHAT HAPPENED, THERE WAS NOTHING YOU COULD HAVE DONE. IF I'D BEEN THERE, MAYBE HE WOULD HAVE PICKED ME INSTEAD... AND THAT WOULDN'T HAVE BEEN YOUR FAULT EITHER.
AND I DIDN'T SAVE THESE PEOPLE. I DIDN'T DEFEND THIS COMMUNITY-- IT HAD DEFENSES.
WE LIVED BECAUSE THE WALLS HELD. IT WAS YOUR IDEA TO PACK THE DIRT AGAINST THEM. YOU ORGANIZED THESE PEOPLE, YOU PREPARED THEM FOR AN ATTACK.
THESE PEOPLE LIVED BECAUSE OF YOU.
RICK, IT... IT'S NOT YOUR FAULT WHEN SOMEONE DIES.
IT'S YOUR FAULT WHEN THE REST OF US LIVE.

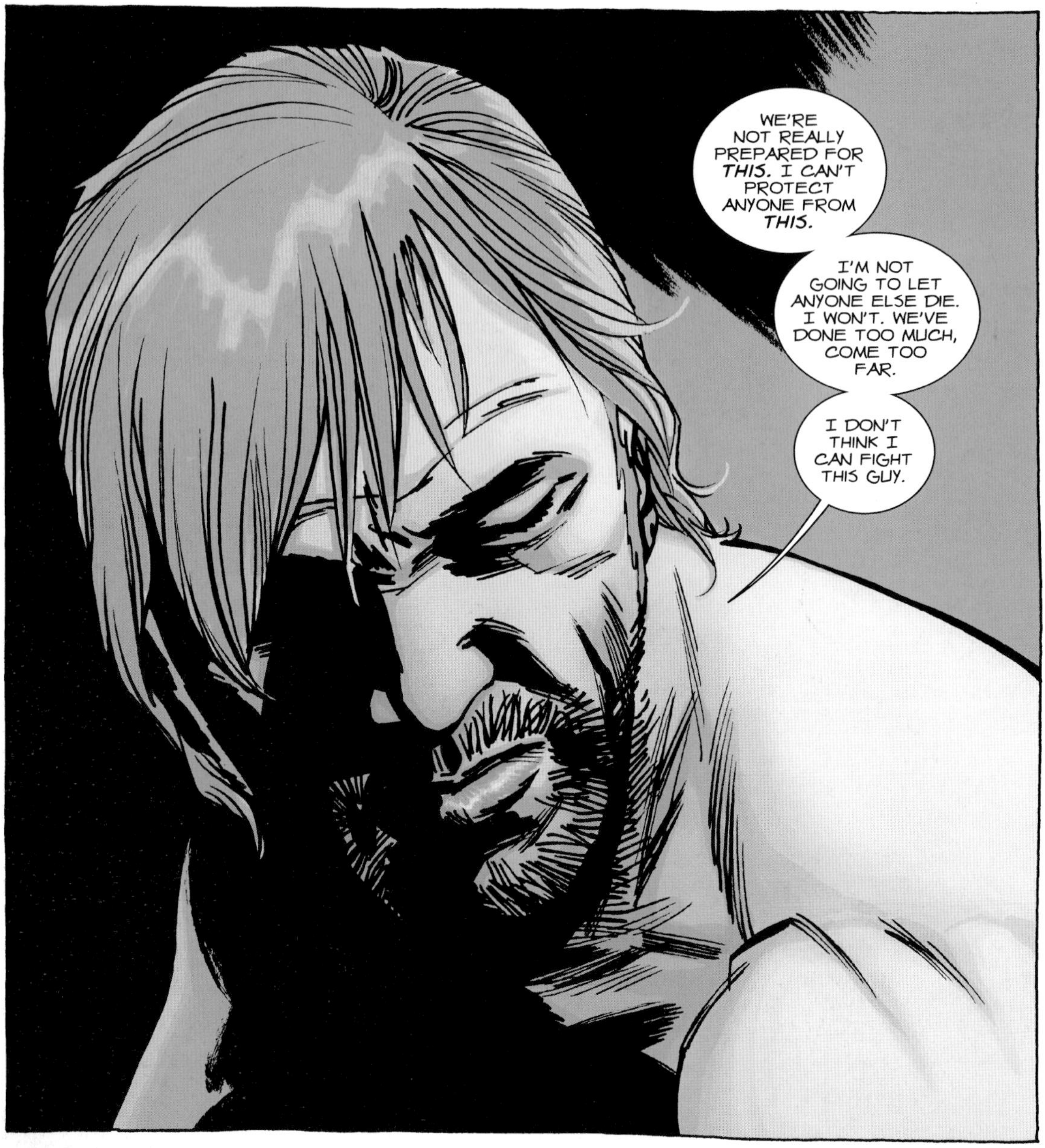
WE'RE NOT REALLY PREPARED FOR *THIS.* I CAN'T PROTECT ANYONE FROM *THIS.*
I'M NOT GOING TO LET ANYONE ELSE DIE. I WON'T. WE'VE DONE TOO MUCH, COME TOO FAR.
I DON'T THINK I CAN FIGHT THIS GUY.

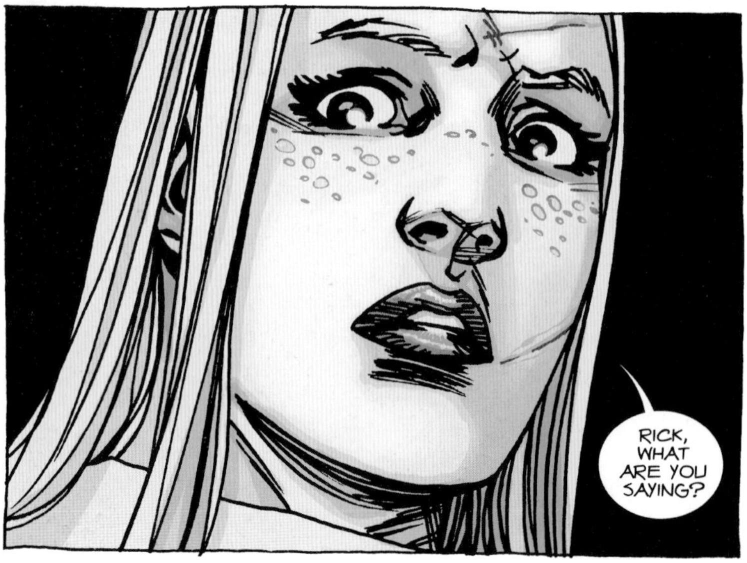
RICK, WHAT ARE YOU SAYING?

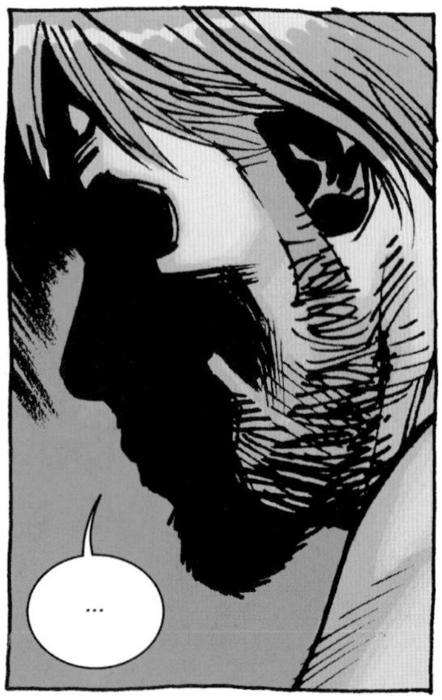
...

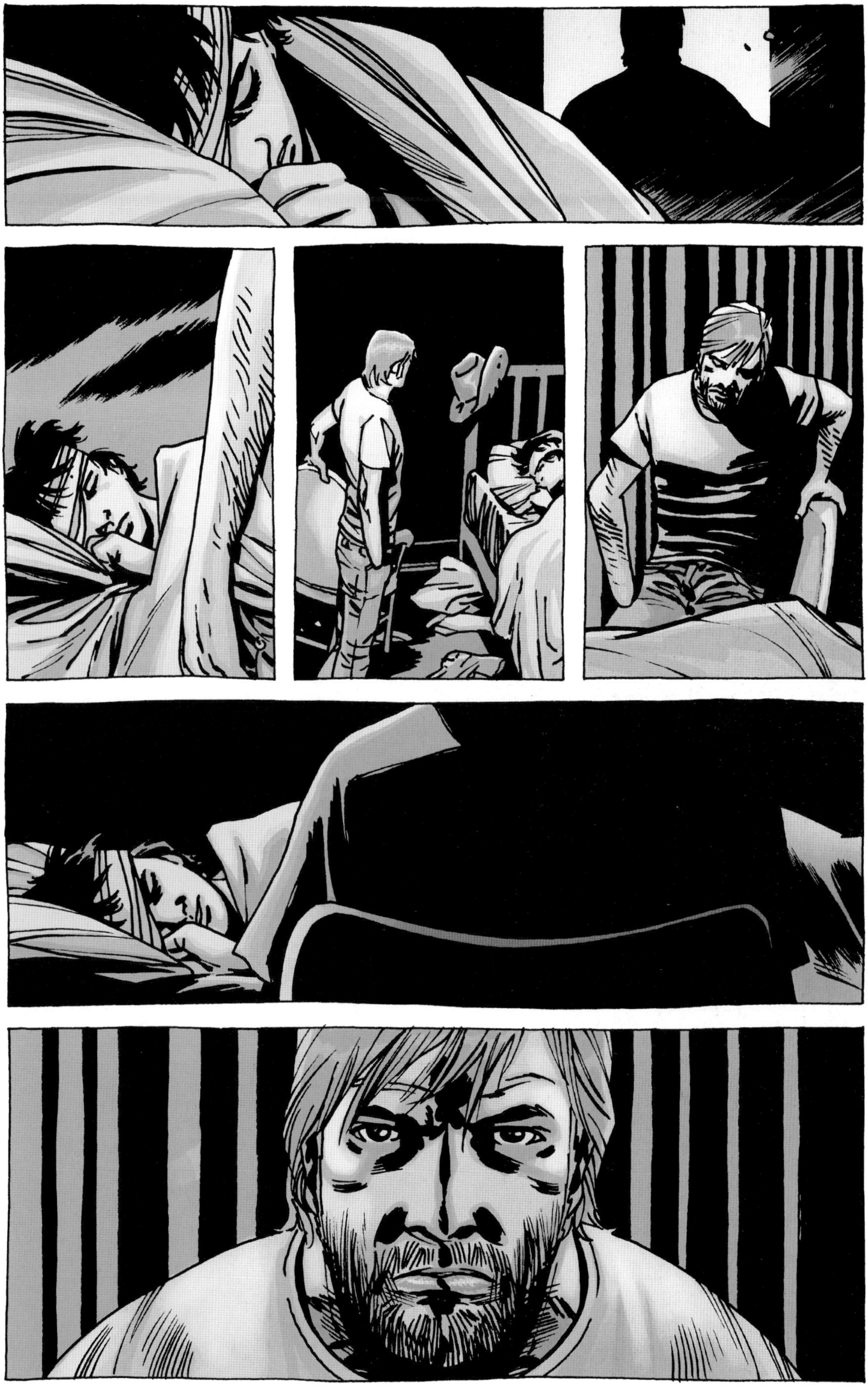

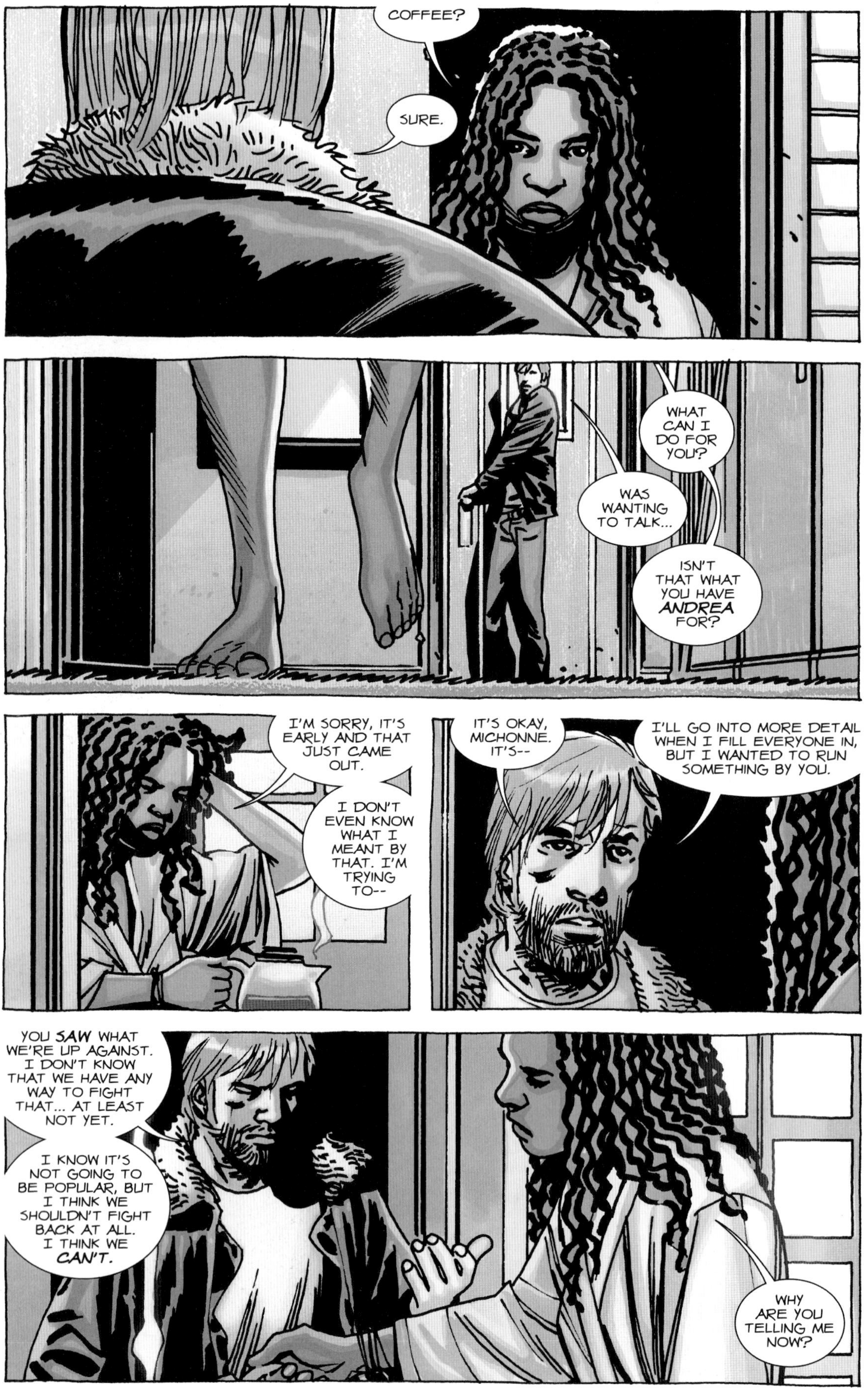
COFFEE?
SURE.
WHAT CAN I DO FOR YOU?
WAS WANTING TO TALK...
ISN'T THAT WHAT YOU HAVE ANDREA FOR?
I'M SORRY, IT'S EARLY AND THAT JUST CAME OUT.
I DON'T EVEN KNOW WHAT I MEANT BY THAT. I'M TRYING TO--
IT'S OKAY, MICHONNE. IT'S--
I'LL GO INTO MORE DETAIL WHEN I FILL EVERYONE IN, BUT I WANTED TO RUN SOMETHING BY YOU.
YOU SAW WHAT WE'RE UP AGAINST. I DON'T KNOW THAT WE HAVE ANY WAY TO FIGHT THAT... AT LEAST NOT YET.
I KNOW IT'S NOT GOING TO BE POPULAR, BUT I THINK WE SHOULDN'T FIGHT BACK AT ALL. I THINK WE CAN'T.
WHY ARE YOU TELLING ME NOW?

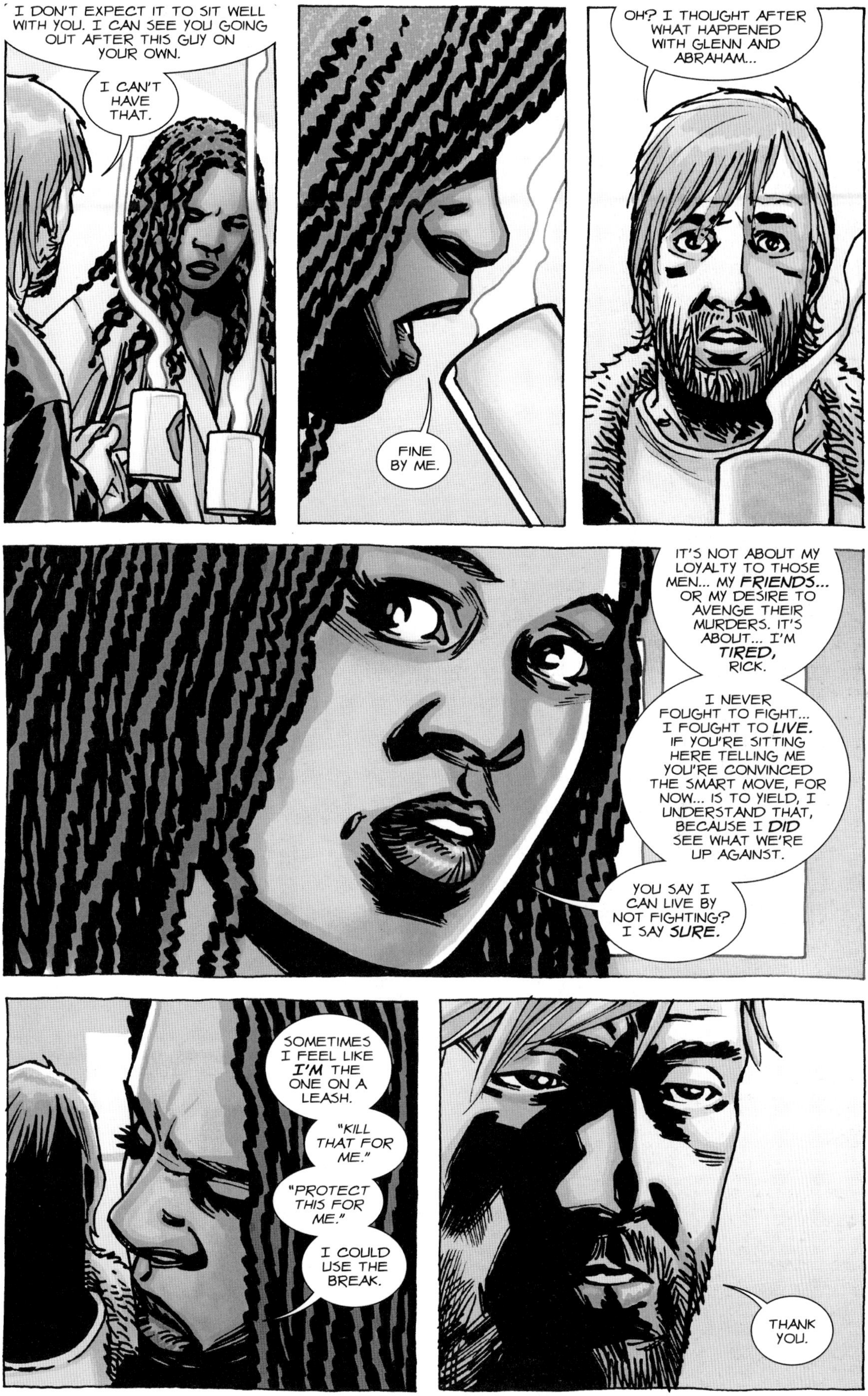
I DON'T EXPECT IT TO SIT WELL WITH YOU. I CAN SEE YOU GOING OUT AFTER THIS GUY ON YOUR OWN.
I CAN'T HAVE THAT.
FINE BY ME.
OH? I THOUGHT AFTER WHAT HAPPENED WITH GLENN AND ABRAHAM...
IT'S NOT ABOUT MY LOYALTY TO THOSE MEN... MY *FRIENDS...* OR MY DESIRE TO AVENGE THEIR MURDERS. IT'S ABOUT... I'M *TIRED,* RICK.
I NEVER FOUGHT TO FIGHT... I FOUGHT TO *LIVE.* IF YOU'RE SITTING HERE TELLING ME YOU'RE CONVINCED THE SMART MOVE, FOR NOW... IS TO YIELD, I UNDERSTAND THAT, BECAUSE I *DID* SEE WHAT WE'RE UP AGAINST.
YOU SAY I CAN LIVE BY NOT FIGHTING? I SAY *SURE.*
SOMETIMES I FEEL LIKE *I'M* THE ONE ON A LEASH.
"KILL THAT FOR ME."
"PROTECT THIS FOR ME."
I COULD USE THE BREAK.
THANK YOU.

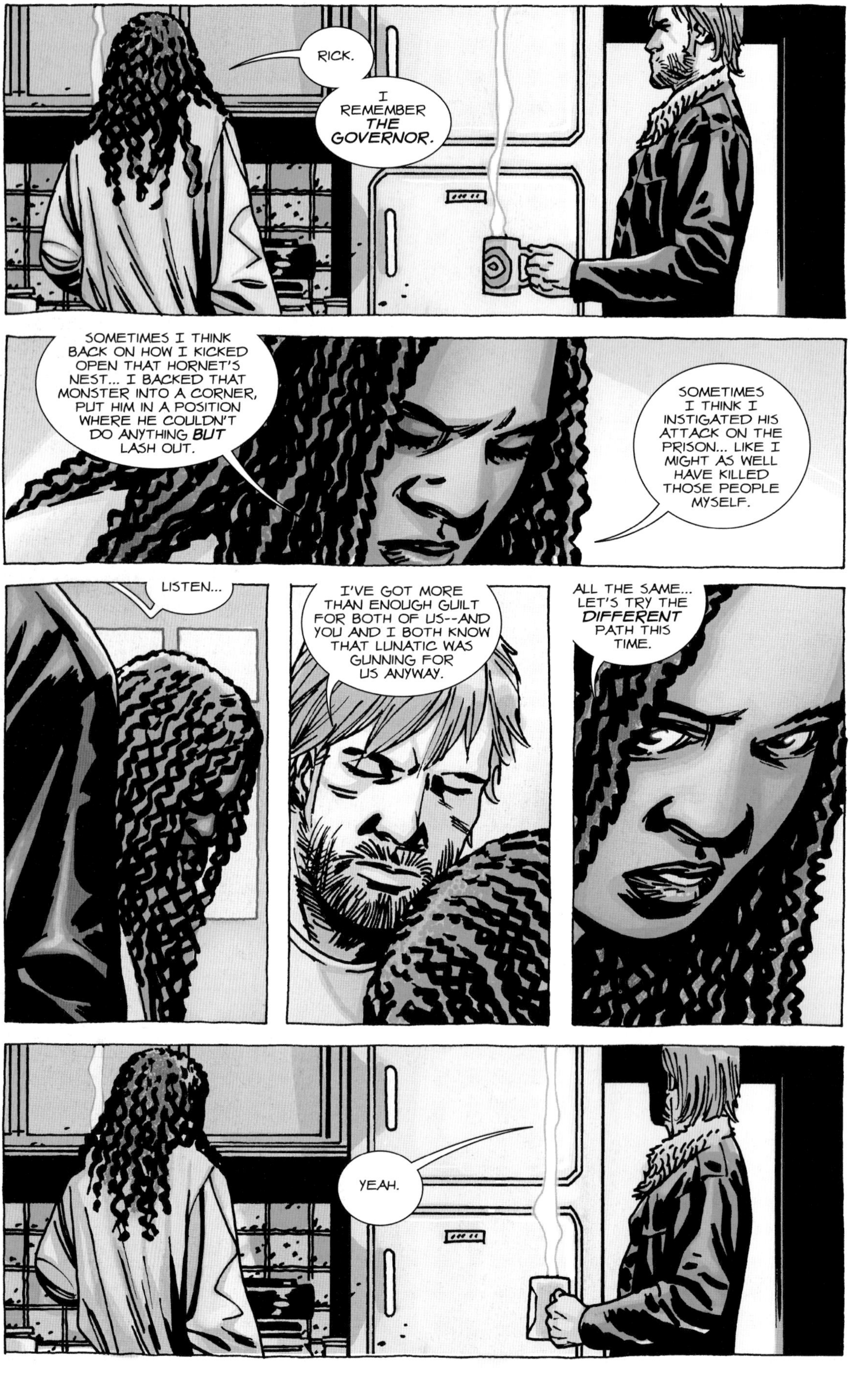

RICK.
I REMEMBER *THE GOVERNOR.*
SOMETIMES I THINK BACK ON HOW I KICKED OPEN THAT HORNET'S NEST... I BACKED THAT MONSTER INTO A CORNER, PUT HIM IN A POSITION WHERE HE COULDN'T DO ANYTHING *BUT* LASH OUT.
SOMETIMES I THINK I INSTIGATED HIS ATTACK ON THE PRISON... LIKE I MIGHT AS WELL HAVE KILLED THOSE PEOPLE MYSELF.
LISTEN...
I'VE GOT MORE THAN ENOUGH GUILT FOR BOTH OF US--AND YOU AND I BOTH KNOW THAT LUNATIC WAS GUNNING FOR US ANYWAY.
ALL THE SAME... LET'S TRY THE *DIFFERENT* PATH THIS TIME.
YEAH.

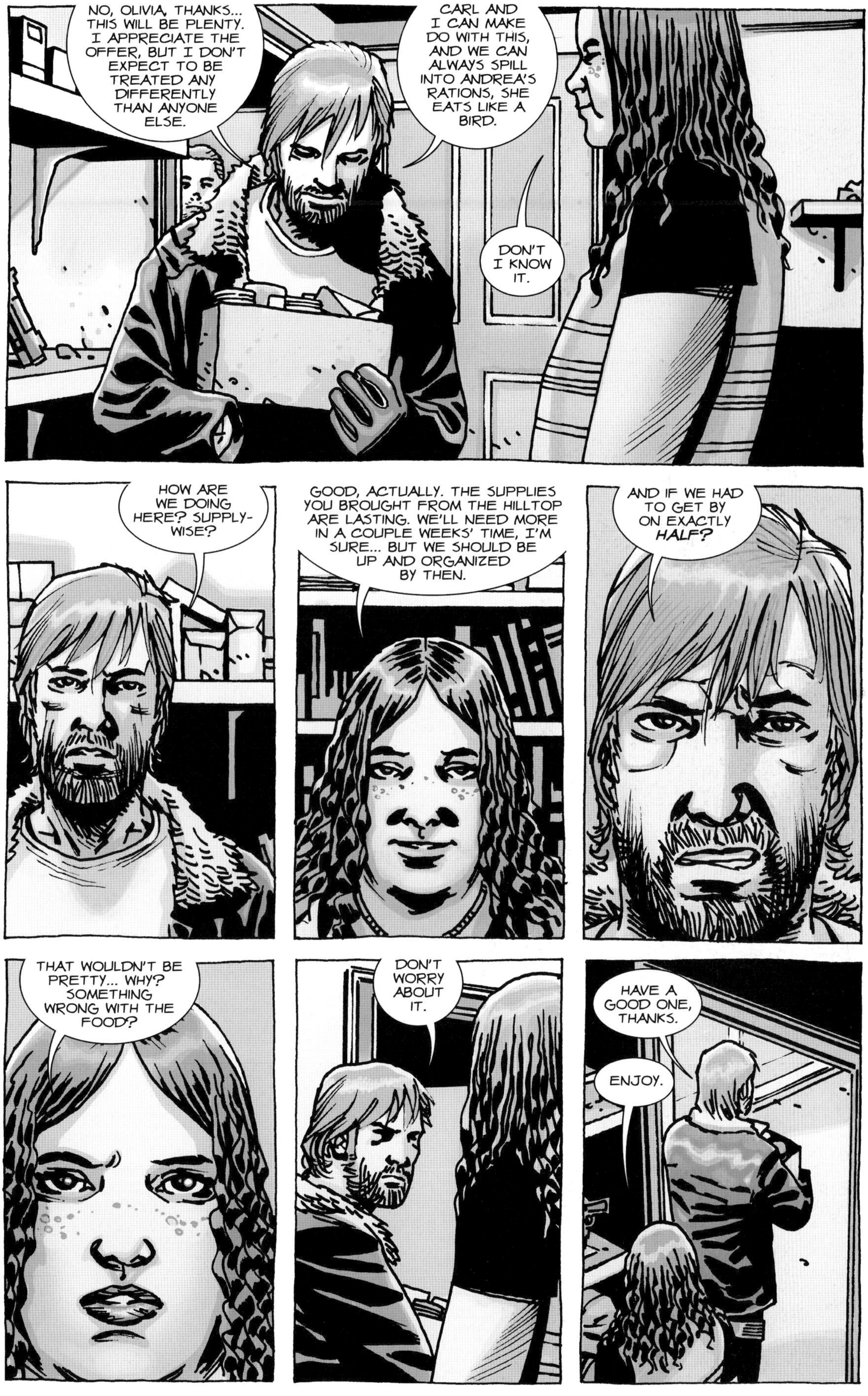
NO, OLIVIA, THANKS... THIS WILL BE PLENTY. I APPRECIATE THE OFFER, BUT I DON'T EXPECT TO BE TREATED ANY DIFFERENTLY THAN ANYONE ELSE.
CARL AND I CAN MAKE DO WITH THIS, AND WE CAN ALWAYS SPILL INTO ANDREA'S RATIONS, SHE EATS LIKE A BIRD.
DON'T I KNOW IT.
HOW ARE WE DOING HERE? SUPPLY-WISE?
GOOD, ACTUALLY. THE SUPPLIES YOU BROUGHT FROM THE HILLTOP ARE LASTING. WE'LL NEED MORE IN A COUPLE WEEKS' TIME, I'M SURE... BUT WE SHOULD BE UP AND ORGANIZED BY THEN.
AND IF WE HAD TO GET BY ON EXACTLY *HALF?*
THAT WOULDN'T BE PRETTY... WHY? SOMETHING WRONG WITH THE FOOD?
DON'T WORRY ABOUT IT.
HAVE A GOOD ONE, THANKS.
ENJOY.

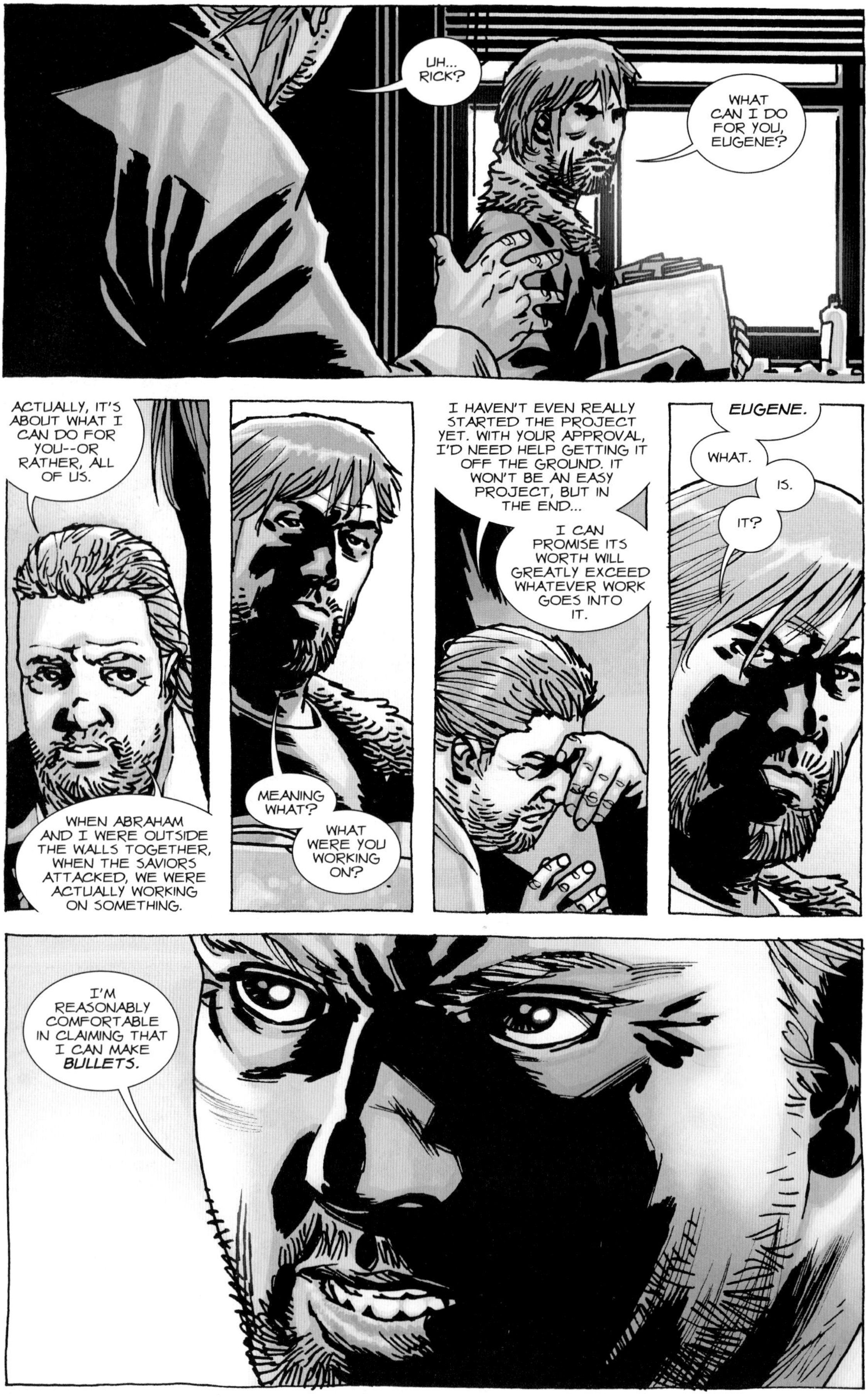
UH... RICK?
WHAT CAN I DO FOR YOU, EUGENE?
ACTUALLY, IT'S ABOUT WHAT I CAN DO FOR YOU--OR RATHER, ALL OF US.
WHEN ABRAHAM AND I WERE OUTSIDE THE WALLS TOGETHER, WHEN THE SAVIORS ATTACKED, WE WERE ACTUALLY WORKING ON SOMETHING.
MEANING WHAT?
WHAT WERE YOU WORKING ON?
I HAVEN'T EVEN REALLY STARTED THE PROJECT YET. WITH YOUR APPROVAL, I'D NEED HELP GETTING IT OFF THE GROUND. IT WON'T BE AN EASY PROJECT, BUT IN THE END...
I CAN PROMISE ITS WORTH WILL GREATLY EXCEED WHATEVER WORK GOES INTO IT.
EUGENE.
WHAT.
IS.
IT?
I'M REASONABLY COMFORTABLE IN CLAIMING THAT I CAN MAKE *BULLETS.*

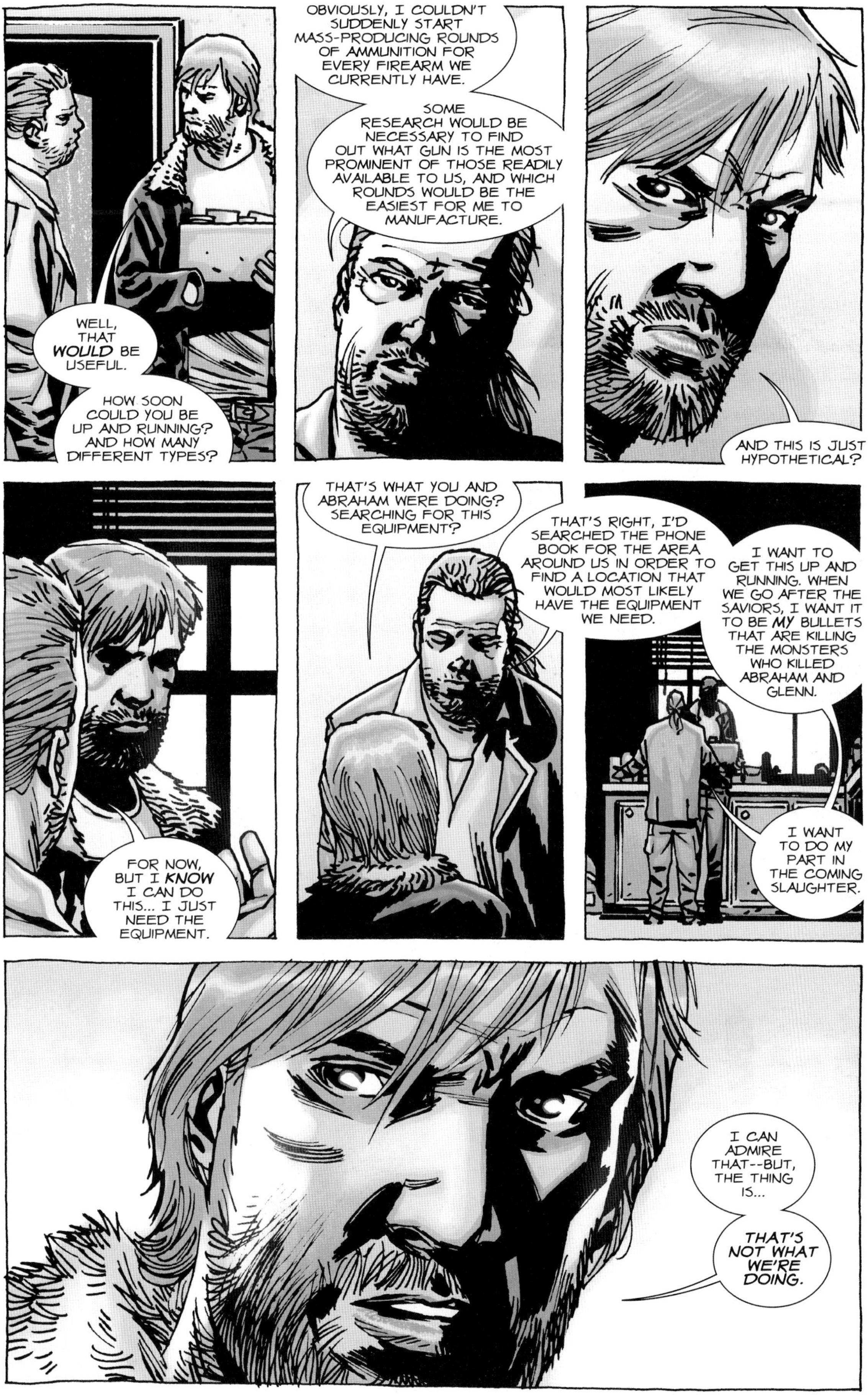

WELL, THAT **WOULD** BE USEFUL.
HOW SOON COULD YOU BE UP AND RUNNING? AND HOW MANY DIFFERENT TYPES?
OBVIOUSLY, I COULDN'T SUDDENLY START MASS-PRODUCING ROUNDS OF AMMUNITION FOR EVERY FIREARM WE CURRENTLY HAVE.
SOME RESEARCH WOULD BE NECESSARY TO FIND OUT WHAT GUN IS THE MOST PROMINENT OF THOSE READILY AVAILABLE TO US, AND WHICH ROUNDS WOULD BE THE EASIEST FOR ME TO MANUFACTURE.
AND THIS IS JUST HYPOTHETICAL?
FOR NOW, BUT I **KNOW** I CAN DO THIS... I JUST NEED THE EQUIPMENT.
THAT'S WHAT YOU AND ABRAHAM WERE DOING? SEARCHING FOR THIS EQUIPMENT?
THAT'S RIGHT, I'D SEARCHED THE PHONE BOOK FOR THE AREA AROUND US IN ORDER TO FIND A LOCATION THAT WOULD MOST LIKELY HAVE THE EQUIPMENT WE NEED.
I WANT TO GET THIS UP AND RUNNING. WHEN WE GO AFTER THE SAVIORS, I WANT IT TO BE **MY** BULLETS THAT ARE KILLING THE MONSTERS WHO KILLED ABRAHAM AND GLENN.
I WANT TO DO MY PART IN THE COMING SLAUGHTER.
I CAN ADMIRE THAT--BUT, THE THING IS...
THAT'S NOT WHAT WE'RE DOING.

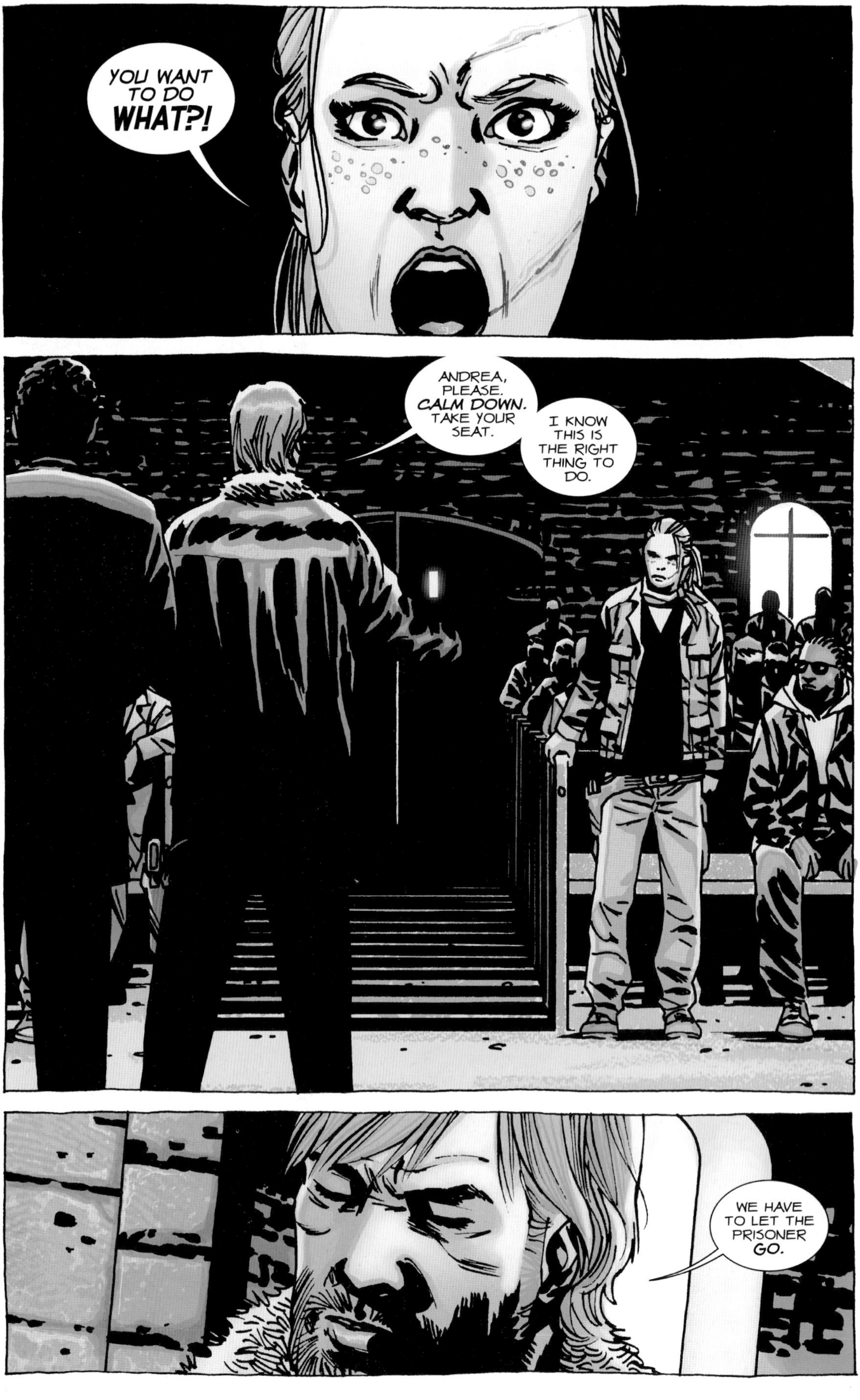
YOU WANT TO DO WHAT?!
ANDREA, PLEASE. CALM DOWN. TAKE YOUR SEAT.
I KNOW THIS IS THE RIGHT THING TO DO.
WE HAVE TO LET THE PRISONER GO.

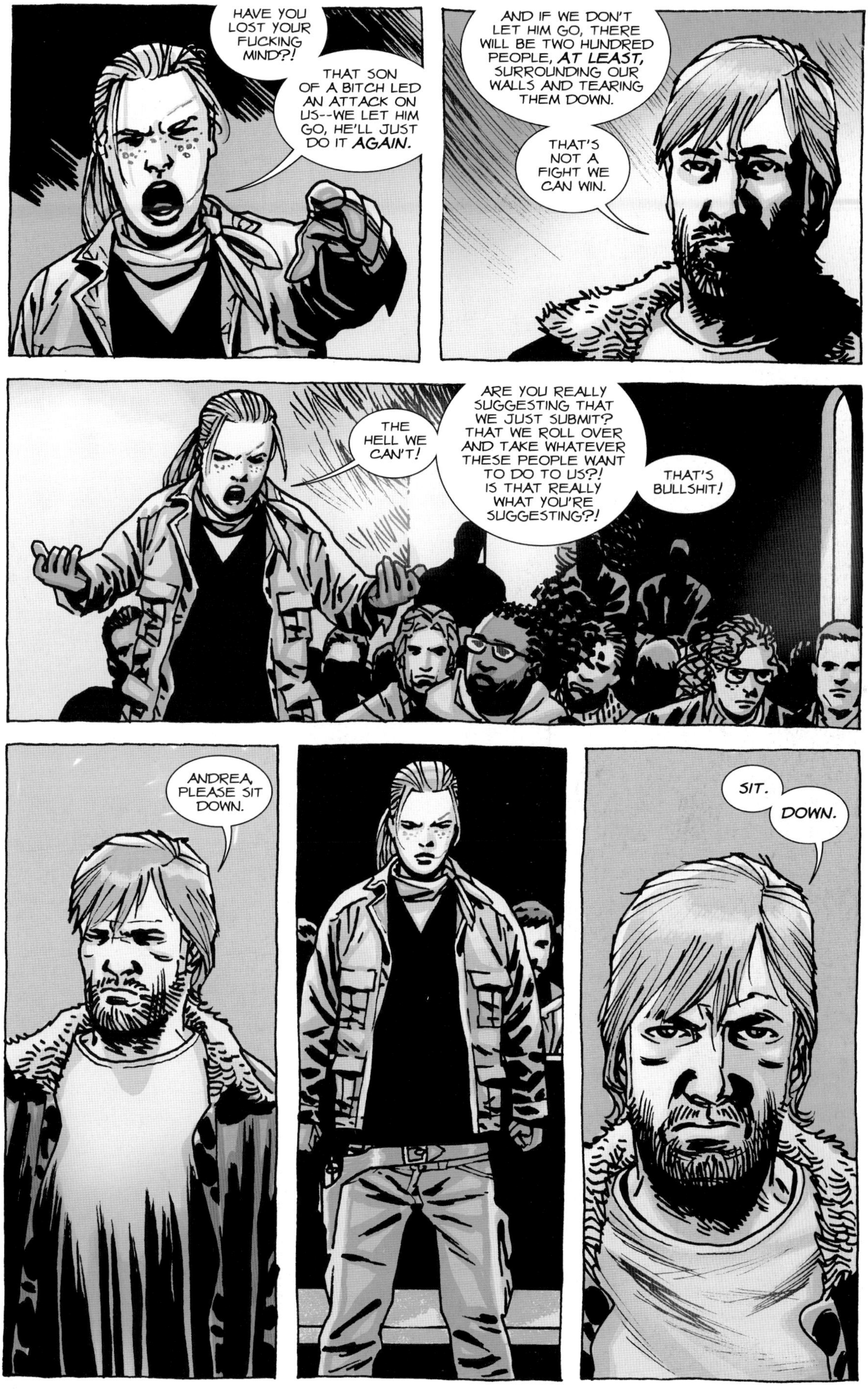
HAVE YOU LOST YOUR FUCKING MIND?!
THAT SON OF A BITCH LED AN ATTACK ON US--WE LET HIM GO, HE'LL JUST DO IT AGAIN.
AND IF WE DON'T LET HIM GO, THERE WILL BE TWO HUNDRED PEOPLE, AT LEAST, SURROUNDING OUR WALLS AND TEARING THEM DOWN.
THAT'S NOT A FIGHT WE CAN WIN.
THE HELL WE CAN'T!
ARE YOU REALLY SUGGESTING THAT WE JUST SUBMIT? THAT WE ROLL OVER AND TAKE WHATEVER THESE PEOPLE WANT TO DO TO US?! IS THAT REALLY WHAT YOU'RE SUGGESTING?!
THAT'S BULLSHIT!
ANDREA, PLEASE SIT DOWN.
SIT.
DOWN.

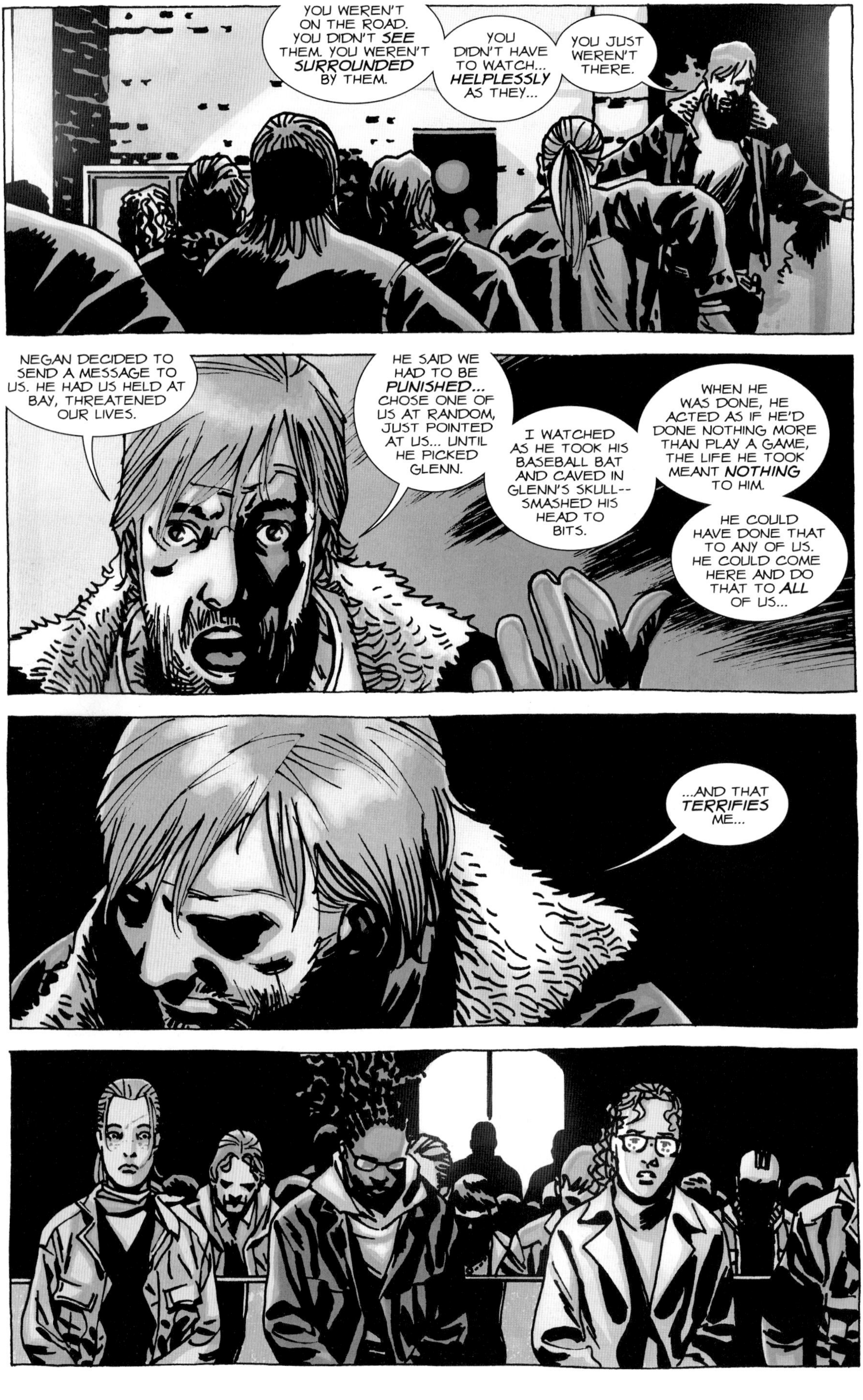
YOU WEREN'T ON THE ROAD. YOU DIDN'T SEE THEM. YOU WEREN'T SURROUNDED BY THEM.
YOU DIDN'T HAVE TO WATCH... HELPLESSLY AS THEY...
YOU JUST WEREN'T THERE.
NEGAN DECIDED TO SEND A MESSAGE TO US. HE HAD US HELD AT BAY, THREATENED OUR LIVES.
HE SAID WE HAD TO BE PUNISHED... CHOSE ONE OF US AT RANDOM, JUST POINTED AT US... UNTIL HE PICKED GLENN.
I WATCHED AS HE TOOK HIS BASEBALL BAT AND CAVED IN GLENN'S SKULL-- SMASHED HIS HEAD TO BITS.
WHEN HE WAS DONE, HE ACTED AS IF HE'D DONE NOTHING MORE THAN PLAY A GAME, THE LIFE HE TOOK MEANT NOTHING TO HIM.
HE COULD HAVE DONE THAT TO ANY OF US. HE COULD COME HERE AND DO THAT TO ALL OF US...
...AND THAT TERRIFIES ME...

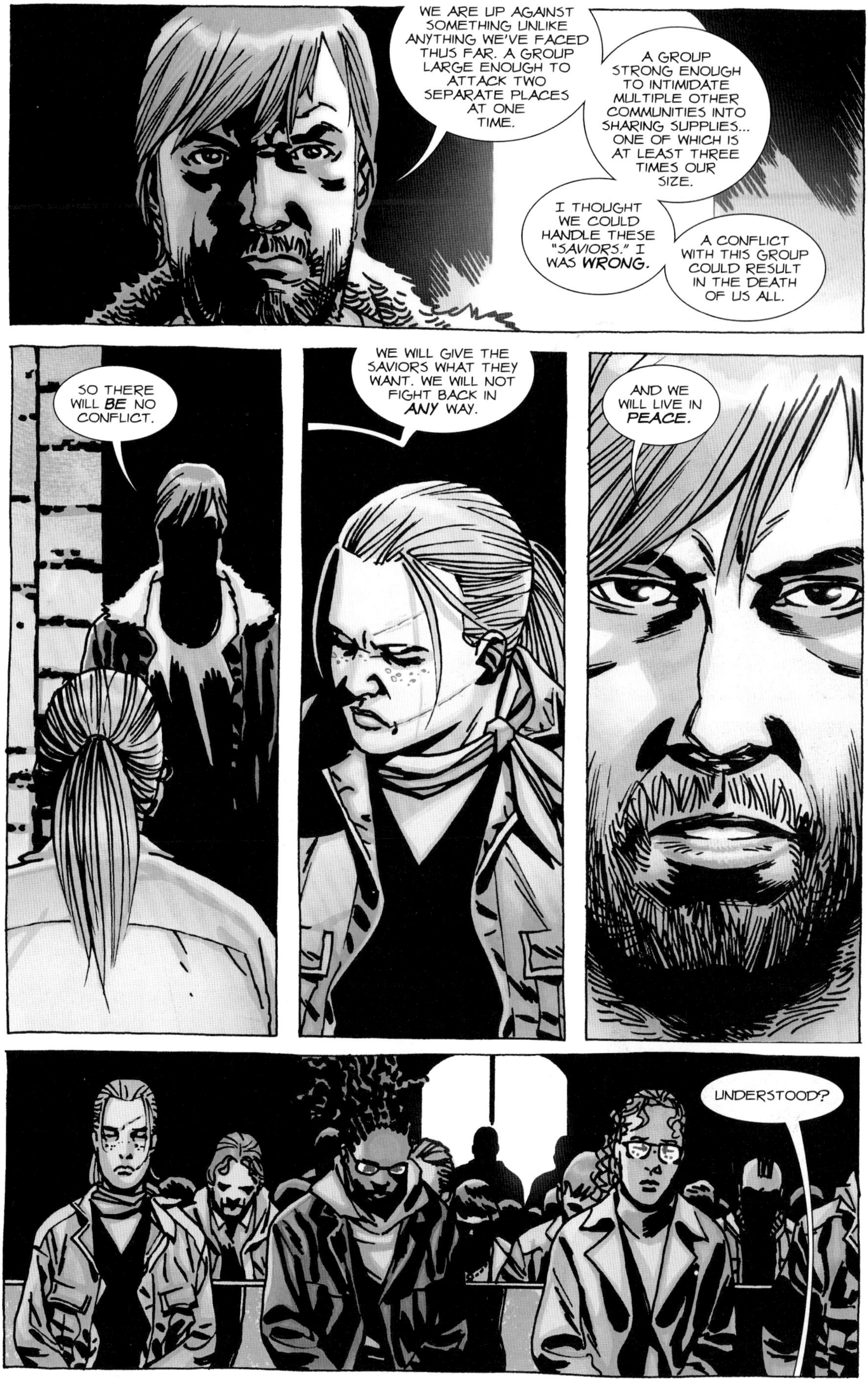
WE ARE UP AGAINST SOMETHING UNLIKE ANYTHING WE'VE FACED THUS FAR. A GROUP LARGE ENOUGH TO ATTACK TWO SEPARATE PLACES AT ONE TIME.
A GROUP STRONG ENOUGH TO INTIMIDATE MULTIPLE OTHER COMMUNITIES INTO SHARING SUPPLIES... ONE OF WHICH IS AT LEAST THREE TIMES OUR SIZE.
I THOUGHT WE COULD HANDLE THESE "SAVIORS." I WAS **WRONG.**
A CONFLICT WITH THIS GROUP COULD RESULT IN THE DEATH OF US ALL.
SO THERE WILL **BE** NO CONFLICT.
WE WILL GIVE THE SAVIORS WHAT THEY WANT. WE WILL NOT FIGHT BACK IN **ANY** WAY.
AND WE WILL LIVE IN **PEACE.**
UNDERSTOOD?

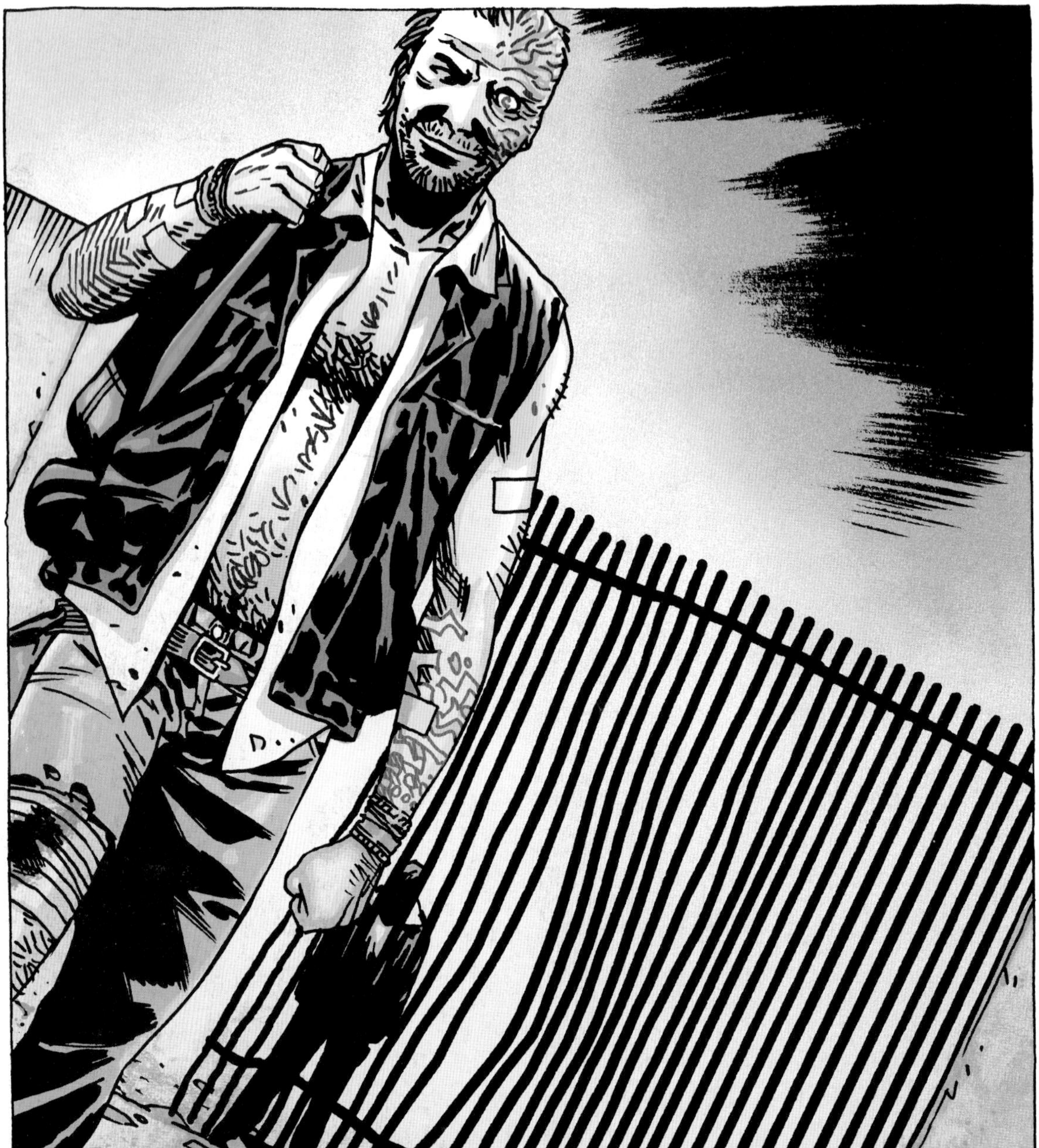

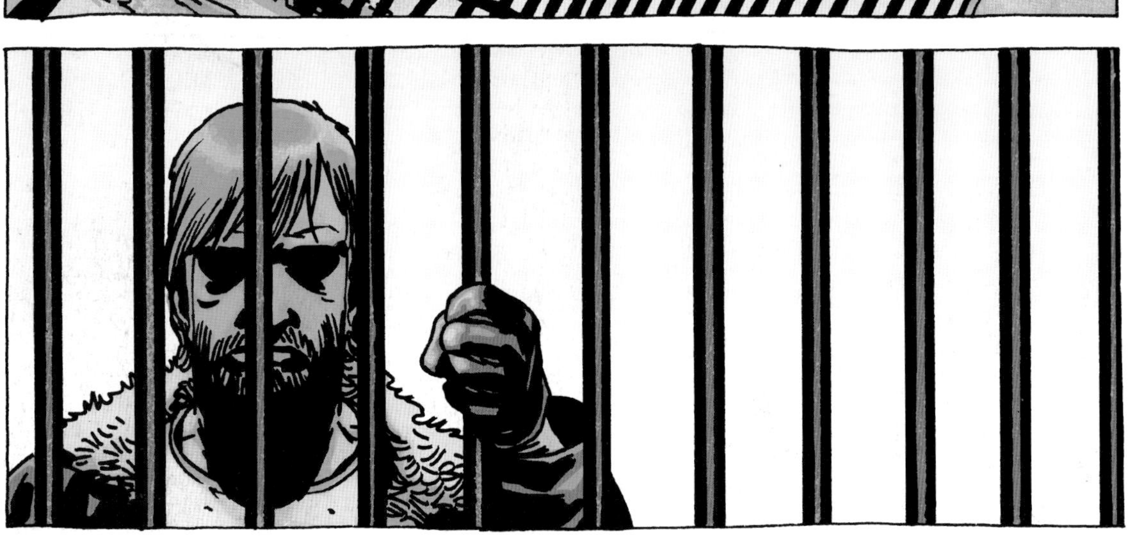

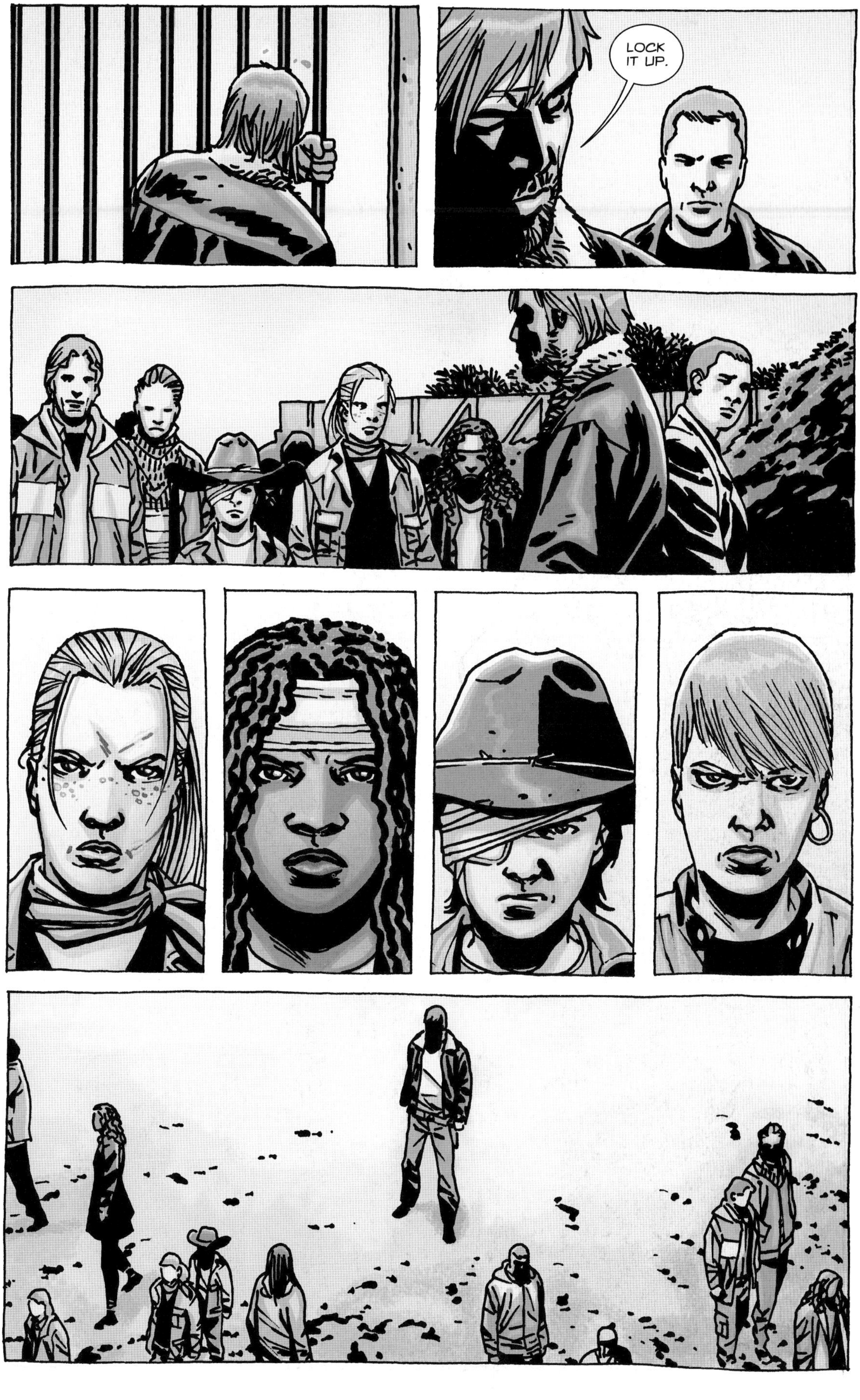
LOCK IT UP.

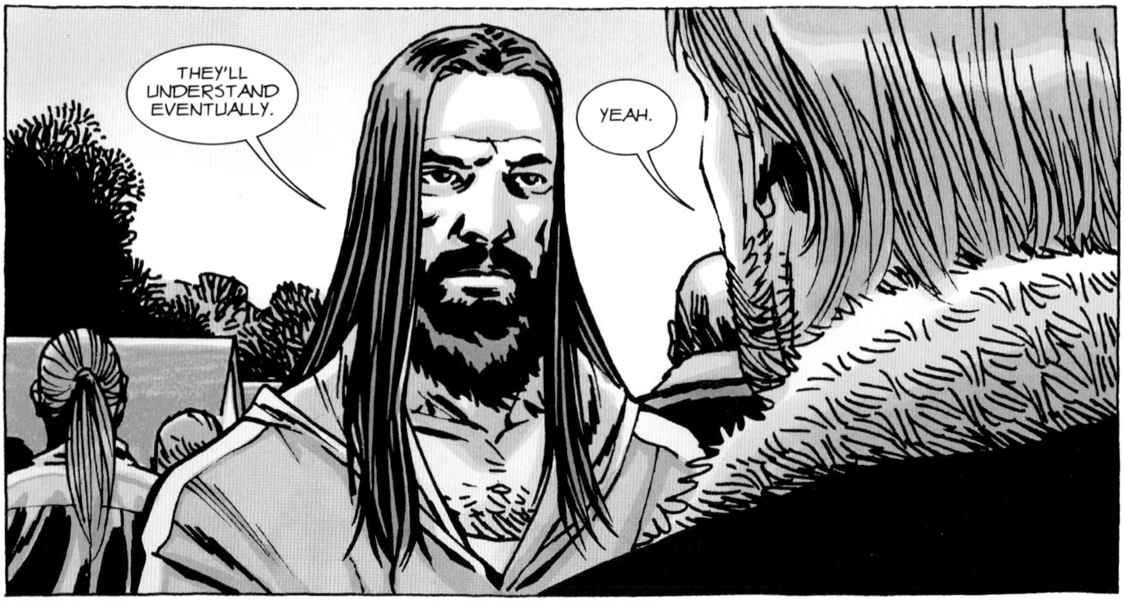
THEY'LL UNDERSTAND EVENTUALLY.
YEAH.
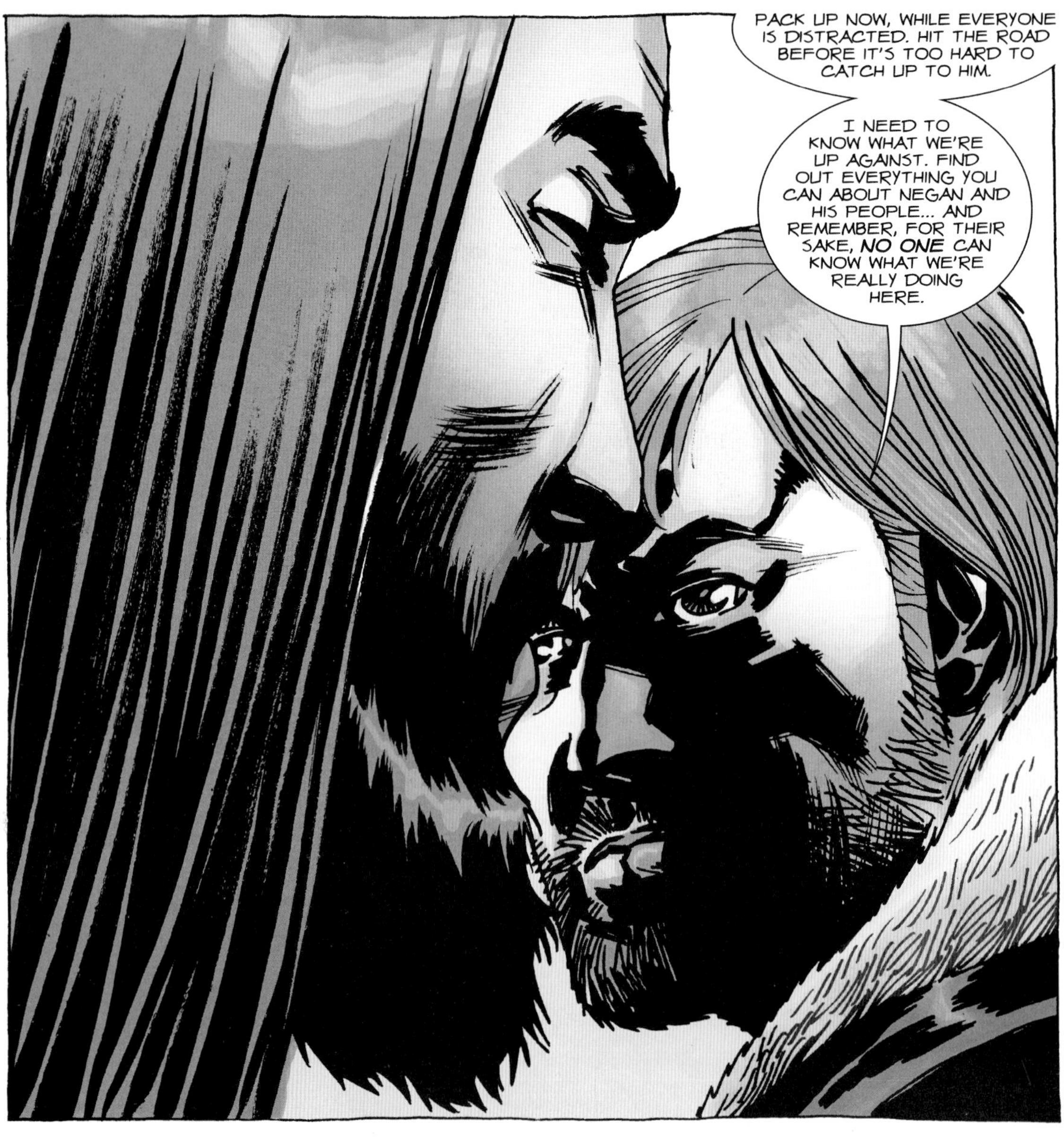
PACK UP NOW, WHILE EVERYONE IS DISTRACTED. HIT THE ROAD BEFORE IT'S TOO HARD TO CATCH UP TO HIM.
I NEED TO KNOW WHAT WE'RE UP AGAINST. FIND OUT EVERYTHING YOU CAN ABOUT NEGAN AND HIS PEOPLE... AND REMEMBER, FOR THEIR SAKE, ***NO ONE*** CAN KNOW WHAT WE'RE REALLY DOING HERE.